Hot, sensual Arabian nights
Dark, brooding strangers

L*o*
DESERT

RESCUED BY THE SHEIKH

Three powerful, intense novels by three
bestselling writers: Susan Stephens, RITA®
award-winning author Liz Fielding &
Alexandra Sellers

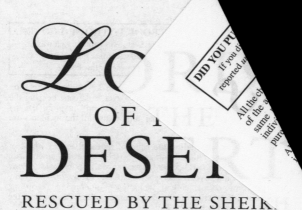

L O
OF THE
DESERT

RESCUED BY THE SHEIKH

SUSAN STEPHENS
LIZ FIELDING
ALEXANDRA SELLERS

aracters in this book have no existence outside the imagination
uthor, and have no relation whatsoever to anyone bearing the
ame or names. They are not even distantly inspired by any
dual known or unknown to the author, and all the incidents are
invention.

RESCUED BY THE SHEIKH
© Harlequin Enterprises II B.V./S.à.r.l. 2010

Bedded by the Desert King © Susan Stephens 2006
The Sheikh's Guarded Heart © Liz Fielding 2006
The Ice Maiden's Sheikh © Alexandra Sellers 2004

ISBN: 978 0 263 87705 2

10-0310

BEDDED BY THE DESERT KING

SUSAN STEPHENS

Susan Stephens was a professional singer before meeting her husband on the tiny Mediterranean island of Malta.

In true romance style they met on Monday, became engaged on Friday and were married three months later. They are still very much in love, though Susan does not advise her three children to return home with a similar story as she may not take the news with the same fortitude as her own mother!

Susan had written several non-fiction books when fate took a hand. At a charity costume ball there was an after-dinner auction. One of the lots – 'Spend A Day With An Author' – had been donated by best-selling Mills & Boon® author Penny Jordan. Susan's husband bought this lot and Penny was to become not just a great friend, but a wonderful mentor who encouraged Susan to write romance.

Susan loves her family, her pets, her friends and her writing. She enjoys entertaining, travel and going to theatre and concerts. She reads voraciously, knits, cooks and plays the piano to relax and can also be found throwing herself off mountains on a pair of skis or galloping through the countryside.

Most of all Susan loves to hear from her readers all around the world!

Look out for Susan Stephens' latest exciting novel, *Master of the Desert*, available in April 2010 from Mills & Boon® Modern™.

CHAPTER ONE

SHE was tempted to take more shots, but her spine was tingling. And that wasn't a good sign when the man she had her camera focused on had a sidekick with a gun slung across his shoulder.

Zara guessed her target had to be one of the local tribal leaders touring the border of his land. But, whoever he was, he was magnificent. Capturing striking images was her stock-in-trade, though wildlife of a different kind had brought her to the wadi—rare desert gazelles and the Arabian oryx, graceful creatures that had been hunted to the point of extinction in some parts of the desert. They had been reintroduced into Zaddara in the early eighties and were said to drink here at dawn. The man was an unexpected bonus.

Zara tensed, realising he had started stripping off his clothes. The temptation to zoom in was irresistible. His torso was hard and tanned an even nutmeg and muscles bulged as he flexed his arms. Discarding his tunic, he let his trousers drop and she gasped as he stepped out of them, completely naked. It was a moment before she realised she hadn't taken a single shot. She made up for it now.

Wildlife photographer to hot-skin snapper? Zara smiled wryly. There was a whole world of opportunity opening up for her here. But she had no inclination to broaden her horizons in that direction even if she could use some of the images she was capturing now in the exhibition she intended to stage when she got back home... An exhibition that was supposed to contain more than wildlife images, Zara reminded herself. She had been hoping to capture something that would help her to forge a closer link with her late parents, not this incredible specimen...

Burrowing deeper into the sand hollow that served as her 'hide', Zara worked as fast as she could, hoping her camera lens wouldn't catch the sun and give her away. She had a living to earn, as well as a past to understand. And the truth about her past lay here somewhere in Zaddara...

Her parents had lost their lives in an oilfield disaster working as geologists for the late Sheikh. Sheikh Abdullah had been a simple man with a simple goal, and that had been to find oil to bring wealth to his impoverished country. Her parents had helped him to do that and had paid for it with their lives. The kingdom of Zaddara was now one of the major oil-producers in the world thanks to them, but the country had a new sheikh, and Sheikh Shahin was said to be far more ruthless than his father. Her late grandparents had always told her Shahin was responsible for the accident that had killed her parents.

Her jaw clenched as she thought about the blood money paid into her bank account each month. As soon as she was old enough, she had formed a trust to hold the money, then used it to fund the schemes she cared about. Recently she'd given a lump sum to a scheme that reintroduced rare species into their natural habitat. She refused to spend a penny of it on herself and had found solace of a sort from using the Zaddaran money to do some good.

Zara felt a shiver run through her a second time. It was a warning. Something wasn't right. Where had the bodyguard got to? Lowering the camera, she knew she shouldn't have allowed herself to become distracted. Capping her lens, she started to shuffle backwards down the slope towards her Jeep.

Shahin's jaw clenched with anger when he heard Aban's warning shout. He was poised on the edge of the wadi ready to dive in. He had waited almost a month for this promise of cool relief. He couldn't believe someone would dare to disturb his privacy now. He was in the middle of the desert. How far must he go to find solitude?

He had chosen the area for his retreat carefully. This place was at least fifty miles from the nearest habitation; only the Bedouin trails of his ancestors, hidden to those unfamiliar with the changing patterns of the desert, passed this way. There shouldn't have been a chance of him coming into contact with another human being. And now this...

Narrowing his eyes, Shahin shaded them against the first low-slanting rays of the sun. Staring up into the dunes, he could see two dark shapes silhouetted against the threatening red sky where there should only have been one. The area might be remote, but the fact that he hadn't checked their surroundings personally was a careless mistake. He could afford no more errors.

Casting another glance into the dunes, Shahin relaxed, seeing his bodyguard Aban had everything under control.

The intruder had been apprehended and it would dent the old man's pride if he were to interfere now. Aban was a good man and he would make sure he retired with honour. The elderly guard had travelled willingly into the wilderness with him to share the privations of a prince. A prince who had for a lifetime cared only for himself, and who must now be a king and father to his people. Only Aban knew the long days and nights of fasting were not just to prepare him to rule, but to drain the pus from a long-standing wound, a wound that even now could make him call out in his sleep and pound the sand with his fists in frustration that the past could not be changed. But if he must live with what he had done, he would learn from it. Diving into the freezing water, he powered across the wadi knowing that when he returned to the capital to be formally recognised by his people as the ruling sheikh of Zaddara he would take on all his father's responsibilities, however challenging. He was ready now.

Vaulting out of the water after his swim, Shahin grabbed the clean ankle-length *thawb* along with the flowing robe left for him by Aban. Adding a *howlis* to protect his head, neck and face from the harsh climate, he deftly fixed the long scarf-like head-covering in place.

A sharp breeze made him turn and in that moment he saw that Aban's captive was a young woman… Aban was holding her by the arm as they came down the dune together and she seemed none too pleased. Turning his face to the horizon, he shut her out. In his mind's eye all he could see now was the ruby-red glow enveloping the desert and the mountains in the far distance standing out in sharp black relief against a crimson sky. This was his land, a cruel land, and he loved it. He would allow nothing and no one to divert him from his chosen path.

The sound of the woman's voice intruded on his contemplation. Her voice was raised in anger and he resented the intrusion. Who was she? What did she want? Belting his robe, he turned to stare as the two figures approached. She was like a young colt walking awkwardly on the sand. Why was she alone in the desert? What type of person took such a risk? Was this journey into one of the most remote regions of the world worth so much to her?

His expression darkened when he saw how poorly she was equipped. Her outfit had no doubt been purchased from some fancy adventure-holiday equipment shop… But where was her survival gear? Where was her water canister? Where was her knife, her rope, her radio alarm…? Where were her flares? Didn't she know the first thing about the desert? Didn't she realise that a sandstorm could cut her off from her vehicle in seconds? Did she think she could snap her way out of trouble with that expensive-looking camera she was hanging on to so desperately?

As he strode towards them all these questions and more were beating a path to his eyes. But as the young woman raised a protective arm to her face he halted mid-stride. *Did she think he was going to hit her?* His expression was enough to make anyone think that, Shahin realised, standing stock still for a moment in silence. The breeze whipped up and took hold of his stark black robe, pressing it against his thighs, thighs that were still burning from his morning exercise. He saw her looking and felt his senses stir.

'Let her go.' He issued the command in a low voice,

but even though he had spoken in the throaty Zaddaran dialect she immediately caught his meaning and her face lit with anger.

'I should think so too!' Furiously she shook herself free from Aban's grasp.

As Aban moved to catch her again he was forced to make a fierce gesture to warn his faithful old servant to let her be. Such autocratic gestures didn't sit easily with him, but if he were to remain anonymous in front of this woman discretion was paramount. 'She's not going anywhere,' he observed, in English this time. 'Bring her to my tent...'

'What?' she exclaimed.

Her incredulity drew a faint smile to his lips as he walked away.

'Come back here!' she cried. 'Who do you think you are, telling me what to do?'

He had to stop, turn around and pacify Aban, before the old man made good the threat he made after this second outburst. It was fortunate for the young woman that she didn't understand the language! Grit, fire, courage, Shahin thought, noting the way she was glaring back at him. His curiosity deepened, but then Aban started to grumble again and, to defuse the situation, he was forced to point out that she was only armed with a camera.

Still muttering, the old man shook his head.

'Come with me.' He addressed her directly, gesturing towards his pavilion. The Bedouin blood running through his veins made hospitality mandatory however unpalatable that might be, and he had vowed to espouse all his father's values, not just cherry-pick them at will.

This time she made no protest. He was impressed by her

self-possession as she walked alongside him, though he could tell Aban was incensed by her easy manner. The old man thought no one should walk next to his king.

The old ways dictated that any guest must be welcomed to his tent for three days and three nights, which wasn't such a bad option in this instance. The young woman had obviously come to the desert seeking adventure—who was he to disappoint her?

As they drew close he could see that she wanted to take some shots of the Bedouin tent. He had to stop her before she went to work. 'No photographs,' he said firmly.

'What?' She didn't believe him at first, but quickly realised he was serious and left the camera to swing on the cord around her neck.

For the first time he had a chance to observe her properly and he could see that, beneath the layer of dirt and grime, she was quite beautiful. Her long hair, caught up in a casual ponytail, was the colour of creamy caramel. There was a hint of gold as well that the dust rising up from the sand couldn't hide…

Dust that had started to lift all around them, Shahin noted with concern. Staring out towards the horizon, he frowned. The red dawn sky had been an early warning of a storm blowing up. 'Move the Jeep to higher ground and stay with it,' he ordered Aban. 'The tents are secure, and I'll check them again before the weather worsens.'

Aban's smaller tent was pitched twenty yards or so from his own, but it was also beneath the same sheltering rocks. There was a third tent in the back of the off-road vehicle that Aban could use until it was safe for him to return.

Turning his attention back to the woman, he saw her

swallow with apprehension. She had caught the urgency in his words and he felt he should say something to reassure her. 'The weather is deteriorating, but you'll be safe here with me. Don't argue,' he warned, when she started to protest. 'You have no alternative but to stay. Aban tells me we have about an hour before the storm hits—and that's if we're lucky.'

'But it only took me two hours to get here from the city—'

Behind the defiance he saw her fear. 'That was before there were dangerous weather conditions to consider. You can't outrun the wind,' he pointed out.

He had no time to waste on persuasion and started off for the temporary structure that had been his home during his retreat, eager to check all the supports and ensure that they would withstand the force of the wind. To his surprise, she ran ahead of him and cut him off.

'If your man's leaving now, I want to leave too. We could travel in convoy—' Her chin tilted at a defiant angle as she held his gaze. 'And why don't you come with us? Why stay here if it's so dangerous?'

Because there were too many memories inside his tent, too many things that had belonged to his parents for him to risk losing them... The tent had been his father Abdullah's before he had claimed his kingdom. There wasn't time to dismantle it now, and so he would stay with it. But that wasn't her business. 'That just isn't possible,' he said coldly. 'And it's too risky for Aban to waste time trying to recover your Jeep. If Aban is to remain safe he must leave right away.' Veering away from her, he walked on.

She chased after him. 'But why can't I go with him?'

'Because Aban won't wait…' And because Aban's traditional values could only be stretched so far. He would be horrified were he to be asked to take charge of the young woman overnight. Aban wouldn't leave his vantage point until he was sure the storm had passed, and who knew how long that would take? He would not risk both their lives in order to appease this young woman's somewhat overdue sense of propriety. If she imagined that the desert was some big beach she was about to be cruelly disillusioned. The desert was a sleeping monster which, when awakened, had the power to destroy everything in its path. The only reason his Bedouin ancestors had chosen this site was because the surrounding rocks and fresh water offered them some protection. For now it was better not to alarm her. He didn't know how she would react if he told her the full extent of their plight. She might panic. She had no idea of the forces involved, or that everything around them was about to undergo the most radical change. He stopped and turned to gaze at the dune. 'Is your vehicle parked up behind that dune?'

'Yes, it is…'

She sounded hopeful and he guessed she thought he had changed his mind about letting her go.

'It's just over the hill, at the base of the dune.' There was a hint of impatience in her voice now.

'On low ground?'

'Of course, didn't I just say so?' Her irritation was mounting. 'I left it where it would be sheltered by the dune.'

'Sheltered by the dune?' A ghost of a smile touched his lips. She didn't have a clue. The storm that was about to hit them would have no respect for hills made out of sand.

'Leave it,' he instructed Aban, seeing the old man's glance swerve towards the dune. 'There's no time for you to climb up there and recover her vehicle. You must get yourself to safety and save our own Jeep.'

Zara wished she could understand the harsh, guttural language. She was way out of her depth. She wanted so badly to leave, but the leader of the two men was planted firmly in her way. Her options were limited. Both of these men walked easily on the sand, whereas the desert boots she had purchased in London gave her no stability at all on a surface she had discovered was as treacherous as ice. They would catch her before she made it to the base of the dune. And if she managed to escape, where would she go? If what this man had said about the storm proved to be right she would have to find shelter. As she gazed around, Zara could only try and visualise the thousands of miles of unseen land that rolled back behind the two men, hostile land with which she was unfamiliar. She had no alternative but to do as he said.

His tent was the size of a small marquee. As they drew closer Zara could see that the sides were made of some heavy woven fabric, which had been dyed a deep red. There was opulent fringing around a tented roof and the fabric was drawn up to a spike in the centre. Missing only a pennant, it reminded her of a medieval pavilion, reinforcing her opinion that she was stepping back in time, with a man who might be dangerous... A very attractive man who might be dangerous. Her heart was thundering—and for all the wrong reasons. She just had to keep telling herself that this was the photo opportunity of a lifetime...

But, as he raised the heavy curtain concealing the entrance to his tent, goose-bumps lifted on her arms. As she hesitated he tipped his chin, indicating that she should enter. The little she could see of his face beneath the folds of black cloth was hardly reassuring. His gaze was as dark and as unbending as iron.

'Come in,' he said impatiently. 'I have no intention of hurting you, if that's what you are worried about. In my country the safety of a guest is a sacred charge.'

Did that sacred charge extend to young women reckless enough to venture into the desert unaccompanied? Zara wondered. It must do, but she gathered from the hard look in his eyes that the prospect of her stay seemed nothing more than tiresome to him. He jerked his chin again and she got a sense of a man who was accustomed to having his smallest whim accommodated the instant he made it known. 'Dinosaur,' she muttered under her breath.

'What did you say?'

His voice had softened to the point where she had to strain to hear it and she shivered involuntarily to think that all his senses might be so keen. 'Nothing…'

His eyes challenged her assertion.

'Come in, or stay outside,' he said as if he couldn't have cared less what she did. 'Either way, I'm going in, and I'm closing down the entrance while I wait out the storm.'

'Are you threatening to leave me out here?'

'Take it any way you want.'

Firmly clenching her jaw, she walked past him into the tent. She saw him staring at her camera and clutched it closer. No way was he taking her camera from her. He might as well have tried to cut off her arm.

She was conscious immediately of the fresh, clean smell inside the tent and the neatness of it all. As she looked around, her eyes found their way back to her host. She noticed he wore a weapon tucked into his belt. She glanced at his face and back again. The long curving dagger looked lethal, but it had a beautifully worked gold hilt and she guessed it was more for ceremonial use than anything sinister. As her heart rate steadied she admired the intricate workmanship and longed to take a photograph of it so she could add it to the record of her trip. Perhaps if she asked politely she might persuade him to let her use her camera for some things in spite of his earlier objections. 'What do you call that?' she said, glancing at it again.

'A *khanjar*. Tradition demands that I wear it,' he explained, confirming her first impression. 'It is meant to represent a Bedouin's honour and is an indispensable piece of equipment in the desert. You never know when you might need a knife…' His dark gaze flashed up.

'Would you object if I take a picture of it?'

'Of the *khanjar*, no…'

The expression on his face left her in no doubt that her image must be confined to the dagger. She was careful to show him, as she narrowed her eyes in preparation for taking the shot, that the picture would be in close up and of the dagger and nothing else. She had no idea what else she might find inside the tent and was keen to respect his wishes in the hope of finding more material for her journal of the trip.

She had guts, he'd give her that. The dagger was beautiful and it pleased him to think she'd noticed it. It had been his father's and he felt Sheikh Abdullah's presence whenever he wore it. It both comforted him and served as a painful reminder that his work outside Zaddara had kept him away from a man he would have liked to know better. *And that now it was too late...* 'That's enough,' he said sharply, wheeling away from the probing lens.

His feelings of regret were not something he wished to share with this stranger.

She flinched at his impatience, but lowered the camera. 'This is what I do,' she explained with a shrug. 'It's all I do. I take pictures...wildlife, indigenous people, unusual rock formations—' She threw up her hands so the camera swung free on its cord around her neck. 'I don't know what you imagine, but I'm no threat to you.'

But was he a threat to her? Zara wondered. In the capital city of Zaddar women were equal to men, but here in the desert different rules applied. She could see that women would be bound by certain restrictions, strength being just one of them. If this man should decide to overpower her... She watched him releasing the bindings that protected the entrance to his tent. Once they were secured inside it, neither one of them would be leaving in a hurry.

It made her angry to think she had got herself into this position. She had researched the trip so thoroughly, reading everything she could lay her hands on, but nothing had prepared her for the vastness of the desert, or the emptiness. Compass, first aid kit, rug and a cold box full of supplies seemed woefully inadequate to her now. But Zaddara was supposed to be completely safe. How was she to know this man would send his armed guard to apprehend her? The thought irked her; his behaviour had been out of all proportion and she decided to challenge him about it. 'Was it really necessary to send a man with a gun after me?'

'I didn't send Aban after you; he took it upon himself to secure the dunes while I was swimming. Would you have me reproach him for doing his job so well?'

'The gun was unnecessary.'

'There are poisonous snakes in the desert,' he countered, 'if you had bothered to check.'

She *had* checked. What sort of amateur did he take her for? But she drew the line at carrying a gun. A camera was her weapon of choice, and she used that and the images it produced to challenge the motives of the people who killed the creatures she had made it her life's work to protect. 'Nevertheless—'

'Nevertheless?'

The rejoinder came back sharp as a whip crack. And it was a mistake to hold his gaze. Having never had her blood pressure raised by a man was no preparation for an encounter like this. The Bedouin was unlike any man she had met before. She could usually judge people from their appearance, but this man was an enigma. Tall and powerfully built, he was tanned a deep bronze and his steely eyes were watchful. He had brought her inside his tent only because he had to. She sensed he was a deeply private man who didn't want her there any more than she wanted to take the risk of being alone with him.

'It was wrong of you to travel so deep into the desert without a companion—'

'I didn't have a companion to bring—' Zara's mouth slammed shut. Why had she admitted to being alone? 'People know I'm here, of course.'

'Of course,' he agreed in a way that suggested he didn't believe her for a moment.

Following him deeper inside, she looked around. As she had first thought, everything was spotlessly clean and orderly and was made comfortable with heaps of intricately embroidered cushions and finely woven rugs. In a variety of rich colours, these were perfectly arranged in piles to relax and recline on. A slender coffee pot made from what looked like beaten silver rested on a simple brazier and the delicious smell made her swallow involuntarily.

'You are thirsty?'

He had barely any accent at all, she realised now, and the rich baritone strummed something deep inside her. Coffee was a good starting point if she was going to strike up a dialogue with him and get to know more about his land and customs. 'I'd love a coffee, thank you...'

How many people got the chance to see inside a real Bedouin tent and find out how a man like this lived? Zara wondered as she moved past him to sit on the cushions he indicated. He made her feel tiny and delicate, which she knew was survival of the species at work. However hard she might try to fight it, her female genes craved his masculinity—and she wasn't fighting nearly hard enough.

The lanterns hanging from the main frame of the temporary structure cast a soft light over the tent's interior and there was another lamp in one corner by what looked like a bed. She inhaled the faint scent of sandalwood appreciatively and found the warmth reassuringly cosy after almost freezing to death on the dunes.

When he offered her a dainty coffee cup full of dark, steaming liquid she was careful not to touch his hand. Taking it, she sipped cautiously. The delicious taste reminded her of rich dark chocolate. She drained it to the dregs.

'More?' he invited.

As he spoke he was unwinding the coils of protective headgear. Zara watched in fascination as a head of hair, thick, black and glossy was revealed. She had to wonder what it would feel like beneath her hands. Jet-black curls caressed his neck and some of the waves had fallen over his forehead so that the hair caught on his lashes. He was an incredible-looking man and the expression in his eyes was both compelling and dangerous; it took all she'd got to look away.

As he refilled her coffee cup and their eyes met she saw a world of experience reflected in his gaze. She found a face so strong it frightened her arousing? Maybe that was because his lips in contrast to his fierce expression were lush and curved with sensual beauty. He was considerably older than she was, perhaps thirty-five, and it only made him seem all the more desirable. Back home she would have been blushing by now and would have looked away, but here the situation was so unreal she felt no such restrictions and stared back boldly.

She had read that the Zaddaran Bedouins were so close to the earth, so in tune with the planet, that they never travelled aimlessly but returned each year to the same locations, using the stars to guide them as well as stone markers they left behind them on a previous trail. They could tell from the few shrubs in the desert when it had last rained and how much rain had fallen, and could find water, recognising by sight and smell whether it was toxic or brackish or safe to drink. What did this man know about her? Anything was possible. As she sipped the hot, dark liquid in her cup a dangerous fantasy swept over her where his strong arms had claimed her, and his fierce, sensual mouth…

'More coffee?'

'Yes, please…' She started out of the reverie with relief. This wasn't a story to which she could dictate some fuzzy romantic ending. She was here with an older man from a very different culture who, fortunately for her, was bound by centuries of tradition that demanded he treat her well. That was the only reason she was here drinking coffee with him, and that was why she would have to leave the very first chance she got.

'Would you care for a bath?'

'A bath?' Zara's mouth fell open as he gestured towards the rear of the tent.

'Another custom…' His eyes were shaded. 'Water is the greatest luxury we have to offer our guests in the desert.'

What he said made sense, but was she running the risk that he was simply adding ever more fantastic 'traditions' to his list?

'Aban heated the water for me before he left. You would be quite private behind that curtain, and I'm sure I could find you a clean robe to wear…'

Zara glanced down. She was extremely grubby. It had been a long drive and then a long wait to capture the images she wanted in the freezing desert dawn. She was still chilled through and uncomfortably gritty in all the wrong places, but that was no reason to behave rashly. 'That's very kind of you, but I couldn't possibly—'

'Why not?'

'Well, I…' She floundered for a moment. 'I don't even know your name.'

He made the typical Arabian salutation, touching his forehead and then his chest in what she thought was a slightly mocking gesture.

'I am a simple Bedouin.'

Which was true, Shahin reflected. All Bedouin were equal according to their custom. Leaders of his people were chosen for their wisdom and judgement, as well as their ability to tread a wary path amidst a society peopled by hard, ambitious men. 'As bathing is considered a great luxury in the desert,' he went on, 'and is one of our most cherished traditions, it would be considered an insult to refuse…'

Maybe that was stretching it a bit, but his bath *was* going to waste. And maybe he had resented her intrusion to begin with, but she was mature and self-possessed in a way he suspected very few people in her situation would be. And now she was here…

'Your tradition?' Zara racked her brain, but she was certain she had read nothing about baths being offered to guests of the Bedouin. She would have been surprised if she had. If water were so precious they would hardly waste it on bathing. But if this man were a tribal leader, perhaps he had his own set of rules. 'You mean this is a tradition of your tribe?'

'My tribe…?' He leaned back so she couldn't see his expression in the shadows.

'I understand if it is…' And then another thought occurred to her. 'But surely your traditions don't prevent you from telling me your name?'

She might be young, but she was shrewd, and he would have to handle her with care. 'My name is unimportant.' He made a closing gesture with his hands.

'To me, it is important. I have to call you something.'

He could hardly believe she was still harassing him. 'You may call me Abbas—' The name flew from his lips before caution could stop him. Abbas had been his mother's name for him. 'It means lion,' he started to explain.

'Of the desert?' she interrupted him lightly. Then, seeing his expression, she dropped her gaze.

But he was under no illusion that she was frightened of him. She wasn't afraid of him, except in a primitive way like any woman who knew a man wanted her in his bed. She feared his masculinity, but she wanted her share of it. She feared him as a man, not as a leader of men. The realisation made him harden instantly. 'The water is warm,' he murmured persuasively.

'And scented with sandalwood?'

He inclined his head.

CHAPTER TWO

YES, all right, this was crazy, Zara fired back at her inner voice. Sinking deeper beneath the scented water naked while her Bedouin was only a few yards away behind a curtain… She would never, *never* behave like this under normal circumstances. But she had been so grubby and un-comfortable, and his promise of fresh warm water on a day when nothing was normal had tipped the balance. Trouble was, she could talk it through inwardly all she liked but that didn't stop her heart racing out of control.

'Are you all right in there?'

Zara hurtled upright at the sound of the deep male voice. The chance she was taking seemed a whole lot bigger suddenly. 'Yes, thank you, I'm fine…' Her voice sounded strained. And where were the clothes he'd promised? What was she supposed to do now? How long could she reasonably remain submerged in rapidly cooling bathwater? Was this Abbas's idea of a joke? Or was he pre-paring her for—? She gasped as a hand appeared around the curtain.

'Here are a couple of towels for you…'

'Thank you…' She could hear another voice now…

Zara tensed, listening. It was an older man! What on earth had she got herself into?

Springing out of the bath, she seized the towels and flung them around her, securing them firmly. Once she was decent, she put her ear to the curtain, which was all that divided her from the two men. They were talking in the husky Zaddaran dialect and she could tell little from their tone of voice.

'Here…'

She started back as Abbas's bronzed hand appeared around the curtain holding some sort of flimsy robe.

'Well, take it…' he instructed impatiently.

'What is it?'

'Something for you to wear?' he suggested bitingly.

Zara watched in fascination as the hand stretched out a little more, revealing a wrist shaded with dark hair. Having located the wooden stand, he let the robe fall over it.

'And here's a veil to go with it…'

Having disappeared again behind the curtain, the hand came back and this time she got a good look at the powerful forearm attached to it… A robe and a veil? What did Abbas think this was—his harem?

'You'll need some fresh clothes,' he pointed out, anticipating her concern. 'Unless you're going to come out of there wrapped in towels, of course.'

'Thank you…' The robe was lovely…pure silk, Zara found on closer inspection. In the softest shade of sky-blue, it was heavily embroidered with the tiniest silver cross-stitch she had ever seen. The matching veil was as light as air, the merest wisp of silk chiffon in the same delicate shade…

'Get dressed quickly,' Abbas instructed. 'I have allowed a man to shelter inside Aban's tent until the storm has passed. I don't want you scaring him half to death—'

'Me?'

'Yes, you... The man's a silk trader, hence your new robe, but the sight of you wearing it would alarm him. Women in the desert usually have more discretion and never appear in public dressed in such a manner.'

But it was all right for Abbas to see her dressed like this? Even as her hackles rose, Zara felt a twinge of guilt. Perhaps it was the only robe the trader had that was suitable and Abbas needn't have troubled to buy it for her. Glancing at her travel-worn clothes lying crumpled on the floor, she realised how grateful she was to have something clean to wear, especially something new and so undeniably feminine... But her doubts returned the moment she slipped her feet into the dainty jewelled mules Abbas had just pushed under the curtain. She had taken a bath in a man's tent in the middle of a desert—a powerful hunk of a man she didn't even know, and now she was wearing a seductive outfit of his choice.

'Do the mules fit? I took a guess at the size of your feet.'

'It was a very good guess.' And if he knew her shoe size, what else had come under his close scrutiny? Zara wondered.

'Are you ever coming out of there?'

Abbas's impatience sent a little shiver of awareness rushing through her. Pressing the robe to her body, she was just checking to see if it was transparent when he spoke again.

'May I?'

Making a last pass with her hands down the front of the robe to make sure she was decent, she straightened up. 'Of course...'

He flung the curtain back.

'Our fashions suit you...'

'It's very kind of you to say so...'

'Not kind at all—a simple fact,' Abbas assured her.

Closing her eyes, Zara inhaled the faint scent of sandalwood and tried not to imagine what could happen in these sumptuous surroundings with her authoritative, seductive host. She thought about the easy command he had over his words, his actions, his body...

What would it be like when they were making love?

Zara banished that thought immediately, conscious that Abbas was still waiting for her. 'I'll just sponge these clothes down and then I'll be right with you,' she assured him briskly. She might be dressed for seduction, but the practical side of her nature always won through. She was keen for him to be aware of that. Pushing the silk chiffon up her arms, she got to work.

She would have to keep a tight rein on her thoughts, Zara reflected, hanging her clothes carefully over the stand to dry out. All these fantasies about harems and seduction were dangerous. Combing through her hair with her fingers, she adjusted the robe so that it hung properly and tried the veil. With the veil on it felt like dressing up—different, fun, glamorous... 'What shall I do about the water in the bath?'

Did he think she was going to leave that for Aban to deal with too? Zara wondered as she came to join Abbas in the tent. Hunkered down by the brazier, he was putting fresh coffee grounds into the pot. As he stared up in frank admiration their gazes clashed, which brought fresh streams of sensation rushing through her veins. She had to let the veil slip in order to clutch the robe a little closer. Shouldn't he look away now? Zara wondered, feeling her cheeks flame. To distract from her discomfort she attacked him on another front. 'I'm surprised you'd allow Aban to carry up water from the wadi just so you could bathe.'

'*I* brought every drop of water up from the wadi. Aban is my man, not my slave.'

She couldn't help but feel a small glow of appreciation at his words. Or maybe the glow had started when she stared at his lips—they were such sensuous lips.

'You have beautiful hair,' Abbas observed softly.

Zara was suddenly conscious of the weight of her waist-length hair and its silky lustre. It felt soft to her touch and the brush of it against her cheek had never felt so sensuous. Even the way it fell into natural waves when it had been washed, which had always annoyed her in the past, seemed suddenly an advantage. She had never thought of herself as beautiful before.

Abbas made her feel beautiful, Zara realised, wrinkling her brow in confusion. She was relieved when he turned away at last. It gave her a chance to study him covertly. But now the glow she had felt moments before raged into an inferno. Heavily shaded with dark stubble, his face was the hardest face she had ever seen...and she just knew that his body, concealed beneath the flowing folds of his robe, would be the body of a fighting man, hard and beautiful.

'I'm going to shave,' he said, picking up a knife. 'Why don't you sit by the brazier and dry your hair while I'm gone?'

'Gone?' She didn't want him gone...not with a storm threatening outside.

'I won't be long—'

'Fine…' She tilted her chin at a confident angle, but something in her voice made him turn to reassure her.

'I'll secure the tent before I leave. You'll be quite safe.'

A fierce gust of wind made the decision for her. 'I'm coming with you.' She grabbed her camera.

'No, stay here and dry your hair—'

'I like to dry my hair outside.'

'Where the air is full of sand? And you don't want sand in your camera, do you?'

Clean out of reasonable excuses, Zara sank down on the cushions again. It was getting progressively darker inside the tent—another indicator that forces were at work over which she had no control. According to Abbas, she wasn't safe outside and she didn't feel safe inside. She was his prisoner as surely as if she were locked inside a cell. And somehow she had to subdue the *frisson* of excitement that provoked.

'Stay here—where you'll be safe,' he repeated as a parting shot.

Did she want to be safe with Abbas?

Reduced to drumming her fingers on the hide couch, Zara was longing to pick up her camera. But she had given Abbas her word. She would ask his permission before taking any more photographs. It was only fair when he was sheltering her from the storm. She couldn't betray his trust. Her heart lurched when he walked back inside the tent and she saw his gaze flick to the camera. It was still in its case just as she had left it. The approval in his eyes sent fire racing through her veins, but even a shave couldn't soften the hard planes of his rugged face. His cheekbones seemed more pronounced than ever, his jaw stronger.

'What are you worrying about?' His brow creased.

'Worried? I'm not worried.' She met his gaze levelly, but the expression in Abbas's eyes added a dangerous spark to the scent of hard, clean man.

She watched him seal the entrance with strong, capable hands. A few robust tugs and he appeared to be satisfied that everything was secure. He moved on around the tent, checking the supports and ignoring her. She should be pleased about that, Zara told herself. The wind had picked up and sand was hitting the sides with an ominous hissing sound. When the tent poles groaned beneath the pressure she began to get worried.

'Are you sure it's safe?' She had to yell to make herself heard above the noise.

'I'm sure—'

'And Aban? Do you think he will have reached safety by now?'

Abbas looked pleased that she had remembered. 'Yes, I checked on him while I was out.' Pulling a satellite phone out of his pocket, he tossed it on to the bed.

She could have rung for help. Why hadn't she thought of it before? 'Could I borrow your phone?' Her mobile was still in the Jeep.

'There's too much static for a call to get through now.'

She hid her disappointment. 'How about the trader?'

'He's safe too—'

And then, before Abbas could say any more to her, a juddering blast made her exclaim with fright.

'Don't worry.' Abbas ran his hand down the ballooning sides of the pavilion. 'This dense fabric is made from camel hair. There's nothing better for keeping out the weather.

And these supporting poles may look flimsy, but they flex to accommodate the force of the gale just like the trunk of a palm tree.' Wrapping his fist around one, he caressed it.

'How long do you think we'll be here?'

'It's impossible to know, so you might as well relax and get used to your confinement…'

Relax? That was easy for Abbas to say—her bones were turning to liquid fire at the thought of being secured inside the tent with him and her heart was vibrating frantically, though not from fear.

'Well, I'm going to relax even if you won't…'

'What are you doing?' Zara stared, unbelieving, as Abbas calmly began shrugging off his robe.

'Getting undressed…' His voice was casual.

'Put your clothes back on again. Now,' Zara ordered hoarsely. Abbas stalked about naked when he was relaxed? Beneath his Zaddaran dignity Abbas possessed an elemental quality that both frightened and excited her. She hadn't got the measure of him and that frightened her too. And now he was testing her she was sure of it. She could lose her mask, tell him the truth—that she was more innocent than she seemed, that life had made her act a lot older than her age, or she could play it cool.

She was relieved when she didn't have to make that choice. Having loosened his robe, Abbas stretched out on a bed of hides and closed his eyes. All she could see now was a glimpse of hard, tanned flesh above the topmost folds of his robe, though where it fell away she could see the loose-fitting trousers he wore beneath…trousers slung low enough to do more than hint at the toned athletic body underneath.

Sucking in a deep, shuddering breath, Zara was almost ready to believe she could feel the warmth of Abbas's naked flesh reaching out to her—warm, fragrant, sandalwood-scented flesh that she longed to feel pressed up hard against her own. Shifting awkwardly on the couch, she knew she was slipping into an even deeper state of arousal. The thought of easing that frustration had crossed her mind... Everything was so unreal—like a day out of time... A day when she could allow herself to be seduced by a man for whom she felt an overwhelming attraction... To have Abbas make love to her... One night of passion with the lion of the desert... And who would know? She was sure Abbas would know everything there was to know about pleasing a woman.

Zara's breathing grew more ragged as she developed her fantasy... A man she didn't know—an older man, an experienced man, a man whose eyes promised exotic pleasures beyond her understanding, a man whose lips she longed to feel all over her body, even those secret places no other man had seen...

But Abbas was a man of principle. He had already proved that by his care for Aban and the trader. There was no way he would touch her while he was treating her as an honoured guest. The best thing to do was to act calmly and normally, as he was doing, and push the dangerous fantasies from her mind.

Reaching into her bag, she drew out a pencil. 'Would you mind telling me what each item of clothing you're wearing is called? I want to be sure I get everything right when I prepare my journal back home.'

Opening one eye, Abbas turned to look at her. An expression of faint amusement flickered across his face, but then he shrugged and, resting his head back on crossed arms, he started to talk.

While her heart hammered away, Zara took refuge in her professional eye. The decoration on his robe was a testament to the skill of the local needle-workers. The gold thread picked up the amber lights in his eyes, something that added to his attraction, and she hadn't noticed before. The dramatic contrast of that and the black fabric of the main body of the robe was a perfect foil for his black hair and for his dark skin tone as well as for his strong white teeth... She could almost imagine them nipping into her flesh...

'Do you have a problem?'

Zara realised she had stopped writing and was gazing into space with a dreamy look on her face. 'No, no, I'm fine.' She drew herself up. 'It's really interesting...' She smiled to encourage him to keep on talking, while she indulged in her fantasy—her nice, *safe* fantasy.

'Perhaps when you return to the city you will buy some eastern clothes to remind you of your time in the desert?' Abbas suggested.

'I'm sure I shall...'

'Though you're more than welcome to keep the robe you're wearing now—with my compliments.'

'This one? I couldn't possibly.' Zara's gaze flew over the intricate workmanship. She guessed the silk robe must have cost a fortune.

'Don't you like it?'

'I love it, but—'

'But?' Abbas pressed. 'You don't accept gifts from

strangers?' he guessed shrewdly. 'So what if I sell it to you? Would you take it home with you then?'

She didn't want to go home yet... And, as for selling the robe to her... Zara's heart lurched as Abbas's lips curved in a way she hadn't seen them do before and her heart stormed into overdrive as she considered the price he might have in mind. 'Do you accept travellers' cheques?'

'I'm a little short of banking facilities, as you can see...' He laughed softly. 'But you could owe me...'

'I'm not sure I'm comfortable with that...' She stood up as she spoke.

'Where are you going?' He sat up.

She had to get away. She had to take a moment to cool down. 'To look outside—'

Springing up, Abbas stood in her way. 'No...'

'No?' She looked at him, and then down at his hand on her arm.

His dark eyes flared, but he spoke softly as he lifted his hand away. 'If you move that curtain the sand will come flying in. The entrance cover must remain as it is until I say it can be opened.'

'So I'm a prisoner here?' Turning away from him, Zara could feel the tension mounting.

'You're here as my guest,' Abbas reminded her.

She could feel him behind her and her pulse responded eagerly to the remorseless beat of his virility. Abbas had thrown an erotic noose around her, which he then pulled tight. 'Let me go,' she warned in a whisper, hardly realising that he wasn't even touching her.

'Or you'll...what?'

She could feel the sweep of his breath across the back

of her neck and had to fight not to tremble. She didn't start breathing again until he stepped away and felt as weak as a puppet when the strings had been let go. And had left her more aroused than ever.

Abbas understood everything about tension—tightening and releasing the invisible cord until it was she who was being driven to make the first move. The blood in her veins had turned to molten honey. Caught in the ambit of Abbas's darkening stare, Zara had to wonder how long she could hold out if it came to it. Abbas was so hard, so elemental, and his robes left so little and yet too much of his powerful frame to the imagination. Rampantly masculine, he was a natural-born hunter... Was she really ready to take him on? And then there was her own lack of experience where sex was concerned to consider... She would almost certainly disappoint him. The elements chose just that moment to intervene. While she was hesitating, the wind gave a terrible roar and, shocked into action, she launched herself into Abbas's arms.

'Sorry—' Gasping with shock, Zara made as if to pull away, but Abbas held on to her. It was a hold so gentle that if she had wanted to she could have broken free at any time...

'Please,' he murmured, brushing her hair with his lips. 'Don't apologise, Adara...'

'Adara?' She raised her eyes to look at him.

Placing one finger over her mouth, Abbas dragged it slowly down over the full swell of her bottom lip as if to remind her how aroused she was... And to tell her that he knew. 'I will call you Adara...'

It meant virgin in his language, but she couldn't know that. It pleased his sense of irony to call her by this name.

Though she was young she had the assurance of a much older woman. His Adara knew what she wanted, and she knew he could give it to her. There would be no complications; she was on the same wavelength he was, and it amused him to see how she squared up to him even now. Her face was flushed and he had to wonder how much of that passion would be channelled into their lovemaking. Nothing was a foregone conclusion and he liked that about her. She was cool and self-possessed, but she could be defiant too and he had never encountered disobedience before. Her unpredictability fuelled his appetite, and would certainly stave off boredom while they waited out the storm.

She collected herself quickly, as he had expected, and he was ready for her. As she went to move away to take her seat on the couch again he made sure their fingers brushed—as if by accident. Her swift intake of breath told him everything he needed to know. And as the moment froze he held her gaze.

CHAPTER THREE

'THE storm is easing...'

As Abbas spoke, Zara watched him move towards the entrance as if the sexual temperature between them had never flickered. Maybe it hadn't for him. Keenly aware of the progress of the storm outside the tent, maybe he was oblivious to the storm he had whipped up inside it. Or was he toying with her? Which one was it?

'If the weather is improving I want to leave as soon as I can...'

'Three days and three nights,' he said, turning to face her.

So he had remembered. 'Your custom?' She raised a brow, wanting him to know she wasn't convinced.

'Custom demands that, having sought refuge here, you must remain as my guest for three days and three nights...' His face told her nothing as he sat down again and arranged his robe around his legs.

'You're serious, aren't you?' She had to drag her gaze away and ignore the heavy throb of anticipation in her lower body.

Raising his head, Abbas levelled a stare on her face. 'I am bound by the customs of my land...'

'But I am not.' It was too shadowy to interpret his expression with any confidence, but Abbas's silence suggested she was mistaken. She didn't press him, knowing he would probably reply that at this moment she was a guest in his land.

Zara found it hard to relax. Abbas's commanding manner had aroused her to the degree where his slightest move made her heart race. He made her long for things that had never mattered to her before, forbidden things. She hardly dared to imagine what it might be like to be held by him, to be cradled in his arms, to be touched delicately, persuasively… As he leaned forward to check the coffee she saw the flare of recognition in his eyes and pulled herself round. 'As soon as the trader leaves, I'm going with him. Even if my Jeep has been lost, it doesn't matter. I'll hitch a lift with him.'

'On his camel? And I think you'll find that he has already gone.'

'But the storm has only just died down…'

'Come with me, Adara…'

When Abbas released the entrance cover Zara uttered a sharp breath of amazement. The desert was peaceful again, but they might have been carried up and brought down in a totally different place. What had happened to the dune where she had been captured, the dune behind which she had sheltered her off-road vehicle? Now all she could see was a flat plain that stretched away into the distance as far as the foothills of the mountains. The sand around the tent had formed into wavelike ripples. The structure was now isolated in a vast expanse of flat featureless nothingness, like a ship floating on a sea of sand…

Looking further, Zara was relieved to see that at least the palm trees clustering round the wadi had survived. But they were bent at such an acute angle their fronds were brushing the water... She found it much easier to walk in the flat sandals Abbas had provided and was suddenly eager to escape the confines of the tent. Hurrying over to the nearest palm, she touched its trunk gently with her hand. 'Will it recover?' She glanced at Abbas, who had come to stand by her shoulder.

'Yes,' he reassured her. 'The trunks of the palm are as flexible as the poles used to support the tent and so they will recover, given time.'

Leaving her, he strode towards the second tent, which had also survived the onslaught of the storm. Picking up her skirts, Zara hurried after him.

There was no sign of the trader or his camel. There was nothing to show that he had been there at all other than a bundle hanging from the fronds of a palm. 'What is it?' Shading her eyes, she looked up into the branches.

'I have already told you that hospitality is instilled at birth in the Bedouin, and so is repayment of the debt.'

Was Abbas sending her a hidden message? Zara wondered, pressing him to continue.

'That cache will contain whatever the trader can safely spare. It is his way of thanking me. But I am honour bound not to touch anything I don't need, the point being I must consider the needs of others over myself.'

His words sent a shiver tracking her spine. 'Perhaps I could copy some prints to send to you when I get home... I have taken some good landscapes...' As she gestured around, Zara felt her offer wasn't enough. 'And I'll send

you a cheque too, of course.' She couldn't bear freeload-
ers and didn't want Abbas mistaking her for one.

'A cheque?'

'Money for the time I've spent here as your guest…'

'I do know what a cheque is. I just wondered why you
should feel it necessary to send one to me.'

'To cover the cost of sheltering me, of course,' she
said, frowning.

'Are you always so scrupulous?'

'Yes.' She held his gaze steadily. 'I never use people and
then just walk away.'

'But you haven't left yet,' he pointed out, 'and I may
need to add something to your account.'

Zara's eyes widened. She didn't know whether to
believe Abbas or not.

He couldn't resist provoking her just a little more. Three
days and nights… It was an outrageous idea, even if he had
based his assertion on ancient lore. Traditions such as that
had never been meant to apply to a situation like this. But
he could hardly blame his ancestors for not factoring into
their thinking one reckless young female who had ventured
into the desert without a chaperon.

And the storm hadn't finished with them yet. This was
only a lull. What he should do was dispatch her to the
spare tent to wait out the weather and then send her on her
way with Aban. But he had been a long time alone in the
desert and he was only human. The girl was strong and self-
assured, mature beyond her years; she knew the score.

He followed her back into the pavilion, noticing how she
resented the yards of material flapping round her ankles.

Having forgotten to pick up her skirts, she looked like an ungainly fawn as she struggled to cope with the flowing robe. Big brown eyes and that shock of golden hair peeping out beneath the veil only added to the illusion. He liked her in the veil; it suited her—softened her.

'Is another storm coming?' she asked anxiously, turning to face him as a gust of wind snatched the veil from her head.

'I think we should go back inside,' he advised.

'If there is another storm, how long do you think it will last?'

For a mischievous moment, as he secured the entrance behind them, he was tempted to leave what he was doing and stride outside to sniff the air. But play-acting wasn't his thing. The truth was, he didn't have a clue. They hadn't taught weather forecasting on his course at Harvard Business School.

'What shall we do to pass the time?'

The innocent question was negated by the look in her eyes and his senses, already sharpened by his days of denial in the desert, raged out of control. He found it ironic that the desert had given her to him. The coincidence of them meeting in thousands of square miles of hostile land was incredible, but she had come to him with the dawn—his virgin, Adara. Fortunately, her manner, her eyes, her body language all assured him she was no such thing. When they were both sated and his mind clear again, he would return to Zaddara and take up his duties. This would be his last self-indulgence before duty claimed him.

And now there was only one thing still plucking at his mind. According to Zaddaran tradition there was no such thing as coincidence; there was only destiny.

She went to check her camera and as he looked at her something inside him softened briefly. 'You may take a handful of photographs if you wish—but only of objects and your surroundings. As an aide-memoire for your trip,' he added. He wasn't prepared for the look on her face of sheer surprised delight and found it gave him pleasure to please her.

'That's very good of you. I promise I'll be quick…' She reached for the camera. 'I know I haven't exactly been the easiest guest. Do you forgive me?'

As she turned her face up to him, he wanted to tell her just how much. The appeal in her eyes made his heart turn over which, as far as he could recall, had never happened before. The offer of the photographs had changed something. It was almost as if an understanding, a bond, had developed between them.

She was scrupulously fair and obviously knew what she was doing. She took a few shots of the tent and some objects and then put the camera away. 'There, I've finished. Thank you…'

His gaze was drawn to her lips, reddened where she had chewed on them while she was concentrating on her work. And now there were questions in her eyes: Did he find her attractive? Did he want her? Did he want her enough to make love to her? The answer to all three was, of course, yes. Her lips were slightly parted and damp where she had moistened them. She wasn't afraid to hold his gaze. She was beautiful and she was ready, and she was waiting for him to make the first move.

'Three days and three nights?' She made it sound like a request. And, as she stared at him, his hunger surged to a new level. He had expected many things of his retreat in the desert, but not this forwardness of a young woman who had appeared out of nowhere like a gift...

'And then we will part asking nothing of each other,' he confirmed.

As silence descended between them they both knew it could only have one outcome. And it was a delicious moment that neither one of them wanted to break. It took a ferocious gust of wind to bring her into his arms and, as she rested her head against his chest, he silently praised the storm for wrestling with the tent.

There was barely enough time to inhale Abbas's delicious scent and feel his warmth seeping through the flimsy fabric of her robe before he swung her into his arms. 'We'd ask nothing of each other?' Zara repeated Abbas's words back to him in a whisper.

'Only this,' he murmured, carrying her towards his bed.

She felt so safe that even the sand rattling against the sides of the tent seemed to be in another world. Her body was tuned to his, waiting for his touch, eager to feed on the passion she knew he possessed. He was so restrained, so controlled; to see him lose that was the only thing she wanted now. When he lowered her to the bed she reached up to draw him down to her. Cupping her face in his warm hands, he kissed her deeply. The taste of him was delicious and addictive, the boldness of his tongue the most thrilling thing she had ever known. She wanted more, more of everything, more of Abbas. She wanted every part of him to be touching her and so she clung to him, pressing herself against him until he was forced to hold her away. She made a complaint at once, asking him, 'Why…?'

Abbas smiled against her mouth. 'Your clothes,' he murmured.

Fortunately, she wasn't wearing many, Zara thought, starting to wriggle her way out of the restrictive robe.

'Let me…'

'And yours,' she ordered, impatient to feel him naked against her.

Abbas had no inhibitions and, as he stripped off his robe, she sucked in an excited breath. He exceeded all her expectations. He was the most beautiful man she could have imagined. Resting her hands on his shoulders, she studied him boldly with the eye of an artist. He was like a living statue carved in bronze, with each muscle and sinew clearly delineated. Stroking him, she revelled in his strength and in the way he quivered beneath her touch. The expression in his eyes when he looked at her with approval was intoxicating. He was so big and so powerful and his muscles rippled as they wrestled together playfully. He allowed her to make all the moves, barely touching her, which in turn was the most arousing thing she had ever known. But he knew how to tease and each caress of his hand, each brush of his fingers, lit a separate fire.

Catching hold of her hand, Abbas drew it to his lips. Zara gasped in surprise when he began to suckle each fingertip in turn. She could feel the sensation all over her skin. Crying out for him to be merciful, she sobbed with relief when at last he let her go, but almost at once she wanted him back again. And, when he would not fall in with her wishes immediately, she balled her hands into fists and pounded them against his chest, calling him angry names until he was forced to capture her wrists in one powerful fist and hold them firmly in place on the pillows above her head.

She drew deeply on the fragrance of his skin and sighed with contentment. And, when at last he released her hands, it was her turn to take control—exploring the hard path of muscle, the inflexibility of bone, her fingers travelling slowly and provocatively until it was Abbas's turn to sigh. She enjoyed the sensation of rough chest hair springing against her finger-pads and smiled to feel his nipples harden beneath her touch. Placing both her hands flat on his chest, she drew them slowly down over his torso across the impressive banding of muscle to where she could feel the heat of his erection.

Brushing him lightly, she pulled away when he groaned with pleasure. She hadn't expected him to be so big. The speed and strength of what was happening to her had not prepared her for this reality. And the reality of a man like Abbas was a great deal more than she had expected.

But then he touched her softly, gently, and her courage began to return. If Abbas could tease, then so could she. And she hadn't finished with him yet...

Crouching up on her knees, she used her long hair to brush back and forth across his body, while Abbas made sounds of appreciation deep in his throat. For the first time she knew the power of her femininity and, growing in confidence, she swept her hair across his ribcage, moving gradually lower.

To see Abbas quivering with anticipation was the most intoxicating thing Zara had ever experienced. She found she couldn't stop watching his erection swell and pulse, and as it did so she felt her own body responding to the same urgent rhythm.

And then he turned her so that now she was beneath him. He kissed her again and she whimpered with long subdued hunger. She was feeling everything she had ever hoped for... Abbas's lips, his tongue, his arms, his hands, teasing her and tasting her, enjoying her as she was enjoying him until she could only cry and laugh and beg him to stop before she begged him for more.

Pausing, he raised his head to stare down at her. 'Make yourself clear,' he instructed her huskily. 'Do you want more, or shall I stop?'

'More,' she commanded him, lacing her fingers through his thick black hair, 'I want more...'

Abbas took control then, lifting her to new levels of sensation until every inch of her was trembling and aware. She believed in that moment that it couldn't get any better until he moved down the bed and did something wonderful. Easing her thighs apart with a gentle touch, he dipped his head and tasted her. And then he brought her floating on a river of sensation with his lips and his tongue and his hands. He knew everything he had to do to please her. And, as she gave herself up to him, he slipped her legs over his shoulders to open her more.

Trusting him completely, she closed her eyes. Her world shrank to encompass just the two of them and the sensation steadily building under Abbas's skilful direction. When the storm broke he was ready for her and held her firmly as she cried out wildly as the waves came at her one after the other and with increasing force, until finally, when she had no strength left, they subsided into tiny, delicious little after shocks.

And then she could only manage a single word. 'More…'

Easing her legs off his shoulders and lowering them down gently to the bed, Abbas moved up to her. It was hard to believe that such a powerful man could be so caring, or could possess such finesse and such tenderness.

Zara thought her body must have melted away, leaving nothing behind it but sensation. Everything she had imagined about arousal beneath the hands of a man had been wrong. This was arousal, this stream of sensation through her limbs, the tears of fulfilment streaming down her face, this heightened sense of awareness, the colours sharper, the noises louder, the taste of Abbas lingering on her lips—delicious, spicy, male. And now she could hardly believe how quickly the hunger was returning again. Combing out her hair in strands of gold as she moved beneath him, she tempted him on…

He couldn't wait to possess her. His impatience was that of a boy's, because that was how she made him feel. She had given him so much more than he had anticipated. He had not expected her to be his sexual equal in both appetite and eagerness, but she had matched him and that was not something he had ever expected to find in a woman.

The taste of her, sweet and delicious, still danced on his tongue and the feel of her skin under his hands was the strongest aphrodisiac he had ever known. The scent of her skin and of her hair reminded him of wild flowers billowing in an English meadow and the look in her eyes was bewitching him. When she called out to him he wanted nothing more than to satisfy her need; she had kindled a fire inside him, which he doubted would ever go out. It took all his strength to pause and reach for protection. But he wanted to protect her in every way. And now she was sobbing softly with impatience for him. It made him smile and made him more determined than ever to tease her for a little longer.

Her eyes widened as he drew himself up and touched her very lightly. As he brushed himself back and forth she drew her legs up to urge him on. He needed no urging, but he would not be hurried. He wanted to look at her first, to drink her in, and to see her blush-pink body throbbing with desire for him. Her nipples were extended and tight with need, her lips parted and her eyes black with the same hunger they both felt. She made no false pretence of modesty and when she writhed provocatively he could see every part of her was swollen and throbbing. She was ready for him.

'Abbas,' she murmured, staring at him through half-shut eyes.

It amused him to think he had never needed prompting before. 'Maybe I should make you wait a little longer?' He pretended to think about it, anticipating her complaint.

'I won't wait. I want you now.' Lacing her fingers through his hair, she drew him close.

But still he held himself back and kept her at a distance so that only their tongues could touch, and then just barely. For all his bravado, he wasn't sure that he could wait much longer, and she was intent on making it harder for him with her stroking, searching fingers...

'Do you submit?' she demanded softly.

The wind answered her, moaning languorously, and

then the supporting timbers joined in, creaking in a gentle rhythm that rose and fell like a pulse.

'Kiss me, Abbas… Kiss me now,' she ordered. They were so close now that the smallest movement of her mouth was enough for their lips to brush.

Drawing back, he prepared to take her.

CHAPTER FOUR

His senses were tuned to the highest level and so he felt her fear before it even showed on her face. It made him pause. And then he saw everything she was feeling reflected in her eyes—apprehension, tension, dread—and drew back sharply.

'Abbas?' She reached for him, wondering what she'd done wrong.

Rolling away, he sat up and, grabbing his robe, he swung it over his head.

'Abbas, what's wrong?'

'Why didn't you tell me?' Turning, he stared down at her.

'I don't understand…' Her face was flushed and her eyes had filled with tears.

'I think you do.' He stood up.

'Did I do something wrong?'

As she pulled up the sheet to cover her naked breasts, he could see that she had lost the air of innocent abandonment and was already ashamed. Cursing, he stood to secure his robe, and it was then, when he needed interruption the least, that he heard the new sound outside.

'Abbas, where are you going?'

'I have to go out…' There was no time to explain. Raking his hair into some sort of order, he could only rail inwardly at himself. He had misread the signs so badly that he had almost seduced an innocent girl. He had allowed desire to rule him and had closed his mind to the truth. Just the thought of what he had almost done sickened him. And now events had taken over and she would be left floundering because their time together had just run out.

'Abbas, please…'

'Can't you hear? We have visitors.' He turned, impatient to be gone, impatient to cut the ties on a situation that seemed suddenly so squalid and depressing that he couldn't wait to get away.

'Engines?' she guessed, her voice faltering.

'Rotor blades of a helicopter,' he informed her briskly, swallowing his emotions. She was struggling to find her way out of a world of sensuality as well as cope with the sudden change in him, while he had to think of the greater good. There was no time to consider his feelings or hers— he had a country to think of. 'Get up and get dressed.'

As he started for the entrance he caught a glimpse of her sinking back on to the bed, ashen-faced. Pressing her lips together hard so she wouldn't cry, she turned her face into the pillow, but not before he'd seen the expression in her eyes. He felt her bewilderment like a reproach. But, as they wouldn't be seeing each other again, it hardly mattered. They would both have to mark this down to experience and put it behind them.

Zara couldn't believe what had happened and for a good few minutes after Abbas had left the tent she couldn't face it either and kept her face hidden in the pillows. But then she grew furious. Why hadn't Abbas had the guts to face up to her and admit that she didn't please him, that he didn't want her and that she fell short as a woman? His brusque manner proved he had no respect for her. Walking out as he had done had left her burning with shame. She felt ugly and gauche, knowing the closeness they had shared, closeness that had been about to become intimacy. Had it been an illusion of her own making? When he walked out there had been nothing left of the tender lover. It was as if a switch had been turned off and Abbas had woken up and wondered what on earth he was doing with her.

Swinging off the bed, Zara pulled the sheet tight and hurried through the curtain to collect her own clothes. She couldn't wait to wash, to dress, to leave the tent and get away from him. She never wanted to see him again.

So much for her adventure with a Bedouin in the desert, Zara raged silently as she dragged on her clothes. The adventure had drifted away on the heels of the storm—the promised three days and three nights had shrunk to fewer than three hours! And during that time she had played out the role of a naïve tourist providing distraction for a prince of the desert while he waited for the weather to improve and his transport to arrive.

Storming out just as Abbas came back into the tent, she tossed the silk robe at his feet. 'Here, take your robe—'

He didn't reply and only stared at her, his face an enigmatic mask that told her he would not be drawn into an argument. She deduced that whoever his visitors might be, they were still waiting for him outside.

'I'll call Aban,' he said, making no move to pick up the

robe. He'll come for you with the Jeep. You can take some fruit for the journey and some water—'

'Is that it?'

'Should there be more?'

The verbal slap in the face stunned her, but she was careful not to let it show. And then Abbas turned away and walked across the tent as if they were two strangers who had only just met and who owed each other nothing.

Picking up another, more formal, robe, he began to put it on. The *jalabiyya* was long and flowing in regal black and, as he fastened the elaborate belt around his waist, she was stung into reminding him, 'Don't forget your *khanjar*...' Lifting the ornate dagger from the stool beside the bed, she held it out to him. 'No Zaddaran Bedouin is properly dressed without one, isn't that right, Abbas? I believe a weapon of this type is meant to represent your pride and honour?'

Ignoring her cold, accusing stare, he took the dagger from her without comment and secured it in his belt. 'I'll make sure some water bottles are loaded into the Jeep for you—'

'I'm sure Aban will have seen to that—'

She wasn't sure that Abbas had even heard her. He walked away without another word, dipping his head to leave the tent, totally in possession of himself, every bit the tribal leader.

Taking one last look around, Zara found that everything that had so recently enchanted her had lost its appeal. She felt like an intruder, an unwelcome guest who must keep hidden for fear of shaming the host. And yet only minutes before the lion of the desert had been sighing beneath her touch. He hadn't wanted to get rid of her quite so quickly then, she thought angrily, picking up her camera.

She could hear snatches of conversation from outside. The men took it in turn to talk and all of them deferred to Abbas. She could hear relief and respect in the voices of his men and her face burned when she heard their laughter. Was she the subject of discussion? If she was, she damn well deserved it.

'Are you ready?'

Zara's head lifted as Abbas walked back inside the tent.

'Aban is waiting for you.' He gave her a brief head to toe inspection as if to check she looked respectable before showing herself outside.

She ignored it. 'What about my Jeep?'

'My men haven't located it yet, but they will.'

'Please thank them for trying.'

She was all business now, her feelings hidden. At least she'd had years of practice doing that.

She was in Zaddara because she'd had a dream that everything would be clearer to her after the visit, and that she would understand why her parents had loved the country so much they had left her behind in England with her grandparents. That dream was dead now.

Zara clutched her camera tightly as she thought about it. She hoarded images like a miser because her grandparents hadn't been able to face photographs of her parents and had removed every piece of memorabilia from their home. When they had died and she had sorted everything out, she had pounced on a dog-eared album stuck away in the back of a drawer—now that was all she had to remember her parents by.

'It's time to go—'

Zara refocused as Abbas spoke. His voice was harsh as if

he had more important things to do than wait for her. 'I'm ready.' She didn't look at him. She didn't want him imagining the tears that always managed to break through her reserve whenever she thought about her parents were for him.

'Your vehicle will be recovered and returned to you in good condition,' he said as she walked past him.

She calmly thanked him and pushed the entrance cloth aside.

'I will have it serviced… At my expense, of course.'

She stopped and let the cloth drop from her hands as she turned to face him. 'I prefer to meet my own expenses. I took the decision to drive into the desert and the vehicle remains my responsibility.'

'As you wish—' He made an impatient gesture as if to say he had no time to argue the point with her.

In the scorching desert light the military helicopter appeared like a sinister black crow perched on the sand and Zara was surprised to see the squad of men in front of it dressed in army fatigues. A shiver of alarm ran through her as one of them came towards her. She backed away as he raised his gun, but he was too quick for her and tried to rip the camera from her hands.

As she fought him, Abbas saw what was happening and issued a brisk command. The soldier released her immediately.

'I must apologise for the zeal of my men—'

'Zeal?' Zara was furious as she brushed down her sleeve where the soldier had held her. 'Bullies, don't you mean?'

'He was only trying to protect my interest—'

'Save it, Abbas, for someone who might be impressed.' Zara's eyes were blazing as she stared at him.

He glanced at the helicopter. 'This is military equipment and it was your camera they took exception to—'

As Zara cradled it protectively, a hot wave of guilt washed over her. Abbas was right to suspect that she had taken some images that he might not want exposed. It had been a reflex action—he had leaned forward into a shot, by which time her finger was already moving…

'You must give it to me,' he demanded.

'Don't be ridiculous.'

'I don't want to make a fuss.'

'Then don't.'

'I'll need your memory cards too.'

'I can't believe you're saying this. Don't you trust me?' She turned her face up to him and was met by a stare from a man she didn't know.

'The memory cards,' Abbas insisted after a pause, 'and your camera. One of my technicians will go through your images and remove anything I don't wish to be shown—'

His technicians? What business was this man in? 'My answer remains the same.'

'Please.' His voice was clipped; his patience was clearly running out.

She risked one last stand. 'Or?'

'Or I will take them from you.'

She couldn't risk damage to her camera. Grinding her jaw, she handed it over.

'Thank you… It will be returned safely to your hotel when we have finished with it.'

She barely heard him. The camera was her lifeline and now Abbas had taken it from her.

She lifted her chin in time to see him raise his hand to his forehead and dip into the graceful Zaddaran salutation.

'*Ma' a salama*…travel safely, Adara…'

She refused to reply and turned her back when Abbas's helicopter finally lifted off. She would not look up. She would not give Abbas the satisfaction of thinking she cared one way or the other where he went. All she cared about was the safety of her camera.

She should never have come to Zaddara, Zara reflected bitterly walking away to escape the sand flurries drawn up by the rotor blades. She hated the desert. She hated Zaddara. She couldn't imagine what had drawn her parents to such a hostile part of the world, though perhaps it did explain why they had left her behind. Who in their right minds would bring a child to such a terrible place? Most of all she hated him—the man who had told her to call him Abbas. If it hadn't been for the wildlife and some earlier images she had managed to transmit to her computer before he interfered, she wouldn't have had anything to show for her trip.

'What?' Zara turned angrily on the elderly guard, who had chosen that moment to nudge her arm. He was only trying to offer her a bottle of water for the journey, she realised, apologising immediately. 'Thank you…'

As his wrinkled face softened into a smile she felt tears prick behind her eyes. She was teetering on the edge of a full emotional meltdown and his kindness made it even harder to hold on. But that was hardly his fault. '*Shukran*— thank you,' she said again, gently.

'*Ghabel nabud*—it is nothing,' he replied, his eyes glinting with pleasure at her attempt to speak his language.

Before climbing into the Jeep, Zara took a last look around. Images of desert gazelles and the Arabian oryx drinking at the wadi would have to wait now—maybe for ever. The beautiful animals had been a symbol, she realised. More than anything they would have helped her to understand her parents' love for this wild, unforgiving land. But the old Sheikh was dead and she had no friends in Zaddara. There was no one at all who could tell her about her parents.

As Zara watched the arid landscape sliding past the dust-caked window she knew it was time to turn her face to the future. It was that or grow more embittered with each passing year. She had tried walking in the footsteps of her parents and she had failed. Zaddara had been their dream and that was something she would never understand. But back in England she would be free of men like 'Abbas' and his leader, Sheikh Shahin. And she wouldn't let either man ruin her life. She would stage her exhibition. She had enough rage-fuelled energy packed inside her to stage a dozen exhibitions. She could already see the outline in her mind… There would be stark images in black and white of dead creatures, their bones picked clean by vultures… Bleached carcasses against a featureless carpet of sand… Warrior faces turned harsh by aeons of savagery and one face in particular…

The cruel truth of an unforgiving land? Yes, that was her lasting impression of Zaddara and it would make a great title for her exhibition.

CHAPTER FIVE

ANY opening was a nerve-racking event. Would anyone turn up? Would they hate the exhibition? Would they drift around and then move on as soon as was decently possible, wearing tight, embarrassed smiles? 'Will all the canapés dry up before the guests arrive?'

'Will you stop fretting, Zara.'

That wasn't a question, it was an instruction, Zara realised as the older of the two men who ran the city centre gallery admonished her.

'What you've created here is stunning. And if you can't see that...' Lambert paused for a theatrical sigh. 'Then I really don't know what has happened to your eye...'

'My famous eye?'

But Lambert had already floated off in the direction of a lily that wasn't quite standing to attention in one of his fabulous displays and missed Zara's cynical remark.

Lambert was right. She was tied up in knots with nerves. She couldn't relax long enough to look at anything objectively. There was a buzz going round the art world, and all because of this... Walking slowly down the lofty gallery, Zara viewed her images critically. They were shown off to good advantage on the stark white walls. She had opted for colour in the end.

Having started the process of examining the images from Zaddara in an angry, resentful mood thanks to all the bad memories associated with the place, she had been forced to think again. She'd found such an abundance of riches on the returned memory cards and knew instantly that the chance to create something extraordinary was within her reach. Far from a sinister portrayal of a harsh land, she had captured colours and character, shapes and textures, and even a rare glimpse of a sandstorm building beneath a cobalt sky. The flash of humour on an old man's face had surprised her, as had the intricacy of the scroll-work on a silver coffee pot, though that had raised her pulse too. The breathtaking craftsmanship of the goldsmith who had worked on the sheath and pommel of a curving dagger had raised it even more. And, lastly, there had been the silhouette of a man, anonymous and unrecognisable to anyone except her. It was the man who had taken her camera and returned it as promised. The man who had told her that his name was Abbas…

When she had first shown her photographs to Lambert and his partner, Gideon, they had been more excited than she had ever seen them. These were the best images she had ever brought them… She was telling the story of a country in pictures… Zara knew both men were passion-ate about their gallery and the young artists they encour-aged, and for both men to insist that if they didn't have space for her exhibition they would make one…. Well, that had been the moment when she had known she had to put prejudice to one side and get back to work.

And now the exhibition was a sell-out. Which was making her really nervous. She checked her watch again. There were only twenty minutes to go...

At ten minutes before the doors were due to open the exhibition lighting flared on, taking over from the work lights. Colour exploded from the walls and, as she looked around, Zara found it hard to believe it was all her own work. It looked like an exhibition of photographs taken by someone who had loved Zaddara, and she had to admit they took her breath away.

She found her gaze drawn to the far end of the room where the image that had become the emblem of her exhibition took up most of the wall. It showed a Zaddaran Bedouin in stark black relief, with the *howlis* he wore wrapped around his head and face concealing all but a sliver of his autocratic profile. It was enough to make her heart pound. Not black and white after all, but in black, crimson and gold, the colours of the desert, Abbas's image dominated the room. It was the first thing people would see as they entered the gallery.

A ripple ran down Zara's spine as she continued to study the picture. The image held such power and resonance, it was impossible to believe that she had lain in his arms and that for a few hours he had been tender with her. This image showed an elemental force, a man who was at home in the desert and the harsh terrain. Like it or not, Abbas *was* the lion of the desert, he was the fire at the heart of the kingdom of Zaddara.

As a ripple of apprehension travelled across her shoulders, Zara checked her watch again. There were only minutes to go before the doors opened. An anxious glance in the mirror proved she looked as pale as a wraith. She should have remembered lipstick and worn something other than black. Only her hair seemed to have life and colour, but it looked untidy—

'Leave your hair alone,' Gideon instructed, swooping on her. 'Dressed all in black without the suggestion of an adornment, if you screw your hair up in a knot you'll be undistinguishable from a vase.'

'Hush, Gideon,' Lambert observed laconically, peering at her through his pince-nez. 'Zara looks extremely elegant.'

'As she is—with her hair flowing round her shoulders.'

Zara seized the chance to slip away. The first chords of the music she had chosen had just crashed around them and that was the signal for the doors to open.

She could feel the vibrations of the music through her feet and, as the horns pealed out, they tore up the air, shaking the atmosphere with an elemental beat. It was an irresistible rhythm, infectious… Giving in to temptation for just a moment, she closed her eyes and threw back her head to bask in the sound. And now the great doors were opening behind her, but still she didn't move. She could feel the chill damp evening air gushing over her as the art world of London crowded in…

Zara preferred to remain anonymous and mingle with the crowd to pick up whatever feedback she could. But, after being jostled a couple of times, she sought refuge in a corner behind one of Gideon's prized vases, almost knocking it over in her eagerness to escape the crush. Flashing a guilty glance at one of the many security cameras, she remembered that there was no one manning the console. Everyone employed at the gallery was working on the floor in one capacity or another and it was a relief to know her clumsiness would have gone unnoticed. But still she made sure to stay out of the range of the camera. Manned or not, she had the oddest feeling that she was being watched…

'Did you see that girl?'

'I'm afraid not, Majesty.' As far as the Zaddaran ambassador could see, the monitor screen was blank, except for the shadow of a large and rather unprepossessing vase. He had been eager to guide the Sheikh's attention towards other screens showing the images he thought the most appealing, but even they needed adjustment to bring the images into focus and, more crucially, Sheikh Shahin wasn't an easy man to guide.

The ambassador stood back quietly, awaiting his next instruction. The screen hadn't changed, he noticed, though the Sheikh was still studying it.

'No matter.' Straightening to his full height, Shahin waved the ambassador forward, directing him to a seating area where coffee had been laid out for them. 'We'll wait until the crowds have gone and then I'll have a private viewing.'

'I could have the gallery cleared immediately—'

'That won't be necessary…' It was an impetuous visit. *The Desert Unmasked*—an intriguing title for an exhibition. Passing the gallery in the diplomatic car, he'd seen the notice and had asked the driver to slow down. A quick phone call from the Zaddaran ambassador to the gallery's owner and they had been admitted through the owner's own private entrance. That was the way he liked it, low-key and discreet. He never threw his weight around.

'The coffee smells good,' he reassured the ambassador, who clearly felt he should be making things happen, 'and I'd rather wait here.' But his relaxed manner was only a mask for his impatience and he had to ease his shoulders as the enforced inactivity started to get to him. He couldn't view the images properly on the screen; he wanted to get close to them… 'Better still,' he murmured half to himself.

'Yes, Majesty?' The ambassador brightened, sensing an instruction was about to be issued.

'Buy it up… It's easier that way.'

'Buy it up?'

'Yes—everything in the exhibition.' Passing the ambassador a box of small red adhesive dots, Shahin tipped his head towards the door. 'Put one of these on each piece. I want them all, Raschid.' He made a brisk gesture to hurry things along. He wanted to be alone *now*.

This impulsive visit to a gallery was a self-indulgence he didn't have time for. On his return from his retreat in the desert, he had made it a priority to discover the name of his ward. After the incident with the girl Adara he had felt the weight of that particular responsibility more than any other. When his father died it had been a shock to learn that a young woman had passed into his care, but he could understand why his father had assumed the responsibility and he was glad of it. He had felt it too important to send an emissary to reassure his ward that all would continue as before, which was why he was in London. He was here to find her, to introduce himself and to explain…

Easing her way through the crowd, Zara fought her way to the steps in front of the stage from where the image of the

Zaddaran Bedouin stood in silent majesty overlooking the room. The signs were good, but she still wanted to test the mood of her audience. She always needed every bit of reassurance she could get. A gift she believed had come out of nowhere didn't give you an anchor to hang on to. It hung like a mirage in the air, a fragile talent that might disappear at any moment…

Halfway up the stairs she could see Gideon at one end of the gallery and Lambert at the other, both with their heads tilted at an authoritative angle as they each granted an audience to the art groupies gathered round them.

It really was going better than she had ever dared to hope. But, just as she was starting to relax, she heard a rumble of discontent…

His ward had moved around like a boat without an anchor after leaving school, which accounted for the fact that his people hadn't managed to locate her right away. His father had let things slide towards the end of his life and there had been no record of any last address. To make it even harder, she had channelled every penny she received from the Zaddaran treasury into a number of wildlife charities.

Taking a photograph from his wallet, he studied it again. The stubborn tilt of the chin, the direct stare into the camera…reminded him of someone else. Blanking his mind immediately, he turned his thoughts to what the young woman in the photograph would look like now. She might have changed her hair colour, her name, anything… Pigtails and braces changed to the casual clothes of a young woman about town would make her unrecognisable to the squad of private investigators he had put on the case. Her school should have been able to provide him with a more recent photograph, but it was too late to worry about that now. He could only hope the detective agency had uncovered something he could use. To date they had told him that it was unusual for an individual to have no living relatives, no close friends or partners, *no one*.

The truth had hurt.

'Majesty?' The ambassador hurried back into the room, conscious that his services might be required.

Shahin raised his hand to maintain the silence. He needed a few more moments of contemplation.

Respectfully, the ambassador bowed his head and waited in the shadows.

Whatever the circumstances of the death of his ward's parents, he held himself responsible. He believed himself to be guilty as charged and that was all that mattered, since his opinion was the one he had to live with, Shahin reflected, slipping into a sombre mood.

To say she was disappointed was an understatement. The party had gone completely flat. People were starting to leave and there was a resigned mood as if a promised treat had suddenly been snatched away.

Even some of the most avid collectors were on the move... It made her feel sick inside to think the gallery would soon be empty when they were only half an hour into the night... Desperate for reassurance, she caught up with Gideon and was surprised he could look so elated. She stood to one side, waiting for him to finish speaking to some people as the majority of their invited guests continued sweeping past her towards the exit.

'Gideon… What's happened?' she asked him the moment they were alone.

'Wonderful news,' he said, putting his arm round her shoulders.

'Wonderful? But how can it be wonderful when everyone's leaving?'

Zara was so deflated she couldn't summon up the energy to resist Gideon when, taking her by the arm, he steered her towards a side room where they could talk in private.

Zara waited until he had shut the door. 'Gideon?' She gazed at him anxiously. 'You can tell me the truth now. Don't they like it?'

'What?' He threw his head back with incredulity. 'Everyone loves it, just as I told you they would. In fact, they're ecstatic and I'm not surprised—'

'Gideon, please…' For once Zara was in no mood for the gallery owner's theatrical flourishes. 'Just tell me what's going on.'

'There's to be a private showing, of course, and it's all arranged—'

'You're not making sense. How can there be a private showing when all these people have received invitations for tonight? You can't just throw them out—'

'I hope you don't think I would be so crass.'

Zara shook her head. 'I don't know what to think.'

'Didn't you notice all the "sold" stickers?'

'No…' She'd been too upset to notice anything. Her attention had been focused on the faces of their guests, not on her exhibits.

'Well, here's the good news.' Gideon patted her arm.

'You are a very lucky young lady. A private collector has approached me with an offer to purchase the entire collection—'

'Everything?'

'Lock, stock and barrel,' Gideon confirmed with satisfaction.

'So that was why everyone was so disappointed—'

'I have to admit our guests weren't best pleased when all the red stickers started going up. I'd already had quite a few enquiries by then—'

'Then why didn't you consult me?'

'You forget, I am acting as your agent.'

'I don't mean it as a criticism, Gideon. But to sell everything to one collector... I'm not in this for the money. You know that—'

'Lucky you.' Gideon pursed his lips. 'Not all of us can afford to be so blasé.'

'I'm sorry. It's just a shock for me, that's all.' Zara was still trying to take in what he'd told her. 'I just wish we could have discussed it before everything was agreed.'

'Opportunities like this don't come along every day.'

Zara was forced to concede, 'You're right. You and Lambert have been good enough to host my exhibition and I realise you're not in this business to indulge me.'

'Good girl,' Gideon said approvingly. 'Now, come with me and meet your patron—'

'He's here now? Where?' she asked as Gideon opened the door on the rapidly emptying gallery.

'Upstairs in my office. He wanted this to be a private visit—no fanfares.'

Zara's heart began to race. It had to be someone important, perhaps one of the fabulously wealthy collectors of art who preferred discretion above flaunting their wealth. 'Do I have to meet him?'

'It's usual for the artist to spare a few moments for their benefactor and I think you'll be pleasantly surprised,' Gideon confided. 'I know I was. And if your conscience is bothering you, please don't be concerned about our invited guests because he has requested a champagne reception at the weekend to which everyone is invited. It will be a celebration of your work. Just imagine that…'

This was the pinnacle of her career to date, so why was she feeling so anxious? It wasn't fair to Gideon, or to Lambert, Zara decided. 'I suppose it will be great if we get on…'

'If you don't meet him, you'll never know.'

Tilting her head to one side, she began to smile. 'You're very persuasive.'

'That's my job,' Gideon reminded her. 'Shall we go up?'

Starting up the flight of stairs behind him, Zara nodded her head. 'Are the monitors on?'

Gideon stopped. 'Why do you ask?' One perfectly manicured hand twitched lightly on the banister.

He didn't want any last-minute hitches, Zara guessed. 'I just wondered—if the collector hasn't even been down to the gallery, what made him buy up all the exhibits?'

'A whim? Who can fathom the minds of the super-rich?'

'I suppose…'

'And you know we always do our very best for you. He said he saw the banner outside the gallery. It made him stop the car—'

'Don't you think you should tell me who it is? Prepare me?'

'I've always loved surprises…' Gideon gave her a wink as they reached the door to his private quarters.

How ironic that she should feel so apprehensive at the thought of losing her images of Zaddara when she had almost destroyed them herself, Zara reflected. But now it looked as though she wouldn't be able to keep a single item from her Zaddaran collection. But this wasn't an ego trip and her charities needed the cash just as much as Gideon and Lambert. 'Okay… Let's get this over with.'

'I'd advise you to put a smile on your face first.'

'Will this do?' She pulled a face.

'We're talking tens of thousands of pounds,' Gideon reminded her in an important whisper. 'But if that's the best you can manage, then I suppose it will have to do.'

As all the tiny hairs lifted on the back of her neck, Zara wondered who she was going to find behind the door of Gideon's office. Gideon was quite relaxed, but that was because he considered his part of the job done. He would hand over to Lambert now to put the gloss on everything and provide the smiles and charm that had made their gallery such a honey pot for the *cognoscenti*.

This feeling inside her was ridiculous, Zara told herself firmly. What did she have to worry about when Lambert could charm the birds from the trees and Gideon had a ferociously sharp mind? Gideon would already be thinking about their next exhibition, believing the money for this one as good as in the bank.

Money had never been her main driver, Zara reflected as she walked down the opulent hallway. One day she hoped to find a home for her work that wasn't dependent on sales, but that would take a miracle. For now she had to work as hard as she could for the best result.

Unlike the studied modernity of the gallery, Gideon and Lambert's private eyrie was a testament to their impeccable taste and joint love of all things luxurious. There wasn't a piece of plastic or a chrome lamp in sight, Zara noted dryly as Gideon led the way across the thickly carpeted hallway. Gideon's real pride and joy was the room they were going into next, the room he referred to as his control pod. It had been designed so that he could view all the exhibits in the gallery, though it took his skill to bring them into clear focus on the monitor screens. It was here she would meet the man who had harvested her images as though they were cans of beans in a supermarket sweep. What would he be like? An obsessive collector, she supposed... Older, and possibly reclusive. 'Who is he, Gideon?'

'My client prefers to remain anonymous—'

'Oh, come on, there must be a name on the cheque. Or is he paying you in gold bullion? Gideon?' Zara firmed her voice. 'What aren't you telling me?'

But Gideon had already opened the door. 'May I present Miss Zara Kingston... The artist,' he announced grandly.

She saw Lambert first, standing beside a short tubby man in a dark suit, which reassured her. But then she saw another man standing in the shadows. He turned as she entered, by which time Lambert was advancing with his arms outstretched in welcome.

'His Majesty—'

'I told you, Raschid... No ceremony here.'

She might not have recognised him at once in the immaculate bespoke suit, but the voice was harsh and cold, exactly as she remembered it.

'Gideon, a chair if you please,' Lambert said urgently as Zara swayed towards him.

They connected at exactly the same moment and recognising her had left him reeling too. He drank her in, drank in the familiar upturned face, wanting desperately for time to wind back so he could undo…so many things. It was too much to take in. He didn't want it to be true. The girl he had glimpsed briefly on the monitor screen was Zara Kingston? But Zara Kingston was his ward. *And his ward was Adara—a woman he had never been able to forget…*

His heart was thudding with the shock of recognition, his thoughts and intentions colliding, robbing him of his usual clear thinking. He couldn't conjure up paternal feeling at will towards his long-lost ward, nor could he bring some safe brotherly affection into play. How could he after their encounter in the desert?

He could see that every inch of her was bunched up with tension, and everyone, except Lambert, who had gone to get her a glass of water, was shifting uncomfortably while they waited to see how matters would play out. But she brought it to a head when she turned a look of utter loathing on him, forcing his hand. 'Leave us everyone…if you please.'

The room emptied quickly, the two men gathering up a clearly flustered Lambert as he hurried back in with a glass of water.

'Leave the water,' Shahin instructed, holding out his hand for the glass.

Once the door clicked shut the silence was complete. She didn't move a muscle. Placing the water on a small table within her reach, he went to stand in front of the flickering bank of monitors with his back turned, wanting to give her a chance to get over the shock.

'Can't you face me, Abbas?'

He turned slowly, absorbing the fact that she was a lot more composed than he had expected. Having got to her feet, she held her ground as he walked towards her, but he could see that every inch of her was wound up like a spring.

'Say your name… Say it!' she hissed at him, her eyes burning with hatred.

'My name is Shahin…Shahin of Zaddara.' Relief swept over him as he spoke the words. He felt like a penitent who had finally lashed himself into oblivion. However much she hated him, and she did, for him this was the beginning of his journey to redemption. The tragedy of her parents' death couldn't be shut away any longer and he had wanted to face it for so long.

The air crackled with tension as they stared at each other. It created a powerful energy between them, energy only he could defuse. He had to think on his feet, think how to keep her calm and get her to listen to him. At the same time he had to hide each one of the tumultuous feelings rising up in him, feelings driven by the fact that she was the only woman he wanted, the only woman he knew now that he could never have.

As he lifted his chin he noticed that she was equally determined to remain in control. Proud, strong, determined—those were words that fitted them both. But if strength was their blessing, it was also their curse because, underpinning all that strength, was the shifting sand of the past.

'Shahin of Zaddara...'

She spoke his name softly and thoughtfully as she stared at him, but it was the simmering restraint of impending hysteria and he wanted to avoid that at all costs. She was off-balance, her mind refusing to accept what was happening. Forgetting all his innermost feelings, it was his duty as her guardian to make sure she came round to accepting that she wasn't alone in the world and that, according to the laws of his country, he, Shahin of Zaddara, was legally responsible for her welfare. 'Zara... Can we talk?'

'Talk?' She shuddered as she looked at him as if what had happened between them revolted her now. Hugging herself defensively, she held his gaze with suspicion, as if he only had to move a muscle for her control to break.

'Zara, please—'

'I can't believe I'm in the same room as my parents' murderer. A man who lied to me... A man who couldn't even tell me his real name! Why was that, Shahin? Was it because your name is reviled and because everyone knows what you did? Or was it because you knew who I was and you tried to seduce me deliberately to put a final act to the tragedy?'

'Don't be ridiculous! How could I know who you were?'

'My visa into Zaddara? Your spies? I'm sure you have your ways.'

Her accusation brought him up short. Her visa into the country... When he'd had an army of investigators on the case? Of course, there had been no special warning at the airport and he had been on retreat. The last thing anyone had expected was that she would travel to Zaddara. They had been looking in the wrong place all the time.

'And how do you explain going under a false name?' she continued scathingly.

'Calling myself Abbas was a necessary precaution.'

'I can imagine—' Taking a step back, she raised her head. 'I want to take a good look at you, Shahin. I want to etch every feature, every inch of you, on my mind so I never forget you. I'm going to hold you *this* close for the rest of my life.' As she held her fist to her chest her eyes left him in no doubt as to her feelings.

'You would be very foolish to do that. Why would you allow something that happened in the past to ruin your future? You should be concentrating on building on this wonderful talent of yours—'

'Advice from you, Shahin?' She made a contemptuous sound. 'Excuse me if I don't take it.'

It was hard to argue with her when he was fighting demons of his own. Had their positions been reversed he would have felt much the same. She could only see what was before her and had no access to the truth. 'Stay,' he insisted as she moved towards the door.

'I've seen enough—'

'You must!' He was not used to being thwarted and moved quickly to stop her.

She looked down with furious resentment at his hand on her arm. 'Take your hand off me, Shahin.'

'Where are you going?' He held his hand against the door.

'I'm going home.' She waited with a lot more composure than he might have expected.

He heard the clock ticking the seconds away as he prevented her from leaving. Were the same thoughts going through her mind? She had been prevented from leaving him once before… Holding her here like this did him no credit. He moved away from the door.

The sound of the door slamming rang in his ears as he eased his head back and closed his eyes. Releasing the air from his lungs in one long ragged stream, he faced the fact that this was only a temporary separation. What alternative did he have but to keep her close? Close enough, without ever being able to touch her. Close enough to see the hatred in her eyes every time she looked at him. If she was ever to find the same path to recovery he had she had to know she wasn't alone and that she could always turn to her guardian for support or advice.

Wasn't this the perfect punishment for him? Wasn't this retribution of a type she could only approve? She would be smiling now if she knew the sentence he had just passed on himself.

CHAPTER SIX

The doorbell distracted her. Dashing tears from her eyes, Zara checked the living room. The room was in a mess and so was she. Gazing at her reflection in the mirror over the mantelpiece, she grimaced. She had two choices: she could pretend to be out or she could fix her face.

Entering the hallway, she slipped into the small bathroom by the front door and ran the cold water. Having dealt with the damage, she patted her face dry and regarded her reflection again. Judging it passable, she straightened herself up and went to answer the door.

Her small modern town house had an excellent security system, which was why she had put a deposit down the moment she received her first decent work-related cheque. The video entry phone was her safeguard at night. She used it now. She sucked in a shocked breath, recognising the face, and then Shahin rang the doorbell again. She could ignore it knowing he wouldn't go away or she could open the door and face him.

'Shahin…'

'Zara… May I come in?'

She left him in no doubt as to her feelings. Standing

back from the door, she made the appropriate gesture for him to enter.

The small hallway led straight into the all-purpose living room. It was living room, dining room and kitchen all in one and she had appreciated the space when she'd bought the house, knowing it to be bigger than the alternatives in her price range. Now it seemed tiny with Shahin standing in the centre of the polished laminate floor. The room seemed to have shrunk around him, drilling home the fact that he was used to spaces on a very different scale.

She didn't ask him to sit down or have a drink, and he didn't patronise her by saying what a nice house she'd got. He was here because he knew he had to tie this matter down and she had let him in because he guessed she never flinched from anything—except once. And he couldn't allow himself to think about that now.

The tension in the small, neat room was palpable. She was mature enough to contain her anger and refuse to let him see how he had affected her, but he wasn't welcome, she made that clear. Without making it obvious, he took a curious look around. He gathered from the lack of personal possessions that she used the house as a hotel, moving endlessly in search of something—an anchor, perhaps. There was only one thing out of place as far as he could tell and that was a litter of photographs spread around the floor. 'You must forgive me for interrupting you…'

'Must I?' Her eyes were hostile.

'I wouldn't have come here, but we must talk—'

'Must? *Again,* Shahin? You seem to forget that I'm not

one of your subjects. I'm a British citizen and I can ask you to leave.'

So why didn't she? He seized the lifeline and pressed on. 'We can't leave things like this. You can't, can you, Zara?' He added an edge to his voice to remind her that the charities she devoted herself to were dependent on the funds from Zaddara.

It proved the tipping point for her. The ice melted and in its place came fire. 'Blackmail now? Why aren't I surprised?' she demanded. 'Whatever you choose to do to me, I won't bend my knee to you, Shahin.'

'That's not what I want. I just want you to understand the past so you can move on.'

'Oh, really? Shahin, the caring citizen? I don't think so. What do you really want, Shahin? What will it take for me to guarantee that money from your treasury keeps on coming?'

She made it sound as if he had gleaned the money from crime, or from the exploitation of those weaker than himself, but he could not allow her to provoke him. 'It's not that simple…'

Her eyes narrowed and he could sense her brain racing as she considered his words and what he wanted. Surprisingly, he guessed she thought none of the possible scenarios entailed her sexual favours. He should have been relieved she thought him indifferent towards her as a woman, but he found himself mildly bemused because she was so beautiful.

'Are you going to tell me what this is about, Shahin? Because if you're not you can leave.' She pointed to the door.

'We need to talk. Neither of us can avoid it, you know that. This has to happen.'

'So you came here to make sure it would?' She looked around as if the house were her sanctuary and he the invader.

'Would you have come to me?'

He had been so careful to keep all the emotion out of his voice and he was surprised to see her eyes fill with tears. Something must have happened before he'd arrived to upset her. As he glanced at the photographs she caught him looking.

'You don't understand anything, do you? You don't understand what you've done because you don't have anything in here...' She clutched her chest. 'You're so busy being a lofty ruler you don't notice the little people on the ground.'

That was so far from the truth it stung him, but he kept quiet, sensing she had to let it out and that there was nothing he could say at this point to console her.

'I saw you looking at the photographs. Would you like to take a proper look?' she cried.

Tears were streaming down her face but she didn't seem aware of them; had she known, he felt sure she would have swallowed them back.

Scooping up a handful, she held them in front of his eyes. 'Take a look, Shahin,' she insisted in a strangled voice. 'This is what you did. You say I must understand the past before I can move on? Well, so must you.'

He couldn't avoid staring at the images...

'That's me at three years old with my grandparents on my birthday...and here's me at four, five and six. Where are my parents, Shahin? Oh, I remember,' she answered for him. 'They were working in Zaddara for you...'

It had been his father, of course, but he didn't correct her.

'Now where's the one of me at seven?' she said in a

much calmer voice as if the storm had passed and her rage was ebbing away. She seemed absorbed in the task of sorting through the photographs.

'Oh, look, here it is,' she said triumphantly, holding it up to him. 'And now it's your turn to tell me what it is…'

Moistening his lips, he gave it a go. 'It's you as a little girl…waiting on a station platform…'

'Yes, that's right. Go on…'

Her voice was calm, and if he hadn't heard the whisper of hysteria just below the surface he might have relaxed. 'You're going on holiday. You're sitting on a suitcase—'

'I was going away to school, Shahin,' she said, cutting him off. 'That was me on my seventh birthday going away to school. I never came home again. You see, my parents were dead by then and I lived with my grandparents. Only they couldn't cope and so your father came up with a solution. Great solution, wasn't it?'

'What do you mean, you didn't come home—surely you had holidays?' But she wasn't listening to him now. She had gone to stand with her back turned to him and was clutching the mantelpiece above the gas log fire. Her knuckles were blue-white with tension. As the enormity of what she'd told him hit him he didn't know what to say. What could he say? What could he do to mend the past? He only knew he couldn't leave her like this.

But as he tried to comfort her she shrugged him off roughly. 'Don't do this to yourself, Zara.'

She made a sound of contempt.

The two sides to his personality battled with each other and the desert won. Dragging her round, he meant to hold her shoulders firmly so she had to look at him, to hear him out—but she landed a double blow on his face before he had time to react. One flat palm and then the next, flying through the air, impelled by desperation and the same longing he felt himself—to once and for all be free of the past.

Capturing her wrists, he held them firmly, bringing her arms down to her sides and holding them there. And when she looked at him with such passion raging in her eyes he did the only thing that felt right—he kissed her fiercely.

She went stiff, as he'd expected, her lips forming a tight barrier she thought he would not cross. But he was stronger and as his will battled with hers she uttered a furious sound deep in her throat. Freeing her wrists, he made the kiss more persuasive. She landed a half-hearted blow with her fists and then another and another, but even as she did that her lips parted and she kissed him back.

But as her fury turned to passion and that passion mounted, his own feelings changed. Repugnance swept over him as he realised what he'd done. He'd kissed his ward in full knowledge of who she was and could find no excuses for his actions this time.

Starting back, he ran his hands down her shaking arms as if that could somehow make everything right again. She was about to say something. He didn't want to hear it.

'Forgive me...' He had to get out.

Zara stood trembling, glad of the mantelpiece to lean against as Shahin strode out of the room. She never felt sorry for herself and the fact that she had broken down in front of Shahin of all people was incomprehensible to her—the fact that he had kissed her and she had let him even more so.

She didn't move a muscle until he slammed the door and only then did she flinch. Her mind was in turmoil. She didn't trust herself to think or move. She was frozen, every part of her locked down.

And then the questions came pouring in. How could she have kissed him? *How?* And how could she have hit him when she abhorred violence of any kind? And then another, more vulnerable voice inside her wanted to know why he had left so abruptly. Did she revolt him?

Zara forced herself to consider the possibility and found it implausible. Shahin had wanted to kiss her. Touching her fingers to her swollen lips, she was forced to accept that she had wanted him to.

And now?

And now her emotions were in absolute turmoil because she couldn't believe she had enjoyed Shahin's kisses quite so much.

The phone rang about an hour later. Zara knew instinctively who it would be. Shahin wouldn't just give up and walk away, conveniently disappear from her life. There was something he had to say to her and, however many doors she slammed in his face, he would find a window and climb through it. And, as her hand hovered over the receiver, unwelcome as it might be, she had to admit to a *frisson* of excitement.

She listened to what Shahin had to say without once interrupting him, but found herself becoming increasingly indignant. He had stirred up a whirlwind and now he was proposing dinner as if nothing had happened. 'No, Shahin—it's too late.'

He ignored the innuendo. 'Supper—half an hour.'

'Shahin, it's almost ten o'clock at night—'

'This can't wait.'

There was command in his tone. He expected her to jump when he gave his orders like everyone else in his world. 'It will have to wait,' Zara said firmly. 'And now, if there isn't anything else…'

'If you want to learn about your parents, you will meet me.'

Every fibre in her body tensed. He had tempted her with the one thing he knew she couldn't resist.

'I'll send my driver to collect you in half an hour,' he said, taking advantage of her silence.

'I haven't agreed to anything—'

'A casual restaurant, no pressure… Busy, impersonal, relaxed.'

Relaxed? Was he crazy? An Arab sheikh in a busy restaurant with all his bodyguards and the protocol that would require…

'Incognito,' Shahin added smoothly, pre-empting her objections. 'We'll wear jeans and enjoy the most discreet protection service you can imagine.'

Go to supper with the man she hated most in the world? He *was* mad.

'Well? Do you want to know what I have to tell you about your parents, or not?'

'You know I do—'

Zara stared at the receiver in her hand as the line went dead. Shahin was a lot harder than the man she had known in the desert. This wasn't her Bedouin Abbas, this was the ruler of a warrior race, Sheikh Shahin of Zaddara, and the Sheikh of Zaddara didn't take no for an answer.

* * *

Zara dressed carefully. Shahin might have said jeans, but she had her pride and that had taken a battering recently. She was wearing slim-fitting jeans with a plain navy-blue sweater and boots. With her hair scraped back into a pony-tail and hardly any make-up, she felt ready for him. No one could accuse her of making too great an effort, but she looked clean and presentable.

As the doorbell rang she grabbed her handbag, not wanting to keep Shahin's chauffeur waiting.

'Shahin...' Zara was stunned as she opened the front door. The very last thing she had expected was that he would come in person to collect her. Instantly she was aware of her bruised lips burning as if he had only just kissed them. 'Were you making sure I turned up?' She knew embarrassment had made her clumsy, but she could think of no other reason why Shahin should come in person to collect her. She regretted the words the moment they left her lips. She didn't want to start the evening on a challenge. She wanted to keep a clear head and make the most of every moment, knowing this might be the only chance she had to find out about her parents.

'I didn't think it right that you should leave the house with a man you didn't know, even if that man was my chauf-feur. I wanted you to feel comfortable right from the start.'

So Shahin had much the same thought in mind. He wanted to keep things cool and polite with everything on an even keel. 'Thank you... That was considerate of you.' She flashed him a thin smile, while her head was still reeling with everything that had taken place between them. Realising she was keeping him hanging on the doorstep, she stood back to let him in. As she closed the door she looked up and down the street, trying to spot his car. It would be oversized and black, with diplomatic plates... 'Did your chauffeur have trouble parking?'

'I gave him the night off.'

'So...'

'We'll be travelling by underground. You don't mind, I hope?'

'The tube?' The station was only on the corner, but she couldn't get her head round Shahin of Zaddara travelling on the underground.

'Unless you'd rather walk?'

'No...no, that's fine.' This was all too casual, too unexpected...

Too clever?

Did Shahin mean to throw her off-balance? He certainly knew how to throw a curving ball, she already knew that. 'I'll just get my jacket—'

She wasn't ready for this, Zara reflected, pulling down her winter jacket from the peg in the hallway. How was she supposed to remain immune to six foot four of solid man who wanted—no, demanded to have a say in her life? A man who could be a prince of the desert one minute and happy to travel on public transport the next. She bitterly regretted losing control in front of him earlier because it didn't exactly put her in a strong position now—neither did seeing him in jeans and a chunky jacket; if he had looked great in a formal suit, in casual clothes he looked sensational.

Shahin was suffering none of her anxiety and appeared to be perfectly relaxed, Zara noticed when she returned to the living room. He was acting as though they were two friends, or work colleagues, meeting up for a casual supper, while her cheeks were blazing and her heart was racing at a ridiculous pace.

'Let me help you with that,' he offered as she started tugging on the jacket over her sweater.

'No, I can manage, thank you. Let's go...' Picking up her keys, she led the way. She didn't want either of them getting the wrong idea about the purpose of the meeting.

The restaurant Shahin had picked was casual, relaxed and about as far removed from the type of place Zara had imagined as it was possible to get. But then she had been surprised by a lot of things about him, not least the way he could change like a chameleon as the situation demanded.

She would do well to remember it, Zara thought as Shahin steered her towards one of the booths where they could expect a degree of privacy.

It would help her to stay calm if she could stop noticing things about him, like how wayward his hair was and how it fell into his eyes until he remembered to push it back. Everyone stared at them as they walked through the restaurant, but she was under no illusion—everyone was staring at Shahin. Not that anyone recognised him; they saw only his power. Shahin gave off a special energy that alerted people to his presence wherever he went.

'This all right for you?' he asked.

'Perfect, thank you...' She sat down, noticing he needed a shave. Although he had probably shaved just before he came out, his hard lean face was already darkened with stubble again. She could imagine the rasp of it against her skin and had to block her mind. She didn't want to be reminded of things that could only distract her, and it was a relief when the waitress came to take their order.

'Would you give us a minute, please?' As Shahin looked at the girl Zara saw her blush.

She couldn't blame the waitress for her reaction. If she hadn't known she was sitting opposite Sheikh Shahin of Zaddara she might have mistaken him for one of his own bodyguards, Zara thought. Like them, Shahin carried an air of danger as well as the power of his blatant sexuality. He was a man of steel, a man of restless energy and, as the young waitress had duly noted, he brought a blaze of glamour to the casual restaurant.

'What's wrong?' His glance flicked up.

A shiver of awareness tracked down Zara's spine as she realised that Shahin always picked up her change of mood in an instant.

'You seem preoccupied?' he prompted.

Preoccupied? Yes! With him! It was so hard to feel angry in surroundings like these—something Shahin had planned, maybe? 'You promised to talk to me about my parents,' Zara reminded him.

'Have you decided what you want to eat yet?'

His voice was like melted honey as he eased back on the padded leather seat, and the waitress was hovering so she couldn't press him now. 'Chicken Caesar and a ginger beer, please…'

'That sounds good to me…' Shahin ordered the same, substituting mineral water for the ginger beer.

They ate eagerly, neither of them having suspected how hungry they were, Zara thought. She certainly hadn't found either the desire or the opportunity to eat during a day that had been packed full of emotion. Glancing up, she wondered whether Shahin had felt the same. Discovering her true identity must have come as a shock to him... His gaze was impenetrable.

When they had both finished eating he surprised her by laying down his knife and fork and starting to talk about Zaddara. It wasn't the subject that surprised her, but the way Shahin began to open up to her. She remained unresponsive to begin with. It wasn't what she wanted to discuss with him. But then she told herself it was a start and that she should find out as much as she could about the country if she was ever going to be able to picture her parents living there.

Against her better judgement Zara found herself drawn in as Shahin started explaining what the kingdom meant to him. Resting his arms on the bleached wood table, he leaned forward in his enthusiasm, his face animated as he laid out his plans.

'But it takes more than talking,' he assured her, 'though we're well into our initial improvements of the infrastructure. Nothing new can be built on any scale until we get that right...'

Zara tried to remain lukewarm; the last thing she wanted was to be ensnared by Shahin's hopes and dreams. But as he talked she realised that everything he wanted was for his people, and she couldn't help but be impressed by the breadth of his vision. It wasn't long before she was prompting him for more information and before she knew it they were exchanging views. She even caught herself smiling in agreement over some of the issues he cared about—education, care of the elderly, better health facilities and improved rights for women. It was only when the coffee arrived that she realised Shahin hadn't broached the one topic they were supposed to be here for.

'Have you changed your mind about pudding?' he suggested when she politely declined as the waitress came forward with her pencil and pad at the ready. 'Another coffee, perhaps?'

'Coffee would be great, thank you. And that was a delicious meal,' Zara added, 'But now we must talk,' she insisted the moment the girl had hurried away.

She felt a tug of concern seeing a glint in Shahin's eyes. Had he planned this all along? Coming out for supper in order to talk had been his suggestion, and now she was pressing him as if she owned the idea. Very clever, Zara reflected tensely, very clever indeed.

Sitting back, Shahin studied her face for a moment and she was forced to hide her feelings. She had to forget tactics and who was doing what to whom and concentrate on making sure Shahin gave her all the information he could about her parents. 'Shahin?' she invited.

'You need to hear what I have to say in context,' he began.

'Yes, I understand that.'

'Do you?' He paused. 'There are certain things you can only understand if you come back with me to Zaddara.'

'Come back with you?' Zara's voice barely made it above a whisper. All she could think was, no wonder Shahin had been so relaxed and at such pains to be an entertaining companion when no doubt he'd known all the time that he was going to drop this bombshell in her lap.

Ice tracked down her spine as she thought about it. A discussion in a local restaurant was one thing—that was in her comfort zone. But leaving England with Shahin to go to a country he ruled, a country where his word was law, was a risk she wasn't prepared to take. 'Surely it won't be necessary for me to come back with you. Things are so easy now—you could email, send photographs—'

'If I believed I could do things that way I would be showing those photographs to you now.'

He let things settle and when he spoke again it was in a voice of reason that was very hard to ignore. 'Once you've made the visit that will be the end of it; you will be able to put the past in context.'

What if it didn't help to explain anything? But would she ever understand what had happened all those years ago if she turned down this opportunity?

She had seen a different side to Shahin in the short time they had been together in the restaurant, Zara reasoned, a human side, and even if she wasn't ready to wipe the slate clean she was impressed that Shahin had proved he shared many of the same goals in life.

'And you should know there's a legacy,' he said, breaking into her thoughts.

'A legacy?' she said in surprise.

'Something of your father's…'

Zara's eyes widened, but then she frowned. 'If it's money, I couldn't possibly take it. You'll have to find a suitable charity…' Any thought of profiting from money her parents had earned for a job that had led to their deaths was unthinkable.

'It isn't money,' Shahin assured her. 'I think you will find it a lot more valuable than that.'

Zara looked at Shahin, wanting to believe him.

'So you'll come back with me?'

A legacy from her parents worth more than money hung between them like a sparkling chalice. Shahin knew she would be unable to resist it, Zara reasoned. He also knew that she was uninterested in material possessions. She hadn't used any of the money from Zaddara for herself, and her home was simple. So the legacy must amount to an emotional journey into the past, which was all that she had ever wanted. But she wasn't prepared to take everything Shahin said at face value and decided to probe a little deeper. 'If my father had left a legacy I'm quite sure I would have heard of it by now…'

'Can you take that chance?'

Zara bit her lip, not wanting him to see how much his offer had tempted her. Shahin might be lord of all he surveyed in Zaddara, but she would exert her will when it came to her father's legacy; she would not have him controlling it. 'Whatever this legacy is, I want it to stay in Zaddara. My parents loved your country, that much I do know. Perhaps I could raise a small monument, something modest. I think they'd like that…'

Her voice had changed and grown small… She had been so sure and confident up to that point, but now her expression was bleak. The truth was, she didn't remember her parents well enough to know what they would have liked and that shamed him. He owed her parents a debt of honour. She had to come back with him so she could understand—not why things had gone wrong, but how much they had achieved. And he wanted her to understand why her mother had decided to leave her in England. But there was another reason, Shahin admitted to himself, and that was he couldn't bring himself to let her go.

'If you come to Zaddara you'll know your parents as well as I do.' He meant well, but as he saw her eyes widen with resentment he knew that all his persuasion had been for nothing, thanks to that one fatal error. She couldn't bear the thought that he, Shahin of Zaddara, the man she held responsible for her parents' death, might know them better than she did.

And then a bad situation turned rapidly worse.

With a mumbled, 'I'm sorry… I shouldn't have come here—' she pushed up from the table, dropping her bag in her haste and scattering the contents across the floor.

As he dipped to help her, she scrambled to hide some photographs from him.

'Don't,' she said furiously, snatching them out of his hand.

'But I've seen the others…'

'And so you don't need to see these.'

It looked as if she kept them with her always, he thought as she stuffed them without looking into the side pocket of her bag. But what she didn't know was that he still had a couple in his hand.

His bodyguards, having spotted the disturbance, had started moving out of the shadows and at the same time a young man from a neighbouring table looked as though he might interfere.

'Call your men off, Shahin!' Zara demanded.

As she leaned across the table to make her point, he found his gaze drawn to her breasts. Some demon inside him demanded to know why he hadn't enjoyed them when he'd had the chance—and then guilt rained down on him.

How could such thoughts be possible when he had accepted the fact that she was his ward? 'Sit down, Zara—' He spoke sharply but discreetly so that only she could hear, knowing there was no time to lose if they were to avoid an unpleasant scene. His bodyguards were within arm's length of the young man. 'Everything will return to normal if you do,' he assured her. 'Turn around. Smile at your young champion. Let him know you're all right. Reassure him, Zara... Now.'

After the briefest pause, she did as he asked and as he saw the man settle back in his seat and the bodyguards melt away he sat down too.

He put the photographs he hadn't given her yet face up on the table between them. 'We shouldn't have any secrets. We have to be honest with each other.'

'I don't want your sympathy,' she said, putting her hand out to take them back.

Quick as a whip, he covered her hand with his own. 'No. I want to see them.'

Her mouth worked. He could tell that the last thing she wanted was another opportunity for him to see her with her guard down. 'No sympathy,' he promised rashly. 'Curiosity, that's all.' He held her stare until she relented.

Picking them up, he realised at once that she must have kept them all, some would say obsessively. It explained a lot about her feeling for the camera he had confiscated in Zaddara. While it had been in his keeping he had felt her anxiety curled around it like a living force and had been glad to get rid of it. He had been more than relieved when she had emailed him to confirm its safe return.

There was one photograph for each year she had been

at school. They all showed a pale, defiant child, her mouth fixed in a rictus grin, surrounded by happy warm-hearted people. They were family photographs—only one of the children was a cuckoo in the nest and it didn't take much insight on his part to know which one. He could see that all the families had gone out of their way to make a child who had nowhere to go for the holidays feel at home. And on each of the photographs she was with a different family. He understood everything now and his heart ached for her.

He was careful to keep every suggestion of emotion out of his eyes as he laid the photographs down again. Leaning forward to look her in the eyes, he insisted, 'Come back with me, Zara. Come back with me to Zaddara…'

CHAPTER SEVEN

THE Ruby Fort...

Zara hadn't known what to expect when Shahin told her on the flight over that this was where they must go if she was to claim her father's legacy.

He hadn't warned her that they would be travelling to the fort on horseback, something he might have rethought had he known she would be sharing his horse. And any thrill of clinging on to Shahin had been more than wiped out by a level of discomfort she could never have imagined in her wildest dreams...

They had been riding for the best part of an hour and every bit of her was saddle-sore. She hadn't known how much longer she could go on. But as Shahin's favourite palace rose out of the empty desert like a mirage she soon forgot about her aching body.

As they drew closer Zara could see ramparts taking shape. Sunset was the time when the palace was at its best, Shahin had said, and he wanted her to see it for the first time just like this...

He was right—it took her breath away.

The colours in the desert were always stunning, but

tonight they were exceptional. The sun hovered on the horizon like a big orange ball, glorious and effulgent, as if to remind the world of its splendour before plunging the land into night. Every colour was exaggerated—the mountains blacker, the sand turning rapidly from ivory to copper, while the sky was a mesmerising mix of lavender and tangerine. And still against this artist's palette of colours the Ruby Fort stood out.

The name alone sounded like something out of a fairy tale and the Ruby Fort did more than live up its reputation. As the name suggested, it blazed red thanks to the countless gems implanted in its walls—gems that had been a gift, Shahin had told her, to his father from the tribesmen who had wanted to show their gratitude to the elderly Sheikh who had laid his wealth at their feet.

'What do you think?' he said, turning his stallion side on to give her a better view.

Before she could answer, he cried, 'Get up, Jal!' and Zara's cry of alarm was lost in a flurry of hooves as Shahin pointed his horse towards their destination. Zara barely managed to lodge her thighs around the stallion's side in time to prevent herself bouncing off. She had been foolhardy enough to try and ease her aching leg muscles by lifting herself a little way out of the saddle and had almost paid for it with a tumble.

'Enjoying the ride?' Shahin asked when he finally reined in.

Gritting her teeth, Zara ground out, 'Great'. How could anyone enjoy riding? Zara wondered. And, as for finding it comfortable… Shahin might be able to sit deep in the saddle, completely at ease, but she felt as if she might possibly be damaged for life.

'Good,' he approved, urging the stallion forward again. 'I told you you'd soon get the hang of it...'

As the horse surged forward Zara clamped her teeth together to stop them rattling in her jaw. She felt like a sack of potatoes and her only wish now was to make it to the fort alive. And the first part of their journey had gone so well—a limousine, a private jet, a royal car waiting for them on the tarmac... Their luggage, Shahin had explained, would be taken on ahead by helicopter. And so she had suspected nothing when the chauffeur-driven royal car had drawn in to his riding stables. She had relaxed by then, fearing helicopters more than anything—except for horses. The green tinge on her face must have given this away and the horse they brought out for her had been swiftly re-stabled.

Resigning herself to the ride, she could see the Ruby Fort was growing even more impressive as they drew closer. When Shahin slowed their mount to a trot beneath the battlements it gave her a chance to appreciate the scale of the palace as well as the care with which it was maintained. As they clattered over the ancient drawbridge Zara's neck was aching from gazing up the towering walls to stare at the crenellated battlements where pennants were flying in honour of Shahin's arrival.

Zara gasped as they rode on through the great gates and entered a courtyard vast enough to house a small village. A mass of white-robed people were waiting there to greet their leader and the moment they saw Shahin they roared their approval, raising their arms in a tide of welcome.

Holding on round his waist, Zara could feel Shahin's

voice vibrating against her hands as he called back to them. Self-consciously, she quickly released her grip.

'Well?' he said, turning to her. 'First impression?'

'Fantastic… I'm overwhelmed,' she said honestly.

Zara was relieved when the stallion slowed to a walk, but her cheeks heated up again when Shahin took him at a deliberately slow pace through the ranks of people. She was provoking considerable interest and knew his people had to be wondering why their leader had a dishevelled woman clinging to his back. Putting a hand to her hair, she quickly straightened it and fixed a composed expression to her face. Then, sitting straight, she tried to look as if riding came naturally to her and she wasn't aching in every part that had contact with the horse. But the truth of it was she was in agony and she couldn't believe anyone was fooled.

Shahin reined in at the foot of the sweeping marble steps. There was a clash of arms as he dismounted and rows of men clad in the graceful robes of Zaddara dipped into a deep bow as he returned their greeting.

Zara realised that she hadn't fully appreciated Shahin's position up to that moment. In the traditional robes he had changed into before leaving the aircraft he was both awe-inspiring and magnificent. She watched with interest as a manservant advanced respectfully. He was carrying a beaten copper tray upon which she could see two tumblers and a jug full of some refreshing drink. Ice clinked enticingly as the man walked closer—and suddenly she couldn't think of anything else but how thirsty she was. Grabbing the horse's mane, she tugged her right leg over its back and started to dismount. Distracted by one of his men, Shahin didn't see what she was doing…

Zara was proud of the neat way in which she was dismounting—until she reached the ground and discovered that neither leg would support her weight.

'Curtseys are unnecessary,' Shahin assured her dryly as she exclaimed with shock. And then, turning to the line of dignitaries, he added, 'May I present Zara Kingston.'

Trying to raise a smile for them and a scowl at Shahin wasn't easy, particularly when she was sprawled in a heap on the ground. This wasn't quite the entrance she had planned. And when Shahin offered to help her up she was forced to admit, 'I don't think I can walk—'

'In that case…'

Zara gasped as Shahin swung her into his arms. Moving swiftly down the line of carefully impassive men, he took her up the steps and in through the grand entrance of his desert home.

'This is your room… I hope you like it?'

Like it? Zara had to cling to the ornately carved back of a sofa when Shahin lowered her to the floor. She still didn't trust her legs to function properly. It was hard to take in everything at once. It was more ballroom than bedroom and the truth was that she felt lost in the vast room.

A sumptuous gilded bed dressed with satin sheets and a crimson quilt was raised on a central platform. There were steps up to the bed and she could only imagine what would happen if she woke up in the night and missed her footing. Several open archways led off to what she supposed must be other rooms, robbing the bedroom of any cosiness it might have had, and hovering in the background a number of serving women were waiting for their instructions. 'This is too much!' she exclaimed softly.

'Don't you like it?'

'It's magnificent, Shahin, but—'

'But?' he demanded.

'Well, don't you have anything smaller?'

'Like a cupboard?'

'No, like a bedroom where I'll feel cosy and where I won't be staring at the shadows and wondering if they're moving half the night.'

He had put her in this suite of rooms for a very good reason. The suite was as far away from his own quarters as it was possible to get in the palace. He wanted her out of his way, out of temptation's reach, and if by settling her into the Presidential Suite was what it took to accomplish that—

'Really, Shahin, I'm not happy about this.'

He had to hide his astonishment that anyone would turn down the opportunity to experience such magnificence. But as she turned her face up, waiting for his response, he suspected she wouldn't be easily persuaded. It forced him to race through the possible alternatives in his mind. It wasn't as if the Ruby Fort was short of rooms, but all the guest rooms were on a similar scale. The smaller family rooms were all situated on his side of the palace.

'It would only be for a couple of nights. You're not planning to stay any longer, are you?' He hoped that would be an end of it.

'I won't be staying overnight if I have to sleep here.'

He should have known she was as stubborn as he was.

'All right, I'll see what I can do. But, in the meantime, why don't you take a bath? I'm sure you'll find the bathroom to your liking.'

'You mean I smell of horse?'

She could imagine what she liked—he had new preparations to make.

'So I do smell of horse. Will someone show me where the bathroom is, please?'

A woman advanced immediately, bowing to him as she drew close.

'Don't worry about finding your way around the palace,' he told Zara. 'I'll have them bring you to me when you're ready.'

On a golden litter? Zara wondered, holding Shahin's gaze. Even then the pictures in her head couldn't compete with the murals on the walls. She wouldn't have been surprised to learn that he had housed her in the harem. 'Shahin—' Her voice stopped him at the door.

'Yes?' He turned to face her.

'Will you show me my father's legacy tonight?'

'Later, Zara… At dinner… We'll talk about it then.'

But she wanted to know about it now, Zara thought, watching Shahin's shadow disappearing through the archway. He had brought her here on the promise that she would be told everything, and now she had to wait again?

'I'm sorry,' she said, remembering the woman waiting to look after her.

'Please let me know if I can get you anything else,' the woman said in perfect English after showing her the bathroom. 'There is a bell here…and here…and here…'

Zara wasn't used to being waited on and felt uncomfort-

able. 'Thank you, I can manage… You've been very kind.'
It was as polite a dismissal as she could think of.

'Shall I have your cases unpacked while you bathe?' the
serving-woman asked her.

'Well, I'm hoping to move to another room, actually—'

'Just one outfit for dinner, perhaps?'

'Thank you… Cream silk pants, and there's a topaz-
coloured blouse on the top of my other clothes…'

The woman bowed and then beckoned to her companions. 'I will return in one hour and take you to the Sheikh,'
she said respectfully.

That sounded ominous, Zara thought, and one hour
didn't leave a lot of preparation time. In fact, it was far too
short when every inch of her was aching after jiggling up
and down on the back of Shahin's stallion. That thought
only grew when she walked into the sumptuous bathroom
and discovered that it was the size of her living room at
home. Clad in night-dark rose-veined marble and lit with
scented candles, it was equipped with every luxury product
she could imagine. There were fluffy rugs underfoot and
a hot tub bubbling gently in one corner with fragrant petals
strewn across the frothy water…

She would just have to put her concerns on hold while
she soaked her aching limbs, Zara decided, throwing off
her clothes.

Bathing in such fabulous surroundings was too good to rush
and Zara left it to the last moment to climb out of the hot
tub. She had to dress quickly to be ready when the serving
woman arrived to guide her through the palace. As she
hurried all her feelings of apprehension came rushing back.

Why hadn't Shahin told her about her father's legacy? She liked to know facts right away so she could deal with them, and she would have preferred to deal with them on her own ground, not Shahin's. Whatever her father's legacy turned out to be, she wanted the opportunity to view it in private. It was too much emotion to share with anyone, especially Shahin. Though, in fairness, everything that had happened since meeting Shahin in the desert had challenged her beliefs regarding him. She had created a monster in her mind, but when she had met the man she had found him too complex to be easily condemned. His magnetism alone made her feel as if she was betraying her parents, but it was hard to know how she should ignore the feelings he provoked. And particularly here at the Ruby Fort she was finding it impossible to forget what had happened between them the last time they had been in the desert…

A discreet tap told Zara the time for thinking was over. She had always known this would be difficult, she told herself firmly. She just had to get on with it, face Shahin and find out what he could tell her about her parents and their legacy.

The marble floors seemed to go on for ever and as Zara walked behind the serving-woman she had plenty of time to regret her decision to return to Zaddara with Shahin. She should have held out in London and insisted he tell her everything there…

Gazing up at the towering golden doors, Zara had to wait until two men in flowing white robes belted in crimson silk opened them for her. They bowed low as she entered and as the serving-woman slipped away Zara couldn't help thinking that she had been well and truly delivered to the Sheikh.

Shahin rose as she entered. Dressed in flowing black silk robes, he looked magnificent. Zara stood for a moment taking everything in. The brilliant room was a perfect frame for his darkly dramatic looks. There were ivory columns decorated with gold leaf stretching up to a stained glass cupola above his head, and the rich jewel shades of the glass were reflected in velvet cushions and plush deep-cushioned couches set around the room. A feast had been laid out for them on a low table and in an alcove musicians were playing softly. The air was lightly scented with sandalwood and candlelight flickered on gold filigree sconces…

It was only then she realised she had left her camera in the room. She subdued the urge to rush back and get it. Polite interest was the most she could afford to show if she didn't want Shahin thinking she was so startled and overawed by her surroundings she couldn't hold a proper discussion with him.

'I thought we'd eat here, seated on cushions in the Zaddaran way…'

He indicated a place where she might sit across from him on a mound of silken cushions. As Zara moved deeper into the room she was conscious of her pulse racing.

'I hope you approve?'

A low table laden with delicious delicacies would divide them. On closer inspection Zara decided it might have been polished bronze or even gold. Whichever, it was quite a contrast from the wine bar she would have gone to at home! She tried to tuck her legs neatly beneath her as Shahin was doing so effortlessly. But her limbs hadn't recovered from stretching over a ton of horse and refused to cooperate so she ended up sitting to one side, trying to look as if she found this comfortable.

She was about to speak when an army of servants, responding to some invisible signal, began to serve them and each time their plates were cleared away another course followed until she found herself becoming edgy. She was deeply conscious of the minutes ticking away and wondered if Shahin intended getting down to the discussion as he had promised. She would have to start the ball rolling, Zara decided, when he finally waved the servants away.

'That was delicious, thank you. And now—'

'Your father's legacy?' Shahin anticipated. 'It's something you need to see, rather than to talk about, Zara.'

Zara bit back her disappointment. She had come this far and her goal was so very close, but she had to be mature and tell herself that after waiting so long she could be patient for one more day. 'I'll see you in the morning, then,' she said, trying to get up.

'I thought we could talk a little first about your exhibition…'

In fairness, Shahin had bought her entire collection of pictures and this was a good opportunity for him to flesh out his understanding of her work, Zara reasoned, sinking down again. 'What would you like to know?'

'What drew you to photography?'

The harmless question allowed her to relax and Zara found herself telling him everything, from the school magazine to the present day. She couldn't help noticing that the excitement she always felt when she talked about her work had not infected Shahin and wondered why he was looking so concerned for her.

'You seem to do so much of this alone,' he commented with a frown.

'All of it.' Zara looked at him quizzically, wondering if Shahin thought everyone had a team of experts to call on as he did.

'Doesn't working alone get to you?'

'No, why should it?'

She was absolutely sincere, Shahin realised, and he could tell that she didn't have a clue what he was getting at. He pushed a little more. 'And when you come home, don't you have friends to come home to?'

She wrinkled her brow. 'Of course I have friends, Shahin. I kept the friends I made at school—wonderful people. But we all lead busy lives. We don't live in each other's pockets, if that's what you mean.'

'So you never feel lonely?'

'I don't have time to feel lonely,' she assured him. 'How can I, when I'm so lucky with my work?' She leaned towards him. 'Shahin, I'm surprised at you. You live a very similar life to me—a solitary life, and you're not complaining...'

The similarities between them had never struck him before, but he realised now, to his surprise, that she was right. People had surrounded him since the moment of his birth, but they were all paid to attend him. Was there anyone he could confide in now that his father was dead? Anyone he could trust enough to be completely relaxed in their company? The answer to that was, of course, no.

The realisation that his ward was not a victim as he'd thought her, someone to be swept up and sheltered, but an independent woman who saw herself in a very different light to the way he did took some getting used to.

'Shahin?' she prompted, anticipating that he would agree with her.

His answer was to press a discreetly positioned call button with his foot.

Had she gone too far? Zara wondered when Shahin didn't answer her right away. She guessed it was the first time anyone had risked comparing their mundane sort of life to his. But even when she ran over it again she could only draw the same conclusion. Was she supposed to suck up to him and humbly agree that of course her life couldn't possibly be compared to that of the ruling Sheikh of Zaddara? She wouldn't take a word of it back. The fact was she loved her life and had thought Shahin was pretty pleased with his... And they did have to work alone for much of the time—that was just the way it was.

Zara tried to get the conversation going again, thinking it time Shahin shared some of his experiences with her. This was supposed to be a two-way conversation and not a trial where she was the only witness. But he appeared to be distracted and, following his gaze, she saw that the serving-woman had returned and was hovering by the entrance.

'A smaller room has been found for you,' Shahin said, standing up. 'I hope it meets your requirements. Fariah will show you where to go.' He dipped into the traditional bow, prompting Zara to get up.

'What about our conversation?' she reminded him.

'It can wait until tomorrow—when we're both feeling rested.'

And, before she could protest that she was wide awake,

he added, 'We leave at dawn. Dress for the desert... Something comfortable with shoes you can walk in.'

Zara's cheeks flamed red as Shahin turned away. The Sheikh had dismissed her, she realised angrily, and there wasn't a thing she could do about it.

CHAPTER EIGHT

THE following morning Zara had too much pent-up excitement inside her to worry about Shahin's curt dismissal the previous evening, or the fact that he appeared to be determined to keep his distance now as they walked together down the palace steps. Having been told to dress for the desert, she was wearing cool cotton trousers with a loose-fitting long-sleeved shirt and desert boots, while Shahin was wearing jeans rather than his long flowing robes. In the past when he had worn jeans she had found it to be a sign that he was relaxed. Eastern dress seemed appropriate for the reigning sheikh—casual dress was Shahin without the trimmings. She hoped this was one of those more relaxed times and that he would open up to her, but his aloofness warned her she might be setting her expectations too high.

A Jeep stood waiting for them in the courtyard and a male servant was standing beside the driver's door holding the keys. Thanking him in Zaddaran, Shahin told her to get in.

Zara stopped dead and looked at him. This journey into the desert to learn about her parents was everything she had dreamed about, but she could not tolerate Shahin's behaviour towards her. She had done nothing wrong. She would rather Shahin gave her directions and left her to find her father's legacy on her own than suffer his brusque manner. 'Not until you tell me where you're taking me—'

'Get in and I'll tell you—'

'Open the door for me and then I'll get in.'

She could tell her defiance still had the power to astonish him. Apparently no one ever argued with the Sheikh of Zaddara. Maybe a good argument was what he needed, Zara reflected—it might help to unbutton him... Maybe it would do them both some good! She felt as if she might burst from holding in all the things she wanted to ask him. She closed her eyes tightly as she fought for control. And then was surprised to hear determined foot-steps striding round to the passenger side of the vehicle. It was an even bigger surprise to see Shahin wave the servant away and open the door for her himself.

'Hurry up,' he said brusquely.

Progress? Zara wondered.

They headed out into the desert and after about an hour or so of driving Zara thought she had never known Shahin so tense. 'Is it far now?'

'This is just the start of your journey.'

Zara decided to skip the innuendo and stick with the facts. 'That's a bit vague for me—how about a destina-tion?' She had to grip the handle on the side of the door to stop herself from falling on top of him when Shahin brought the Jeep to a skidding halt.

'Do you want to know about your parents, or not?' he snapped, holding her angry stare.

'Of course I do—'

'Then understand that this is hard for me too.'

'Hard for you?' All the resentment she had pushed aside came pouring back.

'Yes! Show them some respect!' he said passionately.

His level of concern for two people she thought exclusively her own came as a total shock to Zara and she didn't take it well. 'You dare to lecture me about my parents?'

'If you can't see I'm trying to help—'

'It's a little late for you to help me, don't you think?' Grief, loss, frustration—everything welled up in her at once. 'You were responsible for the death of my parents and, not content with that, you went on to seduce their daughter—'

'And you were so unwilling?' Shahin cut across her. There was only so much he could take and she was testing all his limits.

Zara's face blazed with passion but she held her tongue and gradually the tension inside the confined space fell back again.

'Shahin, I'm sorry,' she said at last. 'You're right. I'm just as responsible for my actions as you are. It takes two to…'

He started the engine. This was hard for both of them— just how hard for him she would never know; he had really cared about her parents, and still felt terrible when he thought about the tragic waste of life.

'We're going deep into the desert,' he explained. 'The place doesn't have a name. But I can get a satellite fix if you would like to see its whereabouts on the monitor screen…'

'Thank you, I'd like that,' she said after a moment, adding, 'What kind of place is it?'

'The first oil exploration site we had here in Zaddara. It's a place you need to see if you're ever going to understand what your parents had to put up with, what brought them here and why they stayed… And, most important of all, why they left you behind.'

He felt her emotion without looking at her and as he drove he tuned in the satellite navigation system so she could see the site on the screen. 'Here,' he said, drawing her attention to it.

'Thanks,' she said as he made some necessary adjustments to the screen.

In his peripheral vision he could see her studying what he'd shown her. He wanted to show her the first camp and explain what the broken-down buildings represented. It wasn't something he could delegate, though admittedly it would throw them together at a very vulnerable time for her. Some base part of him wanted to tell her the truth and have it over with. At one time Zara's father had been considered the finest geologist of his generation but, having turned to drink, he had become reckless and unpredictable. His father, Sheikh Abdullah, had taken a chance on hiring him, mainly because he couldn't afford anyone else. Luckily the calculated risk had paid off for Zaddara, but not for Zara's father or for her mother…

He had always thought Zara's mother a gentle lady with a spine of steel. It was she who had held it all together until the moment her husband, full of drink, had decided not to wait, but to use the faulty detonators after all.

The circumstances didn't matter now, Shahin reflected, ramming his foot down on the accelerator. He held himself responsible for the death of Zara's parents and would always do so. In his naïvety he had believed he could buy detonators cheaper on the black market. His father had picked up the flaw in them immediately and had ordered him back to Zaddara to replace them with quality products from a reputable supplier. He had been nineteen at the time and trying to play his part in rescuing an impoverished country, and in doing so had caused the tragedy. He had rushed from the desert to Zaddara and back again in a single day to replace the equipment but had been too late. It was a miracle his father had survived. But he had killed Zara's parents as surely as if he had fired the faulty detonator himself. Whatever anyone else thought, he would never forgive himself for that.

'Would you like me to take over the driving for a bit?'

His ward's question made him leave the past and drew a smile to his lips. 'I think I can handle it…'

His smile deepened at her murmured exclamation and he had to wonder what he had to do to stop wanting her… If it hadn't been right before, when he hadn't known who she was, it was even less so now. But nothing, not even the fact that she was his ward, seemed to make the slightest impression on him.

Swinging the wheel, Shahin pointed the Jeep towards the deepest and most hostile part of the desert. It had taken great courage for her parents and his father to explore this particular region in the early days before any form of infrastructure had been put in place and he wanted Zara to know that. He had to concentrate on getting there and forget how many things he wanted to do with her, to share with her, and that they beat at his brain every waking moment. Each time he was with her like this, within touching distance, was only ever going to remind him that she was out of his reach.

* * *

It was just a collection of ramshackle buildings. They had been driving deeper and deeper into the desert and all the time she had been straining to catch her first sight of... Well, that was just it, Zara realised—she hadn't really had a clear idea of what to expect, but this wasn't it.

She felt shivery as she climbed down from the Jeep and then foolish as tears pricked her eyes. But nothing could have prepared her for treading the same land, seeing the same horizon, staring at the same sky that her parents had. Talking, asking questions... None of that filled in the gaps like this collection of time-scarred trailers. But, instead of providing answers, the exploration site only provoked more questions... How could her parents have existed here? How could they have left their small child for this? She didn't understand and she wanted to so badly, yet now she was here there didn't seem any hope she would find any of the answers to her questions.

The site was just so desolate, Zara thought, hugging herself as she looked around. Then she noticed Shahin staring at her and remembered he had been driving for hours... She couldn't let him see how disappointed she was.

Seeing her looking at him, he came around the Jeep and put his arm across her shoulders to urge her forward. 'This building was where your parents lived...'

Shahin's brief, comforting squeeze worried her and she braced herself for what might come next. She turned as always to her camera. 'Do you mind?' she said, lifting it. 'I'd like to make a record...'

'Of course,' he said, standing back as she ran off a series of shots.

However unpromising the trailer looked, she wanted

him to know she was all right. And she did want a record of everything so that perhaps in time she could understand. Having finished, she headed off towards the door. But when she reached it she hesitated, waiting for Shahin. It took her a moment to gather her resolve.

He opened the door for her and then stood back.

Zara's first impression, aside from the overwhelming heat as she stepped inside, was disappointment. Disappointment and frustration… There was just a table, three plastic chairs and a stiff broom that somebody had left leaning against the wall. The sight of the broom gave her a pang… It was as if the person who had left it would be back any time now, but the lack of personal touches, of personal possessions, made her feel as if she had been robbed.

Judging the moment right, Shahin walked across the room and opened another door. Without needing to be asked, he sensed her need to be alone and didn't attempt to follow her as she went to explore.

It was a bedroom… An iron bed was pushed up against the wall and through another smaller opening she could see a basic bathroom. Remembering her own opulent quarters back at the Ruby Fort, Zara grimaced. 'Is this it?' she whispered.

'No, this is just the beginning,' Shahin assured her. 'I thought you should see how it was for them when they first set up camp. The place grew, of course, as the work progressed…'

She looked out of one of the windows when Shahin pointed and saw more buildings.

'This was the first portable building on site,' he explained.

'Thank you for showing it to me… '

'You know how they had to live now—how hard it was for them.'

What wasn't he telling her? Zara wondered. 'And?'

'How tedious it was for them back then when they had finished work for the day… No satellite phones, no TVs, no outside communication of any kind, unless they had visitors… And I'm guessing even playing cards and reading palled after a while.'

Zara was sure Shahin was hiding something and if there had been problems caused by stress and isolation she wanted to hear about them. 'But my parents had each other,' she pointed out, 'and then there was your father…'

Shahin refused to respond to her prompt. 'I hope this tour will help you get everything in perspective,' he said economically as he made for the door.

Zara followed him. 'I knew it was going to be basic…' She still hoped to prompt him into revealing why he had suddenly withdrawn into himself.

'It's more than a lack of amenities that makes life in the desert so hard,' Shahin explained. 'It's the emptiness, the space…' He stood by the open door, looking beyond them to where the horizon was smudged by a heat haze. 'It's gets very lonely out here…'

'But there are more buildings,' Zara pointed out. 'Weren't there more people?'

'We couldn't afford any more people, but the buildings sprang up as the work continued. There was a lot of equipment and that needed storage space.'

'Can we go and see those buildings now?'

'Of course…'

The largest of the buildings had been used as a makeshift

recreation hall, Shahin explained. It was here that Zara would find quite a few things belonging to her parents…

She prepared herself mentally, but when Shahin hesitated outside the door she found her confidence draining away. 'What's the problem?' she pressed.

'Nothing…' Shahin looked deep into her eyes. 'I thought you might want to look around here on your own, that's all…'

'Good idea…' She forced a light note into her voice.

He released the catch without opening the door fully. 'I'll be waiting for you in the Jeep.'

He got halfway to the Jeep and then turned back. He couldn't leave her. Whatever demons he might be fighting, someone had to be there for her—he had to be there for her.

He was feeling everything a guardian should feel, Shahin told himself, walking faster. She'd been on her own for five minutes—five minutes too long.

Treading carefully, he made it to the door and stilled his breathing to listen. Racking sobs, almost completely smothered… He guessed she had her head buried in her arms; she never wanted anyone to know how she felt. He didn't hesitate. Maybe it was an intrusion, but it was something he had to do. He found her sitting in the centre of the floor, leaning against the leg of the dusty pool table and, surrounding her like a moat of memories, were the photographs he knew she would find. 'Zara…'

'Leave me… Please, Shahin. I want to be alone.'

'I thought you should know where your own talent comes from…' She didn't ask him to leave so he pressed on. 'Your father was a brilliant photographer, as you can see…' When his hand wasn't shaking too badly to hold a camera, Shahin remembered grimly, keeping that thought to himself. 'He kept a record of everything that happened on site from day one—'

'Just as I would have done…' She forced a smile as she looked at him and then gathered the photographs in. 'These are wonderful…'

As she picked up a handful of photographs to study them, he knew the time had come to tell her everything. 'Searching for oil saved my father at a time when he was out of his mind with grief at the loss of my mother in a smallpox epidemic…'

'Oh, Shahin, I had no idea…'

The way she so quickly forgot her own concerns touched him deeply and he knew he could hold nothing back from her. 'It was particularly ironic that since the day he took the throne my father had fought to raise the standards of health care in Zaddara. But there was never enough money. He believed oil was the answer and that was when he brought your parents on board. He couldn't offer them much, but they shared the same vision…'

'So the continuing health risks explain why I was left behind in England when they came to work here?'

'Exactly,' Shahin confirmed, feeling they had drawn closer than they had ever been in that moment.

'Go on,' she pressed.

'This was their headquarters—no air-conditioning, no heating… Freezing cold at night and dangerously hot during the day. My father used to sleep on that old camp bed over in the corner, while your parents used the mobile home you've already seen. They lived in primitive conditions, but there was no money to spare. It was an all or nothing venture for them.'

'So I share the same thirst for adventure…'

'Yes, I think you do,' he agreed.

'And what were they like?' she asked eagerly. 'Can you tell me? Do you remember?'

He thought how best to phrase it before saying, 'Of course I do. Your father was a brilliant man, fiery and impetuous… Your mother far less so. She was his rock.' She'd had to be strong, Shahin remembered, she'd had a lot to put up with. 'But as far as diplomacy went?' He was longing to make it easier for her. He wanted Zara to understand where she came from, but he wanted to leave her with happy memories of her parents; they had done so much for his country. 'Your mother always said exactly what was on her mind,' he confided, hoping to lighten the mood.

'You're saying diplomacy wasn't her strong point?'

'Does that remind you of anyone?'

She almost smiled. 'How did she behave towards your father?'

'As if being the ruler of a country was no big deal.'

And now she did smile, but she looked away.

'Shahin,' she said at last, 'I think it's time you told me about the accident…' Her voice was low and quite steady, but she wasn't quite ready to look at him.

He was determined now to take the line that would hurt her the least. 'You know about the faulty detonators.'

'And you knew too,' she said softly.

'We all knew they were faulty,' he admitted. 'My father had detected the fault and had insisted they be locked away until they could be safely destroyed. He sent me back to Zaddara to buy more.'

'So, what went wrong?'

'I wasn't here, but…'

'My grandparents were quite clear that it was your fault.'

'I'm not trying to mislead you. I take full responsibility.' He refused to make excuses for himself. 'I bought the faulty batch cheaply from a man who worked in army ordinance. I thought I'd done a good deal. I never dreamed there'd be anything wrong with them.'

'You were young—'

'I was nineteen. But, young as I was, I would never have knowingly risked lives to save money.'

'So what did happen?'

He phrased it carefully. 'Your father was eager to get on with things…' Then he paused.

'Do you mean he took a chance and broke into the place where the detonators were being kept? Shahin,' she pressed when he hesitated.

He wasn't comfortable with telling her that this was exactly what had happened. 'He was close to finding oil…'

She frowned. 'And you didn't get back in time to prevent him from using the faulty detonators?'

'I shouldn't have bought them in the first place.' Emotion made his voice harsh.

Zara paused for a second, considering what she had heard. 'However long it took you to get back after concluding the new deal, my father had no right to break the locks, nor was there any excuse for him using detonators he knew to be dangerous.'

He could say nothing, because her father had been

drunk. He had been blown clear by the explosion and had died later in hospital, while her mother had perished in the fire. His father, Sheikh Abdullah, had been lucky. He had been standing where they were now, taking delivery of some more equipment. He wouldn't tell her everything, Shahin decided. There was nothing to be gained by telling her the truth about her father and breaking her heart all over again. 'We all made mistakes that day,' he said simply.

'And you still blame yourself for taking so long to get back here? It's a long drive to Zaddara, Shahin.'

'I know that…' He ground his jaw; he didn't want her making excuses for him, but still she had a right to know. 'I drove to the capital and back in less than twenty-four hours. In that time I sourced the new detonators, had them checked and arranged payment.'

'You did all you could—'

'I hold myself responsible to this day,' he said, cutting across her. 'I know money was short and we were so close to finding oil we could almost smell it, but I was offered a deal and at the time it seemed the only way we could push things forward. I sold the Jeep to pay for the new detonators when I arrived in Zaddara and then I rented it back from the man I sold it to, to make the return journey. That's how hard up we were—'

'But oil was found?'

'Yes, in one final irony, the explosion that killed your parents uncovered oil. But, as we both know, it was discovered at far too high a price and, whatever you or the world thinks of me, I will never forgive myself.'

She sat in silence on the floor, surrounded by her

photographs, until at last she whispered his name and looked up at him.

'Yes?'

'I want to thank you for your honesty… I know you believe you were to blame, but you were all adults, and all responsible for your actions. You were only nineteen, trying to do the best you could for your financially crippled country. And if my father had only waited for your return the accident need never have happened…'

He was determined to protect her. 'Don't feel you have to absolve me.'

'But I must,' she insisted, 'because you will never forgive yourself until I do. The accident was my father's fault, Shahin. His eagerness killed him, not you. And you mustn't blame yourself any longer.'

He needed no more absolution than those words. And he was glad for Zara's sake that she had been able to accept his account of her father's part in the tragedy. What good would it have done to tell her that her father had been drunk and that alcohol had prompted him to take the fatal risk? It would taint her memory of him, and that was all. 'Thank you,' he said with more feeling than she knew. And then, because he couldn't leave her sitting on the floor a moment longer, he drew her to her feet.

Emotion grabbed him when he saw she was still holding some of the photographs to her chest. 'They've been waiting for you—' He had to turn away.

'Yes, and now I understand who I am,' she told him simply, 'thanks to you, Shahin.'

As she spoke she touched one of the photographs and there was such an expression of longing in her eyes that, without thinking, he drew her close. He could feel her trembling as he stroked her hair and as she pressed into him it was as if she needed to feed on his strength. He stroked her back, willing her to relax, until with a ragged sigh she turned her face up to him.

She was waiting for him to kiss her, he realised. Their faces were just inches apart. He tried to force himself not to look at her lips—lips that were softly parted and moistly inviting… But taboo. He settled for a quick hug, releasing her while he still had the will to do so. And when she wasn't quite quick enough to hide her bewilderment, he thought quickly and said, 'Come on… There's something else I want to show you—'

'What is it?'

She looked so worried. And who could blame her when the sexual chemistry between them was snapping like an overloaded power line?

Slipping his hands into the pockets of his jeans before he could be tempted to take her hand, he said, 'Wait and see… I think you're going to like it—'

As Zara stood with Shahin outside the largest of the buildings she wondered what secrets it held… And why was Shahin edging away from her? It didn't make sense. After stripping away years of hurt and anger in the past hour he couldn't think she still blamed him for the accident. She felt a profound sense of loss as she walked around the site, but the only anger left in her was for the people who had supplied the faulty detonators.

'This was going to be an exhibition hall—'

She looked up as Shahin began speaking again.

'It was something they always joked about,' he went on. 'They used to say all they had to exhibit were blisters on their hands, but that one day it would be different... They were far-sighted people, Zara, your parents and my father. They could see past their difficulties to a future when Zaddara would be prosperous and they knew that the next generation would want to know what their country's wealth had been founded on.'

She could never hear enough about the past, and even more so now, Zara realised, because it was a heritage she shared with Shahin.

'I want to use those photographs you found back there,' he explained. 'I want to exhibit them—with your permission, of course. In fact, why don't you help me with the project? You've got the know-how and perhaps we could involve Gideon and Lambert?'

'They'd like that...' She hadn't expected Shahin to push things along at such a pace. Now she understood why the kingdom of Zaddara was rising like a phoenix out of the desert since Shahin had taken control.

'We'll have the pictures,' he went on, 'and then we'll bring all the artefacts out of storage and create a museum—'

'Shahin, that's a wonderful idea...' It was impossible not to be swept away by his enthusiasm, but as she rested her hand on his arm to show her appreciation he moved away. He was in the middle of sharing his vision with her, Zara reasoned, and let it go.

'I can see your images of Zaddara here, can't you?' He turned to look at her.

'Yes, I can,' she admitted. It was everything she had ever dreamed of...and what both sets of parents would have wanted. As emotion swept over her she tried to hug Shahin and was shocked by the brusque way he shook her off.

Zara couldn't believe she had misread the situation so badly. She was stunned by the fact that Shahin found her gesture of affection so distasteful.

'Where are you going?' He stepped in front of her as she tried to leave.

'I'd like to go back to the Jeep—'

'But I haven't finished showing you round yet—'

'I've finished looking.' The expression in her eyes left him in no doubt that she was serious.

'There's something I have to tell you…'

'Something else?' Her mouth tightened. She couldn't think of anything so important that Shahin had to stand in front of her like this.

Pulling a document out of his back pocket, he handed it to her. The royal crest of Zaddara was prominently displayed on the thick cream vellum.

'What is it?'

'Why don't you read it?'

Filled with curiosity, Zara turned away from Shahin. After a few moments she wheeled back again, laughing in disbelief.

'Why are you laughing?' Shahin demanded quietly.

'Because this is absolutely ridiculous… Because I have no intention of holding to an agreement like this—' She thrust the document towards him.

'It's a legal document,' he said, refusing to take it. 'It's not up for discussion.'

'Legal here in Zaddara, maybe…'

'I think it's better if you keep it, don't you?' he said calmly when she tried again to hand it to him. 'For your records…'

'I don't want it.' She tried to give it to him again and, when he refused, exclaimed, 'If you won't have it, it can go in the bin.' She looked around and, finding no bin to put it in, she screwed it into a ball and flung it down on the floor at her side.

'Destroying the document means nothing,' Shahin told her calmly. 'The facts contained within it hold firm.'

'Facts?' she exclaimed in outrage. 'The only fact is that that is the most preposterous piece of patronising cant I've ever read.'

'I'll leave you to think about it for a moment, shall I?'

'I don't need a moment,' Zara assured him, turning away. Her cheeks were on fire. She couldn't remember ever feeling quite so worked up. Sheikh Abdullah had been her guardian and now Shahin had inherited that role? What was worse, according to Zaddaran law, Shahin would remain her guardian until she reached the age of twenty-five.

She wouldn't accept it. It was that simple.

CHAPTER NINE

'How old are you, Zara?'

Shahin addressed the question to Zara's hostile back.
His tone was so reasonable it only made her angrier. 'You
know how old I am. My date of birth must be written on
your precious document—'

'How old?' he asked her again in the same level voice.

Shahin must have known she wouldn't accept this, Zara
raged internally. Did she need a guardian? *Did she?* And
then the penny dropped… This was why Shahin had been
so distant with her since he'd kissed her. This was why he
was avoiding physical contact with her like the plague. He
could attribute a moment's loss of control to any number
of things, but more than that was unthinkable as far as
Shahin was concerned. But why couldn't he have been
straight with her from the start? 'I'm twenty,' she told him
fiercely, still stinging from his distant manner, 'As I'm
sure you know—'

He ignored her fury and continued in the same reasonable voice. 'So we have five years to make this work.'

'Five years? Don't tell me you intend going through
with this?'

Shahin's silence assured her that he had every intention of doing just that.

'But I never had any personal contact with your father. So why should we change things now? The money from Zaddara has always been paid on time without my ever meeting Sheikh Abdullah—'

One ebony brow rose. 'That sounds like a very mercenary arrangement to me... I fully intend to take an interest in my ward's life, as I hope she will in mine—'

'She? This is me, Shahin,' Zara reminded him furiously. 'And don't you dare make it sound as if all I care about is money. You know as soon as I could support myself I channelled every penny of the Zaddaran funds into my charities.'

'But the money was paid—' he flashed back softly.

Anger was getting her nowhere, Zara realised. Taking a deep, steadying breath she tried to reason with him. 'I can't believe you'd want to enforce this agreement, or that you'd expect me to go along with it.'

'I'm not above the law, whatever you might like to think, and if I flaunt this official order, or allow you to do so, what does that say to my people?'

'But this is wrong. Can't you see that?'

'Not in Zaddara; here it is the law.'

'Then the law will have to be changed.'

'That's not as easy as you think, and even if it could be changed it wouldn't be a quick fix. What we have is a binding contract between us. I don't want to argue with you—'

'Then let me out of this agreement, Shahin,' she said, cutting across him. 'I'm my own woman, responsible for myself. You know that...' Ward and guardian was one relationship between them Zara knew was never going to work.

Shahin's expression darkened. 'I thought my bringing you here had set things straight between us.'

'Don't, Shahin,' Zara warned. 'Bringing me here isn't a blanket solution for everything…' Even as she made the complaint and did everything in her power to push him away, her heart yearned for him. She hadn't suspected the depth of her feelings for Shahin until this moment, Zara realised, and the irony wasn't lost on her. Shahin was further out of her reach now than when the great chasm of her parents' death had stood between them.

'What about our museum?'

She faced him calmly, knowing that if she stayed on in Zaddara and helped Shahin to create a showpiece museum their relationship would be platonic—that was what he was telling her. But the project they both cared so much about would be completed. It was agony to balance a long held dream against another, no less intense for the fact that it had so recently come into her life. But in the end, Zara accepted, she could only do what was right. 'A museum that would stand as a monument to our parents…' The slight inflection in her voice turned it into a question.

'Of course…'

Shahin kept his expression neutral as he waited to see what Zara would say. She had suffered two surprises, two traumas, in quick succession. He had been wrong to be surprised by the intensity of her reaction. And now he had to wait and see if she had as much character as he thought. To stay true to his original intention he must remember that his intention had been to find his ward to explain that he would be taking over her guardianship, and to reassure her that everything would remain the same…

His jaw clenched at that. *How could it remain the same?* It must, he ordered his inner voice. 'You would have separate accommodation, of course,' he informed her. 'And, naturally, you would have a voice in all the decision-making.'

'A voice?'

He had to hide his feelings at the small victory, but adrenalin was pumping through his veins at the thought that she might stay. She had to stay. He needed her input, her expertise… 'An equal voice to mine,' he amended, moving away from the door. The project would be nothing without Zara's fire, her creativity, her vision… For that alone he would put up with her challenging him every inch of the way. It was worth it to build something so special and unique. But now he wanted her answer. 'Will you stay? Yes or no?'

The look she gave him left him in no doubt that it wouldn't be an easy ride for him. And then she spelled out the specifics.

'To create a museum that would celebrate my parents' achievements and those of your father? Yes, I'll stay for that.'

A second rush, bigger than the first, ripped through him. Duty would make this work. It had always kept him focused in the past. He had vowed to serve his country and they would be so busy once the project kicked off that neither of them would have the opportunity to think about personal considerations. Transforming the old building into a world-class gallery would take every moment of their time… But it would take a day or two to get everything in place, a day or two during which both of them must be kept fully occupied. And then he hit upon a solution…

'Where are you going?' she called after him as he headed off.

It pleased him to think she was calling him back and he didn't stop or slow his pace.

She ran faster than he had ever imagined she could on the sand and was there, staring him in the face, by the time he reached for her door handle. He hid his surprise and didn't waste time talking. 'Get in…' He left her to clamber in and shut the door for herself.

She flared a look at him as he sprang in beside her and surreptitiously clung on as he slammed the door and gunned the engine.

'Where are we going? I think you'd better tell me. Or is this another of your surprises, Shahin?'

He was taking her to a place where she could relax, making it easier for him to persuade her to accept the contract between them.

'You could say that…' He swung the wheel.

'So,' she prompted doggedly, 'where are you taking me?'

He ground his jaw, knowing this wouldn't stop until she got everything out of him. 'To my desert encampment—' To counter her stunned silence he added, 'Not the camp site where we first met—this is a different place… I hope you like it.'

'I hope I do too.'

Her voice augured trouble if she didn't! But it pleased him to keep the surprise to himself for now. He wasn't taking her to a spartan Bedouin tent but to his favourite place of recreation—a desert encampment where he was able to indulge himself far away from prying eyes and where Zara would see the obvious benefit of being his ward.

Just as he expected, when they crested the hill she exclaimed in amazement. He pressed her for a reaction.

'It's hard to imagine all this is here after…'

As her voice tailed away he guessed she was thinking about the desolation of the oil exploration site where their parents had lived and worked. But they had all worked for an outcome like this…this was Zara's heritage as much as his and she had every right to share it with him.

After a pause she asked him why the exploration site had been allowed to get into such a state.

'In his later years my father couldn't bring himself to go there. It upset him too much…'

'I'm sorry. I should have realised…'

'But restoring it is at the top of my agenda,' he reassured her.

And mine, her eyes seemed to tell him.

'So… What do you think?' Drawing the Jeep to a halt on the hill, he leaned his elbows on the steering wheel to stare out over the luxurious encampment.

'It's amazing…'

Her enthusiasm gave him a warm glow of pleasure. He was so keen to help her look to the future.

'It's not what I expected at all,' she went on. 'It looks so…'

'What?' he prompted, his lips tugging up in a grin, 'Fabulous? Regal?' She was right to be surprised—no one knew of this place except his most trusted advisors.

'Are you teasing me?'

He was so pleased by her lightened mood that he laughed, enjoying her surprise. He couldn't wait to get down to the camp and start spoiling her.

In the soft evening light the canopied pavilions were pale shadows against a lilac-coloured sky. The sand had deepened to mustard-yellow and the naked torches added exclamation marks of flaming crimson to the peaceful scene. The colours alone were spectacular, but just for once Zara had forgotten to raise her camera, Shahin noticed. Dusk was a very special time in the desert, but it looked as if she would have to come again to take her photographs...

The rush of pleasure that thought gave him augured badly for reining in his feelings where his ward was concerned. He realised he was already planning her next visit to this very private and sybaritic retreat.

The pavilions were clustered around the most beautiful stretch of sapphire water Zara had ever seen. 'Oh, look...' Her heart thundered with excitement to see birds skimming the surface of the oasis. There were men flying falcons, she realised, and beyond them camels standing in a palm-shaded paddock. And then she saw the horses and her smile died abruptly.

'You're going to learn to ride,' Shahin confirmed, as if this was the greatest gift he could bestow on her.

'Oh...wonderful.'

'And you're going to have the very best instructor there is.'

'You?'

He frowned. 'Of course me...'

As Zara's heart picked up speed she didn't want to think if apprehension or excitement was the cause of it. But maybe learning to ride wouldn't be such a bad thing after all...

Was this her tent? No. How could this be called a tent? Zara wondered, turning full circle beneath the vaulted ceiling.

The pavilion into which she had just been shown was absolutely stunning. It was impossible not to feel pampered the moment she walked beneath the canopied entrance.

Shahin had been right to say she would find this a very different experience to his Bedouin tent. Gazing around, she guessed the furniture and all the beautiful ornaments must be antique and suspected that many of them were priceless treasures. The room was scented with exotic aromatics and candles flickered in what she was sure were solid gold holders. The bed was of a type she had never seen before except in a magazine. Huge and circular, it was dressed with crimson satin covers beneath a mirrored canopy.

As she crossed the room to explore the rest of her accommodation, she trailed her fingertips over sumptuous fabrics and jewelled *objets d'art,* hardly able to believe that all these riches had been brought into the furthest reaches of the desert to satisfy one man's desires. It showed another and far more intriguing side to the serious-minded Sheikh of Zaddara…

As her heart drummed a warning, Zara forced her attention back to her surroundings. Better not to think about Shahin in any light other than His Royal Aloofness—unless she wanted another knock back during her stay.

If she had thought the bedroom of her suite fantastic, the bathroom exceeded all Zara's expectations. Cloaked in ivory pink-veined marble, there was a hot tub big enough for two and a walk-in shower. Through another doorway she discovered decking, beyond which her own private swimming pool glinted in the fast fading light. The wrap-around veranda overlooked the oasis, which was softly lit by torchlight now. Then she noticed that a table had been laid for her, complete with fresh fruit punch sitting on a bed of ice and delicious-looking canapés.

'Do you like it?'

At the sound of Shahin's voice every part of Zara's body tingled. He was standing directly behind her and when she turned she saw that he had already changed out of his jeans and was wearing a flowing robe. The scent of his cologne teased her senses and because his ebony hair was still a little damp she knew he must have used the time to take a quick shower. 'I like it very much…' In the muted light his robe, beaded discreetly black on black around a deeply slashed neck, showed off his tanned, toned body in a way that stole her breath away.

'Good,' he said, hopefully missing out on the fact that she was somewhat distracted.

She had to try very hard not to react when he came to stand by her side.

'This is where we will indulge ourselves before getting down to work,' Shahin explained.

'Indulge ourselves?'

'In vigorous exercise,' he said as if that were obvious. 'That way we can free our minds for the work that lies ahead of us.'

Very commendable, Zara thought wryly.

'Why are you smiling?'

Because the thought of vigorous exercise with Shahin had a certain appeal. And because she'd plucked out three words from what he'd said, Zara thought mischievously, and given them a meaning all of her own… Indulge. Exercise. Vigorous. 'Perfect,' she said aloud. 'I mean, it's perfect here,' she said when he looked at her with suspicion. And then, widening her eyes, she added earnestly, 'And I'm sure a vigorous workout will give us both the best possible start.'

'Good. In that case we will start your riding lessons tomorrow at dawn.'

'At dawn?' Zara bit her lip. She wasn't sure she wanted to wait so long.

'The horses have been fed,' Shahin explained to her, smiling at her eagerness. 'They need to rest now. But don't worry,' he added, thinking no doubt to console her, 'we'll be ready to ride out at dawn, before the sun makes things too uncomfortable…'

If there was one thing she had learned from fending for herself it was that she couldn't sit around waiting for things to happen—she had to make them happen, Zara reflected. 'Couldn't we start my lessons tonight?'

'Ride in the moonlight, do you mean?' Shahin frowned.

Zara held her breath.

'You're not sufficiently experienced to take the risk—riding at night can be tricky'

'Then how shall I ever become experienced if you do not teach me?'

Raising his head to the stars, Shahin cursed softly in Zaddaran.

So he had got the point. 'Shahin?' Zara felt a thrill of anticipation as she pressed him. She wasn't letting him off the hook now.

But just when she was confident he'd got the message, his face changed. 'What are you trying to do to me, Zara?'

Firming her jaw, she stared him out.

'Don't you know who I am?' His voice was low and rough and he gripped her arms in his passion.

'If I ever forget I'm sure I can rely on you to remind me, your royal highness—'

'Forget my title! I'm your guardian! You're my ward! How do you expect me to overlook that fact?'

'I think you'll find there's plenty of historical precedent for—'

'For what?' He cut her off brusquely. 'You're still a child—'

'I'm twenty years old,' Zara argued fiercely. 'I'm a woman, Shahin, even if you can't see it. I'm old enough to know what I want—'

She was right. And she was everything a woman should be and never had been. They had all been too eager, too obvious, too desperate, but Zara fought him every inch of the way. There was nothing desperate about her—other than her desperation to have her own way and defy him at every turn. But he loved the fire, the fight he could see in her eyes. 'And you know what you want?' he mocked, unable to resist the temptation to provoke her.

'Yes I do!'

'And what's that?'

'You…'

They glared at each other for a moment as if hate and not passion had fuelled the exchange. The air was charged and alive with danger and Shahin knew he was battling an enemy he had no hope of defeating, because that enemy was himself.

He kissed her brutally, hard, as if the guilt was pouring out of him and she had to absorb it and make it right. But, whatever it said about Shahin's feelings for her, he could not possess more determination than she did to have him make love to her. She was all sensation, caught up in passion, need, love, desire… This was her man and she had laid claim to him.

Was it wrong for a guardian to love his ward? Who said it was wrong? Who had the authority to pass judgement? Could a man-made law stand between lovers? Who dared to deny fate?

Zara thought her heart might burst with happiness when Shahin swung her into his arms.

Now she was lying on the bed he kissed her gently and stroked her hair, but she cried out in disappointment. She was ready for him. She had been waiting so long she didn't want to wait a moment longer. He knew she wanted fast relief, but he knew better. Her lips might be plump, her nipples thrusting towards him through the fine fabric of her shirt, but he would refuse her what she craved. He would tame her a little first and show her the benefits of patience.

Capturing Zara's wrists in one fist, Shahin brought them over her head and rested them on the soft bank of pillows.

'Don't stare at me as if I might break,' she complained.

His lips curved with amusement. 'Don't touch, hold back, or you might break… Is that what you think I'm doing?' he teased her in a low voice.

'Shahin!' she warned him furiously as he dropped kisses everywhere on her face except her mouth. Her frantic need for sex was arousing him more than he had ever known.

'You're looking at me as if I'm one of your delicate ornaments…'

'Would you rather I was rough with you?'

'Yes…'

'Well, you're going to be disappointed.' He had to ignore the angry sound she made deep in her throat and concentrate on keeping her still.

The pain she had read about would all be over in a moment, Zara reasoned. What was Shahin waiting for? Did he think she couldn't stand it? She would bear anything to have him claim her, as she had claimed him. She wanted all of him and she wanted him now, every part of him. At first, as she writhed beneath him, she thought he was holding her still so he could lecture her on the error of her ways—perhaps lay out another, more prosaic, exercise schedule for the next day… But when Shahin dipped his head and ran the tip of his tongue across the full swell of her bottom lip with tantalising steadiness she realised that this was all part of the foreplay and her senses roared to a higher level still.

Her lips were so sensitive after his earlier rampage she cried out in excitement, and then groaned with sudden pleasure as he rasped the stubble on his cheeks against her neck. She arced her body to find contact, but he cleverly moved away, denying her the touch of his hands and the possessive thrust of his tongue until she was going mad for him. Could anything be more arousing? She writhed shamelessly, hunting for relief, even from the friction of her thighs and from the pleasant sensation of her hips moving on the cool white sheets. But Shahin refused to be hurried and her actions only deepened the half-smile on his lips.

'And that was your first lesson, little one,' he told her, apparently unmoved by her sharp growl of complaint.

'To wait?' She challenged him angrily. But he only gave

her impatience a moment's hearing before teasing her with his tongue again. A sigh of delight poured out of her as Shahin began to toy with her ear lobe, and he soon had her angling her head, wanting more. When he pulled away she moved sinuously beneath him... And, with her hands still trapped in his fist, she stretched out her body to lure him on— arching, sighing, trying everything she knew to make him forget his wretched rules on control. Which got her nowhere.

When at last he let her go it was to start unbuttoning her shirt, which he did with a tantalising lack of urgency. She thrust her breasts at him, eager to show them off and have him approve them. She couldn't wait to see the look on his face when she was naked and he could dip his head to suckle. But as she lifted her shoulders from the bed to speed things up, he pressed her down again. And all the time Shahin's eyes were burning into her, assuring her that he knew how much she wanted him and that the more she urged him to hurry, the longer he was determined to make her wait.

CHAPTER TEN

'WHY are you holding back like this, Shahin?' Zara challenged him impatiently.

'Holding back?' His voice was husky. 'There are certain benefits to delay, as you will discover when you are more experienced...'

'Are you patronising me?'

'Would I?'

She ignored the obvious and went for the subject closest to her heart. 'And shall I grow more experienced beneath your hands?' She felt a sense of power seeing a muscle jump in his jaw. 'How much do you want me, Shahin?'

His answer was to take her mouth with mind-numbing thoroughness while he chafed her nipples beneath the flimsy lace of her bra.

Lifting his head, he teased her cruelly. 'Let me think...'

As she cried out Zara knew that her bra had proved no defence against Shahin's determined assault, and that both her lips and nipples were swollen with arousal by the time he had released her.

Slipping his hands behind her back, he freed the catch on her bra and cast it aside... And then the real torture began. Her nipples, already standing to attention beneath his appreciative inspection, tightened still more when he leaned forward to tease them with the tip of his tongue. She was so sensitive that when he drew the first bud into the heat of his mouth and laved it with his tongue she had to try again to make contact and bucked beneath him, not caring what he thought of her. But Shahin had left his hands free to press her down, to control her, to hold her steady while he prepared her for what was to come next. And when she was reduced to sobbing with pleasure he silenced her cries with a kiss.

And now the longing to touch him, to please him had grown stronger inside her. She wanted to weave her fingers through his hair and keep him close. 'Release me,' she commanded the moment their lips parted.

'I will, after this…'

Zara couldn't believe the sensation when Shahin began to stroke her belly and, with a sharp cry, she ground her hips against the bed. Fire raced through her veins as his fingers teased her—fire that ended in a feather-touch of warmth that caressed each nerve-ending as she bucked mindlessly beneath him in the hunt for a more intimate assault.

Shahin's answer was to dip his fingers beneath the waistband of her briefs, searching, teasing, but never quite reaching the place she wanted him to be. But then he removed his hand and, with studied deliberation, opened the fastening on her trousers and laid them wide.

'Take them off,' Zara instructed him, lifting her hips from the bed.

Shahin laughed softly, but he did as she asked. 'And now?' he demanded, staring into her eyes.

Lacing her fingers through his hair, she whispered, 'And now you kiss me…'

'And how is that?'

'Like this…' Drawing him to her, she teased the seam of his mouth with her tongue and then planted a soft kiss on his bottom lip. 'And like this…' Another on his top lip… 'And like this…' She softly captured the full swell of his bottom lip between her teeth. 'And finally…like this.' Angling her head, she slipped her tongue into his mouth. As their tongues clashed, she sucked on his shamelessly, delighting in it, shivering with arousal as Shahin clasped her in his arms.

'And now?' he prompted, humour glinting in his eyes.

'Don't pretend you don't know…'

'But I'm enjoying my lesson,' he complained huskily.

And so she gave him the next lesson, drawing his robe slowly up his body—until her bluff was called and she stopped abruptly.

'Does it surprise you that I wear nothing beneath my robe?' Shahin demanded with amusement.

She couldn't stop staring at his arousal, but somehow managed to drag her gaze away. 'Nothing would surprise me about you,' she offered boldly.

'It is much more comfortable to go commando in the desert.'

'I'm sure it is. And much more convenient, perhaps?'

'Of course,' he agreed.

Tumbling her on to her back, Shahin moved into the dominant position. Slipping his hands down beneath her briefs, he cupped her buttocks. Zara gave a little cry of excitement, but he hadn't finished with her yet. Parting the softly yielding cheeks, he released them… And then, just when she was thinking she couldn't be more aroused and that he couldn't expect her to sustain this level of stimulation a moment longer, he did it again…

'I hate you,' she panted feverishly. 'You're too cruel—'

'I know,' Shahin whispered against her mouth.

But his eyes were dancing with laughter, Zara noticed as he used his thumbs to stroke and tease her thighs apart. 'I can't stand it…'

'Yes, you can,' Shahin insisted, kissing away her sobs of frustration, 'and you must…'

'Then you must allow me to undress you…' She didn't wait for his reply. Grabbing the edge of his robe, she tugged it over his head.

And gulped. His body was as stunning as she remembered… Only this time she saw that his belly was as hard and well muscled as his torso. He glowed with vigour and with strength like polished copper in the lamplight. She was careful to edit her inspection, not sure she was ready for a second look. And then she felt a flicker of fear seeing the power in his thighs… Would he be too big for her? Too demanding? *Would she disappoint him?*

Reaching up to safer ground, she ran her fingers lightly over the wide spread of his shoulders and on again down his arms. She wanted to tease Shahin as much as he had teased her. She found his nipples and toyed with them, pleased to hear him sigh, pleased to feel them harden as she nipped them between her thumb and forefinger.

Shahin pulled away. 'And so you want to play games with me?'

'It's only fair,' Zara pointed out. She felt so small against him, so helpless. And yet when Shahin groaned beneath her hands she felt so strong. When he sighed, when he was forced to pull away because he couldn't bear the level of pleasure she was giving him, she wanted to deal out more of it.

She wanted more of him. And then she remembered the first time, remembered tasting him...

Pressing Shahin down on the bed, Zara ran her hand over his flat belly. Closing her eyes so the sight of him fully aroused would do nothing to deter her, she brushed her hands against him. She found him as she had expected, thick, hard and pulsating beneath her touch. His groan made her smile and grow in confidence. She could feel him becoming harder and starting to flex beneath her touch. It was impossible not to think about that delicious action occurring inside her. It took both her hands to encompass his girth now and as she gripped him she had to wait a moment in order to gain courage enough to explore further... And then she traced his length, from the nest of springing curls to the silky tip so beautifully formed, so perfect for slipping inside her...

'Do I please you?' he murmured.

She couldn't possibly tell him how much. 'Yes, you do...' But she was coming to believe that he was far too big for her. But she wanted him so badly... And then her mouth closed over him and she tasted him. It thrilled her to feel him thrusting deeper into her moist, silky warmth. She wanted to please him, but she was frightened too. Now the moment of truth was here she was frightened of Shahin possessing her as a man must possess a woman. But this was a way to please them both, Zara convinced herself. And she loved the taste of him, the texture of him beneath her tongue, the strength, the power, the raised veins that pulsed with life...

'Are you frightened of me?' Drawing back, Shahin lifted her up the bed. 'Zara?' He made the whispered demand staring into her eyes so she had no escape. 'Do you believe I would hurt you?'

Her eyes filled with tears as she stared at him. He knew so much about her. But maybe there was something else holding him back. 'Did I do something wrong?' Her cheeks burned beneath his scrutiny, but then warmth flooded through her when she saw the tenderness in his eyes.

'You did nothing wrong... But something tells me you're drawing back, you're postponing the moment when—'

'No, I—' Placing her finger across his lips, she shook her head. But Shahin quickly took hold of her hand and kissed her palm.

'I understand,' he whispered. Drawing her down beside him in the bed, he stroked her and soothed her until she began to respond, slowly at first, but then with increasing ardour as her body cried out for his touch.

'If you want me to stop,' he murmured, 'you only have to tell me that you've changed your mind.'

To each of the questions in his eyes she answered no. There was such warmth and such tenderness in Shahin's eyes and she held his stare until she knew that he was no longer in any doubt in his mind that her resolve was fixed.

'Then shall I prepare you?' He drew her excited gasp into his mouth, kissing her deeply as he cupped the swollen mound between her legs over the cobweb fabric of her briefs. His fingers strayed a little, but never enough, and he always managed to evade her best attempts to lure him on.

As he stripped off her briefs she moved eagerly to help him. She had no inhibitions left that had not been overtaken by hunger. She wanted him so badly she drew her knees back in anticipation and, locking her hands behind Shahin's waist, closed her eyes.

Zara cried out softly, not sure that she could survive the pleasure, as Shahin delicately began to touch her most sensitive place.

'Is that good?'

Shahin didn't need an answer as she moved beneath him. He heard her sighs and saw the pleasure he was giving her reflected in her eyes. But she wanted to please him too. 'Make love to me, Shahin... I want you so badly. Oh, please, Shahin, I love—'

He cut her off with a kiss and absorbed the cry she made as he entered her. He moved slowly to possess her in the most sensitive way she could have imagined...

'Am I hurting you?'

The truth was he would have hurt her more had he stopped. Her answer was to rock back on her hips, affording him greater access.

Cupping her face in his hands, Shahin kissed her deeply, tangling his tongue with hers before plunging into the dark secret warmth of her mouth. He stopped once briefly when she cried out. But the moment soon passed and her eyes cleared again.

'Are you all right?' he demanded huskily, dropping kisses on her eyelids.

'Please...' It was the one word she could manage, the

only word that perfectly expressed her wishes, and so he moved deeper until her muscles closed around him and he inhabited her completely.

And then at last he moved, side to side without withdrawing, rolling gently to massage the very place that had waited so long for his attention. She couldn't hold back, she didn't want to... She had become greedy for him, greedy for Shahin and all the pleasure she knew he could bring her. She thrust her pelvis against him, grinding hungrily, so incredibly aware and sensitive... She didn't even hear herself calling out for satisfaction—ordering him, begging him, because her heart was thundering so loudly in her ears. Her skin was warm and her fingers dug into him, into his buttocks, driving him, encouraging him... And then light enveloped her, exploding in her head in a starburst of sensation that left her oblivious to her surroundings. And then, as she slowly grew conscious again to those things that existed outside the pleasure vortex, Shahin began to move.

He thrust steadily, bringing her with him, raising himself on stiff arms so he could watch the pleasure unfolding on her face. Growing accustomed to his rhythm, she rose to meet him, moving with him, working her hips to draw him deeper, while his warm hands cupped her buttocks to support her and hold her in place. She responded eagerly as he pleasured her, catching hold of him and then splaying her fingers against his chest as he moved faster. She wanted every inch of her to be in contact with Shahin, but he misread the signal and, taking it as a warning sign, drew back.

'I just want to feel every part of you,' Zara reassured him.

His lips tugged up in a smile. 'Like this?' he suggested, moving deep. As she groaned with pleasure he withdrew so that it was like starting over again when he took her the next time. And then he wouldn't stop teasing her and made her wait a little longer and a little longer for each new assault until she was thrashing helplessly beneath him.

'Don't tease me, Shahin—' Taking hold of his hips, Zara showed him clearly what she wanted.

'Like this, then…' He set up a fast pace that had her gasping with pleasure and surprise.

'Oh, yes…yes…' She clung on as he thrust over and over, building up the pleasure until she knew it had to find an outlet again. She heard someone wailing with anticipation, calling out excitedly, someone moaning rhythmically and making guttural animal sounds down low in her throat, sounds that rang to a primitive beat until the world and everything in it dissolved once again into pleasure.

'I don't think I need to ask if you enjoyed that,' Shahin murmured against her ear. 'In fact, I only have one question for you…'

'And what's that?' Turning her face up lazily, she looked at him.

'More?'

With a wanton sigh Zara wrapped her legs around his waist.

CHAPTER ELEVEN

IT WAS only necessary to give the slightest indication with his thighs for Jal to respond. Plunging forward eagerly, ears pricked, the stallion's polished hooves pounded the sand, eating up the distance between the encampment and the mountains beyond the plain. It would take an hour of hard riding for him to get there, an hour in which to excise his demons…

Leaning low over Jal's neck, Shahin pressed him on. By the time they arrived at the source of the underground stream where Jal could drink and rest in preparation for the homeward journey, he had to be ready to face facts.

And find an answer?

With a fierce sound, Shahin loosened the reins, allowing the horse his head; he didn't expect a miracle.

The moment they arrived he sprang down and went to break off fistfuls of the coarse, dry grass that somehow managed to survive in the shadow of the granite outcrop. The horse's dark hide was flecked with sweat and, bunching the grass, he rubbed him down vigorously. He hadn't wasted time on a saddle, but a fiery horse like Jal was better ridden with a bridle, or like a wayward woman would rush heedlessly into danger…

No one could accuse Zara of being wayward, Shahin reflected grimly. In fact, she was anything but. She had hidden her inner passion beneath a cloak of good sense and caution, and it was he who had shown her another path, a dangerous path, an erotic path…

Picking up the reins, Shahin began walking the horse, talking to him soothingly as Jal snorted his impatience to reach the water. 'Not yet,' Shahin whispered in one quivering ear, pulling the forelock out of his stallion's eyes. 'First you must cool down…'

As he paced with the horse, Shahin wondered if he could despise himself more. It wasn't the fact that Zara was his ward that troubled him, for as she had pointed out that problem was not insurmountable. There were precedents for relationships and even marriages between ward and guardian. It was that having discovered a beautiful and inviolate flower he had trampled it underfoot. Desire had blinded him to duty, to moral scruples—he hadn't given a thought to what would happen next. But the future had hit him in the face when he had woken to find her sleeping at his side. He had known then that he could not allow the susceptibilities of a man to interfere with the duties of a king.

In other countries a man might marry a princess, or a prince a secretary, but in Zaddara such a thing was unthinkable. The ruling sheikh must marry someone appropriate—a virgin from a neighbouring territory in an arrangement that would bring benefits to both parties. That was what he had decided he would do long before he had met Zara Kingston. Privilege came with a price and his account had just fallen due.

'Shahin?' Feeling the empty space on the bed beside her, Zara opened her eyes. Thin strands of sunlight were spilling into the pavilion, falling in silver streaks across the bed. At first she thought dawn must be rising over the desert and she was waking in good time for the dreaded riding lesson, but then she realised that the heavy silk curtains were still drawn and only fingers of light were seeping through.

Sitting up, she looked around and then stayed still to listen. She hoped to hear the shower running or the sound of strong limbs plying the cool waters of the private pool. But she was alone and the silence was heavy and complete.

Her body, still languid from sleep, was throbbing from the effects of so much lovemaking. Thinking about Shahin made her smile and, tugging off one of the sheets, she wrapped it tightly round her naked body and slipped out of bed to go and look for him.

Padding across the cool floor to the double doors leading on to the veranda, she opened them and paused a moment to enjoy the gust of warm air that greeted her. She couldn't believe she had slept so long. It must be almost noon, she guessed, gazing up into a flawless cobalt sky.

Her discarded clothes were still strewn across the floor like an obstacle course, she noticed with amusement, picking her way around them for a second time. Flinging herself down in contentment on to the tangle of silk and satin covers, she caught sight of her reflection in the mirrored canopy. Her cheeks flushed red as she remembered... But where was Shahin?

He had left nothing behind him in the room, Zara noticed. It was as if he had never been there at all and she had imagined everything... Was that what he wanted her to think? Her stomach clenched with anxiety as she thought about it... But then the sound of a horse's hooves brought the smile back to her face and, slipping off the bed, she hurried back to the open door.

Feeling a rush of excitement as she identified the horse and rider, Zara knew what must have happened. When she hadn't woken at dawn as they had agreed, Shahin had gone riding without her. Being considerate, he hadn't wanted to wake her....

Walking out on to the veranda, she shaded her eyes and waved, secretly glad that she had missed her first riding lesson. She would only have held them back, Zara reflected, admiring the way Shahin rode the stallion as if he were part of the horse.

Jal was walking at a steady pace as horse and rider approached the encampment. Thanks to Shahin's concern for the animal, Zara thought. It was hot now and Shahin would never overwork his horse. He must have left very early to give the stallion such a good workout, she realised, seeing Jal's usually glossy hide was coated in dust.

Hurrying inside to shower and make herself presentable, Zara found it hard to contain her excitement. She couldn't wait to be with Shahin again. Their relationship had changed irrevocably and she only had to remember the look in his eyes when he'd held her in his arms for the thrill of desire to return.

She couldn't wait to tell Shahin how much he meant to her when they fell into each other's arms. That would give him the opportunity to confide that he felt the same... He always held back when it came to expressing his feelings, but today she felt confident that all he would need was a tiny push.

He had been so gentle with her, so loving and passionate, and in return she had given him everything. Shahin had made her first experience of lovemaking beautiful... Though, looking back, she could see that she had tensed at the crucial moment and might have spoiled it for him.

She would be able to reassure him about that too and tell him it had been everything she had hoped for and more... She couldn't wait.

From the moment Shahin entered the room Zara was filled with a sense of foreboding. Had he left her to sleep or simply decided to leave her? The expression on his face made her think the latter might be the more likely explanation.

He stood by the door with his whip and riding gloves in his hand, as if to emphasise the fact that this would only be a short visit. She might be naïve, but she wasn't naïve enough to think that he had come straight from the stables because he couldn't wait to see her. His body language assured her that wasn't the case. No. He was impatient to get whatever he had come to say to her over and done with. He must have woken at her side and regretted everything that had happened. Her dream had been Shahin's nightmare...

Shivering a little, she forced herself to meet his gaze. Everything she hoped not to see was in his eyes. He had enjoyed her and he would never forgive himself for that. And, quite possibly, he believed she had led him on...

What could she do? She would not feel ashamed and she did not regret what had happened. So should she give in without a fight? As he stared at her she felt as if a huge gulf had widened between them. And the feeling made her all the more determined to prove him wrong. She hadn't come all this way in her feelings for him to turn back now. She wasn't a coward and she wouldn't run from love. Why would she, when she had been searching for love all her life?

She would tell him how she felt and that she understood his reservations. It was up to her to put their feelings into words. Shahin's life had been channelled into duty and maintaining his dignity, which made it impossible for him to express his emotions freely. She understood that and she also understood that reserve like his couldn't be broken down all at once. Everything would be right again when she told Shahin how much she loved him…

'What are you saying, Zara?' As he looked at her and saw the love shining from her eyes, he wondered how he could ever have imagined his guilt could be mitigated by a taxing ride. It had just come flooding back, only now it was redoubled.

Confidence radiated from her as she told him again, 'I love you…'

The honesty blazing from her eyes emphasised how young she was, how innocent. He should have anticipated this because, however wise she appeared, however strong and determined, she was inexperienced in every way. For all her talk of independence, of carving a life for herself, she was unworldly, and he had taken advantage of that fact and had ridden roughshod over her dreams. And now, at the very moment when she declared her love for him, he must abuse her trust in him one last time.

'You mustn't say that,' he murmured gently, removing her hands from his shoulders. She had laid her head on his chest so trustingly he felt ashamed. But, whatever she had conjured in her mind, this was the moment when he must kill her hopes once and for all.

'I know you find it difficult to say what's in your heart,' she said, staring up at him, refusing to acknowledge the coolness in his gaze.

'Zara, please... Don't make this any harder than it has to be.'

'What do you mean?' The glow lasted for barely an instant and then abruptly it vanished and her face crumpled. 'Don't you want me, Shahin?'

'You know I do...' He turned away to gather his thoughts. He had been conveniently blind to how vulnerable she was, but now he had to face the fact that he had slept with her and that he shouldn't have and that, having been the first, he had taken something from her that could never be restored.

There was only one way he could help her now and that was to convince her that she was better off without him in any romantic sense and that a working arrangement, along with a strict guardian/ward relationship was the most she could expect. 'Of course I want to be with you,' he said with a false air of optimism. 'We're going to be working together, aren't we? But—'

'But?'

Her gaze was razor-sharp and she picked up his meaning fast. Her eyes might hold hurt, pain and disillusionment, but she would not be lightly dismissed. She had hoped for so much more than he could give her, but that didn't mean she was a fool. 'But… You must see that an intimate relationship between us can never work,' he said plainly.

'Oh,' she said thoughtfully, as if she might be giving some consideration to his words.

He drove on. 'You'd have a poor life with me, Zara… I'm bound by duty; I'm not free to follow my own inclinations—'

'As you did last night…'

She spoke so gently he didn't take it as a warning and, in his desire to avoid revisiting anything to do with the passionate night they'd spent together, he gave a humourless laugh. 'You'd be miserable as my wife.'

'Your wife?' Her surprise was obvious. And then another expression came into her eyes: disbelief, rapidly followed by contempt that he should, out of desperation or a desire to be rid of her, place what *might have been* on so high a level.

'Yes, I respect you too much to…' He hunted for the right words, words they might both find acceptable. *To make you my mistress* felt wrong, sordid under these circumstances.

But before he had the chance to finish the sentence she demanded, 'Don't you feel anything for me, Shahin?' Her eyes were full of tears, but her tone was angry.

'Of course I do. But—'

'But?' She cut across him passionately as if she loathed the word. 'Have I just made a complete fool of myself, Shahin?'

'No, of course you haven't!'

'I think I have,' she said stubbornly.

'Zara, you must know that what we have is—'

'What?' she said, cutting across him coldly.

'Well, it's wonderful.'

'Wonderful?'

'But it can't go anywhere. Can it?' he demanded gently, appealing to her common sense. 'You know the position I'm in—'

'Would that be your position as ruling Sheikh of Zaddara, your position as my guardian, or your position in my bed? You'll have to excuse me here, Shahin—' She clutched her arms as she shook her head. 'Only I'm getting a little confused—'

'Don't do this to yourself.' He reached out to her, but she pulled away.

'What? What am I doing to myself, Shahin? Am I facing up to the truth, perhaps?'

'It doesn't have to be like this—'

'So how should it be? What was I for you, Shahin? A workout? Part of your exercise regime? What? Where do I fit into your life?'

'Don't talk like that, Zara. Don't demean yourself—'

'Demean myself?' she scoffed. 'You're doing a pretty good job of that without my help.'

'Zara, please—'

She knocked his hand off her shoulder. 'Is this how guardians behave in Zaddara? Before I got here I guessed your country might be behind the times, but I never dreamt the ruling sheikh would still exercise *droit de seigneur!* Do you make a habit of trying out all the available virgins, or am I the first of this new reign? Well?'

Tears were streaming down her face, making her look more vulnerable than ever.

'Answer me, damn you!' she railed at him.

'What did you think would come of this? You must have known you couldn't stay here long-term. What would you be? What would you do?' The blood drained from her face as he hammered each of the nails into the coffin holding her dreams. 'And you were right,' he admitted, 'you could never be my wife. And it's unthinkable that you would be my mistress—'

'No, I suppose I couldn't be both your mistress and your ward,' she observed scathingly. 'But one day you will marry, Shahin.' She bit down on her lip and it took her a moment to gather her thoughts again. And then she said bitterly, 'You will have to take a wife, if only to continue the royal line—'

The way she said 'royal' made it sound like some aberrant strain of human being.

'The woman who agrees to be my wife will have to be an exceptional human being,' he conceded. 'The responsibility alone will be stifling…' He hoped she would see that he couldn't possibly subject a free spirit like Zara to a life sentence of duty and protocol. He looked at her again, beseeching her with his eyes to understand as he waited for her to react, to say something…

'Your wife…' She went white. And, rather than rail at him, she covered her mouth with her hand and everything she was feeling inside poured out. 'I won't be able to bear it…'

That she could be so open with him after everything they'd said to each other shocked him. She had so much raw emotion inside her and there was no self-belief or inborn arrogance to hold it in. He longed to help her, to comfort her, but when he tried to touch her, her hand shot up to ward him off.

'You have no idea what marriage to a man like me would involve—'

'Oh, no?'

He watched the strength pour back into her tear-stained face.

'Wouldn't it involve love and laughter and children, Shahin? Wouldn't it involve working together, side by side, for the good of the people of Zaddara? Don't shake your head at me, Shahin. It's you who needs help. You're more damaged than you know. You may be a giant of a man, a sheikh who is wealthy beyond imagining, but you're poor inside. In here—' she punched her chest '—you're emotionally dead!'

'Don't be ridiculous, you're overreacting—'

'Oh, I'm being ridiculous?' Shaking her head, she smiled, but it was a sad smile. 'You're the one who's being ridiculous, Shahin. You're not capable of love and you can't see that what that means is that you have nothing to offer your people. Yes, they want duty, but they want your love too. People need love, Shahin. No one understands that better than me.'

He was stunned by what she had said, but even so he had to let her go. And the only way he could drive this to a conclusion was by withdrawing from her and by standing on his dignity. 'Unfortunately, Zara, you're too young to know the difference between a schoolgirl crush and love.' He controlled himself with difficulty as a fresh stream of tears poured down her face. He willed her to be angry with him, to lose control, to express her hatred for him, but instead she was suddenly quite composed.

'I think we both know I'm all grown up, Shahin,' she said softly.

She had collected herself with such strength of will he flinched in the face of her sad reproach.

'Don't you think I've waited long enough for love to know love when I find it?' she said.

Her honesty was so brutal he couldn't fail to be moved by it, but as he pushed caution aside and went to take hold of her to comfort her, she shook him off.

'Don't…touch…me!'

'Zara, don't do this…' He followed her across the room and stood watching in silence as she started stuffing her clothes into a bag.

'I'm already doing it, Shahin. All you have to do is find someone to take me back to the capital. I'm flying out of Zaddara the first chance I get. I take it you can organise that much for me without it trespassing on your precious pride?'

'Of course I can…' For the first time in his life he was at a loss to know how to stop events rolling forward without his guiding hand deciding which direction they would take. 'But what about the exhibition?' He was willing to pull out all the stops to slow things down. 'What about the work we planned here in Zaddara? What about the memorial to your parents?' As she flashed him a glance he knew it was a cheap shot. And she didn't let it pass her by.

'The memorial to my parents?' Lifting her head, she stared at him and he saw then the full extent of the damage he'd done. Hurt brown eyes shamed him as she pressed her hand against her chest. 'The memorial to my parents is in here, Shahin. I don't know why I didn't see that all along.'

'But we have a chance to build something special in

Zaddara, something that will stand as a memorial to my father, as well as to your parents, a living monument that will show their struggle—'

He was wasting his time. She was looking at him as though he were mad to think they could ever work together now. But conceding defeat wasn't a concept he recognised. 'We have a chance to create a gallery of images that will stand as a guiding principle for all the young people of Zaddara—'

'You still think of me as one of those "young people", don't you, Shahin? You can't see that life makes some people grow up faster than others. You don't understand that some of us must take on responsibility at a much younger age than other people because we have no choice... And that it doesn't mean we need your pity,' she raged in case he hadn't got the message.

The look she gave him spoke of the childhood that had been stolen from her and the way she had rebuilt her life without anybody's help.

He had to mend bridges and fast. 'I thought—'

'You thought you'd talk to me about guiding principles and I'd be pacified. You thought if you made me see the bigger picture everything would be okay. But I do see the bigger picture and it's still not okay.'

'So what about our gallery?'

'*Your* gallery, Shahin. The Zaddaran gallery of historic images where, no doubt, I'd always be a welcome visitor.'

'Of course you'd be welcome. How could you not be welcome when most of the work will be yours and the rest of it your parents'—' He stopped as she frowned. A bad feeling was growing in the pit of his stomach.

'That's something else we have to talk about. As far as my parents' things are concerned, I want to have them shipped home to England. I presume that even you wouldn't deny me that much?'

He needed time to think how to get round this. And found none. 'If that's what you want?'

'It is.'

There was nothing left him but the authority card, which he now played. 'You're right, we do have to talk about this before you make any rash decisions—'

'I'm not being rash, Shahin, I've made up my mind. We just did all the talking we're going to do—and they're coming home with me.'

'You're still my ward. You'll need my authority to remove them from Zaddara.'

'In that case…' She remained quite calm. 'I think I should also tell you that the collection you bought at the exhibition is no longer for sale.'

'But I already bought them. The shipping is arranged.'

'Then un-arrange it. The exhibits aren't for sale. I just took them off the market.'

'You can't do that—'

'I just did.' And then everything she was holding back welled up in her eyes. 'The artist changed her mind, Shahin. Fickle, women, aren't they?'

His jaw worked as he fielded the verbal jab. 'But I've already paid for all the pieces in your collection.'

'Your money will be returned to you in full.'

'By Gideon and Lambert?' His voice hardened.

Zara faltered momentarily. She hadn't taken account of her sponsors, he guessed.

'I'll talk to them,' she said finally.

Her voice was dry and he guessed she was calculating the amount of money it would take to buy them off. Gideon and Lambert levied a sizeable commission on anything sold in their gallery—and that didn't include the generous mark-up they added to the 'for their eyes only' price list. He was willing to bet Zara would receive less than a tenth of what he'd paid for her exhibits by the time the wily gallery owners had finished deducting for this and that. Whatever his personal feelings, he couldn't stand by and see her fleeced. 'Very well... I have no wish to keep them if you feel so strongly about them, but maybe I should handle that side of things for you.'

'How would you do that?' she asked him suspiciously.

'I'll make sure the exhibits are released into your hands and compensation paid to the gallery. What?' He had expected her to be grateful, reassured even, but now she looked more worried than ever. And then he remembered how small her apartment was and that some of her exhibits were over twelve feet tall. 'Perhaps I could ask my people in London to find you an exhibition hall—'

She gave a humourless laugh.

'Okay, I guess that won't be easy, but we'll think of something else...' At least she was listening. 'There's always the embassy—' He had to admit to a flush of pleasure as he thought of it, because now she was looking at him with real interest. 'You have a substantial fan base,' he went on. 'And I dare say a change of venue from hip gallery to an exotic eastern location conveniently located in the centre of London would bring people flocking to the exhibition.'

She was in no hurry to dispute any of the points he'd raised, Shahin realised thankfully, and so he pressed for a conclusion. 'What do you think?'

What did she think? That Shahin was more securely locked in the past than she was. That he refused to accept that at twenty she'd had more life experience than many people twice her age. That they loved each other. She was utterly confident on that point, but again, he couldn't or wouldn't accept it. Shahin needed somebody strong and resourceful to stand at his side, but he wouldn't see that she would work tirelessly in the service of the country he loved, the country her parents had loved and the only place, she had begun to realise since seeing where her parents had lived, that she might ever have a chance of calling home.

Could she forget everything that had happened between them in order to house her work? Or should she harbour a grudge against Shahin and throw her career into jeopardy? He had offered her a way out of her immediate difficulties and if she could remove emotion from the equation it should be possible to go forward from this with her head held high. 'Thank you… That's a very generous offer; I'd like to take you up on it.'

CHAPTER TWELVE

ZARA had quickly come to think of the Zaddaran embassy as a haven of warmth and welcome in the heart of chilly London. Considering her history with the country's ruler, that was quite an accolade. Muffled up to the nose in scarf and jacket, she slipped inside the heavy front door, acknowledging the security man with a bright smile. But beneath it she was worried. The year was drawing to a close and with it her tenure on the embassy ballroom. She couldn't complain; she'd had use of the ballroom for well over a month, but her exhibition would have to be removed to make room for the concerts that were always a highlight of the London holiday season.

As ruling sheikh Shahin would be arriving soon to act as host for the festivities... Zara couldn't pretend she hadn't looked over her shoulder every day since the first of her exhibits had gone up in the hope that he might walk into the ballroom and surprise her. There was nothing subtle in the way she felt about him. He'd hurt her and discarded her, but love like she felt for Shahin wouldn't conveniently go away and, no matter how many times she told herself that it was wasted on a man who couldn't see beyond his duty to a country, her love for him remained undiminished.

Did he ever think about her? Zara wondered as a smiling attendant took her scarf and coat. Did the Sheikh of Zaddara feel the same sense of loss she did, or had Shahin simply shut her out of his mind?

She would never know. And now she had to make arrangements for her exhibition to be stored somewhere else, which would cut a huge chunk out of her budget and leave her wildlife charities without the level of funding they required. But before she turned her mind to that problem she had one last chance to walk around her exhibition and enjoy it before the general public were admitted.

Shahin hesitated outside the ornate doors leading into the embassy ballroom, knowing he should have stayed away. He should have waited another few days and then she would have been gone. But he couldn't resist seeing what she had done with the exhibits. Or at least that was his excuse for being in London a week early. The truth was, he couldn't stay away. And now he was dithering in front of one of his advisors like a youth who didn't know his own mind.

'How long has she been in there?' His voice was firm as he turned to his aide-de-camp in London. He was playing for time, steeling himself. Preparing to see her again after all this time wasn't as easy as he had imagined. She was unpredictable; she could always surprise him; he had no idea how she would greet him.

'Not long, sir. Perhaps twenty minutes…'

Twenty minutes on her own… What was she thinking, remembering? 'Thank you… That's all…' Shahin sensed, rather than saw his aide bow and then back away discreetly leaving him alone. Easing his neck in the immaculately starched white collar, he sucked in a steadying breath before opening the door.

She was standing in the centre of the dance floor with her back to him. The scale of the room made her seem smaller, more fragile than ever. She wore a calf-length skirt with boots and a roll-neck sweater—all in black, as if she were in mourning, and her hair fell loose in a glimmering cascade to her waist. She looked as young as ever, and just as vulnerable.

She remained absolutely still, though she must have heard the door open. He wished he could see her face... But he could see how stiff her shoulders had suddenly become and how rigid her back.

She knew it was him... 'Zara...'

Her shoulders eased as he spoke, almost as if she had been expecting him, and then she turned and all the tension he had expected to see in her face drained away. Her eyes glowed with love and her smile lit up the room. She came towards him with her hands outstretched, as honest and as open in her feelings towards him as she had ever been.

'Hello, Shahin...'

When he first heard her voice again, speaking his name, he couldn't put his feelings into words. She transformed him—her lack of guile, the omission of any rebuke or bitterness in her tone, when she had every reason to hate him for what he'd done to her. 'Zara...' Taking her hands in his, he raised them to his lips. And then, because he couldn't resist forces stronger than himself, he took her in his arms and held her close.

'Can I show you round?' she asked, staring up into his eyes when he finally released her.

Her composure, her absolute certainty that he would come to see her exhibition, her trust in him, her sincerity touched him, shamed him, made him face up to the fact that he loved her beyond anything else in his existence. 'I'd like that…'

His throat was raw from holding back his feelings by the time he had completed the circuit of her exhibits. He had never been so deeply moved. She had enlarged all the early photographs of her parents with his father… And they were young again, their faces full of confidence and laughter in the midst of all their struggles. There was no sign of her father's alcoholism in any of the images, and for that he was eternally grateful and had cause again to be glad that he hadn't told her everything he might have. All he could see in those old prints was youthful fire and zest for life… It had all been theirs and she had brought it back to life again. Her love for his country showed in every image. All the artefacts that had been rescued from the old cabin were beautifully displayed, with carefully thought out notes to explain their provenance…

'Do you like it?'

'Like it?' His voice sounded tight. 'You've done a great job…' *A great job?* Was that the best he could come up with?

'It's been a sell-out. We've raised thousands for Zaddaran charities.'

'*You've* raised thousands,' he corrected her. 'And I can't thank you enough…' He sounded so stiff, so formal.

'Don't thank me…' She laughed. 'You gave my exhibition a home, remember?'

'Still, I would like you to accept my thanks…'

'Of course…' She stared into his eyes.

'And so…'

'And so?' she pressed, still smiling.

'I'd like you to have dinner with me,' he blurted, wondering at his sudden loss of assurance. The thought that she might well refuse him was frightening.

'With my guardian?'

She needed clarification. He owed her that much. 'Will my ward accept?'

There was the smallest flicker of adjustment in her gaze, but she quickly recovered. 'It would mean a lot to me if we could part as friends, Shahin.'

'Yes…' He gathered himself. 'Me, too.'

They didn't go out to a restaurant that evening, but at Shahin's invitation ate dinner in his apartment at the embassy, which played into her hands. It was quiet and private in the wood-panelled sitting room. The muted masculine colours, deep-cushioned seating and roaring fire made everything cosy, Zara thought with approval, looking round. It was smaller than she had expected, but perfect. 'This is lovely…'

'I'm glad you think so… And I hope you're hungry.' Glancing at the feast that had been laid out for them, Shahin smiled.

'Starving.'

He had no idea, Zara thought, keeping her expression strictly neutral.

As always, Shahin looked magnificent in his flowing black robes and she knew enough about him now to know that, apart from the trousers secured only by a loosely tied drawstring, he would be naked underneath.

Swallowing hard, she had to accept that since meeting Shahin both diplomacy and caution, once her strong points, had been thrown to the wind. And, having decided on a plan of action, it was time to put it into effect. 'Will we be disturbed?' she asked innocently.

Shahin's face grew serious. 'I hope you know that if you ever need to speak to me in private, Zara—about anything,' he emphasised earnestly, 'you only have to ask.'

'I'm asking...' She tried to look as if she had something really serious on her mind.

'Go on,' he encouraged, sitting forward so she had a great view down the slashed neck of his robe to the hard bronzed body underneath.

'What is it, Zara?'

His voice was deliciously cajoling and filled her with conviction that she was doing the right thing. 'It's not easy...' She bit her lip.

Holding her gaze, Shahin picked up the phone.

'What are you doing?' Zara couldn't believe she was managing to keep the shake out of her voice.

'Making sure we're not disturbed—' Turning from her, he rapped out a few words in Zaddaran.

'Thank you...' She had to clench her fists at her sides to keep from laughing. Her plan was unfolding without her having to do a thing. If it all went so well...

'Now,' Shahin said, smiling reassurance, 'Why don't you tell me what's worrying you...?'

If you won't change, then once again I shall have to make you, Zara thought, holding his gaze. There's your answer, Shahin. So perhaps it's you who should be worried, because I don't have a cut-off point where I give up. I never had anyone to teach me how to accept defeat, which is quite a bonus when you think about it. 'It's a little involved...' She sighed.

'I'm listening...'

Shahin sat back to show her how relaxed he was. But that didn't last long. 'Zara, what are you doing?' He shot up, his amazed gaze following her hands as she stood and swept off her lacy cardigan.

Her breasts were accentuated in the tight-fitting top she wore underneath. 'Don't you think it's a little hot in here, Shahin?'

He couldn't look away, which was good, and so she smoothed her hands down over her body from her breasts to her waist, and then on over her hips and finally her thighs. Easing her neck, she levelled a gaze at him and found him motionless, staring at her, mesmerised.

'I could open a window if you're too warm,' he suggested faintly.

'That won't be necessary. Hot is good...'

That moment, as Shahin stared at her in silence and she couldn't read his mind, was the longest moment of her life.

They came together like an elemental force—the need to touch, to feel, to kiss, to possess, overwhelming every rational thought for both of them. Shahin had her clothes off in moments and Zara made short work of his.

Holding her to him, Shahin backed her towards the fur rug in front of the fire. But she couldn't wait to get there and, throwing her arms around his neck, she sprang up and wrapped her legs around his waist, leaning back so he had no alternative but to do as she demanded. Sinking deep with an animal roar, it was Shahin's turn to throw his head back in ecstasy as she closed her muscles around him and held him tight.

'You're mine,' she told him fiercely. And then she moved her hips with strong, deliberate thrusts, daring him to argue.

'Good...so good,' Shahin moaned, allowing Zara to dictate the pace. Completely naked, he stood firm in the middle of the room, supporting her weight with his strong hands clamped around her buttocks as she took him firmly and deeply, over and over again, driving them both to the peak of ecstasy. He cried out first and then she followed an instant later.

He had lost control. He had never done that before. Not once. And never like this. But he was shaken to the core. Kissing her gently, he inhaled the fragrance of her hair, wondering how he had lived without her sweetness. Laying her down gently on the soft fur rug, he sank into her as if they had been lovers for ever. She was so small and yet they fitted together so well, and they already knew that this was something neither of them had the power to resist.

'You're mine, Shahin... Mine,' she gasped, clinging to his arms as he pleasured her.

He didn't doubt it. She was a lioness, a queen, and the only mother he could ever want for his children...

'I want your child, Shahin...' She looked straight into his eyes as if she had a window into his soul. 'Fill me, make me yours...'

His answer was to kiss her deeply, slowing the pace of their lovemaking so that she could feel the depth of his love for her first. The desire to make love to her, really make love to her, was overwhelming. They would never be parted again. That was a vow he made to himself and would make to Zara in every way he knew. They would stay together always—that was what both destiny *and* his heart had decreed.

But for now… She was already grinding against him, asking for more. Cupping him, she nursed him, stroking him into a frenzy of desire. He was her slave and could only thrust deeper and faster in response to her coaxing, and only just managed to hold back when he saw the look of astonishment in her eyes that always marked the first wave of her climax. She clung to him, bucking convulsively as he found his own savage release, and when she softened against him this time he found it was his eyes that had filled with tears.

An ironic half-smile touched his lips as she looked at him, and when he saw the wonder and sheer exhilaration in her eyes he confirmed, 'Yes, emotion… Something new for me.'

'Something new for the man who has everything?' she teased him gently.

'I had nothing before I had you,' he assured her fiercely, his voice thickening.

'It's very lonely at the top of the mountain, isn't it, Shahin?'

'Not any longer,' he said, capturing her hand as she stroked his face. Pressing a kiss against her palm, he smiled deep into her eyes. 'I think I've found someone who can bring me down to earth…'

'You only think?' Zara reprimanded him. 'Then I shall have to convince you…' But, before she could make good her threat, Shahin moved on top of her and, pressing her into the rug, he took her again.

* * *

The Ruby Fort was filled with light as Zara descended the central staircase flanked by Lambert and Gideon. They worked for her now, having taken on the responsibility of marketing her work to a wider audience, as well as directing all their wealthy art buff friends to the magnificent new gallery she had created in Zaddara. All the proceeds from the sale of her images were directed into her charities, and all the proceeds from her gallery in Zaddara went to support the many causes there, for which she and Shahin had taken on joint responsibility.

Shahin stood waiting for her now, his dark eyes burning with love as he stared up at her. Dressed in all the splendour of his rank, he was a formidable, awe-inspiring sight—to everyone but her, Zara mused, trying, but not quite succeeding, to keep the smile from her lips. It was a look only they could share, and only they could interpret. It was a look that spoke of secrets between them, of intimacy and mischief and pleasure. It reminded her that now she had unlocked the door for him, they were both free.

She had protested when he had invaded her room earlier as she was being dressed for the ceremony, and his answer as always had been to dismiss the servants…

'But my hair,' she had protested weakly, as he'd eased the gossamer folds of silk over her head.

'Can be redone,' Shahin had reminded her, sweeping her into his arms.

And then later, when he had shown her the contents of the small velvet box he had with him, she had gasped, 'What is it?'

'Well, it's big, bright and sparkly,' Shahin observed. 'You tell me.'

'And cost the gross national product of which country?' Zara teased him back. 'It's incredible,' she said, reverently touching her fingertip to the huge cushion-cut diamond. 'But do I lay my head on it, or rest my chin on it?'

'You wear it on your finger,' Shahin said, flashing her a mock reproving glance. 'Like this…' Taking the ring out of the box, he placed it on her wedding finger.

'But I didn't…'

'What?' he prompted. 'Expect it? Ask for it? All the more reason for me to give it to you…'

'Will I be able to lift my hand while I'm wearing it?' She opened her eyes very wide.

'I'm sure that should be possible. Shall we have a trial run?' Shahin suggested wickedly.

'It seems you're right,' she said happily, reaching for him…

And now this, the full pomp and ceremony of a royal wedding at the Ruby Fort—after a scant fifteen minutes in which she'd had to shower, rearrange her hair and throw on the most fabulous wedding dress before racing down the endless palace corridors with her attendants in hot pursuit.

She didn't have any relatives to stand up for her and didn't even know half the people, but none of that was important because there was only one person who mattered and he was waiting for her at the foot of the stairs.

Catching hold of her hands, Shahin drew her close, ignoring the whispered words of his aide-de-camp. The man had laid out a very detailed wedding plan, telling him exactly how he should proceed. No Sheikh of Zaddara had ever defied tradition before, or had even wed in public before… But then no Sheikh of Zaddara had ever married his ward before, Shahin reflected, a muscle working in his jaw as he thought about the special treats he had in store for Zara at the desert encampment, where they would be spending their honeymoon.

She'd had no experience of small, thoughtful gifts given to her by someone who loved her as deeply as he did, but all that was about to change. Her life would be transformed… He couldn't wait to see her face when she walked into the privacy of their bridal suite. Would she like the chest of fabulous jewels best, or the full selection of scents and beauty products waiting for her in the bathroom? Perhaps it would be the racks of designer clothes in the dressing room, or possibly the feast he had ordered to surprise her. He'd had the very best chefs and pâtissières flown in from Vienna and Milan to cater for her every whim.

He already knew the answer, Shahin realised, amused to hear a gasp go up as he kissed his bride on the lips. They liked each other, loved each other and enjoyed each other more than anything else the world had to offer them.

'So you do dare to kiss me in public,' she whispered so that only he could hear.

'You should know better than to dare me…' It had been one of her demands for compensation when he had forced his way into her suite of rooms while she had been dressing earlier—and a challenge he had found no difficulty in accepting, or in making good. 'Did you ever doubt me?'

'Never,' Zara admitted, fixing her love-bright eyes on him.

'Shall we?' he invited, taking her soft pale hand in his. 'We mustn't keep our wedding guests waiting,' he reminded her, leading her forward into the light.

* * *

Zara couldn't wait to be rid of the ceremonial guard who had formed behind them. The limousine had taken them as far as the edge of the desert, where Shahin's Jeep was waiting, and now he was going to drive them to his luxury encampment beside the oasis. No guards, no protocol… Heaven. There would just be a skeleton staff to care for them—and this was a new tradition, Shahin had informed her, that would have to be strictly observed every couple of months.

'And for at least a week each time,' Zara had suggested.

'For at least three days and three nights,' Shahin had teased her, reminding her of the pact that had been made when they had first met.

'Must they march with us to the Jeep?' Zara protested, glancing up at Shahin. 'I can't keep in step.'

'You don't have to keep in step,' he reminded her. 'It's up to them to keep in step with you…'

'That only makes me feel worse. And—'

'And?'

'Well, if they're the royal guard, sworn to protect your person with their life, and they all have to march behind you—'

'Yes?'

'What if someone shoots you from the front?'

'Good point,' he murmured dryly. 'I'll have the royal protection programme placed on your desk on Monday morning—'

'I have other plans for Monday morning…'

'I'm relieved to hear it,' He reached across her before any of his men had the chance to open the passenger door of the Jeep for her. 'Now, get in. I'm in a hurry.'

For once she didn't feel like arguing with him.

* * *

He hadn't expected her to burst into tears.

'Shahin, I can't wear all this…'

'Not all at once,' he agreed mildly, enjoying the sight of her holding armfuls of precious jewels up to the light. 'That would be a gross abuse of good taste.'

'You know what I mean… And don't tease me. I'm serious. I've brought you so little—'

'So little? You call the most marvellous images of my country so little? You call your energy to change things, including me, so little? You call love, laughter and a wonderful future so little? You're right,' he said finally, pretending to frown, 'I have every reason to be dissatisfied…'

'Shahin,' Zara reprimanded him softly, brushing the inky locks of hair from his eyes. 'You have to stop teasing me—'

'Not sure I can…'

'But there is one more thing…' She let the jewels slide back inside the casket.

'What is it?' he asked, reclining back on the silken cushions with his hands folded behind his head. He loved just looking at her, filling his eyes with her… He would never tire of it. It was enough for him. It was the only gift on earth he desired.

'I'm not sure if this strictly qualifies as a gift, or if you'll think I'm—'

'Zara…what are you trying to say?' he drawled, noticing she had begun to wring her hands with anxiety.

'This…'

Coming to lie beside him, she placed his hand on her belly.

'What are you telling me?' He searched her eyes.

'I think you know, Shahin…' Pressing her lips together, she waited.

'You mean? Oh, my darling…' Kissing her, Shahin knew instantly and couldn't understand why it hadn't registered before. She even tasted different—warmer, sweeter, full of femininity…and impending motherhood. 'You've made me the happiest man on earth… So why are you crying?'

'I'm overwhelmed by everything you've given me… What?' she asked, staring at the box of tissues Shahin handed her.

'You'd better arm yourself with another wad of tissues in that case, before you read this,' he suggested dryly, handing her an envelope.

'What is it?'

'Your wedding present…'

'But you've already given me too much…'

'And you've given me the greatest gift of all, which is your love. Now, open the envelope.'

Drawing the single sheet of paper out of the thick vellum envelope, Zara read the document through carefully. Shaking her head in disbelief, she read it through again. '"The breeding programme I've set up in Zaddara in your name…"' Pausing, she gazed at Shahin, then, reading out loud, she continued, '"Gazelles, Arabian oryx and other rare creatures… As patron you will be expected to take a very keen interest. I hope you won't find your duties too onerous…" Oh, Shahin…' Leaping up, she flung herself into his arms. 'I love you so much.'

'No more than I love you, my Adara…'

'I don't think you can call me that any longer,' she reminded him.

'Perhaps not…' Shahin's lips pressed down as he pretended to think about it. 'No, your name is Zara, which in

Greek means "bright as the dawn". You came to me with the dawn, and now—'

'You can't get rid of me?'

'You just spoiled a very romantic moment,' Shahin murmured, nuzzling his stubble against her neck in the way he knew she loved.

'Don't worry,' Zara murmured, tracing the planes of his face with her fingers. 'There are going to be plenty more opportunities for you to practice your new found romancing skills…'

'As there will be for you to practice your new skills,' Shahin promised Zara, tumbling her on to her back.

'For ever?' she murmured against his mouth.

'Oh, a lot longer that that, I should think,' Shahin whispered, silencing his beloved wife with a kiss.

THE SHEIKH'S
GUARDED HEART

LIZ FIELDING

Liz Fielding was born with itchy feet. She made it to Zambia before her twenty-first birthday and, gathering her own special hero and a couple of children on the way, lived in Botswana, Kenya and Bahrain – with pauses for seeing pretty much everywhere in between.

She finally came to a full stop in a tiny Welsh village cradled by the misty hills and these days mostly leaves her pen to do the travelling.

When she's not sorting out the lives and loves of her characters, she potters in the garden, reads her favourite authors and spends a lot of time wondering… "What if…?"

For news of forthcoming books – and to sign up for her occasional newsletter – visit Liz's website at www.lizfielding.com

Look for Liz Fielding's exciting new romance,
A Wedding at Leopard Tree Lodge, **coming to you from Mills & Boon®**
Romance in May 2010

CHAPTER ONE

Lucy Forrester wasn't fooled for a minute. The insubstantial shimmer of green was a mirage.

She'd read everything she could about Ramal Hamrah, the desert. Mirages, she'd learned, were not the illusions of thirst-maddened travellers, but occurred when refracted light mirrored distant images—oil tankers, cities, trees—making them appear where they had no business to be, only for them to evaporate as the earth revolved and the angle of the sun changed.

It happened now, the momentary vision of eye-soothing green vanishing before her eyes. But even a mirage was enough to distract her from her unthinking rush to confront the man who'd betrayed her. Just because there was no traffic—no road—didn't mean that there were no hazards.

She checked the satellite navigation system, adjusted her direction slightly, then forced herself to relax her white-knuckle grip on the steering wheel a little. Look around, take her bearings.

Not that there was much to see apart from the mountains—clearer, sharper now that she was on higher ground away from the coast. There was nothing green here, only the occasional scrubby, dust-covered bush in an otherwise dry and empty landscape.

Her eyes, seared and aching from a sun that mocked her delicately tinted sunglasses, felt as if they were filled with sand and she would have welcomed another glimpse of the cooling green. Even an illusion would do.

Dehydrated, hungry, she should have realized that she'd need more than rage to sustain her, but her bottle of water had long been empty. And, shaken to bits by her charge across the corrugated surface of the open desert, her entire body felt as if it had been beaten black and blue.

She didn't understand it. According to the map, it was no more than a hundred and fifty miles to Steve's campsite. Three hours, four at the most. She should have been there long before now.

She closed her eyes momentarily, in an attempt to relieve them. It was a mistake. Without warning the 4x4 tipped forward, throwing her against the seat-belt as the ground fell sharply away in front of her, wrenching the wheel from her hands. Before she could react, regain control, the front offside wheel hit something hard, riding up so that the vehicle slewed sideways, tipped drunkenly, and after a seemingly endless moment when it might, just, have fallen back four-square on the ground, the rear wheel clipped the same unseen rock and the world tipped upside down.

Only the bruising jolt of the seat-belt against her breast-bone, shoulder, hip, stopped her from being tumbled around the interior like washing in a drier as the vehicle began to roll.

It didn't stop her arms from flailing uncontrollably, bouncing against the wheel, the roof, the gear stick. Didn't stop her legs from being pounded against the angles of a vehicle built for function, rather than comfort. Didn't stop everything loose from flying around, battering her head and neck.

It seemed an eternity before the world finally stopped turning and everything came to a halt.

For a while that was enough.

When, finally, she managed to focus on her surroundings, the world was at an odd angle, but the silence, the lack of any kind of movement, was deeply restful and Lucy, glad enough to rest quietly in the safety cage of her seat-belt, felt no urgent need to move.

At least the green was back, she thought. Closer now. She tried to make sense of it through the crazing of the safety glass.

Trees of some kind, she decided, after a while. It was the fact that they were upside down that had confused her. That they were below, rather than above a high wall.

Had she stumbled across the Hanging Gardens of Babylon?

No, that couldn't be right. Babylon wasn't in Ramal Hamrah. It was... Somewhere else.

Maybe she was dead, she thought dispassionately.

Heaven would be green. And quiet. Although the gate she could see set into the wall was not of the pearly variety promised in the fire-and-brimstone sermons preached at the church her grandmother had attended, but were carved from wood.

But then wood was, no doubt, more precious than pearls in a place where few trees grew.

Wall and door were both the same dull ochre as the desert. Covered with centuries of wind-blown dust, they were all but invisible unless you were looking directly at them or, as now, intense shadows cast by the lowering sun were throwing the carvings into relief.

The angel looked real enough, though, as he flew down to her on wings of gold.

Gradually tiny sounds began to impinge on her consciousness. The ticking of the engine as it cooled. Papers fluttering. It was her diary, she saw, lying amongst the jumble of stuff thrown from her bag, the pages riffling in the wind, blowing her life away. She closed her eyes.

Moments, or maybe it was hours, later she opened them to a pounding beat that sounded oddly familiar but which she couldn't quite place. And the slow drip, drip, drip of something leaking.

Coolant or brake fluid, she thought.

She ought to do something about that. Find the hole, plug it somehow or she'd really be in trouble...

Stirred from her dazed torpor, she began to tug feebly at the seat belt but was brought to an instant halt by a searing pain in her scalp. Confused, in pain as a hundred smarts, bruises and worse were jolted into life, she kept still, tried to focus her energy, find the strength to reach the release catch, free herself, without tearing her hair out by the roots.

Then the smell of petrol reached her.

Petrol dripping on to hot metal...

It was a wake-up call to the danger she was in; forget heaven, she was at the gates of hell and raw, naked fear overrode pain as she struggled to twist herself around to hit the seat belt release.

Her sweaty fingers slipped as she tried to make contact and, as the smell of petrol grew stronger, she panicked, throwing herself against the restraints—

'Hold still, I've got you.'

She heard the words, but they didn't penetrate the thinking part of her brain as she fought to break free.

'Don't move!'

It wasn't the harsh order that shocked her into motionless silence, or the fierce, hawk-like features of the man who gave it. It was the gleaming knife blade, so close to her face that she could almost taste the metal at the back of her throat.

It was one shock too many.

* * *

Hanif al-Khatib cursed as the woman fainted dead away, then braced himself to catch her as he cut her free from the seat belt, trusting to luck as to whether he did more damage as he hauled her dead weight up through the open window of the 4x4 and on to his saddle. The smell of petrol filled the hot air and there was no time to waste doing the thing gently as, holding her limp body tight against him with one arm, he urged his horse to safety.

When the vehicle burst into flames he was still close enough to feel a flare of heat that made the desert air seem momentarily icy.

Time passed in a blur of pain. Lucy heard voices but could not understand what they said. The only comfort was in the dusty cloth beneath her face, the steady beat of a human heart, soft reassuring words. Someone was holding her close, not letting go. With the part of her brain that was still functioning, she knew that as long as he held her she would be safe.

Nothing short of an emergency would have induced Hanif al-Khatib to set foot in a hospital. He hated everything about them—the smell, the hushed careful voices of the staff, the high-tech sound of machines measuring out lives in bleeps rather than heartbeats. Announcing death in a high-pitched whine that drilled through the brain.

The overwhelming sense of guilt…

His aide had done his best to keep him away from the emergency room, to persuade him to remain in the desert, assuring him that he could manage.

He didn't doubt it; Zahir was more than capable, but he came anyway, needing to assure himself that everything necessary was done for the woman. And because a lone foreign woman driving across the desert as if the hounds of hell were after her had left him with the uneasy suspicion that there was more to it than a simple accident.

Since he hadn't delayed to change his clothes and they, and the *keffiyeh* wound about his face, bore the dust of a day's hunting, no one had realised who he was and that suited him well enough. The last thing he wanted was to attract the attention of local media; he valued his own privacy and the young woman he'd rescued was unlikely to welcome the attention, speculation, that being brought into casualty by the son of the Emir was likely to arouse.

He'd left all direct contact with the hospital staff to Zahir, staying in background, content to be thought nothing more than muscle brought along to carry the woman pulled from the wreck of her vehicle.

Nevertheless, the arrival at the hospital of a helicopter bearing the Emiri insignia would have raised more than passing interest and he was eager to be away. Just as soon as he satisfied himself that the woman was not seriously injured, would be properly cared for.

He turned from the window as Zahir joined him in the visitors' room. 'How is she?'

'Lucky. They've done a scan but the head injuries are no more than surface bruising. At worst, mild concussion.'

'That's it?' He'd feared much worse. 'She was fainting, incoherent with pain in the helicopter,' he pressed.

'She's torn a ligament in her ankle, that's a world of pain, and she took quite a battering when the vehicle rolled.'

'That's lucky?'

Zahir pulled a face. 'But for you, Excellency, it would have been a lot worse.'

'I was simply the nearest. The first to reach her.'

'No one else would have risked riding straight down the *jebel* as you did.'

The boy did not add that no one else had had so little regard for his own safety, although he was clearly thinking it. Not true. With a broken neck he would have been no use to her.

'The woman owes you her life.'

He dismissed the idea with an impatient gesture. 'Is she being kept in the hospital?'

'That won't be necessary,' Zahir said. 'She just needs to rest for a few days.' Then, 'I've informed the pilot that we're ready to leave.'

Hanif had done his duty and now that he knew the woman would make a full recovery there was nothing to keep him. Except that she had looked so fragile as she'd struggled to free herself.

'You've spoken to someone at Bouheira Tours?' he asked, pushing the image away. 'They have contacted her family? Someone is making arrangements to look after her, get her home?'

Zahir cleared his throat. 'You need not concern yourself, Excellency,' he said. Then, forgetting himself in his anxiety to leave, 'We need to go, Han, already rumours are flying around the hospital—'

He didn't ask what kind of rumours. A foreign woman had been brought to the hospital in a helicopter used by the son of the Emir. What they didn't know, they'd make up.

'Put a stop to them, Zahir. The girl was found by a hunting party, my staff offered humanitarian aid. I was not involved.'

'I'll do what I can.'

'So?' he persisted. 'Who is she? Does she work for this company? Or is she just another sand-surfer, tearing up the desert as if it's her personal playground?'

He hoped so. If he could write her off as some shallow thrill-seeker, he could forget about her.

'The tourist industry is becoming an important part of our economy, Excellency—'

'And, if so, why was she travelling alone, in the wrong direction to anywhere?' Hanif continued, ignoring Zahir's attempt to divert his attention.

Too inexperienced, too young to hide what he was thinking, his young cousin hesitated a moment too long as he decided just how much to tell him. Just how much he dared leave out.

Hanif moved to the nearest chair, turned, sat down with a flourish that no one could have mistaken for anything but regal and, with a gesture so slight as to be almost imperceptible, so imperious that not even a favoured cousin would dare ignore it, invited the boy to make up his mind.

'Sir—' Zahir swallowed, saw there was no help for it and finally admitted the truth. 'Bouheira Tours say they have no idea who this woman might be. She does not work for them and they were adamant that she could not be a client. They have no women in any of the parties booked this week.'

'Yet she was driving one of their vehicles.' He waited. 'Their logo was emblazoned on its side. Desert safaris, dune-surfing,' he prompted.

'I made that point.'

'Who did you speak to?'

'The office manager. A woman called Sanderson. The man who actually owns the company, Steve Mason, is in the east of the country, guiding a party of archaeologists who have come to look at the ancient irrigation systems.'

'She was heading too far north to have been joining them.'

'She may have been lost.'

'Surely their vehicles are fitted with satellite navigation equipment?' Zahir made no comment. 'So, what explanation did this Sanderson woman have for the fact that a woman she'd didn't know was driving one of their vehicles?'

'She didn't. She said we must be mistaken. That none of their vehicles is missing. She pointed out that there are other companies running desert trips. That, since the vehicle was burned out, we may have been mistaken.'

'You were there, Zahir. Do you believe we were mistaken?'

Zahir swallowed. 'No, sir.'

'No. So, when you assure me that our casualty is to be looked after, what exactly did you mean? That the hospital will contact her embassy where some official will draw up a document requiring her to repay them the cost of medical treatment and repatriation before they'll do a damn thing to help her?'

'I assumed you would wish to have her treatment to be charged to your office, sir. Other than that—'

'Always assuming that she can prove her identity,' Hanif continued as if he hadn't spoken. 'Her nationality. It might take some time, since everything she was carrying with her was incinerated. Who will care for her in the meantime?'

'You saved her life, Han. You have done everything required.'

'On the contrary, Zahir. Having saved her, I am now responsible for her.' A situation he would have otherwise, but to wish that he hadn't become involved would be to wish her dead and that he could not do. 'Who is she?' he demanded, as keen as anyone to see an end to this. 'What's her name?'

'She gave her name as Lucy Forrester.'

'Did she say where she was going?'

'No. It was because she seemed so confused that they ordered a scan.'

'And the doctor says she can be discharged?' Then, on his feet and at the door before Zahir could open his mouth, he said, 'Never mind. I'll speak to him myself.'

'Sir!'

Hanif strode down the corridor, ignoring the boy's anguished plea.

'Excellency, it is my duty to insist—'

As he turned on him the boy flinched, stuttered to a halt. But he bravely stood his ground.

'You've done everything that is required,' he repeated. 'There can be no doubt that she's British. Her embassy will take care of the rest.'

'I will be the judge of when I have done everything required, Zahir.' Then, irritably, 'Where is he? The doctor?'

'He was called to another emergency. I'll have him paged for you.'

'No.' It wasn't the doctor who held him where he least wanted to be, but his patient. 'Where is *she*?'

There was another, almost imperceptible, pause before, apparently accepting the inevitable, Zahir said, 'She's in the treatment room. The last door on the left.'

Lucy Forrester was looking worse, rather than better than when he'd carried her into the A and E department.

In his head, he was still seeing her in that moment before she'd fainted, with long hair spread about her shoulders, fair skin, huge grey eyes. Since then the bruising had developed like a picture in a developing tank; her arms were a mess of ugly bruises, grazes, small cuts held together with paper sutures and there was dried blood, like rust, in her hair.

The hospital had treated her injuries—her right leg was encased below the knee in a lightweight plastic support—but the emergency team hadn't had time to do more than the minimum, cleaning up her wounds, but nothing else. Pre-sumably that was the job of the ward staff.

For now, she was lying propped up, her skin clinging to fine bones, waiting for someone to decide where she was going. She looked, he thought, exhausted.

Her eyes, in that split second before she'd lost conscious-ness, had been wide with terror. Her first reaction now, starting, as if waking from a bad dream, was still fear and, without thinking, he reached for her hand. Held it.

'It's all right, Lucy,' he said. 'You're safe.'

Fear was replaced by uncertainty, then some other, more complex, emotion that seemed to find an echo deep within him.

'You saved me,' she mumbled, the words scarcely distin-guishable through her bruised, puffy lips.

'No, no,' he said. 'Lie back. Take your time.'

'I thought… I thought…'

It was all too clear what Lucy Forrester had thought, but he did not blame her. She'd been hysterical and there had been no time for explanations, only action.

He released her hand, bowed slightly, a courtesy that would not normally be afforded to any woman other than his mother, his grandmother, and said, 'I am Hanif al-Khatib. You have friends in Ramal Hamrah?' he asked. Why would a woman travel here alone except to be with someone? 'Someone I can call?'

'I—' She hesitated, as if unsure what to say. She settled on, 'No. No one.' Not the truth, he thought. Not the whole truth, anyway. It did not matter.

'Then my home is at your disposal until you are strong enough to continue your journey.'

One of her eyes was too swollen to keep open. The other suggested doubt. 'But why—?'

'A traveller in distress will always find help, refuge in my country,' he said, cutting off her objection. He was not entirely sure 'why' himself, beyond the fact that he had not rescued her from death to abandon her to the uncertain mercy of her embassy. At least with him, she would be comfortable. And safe. Turning to Zahir, he said, 'It is settled. Make it happen.'

'But, Excellency—'

Hanif silenced him with a look.

'Go and find something warm for Miss Forrester to travel in. And send a nurse to clean her up. How could they leave her like this?'

'It may be a while,' his cousin said, disapproval practically vibrating from him. 'They're rushed off their feet in A and E.'

Lucy watched as her Samaritan impatiently waved the other man away before turning to the cupboards where dressings were stored, searching, with growing irritation until he finally emerged with a stainless steel dish and a pack of cotton wool. He ran water into the bowl, tearing off chunks of cotton and tossing them in to soak.

'I'm not a nurse,' he said, turning to her, 'but I will do my best to make you more comfortable.'

'No,' she said, scrambling back up against the raised headboard. 'Really, there's no need.'

'There is every need,' he said. 'It will take Zahir a little while to organise the paperwork.' He didn't smile, but he was gentleness itself as he took one her hands, looking up in concern as she trembled. 'Does that hurt?'

'No,' she managed.

He nodded, as if that was all he needed to know, and began to gently wipe the damp cotton pads over her fingers, her hands, discarding the pads as each one became dirty.

And it was, after all, just her hands.

It was nothing, she told herself. She wouldn't object to a male nurse doing this and the man had saved her life. But his touch, as he carefully wiped each finger as if they were made of something fragile and fine, did something unsettling to her insides and a tiny sound escaped her. Not nothing...

He glanced up enquiringly and she managed to mouth, 'It's okay.'

Apparently reassured, he carefully washed away the dirt and dried blood from the bruised back of her hand before turning it over to clean the palm. He moved to her wrist, washed every bit of her arm with the same care.

Then he began again on the other hand. Time was, apparently, of no importance.

He emptied the bowl, refilled it. 'Fresh water for your face,' he said, and she swallowed. Hands, arms were one thing. Her face was so much more personal. He'd have to get closer. 'I... Yes...'

'That's too hot?' he enquired, as she jumped at the touch of a fresh pad to her cheek, let out an incoherent squeak.

'No...' The word seemed stuck in her throat but she swallowed it down and said, 'No, it's just...' It was just that her grandmother's brainwashing had gone deep. Bad girls let men touch them. In her head she knew that it wasn't like that, that when people loved one another it was different, but even with Steve she'd found the slightest intimacy a challenge. Not that he'd pressed her.

He'd assured her that he found her innocence charming. That it made him feel like the first man in the world.

Innocent was right. No one but an innocent booby would have fallen for that line.

While she knew that this was different, that it had nothing to do with what her grandmother had been talking about, it didn't make it any easier, but she managed a convincing, 'It's fine...' refusing to let fall tears of rage, remorse, helplessness— a whole range of emotions piling up faster than she could think of words to describe them. After a long moment in which the man waited, apparently unconvinced, she said, 'Truly.'

'You must tell me if I hurt you,' he said, gently lifting the hair back from her face.

All she wanted was for him to get on with it, get it over with, but as he gently stroked the cotton over her skin it was just as it had been with her hands, her arms. He was tenderness itself and her hot, dry skin, dehydrated and thirsty, seemed to soak up the moisture like a sponge.

'I'm just going to clean up your scalp here,' he warned. 'I think you must have caught your hair when you were struggling with the seat belt.' It stung a little. Maybe more than a little because he stopped, looked at her and said, 'Shall I stop?'

'No. Really. You're not hurting me.' Not much anyway.

Pride must abide.

Words chiselled on to her scalp.

He lifted her long tangled hair, holding it aside so that he could wash the nape of her neck, and she gave an involuntary sigh. If she could only wash her hair, she thought, she'd feel a hundred times better.

'Later,' he said. 'I will wash your hair tomorrow.'

She was smiling into the soft wool *keffiyeh* coiled around his neck before she realized that he'd answered her unspoken thoughts. She considered asking him how he'd done that. Then waited. If he was a mind-reader she wouldn't need to ask...

There was a tap on the door and someone called out.

He rapped out one word. He'd spoken in Arabic but the word was unmistakable. *Wait.* Then he laid her back against the headrest and she whispered, '*Shukran.*' Thank you.

She'd bought a teach yourself Arabic course, planning to learn some of the language before joining Steve. She hadn't just want to be a silent partner. She'd wanted to be useful. A bit of a joke, that. She'd served her usefulness the minute she'd so trustingly signed the papers he'd placed in front of her.

Hanif al-Khatib smiled at her—it was the first time, she thought. The man was so serious... Then he said, '*Afwan,* Lucy.'

Welcome. It meant *welcome,* she thought. And she knew he meant it.

In all her life, no one had ever treated her with such care, such consideration, as this stranger and quite suddenly she was finding it very hard to hold back the dam of tears.

Obviously it was shock. Exhaustion. Reaction to the accident...

She sniffed, swallowed. She did not cry. Pain, betrayal, none of those had moved her to tears. She'd learned early that tears were pointless. But kindness had broken down the barriers and, embarrassed, she blinked them back.

'You are in pain, Lucy?'

'No.'

He touched a tear that lay on her cheek. 'There is no need to suffer.'

'No. They gave me an injection. I just feel sleepy.'

'Then sleep. It will make the journey easier for you.' Then, 'I will return in a moment,' he said.

She nodded, her mind drifting away on a cloud of sedative. She jerked awake when he returned.

'I hope you will not mind wearing this,' Hanif said, helping her to sit up, wrapping something soft and warm around her, feeding her arms into the sleeves.

She had no objection to anything this man did, she thought, but didn't have the energy to say the words out loud.

* * *

'How is she?'

Hanif had left Zahir in Rumaillah to make enquiries about his guest and now he roused himself to join him in the sitting room of the guest suite.

'Miss Forrester is still sleeping.'

'It's the best thing.'

'Perhaps.' She'd been fighting it—disturbed, dreaming perhaps, crying out in her sleep. It was only the sedatives prescribed by the hospital keeping her under, he suspected. 'What did you discover in Rumaillah? Was the embassy helpful?'

'I thought it better to make my own enquiries, find out what I could about her movements before I went to the embassy. If you want my opinion, there's something not quite right about all this.'

'Which is, no doubt, why you tried to dissuade me from bringing her here,' Hanif replied, without inviting it.

'It is my duty—'

'It is your duty to keep me from brooding, Zahir. To drag me out on hunting expeditions. Tell my father when I'm ready to resume public life.'

'He worries about you.'

'Which is why I allow you to stay. Now, tell me about Lucy Forrester.'

'She arrived yesterday morning on the early flight from London. The immigration officer on duty remembered her vividly. Her hair attracted a good deal of notice.'

He didn't doubt it. Pale as cream, hanging to her waist, any man would notice it.

Realising that Zahir was waiting, he said, 'Yes, yes! Get on with it!'

'Her entry form gave her address in England so I checked the telephone number and put through a call.'

'Did I ask you to do that?'

'No, sir, but I thought—'

He dismissed Zahir's thoughts with an irritated gesture. 'And?' he demanded.

'There was no reply.' He waited for a moment, but when Hanif made no comment he continued. 'She gave her address in Ramal Hamrah as the Gedimah Hotel but, although she had made a booking, she never checked in.'

'Did someone pick her up from the airport, or did she take a taxi?'

'I'm waiting for the airport security people to come back to me on that one.'

'And what about the vehicle she was driving? Have you had a chance to look at it? Salvage anything that might be useful?'

'No, sir. I sent out a tow truck from Rumaillah, but when it arrived at the scene, the 4x4 had gone.'

'Gone?'

'It wasn't there.'

'It can't have vanished into thin air, Zahir.'

'No, sir.'

Hanif frowned. 'No one else knew about it, other than the woman at Bouheira Tours. What did you tell her?'

'Only that one of their vehicles had been in an accident and was burnt out in the desert. She was clearly shaken, asked me to describe it, the exact location. Once I had done that she said that I must be mistaken. That the vehicle could not belong to them. Then I asked her if Miss Forrester was a staff member or a traveller booked with them and she replied that she'd never heard of her.'

'She didn't want to check her records?'

'She was quite adamant.'

'Did you tell her that Miss Forrester had been injured?'

'She didn't ask what had happened to her and I didn't volunteer any information.'

'Leave it that way. Meanwhile, find out more about this tour company and the people who run it. And Zahir, be discreet.'

CHAPTER TWO

THE room was cool, quiet, the light filtering softly through rich coloured glass—lapis blue and emerald, with tiny pieces of jewel-bright red that gave Lucy the impression of lying in some undersea grotto. A grotto in which the bed was soft and enfolding.

A dream, then.

Lucy drifted away, back into the dark, and the next time she woke the light was brighter but the colours were still there and, although she found it difficult to open her eyes more than a crack, she could see that it was streaming through an intricately pieced stained glass window, throwing spangles of colour over the white sheets.

It was beautiful but strange and, uneasy, she tried to sit up, look around.

If the tiny explosions of pain from every part of her body were not sufficiently convincing, the hand at her shoulder, a low voice that was becoming a familiar backdrop to these moments of consciousness, assured her that she was awake.

'Be still, Lucy Forrester. You're safe.'

Safe? What had happened? Where was she? Lucy struggled to look up at the tall figure leaning over her. A surgical collar restricted her movement and one eye still refused to open more than a crack, but she did not need two good eyes to know who he was.

Knife in his hand, he'd told her to be still before. She swallowed. Her throat, mouth were as dry as dust.

'You remember?' he asked. 'The accident?'

'I remember you,' she said. Even without the *keffiyeh* wound about his face she knew the dark fierce eyes, chiselled cheekbones, the hawkish, autocratic nose that had figured so vividly in her dreams.

Now she could see that his hair was long, thick, tied back at the nape with a dark cord, that only his voice was soft, although the savage she'd glimpsed before she'd passed out appeared to be under control.

But she knew, with every part of her that was female, vulnerable, that the man who'd washed her as she lay bloody and dusty on a hospital couch was far more dangerous.

'You are Hanif al-Khatib,' she said. 'You saved my life and took me from the hospital.'

'Good. You remember.'

Not that good, she thought. A touch of amnesia would have been very welcome right now.

'You are feeling rested?'

'You don't want to know how I'm feeling. Where am I?'

Her voice was cracked, dry, and he poured water into a glass then, supporting her up with his arm, held the glass to lips that appeared to have grown to twice their size. Some water made it into her mouth as she gulped at it. The rest dribbled down her chin, inside the collar.

He tugged on the bow holding it in place and removed it, then dried her face, her neck, with a soft hand towel.

'Should you have done that?' she asked nervously, reaching for her throat.

'Speaking from experience, I can tell you that the collar doesn't do much good, but the doctor advised keeping it in place until you were fully awake.'

'Experience? You crash cars that often?'

'Not cars. Horses.' He gave a little shrug. 'Perhaps it would be more accurate to say that they crashed me. Polo makes great demands on both horse and rider.'

'At least the rider has the choice.' Then, 'Where am I? Who are you?' His name and 'safe' told her nothing.

'When I lived in England,' he said, 'my friends called me Han.'

'When I lived in England...'

Her brain felt as if it was stuffed with cotton wool, but she was alert enough to understand that this was his way of reassuring her that he understood western expectations of behaviour. Why would he do that unless she had reason to be nervous?

'What do your enemies call you?' she snapped back, pain, anxiety, making her sharp. She regretted the words before they were out of her mouth; whatever else he was, this man had saved her from a terrible death. But it was too late to call them back.

His face, his voice expressionless, he replied, 'I am Hanif bin Jamal bin Khatib al-Khatib. And my enemies, if they are wise, remember that.'

Her already dry mouth became drier and she shook her head, as if to distance herself from what she'd said. Gave an involuntarily squeak of pain.

'The doctor prescribed painkillers if you need them,' he said distantly.

'No,' she said. 'Thank you.' She was finding it hard enough to think clearly as it was and she needed all her wits about her. Needed answers. 'You told me your name before,' she said. Only this time there was more of it. Steve had explained about the long strings of names and she knew that if she could decipher it she would know his history. '*Bin* means "son of"?'

He bowed slightly.

'You are Hanif, son of Jamal, son of...'

'Khatib.'

'Son of Khatib, of the house of Khatib.' The name sounded familiar. Had Steve mentioned it? 'And this is your home?'

Stupid question. Not even the finest private room in the fanciest hospital had ever looked like this. The carved screens, folded back from the window, the flowered frieze, each petal made from polished semi-precious stone, furniture of a richness that would have looked more at home in a palace...

'You are my guest, Miss Forrester. You will be more comfortable here than in the hospital. Unless you have friends in Ramal Hamrah with whom you would rather stay? Someone I could contact for you?' he continued. 'We tried calling your home in England—'

'You did?'

'Unfortunately, there was no reply. You are welcome to call yourself.' He indicated a telephone on the night table.

'No.' Then, because that had been too abrupt, 'There's no one there.' No one anywhere. 'I live alone now. I'm sorry to be so much trouble,' she said, subsiding into the pillows, but not before she'd seen the state of her arms. The cuts had been stuck together, the grazes cleaned, but the effect was not pretty.

'Don't distress yourself. They'll heal very quickly. A week or two and they'll be fine.' Then, 'Are you hungry?'

'I don't want to put you to any more trouble,' she said. 'If I could just get dressed, impose on you to call me a taxi.'

'A taxi?' He frowned. 'Why would you need a taxi?'

'To take me to the airport.'

'I really would not advise it. You should take a day or two to recover—'

'I can't stay here.'

'—and it will undoubtedly take that long to replace your passport, your ticket. I'm sorry to have to tell you that everything that you were carrying with you was destroyed in the crash.'

'Destroyed?' Without warning she caught a whiff of petrol amongst the mingled scents of sweat, dust, disinfectant that clung to her. 'They were burned?' And she shivered despite her best effort not to think about how close she had come to being part of the conflagration. 'I need to see someone about that,' she said, sitting up too quickly and nearly passing out as everything spun around her.

'Please, leave it to my aide. He will handle everything,' he assured her. 'They will be ready, *insha'Allah,* by the time you're fit to travel.'

'Why are you doing this?' she demanded. 'Why are you being so kind to me?'

He seemed surprised. 'You are a stranger. You need help. I was chosen.'

Chosen?

She put the oddity of the expression down to the difference in cultures and let it go, contenting herself with, 'You pulled me out from the car wreck. For most people that would have been enough.' Then, realising how ungrateful that must have sounded, 'I know that I owe you my life.'

That provoked another bow. *'Mash'Allah.* It is in safe hands.'

For heaven's sake! Enough with the bowing...

'I'm in no one's hands but my own,' she snapped back.

She might owe him her life, but she'd learned the hard way not to rely on anyone. Not even those she'd had a right to be able to trust. As for the rest...

'We are all in God's hands,' he replied, without taking offence, no doubt making allowances for her injuries, shock, the fact that sedatives tended to remove the inhibitions. Her grandmother hadn't held back when she'd finally surrendered to the need for pain relief. A lifetime of resentment and anger had found voice in those last weeks...

'I'm sorry,' she said carefully. 'You're being extremely kind. I must seem less than grateful.'

'No one is at their best when they've been through the kind of experience you've endured,' he said gravely.

This masterly, if unintentional, understatement earned him a wry smile. At least it was a smile on the inside; how it came out through the swellings and bruises was anyone's guess.

'You need to eat, build up your strength.'

She began to shake her head and he moved swiftly to stop her. 'It would be better if you did not do that,' he cautioned, his hand resting lightly against her cheek. 'At least for a day or two.'

She jumped at his unexpected touch and he immediately removed his hand.

'What can I offer you?'

What she wanted most of all was more water, but not if it meant spilling half of it down herself like a drooling idiot.

Maybe she'd said her thoughts out loud, or maybe he'd seen the need in her eyes as she'd looked at the glass, because he picked it up, then sat on the edge of the bed, offering his arm as a prop, but not actually touching her. Leaving the decision to her.

'I can manage,' she assured him, using her elbows to try and push herself up. One of them buckled beneath her and all over her body a shocking kaleidoscope of pain jangled her nerves. Before she fell back he had his shoulder, his chest, behind her, his arm about her in support, taking all her weight so that her aching muscles didn't have to work to keep her upright.

'Take your time,' he said, holding the glass to her lips. Raising her hand to steady it, she concentrated on the glass, avoiding eye contact, unused to such closeness, such intimacy. He did not rush her, but showed infinite patience as, taking careful sips this time, she slaked what seemed to be an insatiable thirst. 'Enough?' he asked when she finally pulled back.

She nearly nodded but remembered in time and instead glanced up. For a moment their gazes connected, locked, and Lucy had the uncomfortable feeling that Hanif bin Jamal bin Khatib al-Khatib could see to the bottom of her soul.

Not a pretty sight.

Hanif held the glass to Lucy's lips for a moment longer, then, easing her back on to the pillow, turned away, stood up. Her body had seemed feather-light, as insubstantial as gossamer, yet the weight of it had jarred loose memories that he'd buried deep. Memories of holding another woman in just that way.

Memories of her dark eyes begging him to let her go.

From the moment he'd cut Lucy Forrester free of the wreck she'd been attacking his senses, ripping away the layers of scar tissue he'd built up as a wall between himself and memory.

She smelt of dust, the hospital, but beneath it all her body had a soft, warm female scent of its own. He'd blocked it out while he'd held her safe on his horse, cradled her as she'd whimpered with pain, drifting in and out of consciousness in the helicopter, other, more urgent concerns taking precedent. But now, emergency over, he could no longer ignore the way it filled his head. Familiar, yet different.

He could not tell if it was the familiar or the different that bothered him more. It did not matter, but he clung to the glass as if it was the only thing anchoring him to earth as he took a deep steadying breath.

He was no stranger to the sick room, but this was more difficult than he'd imagined. Dredging up the poignant, painful memories he'd worked so hard to obliterate from his mind.

She is different.

And it was true. Noor had been dark-eyed, golden-skinned, sweet as honey. The unsuspected, unbreakable core of steel that had taken her from him had lain well hidden within that tender wrapping.

Lucy Forrester was nothing like her.

The difference in their colouring was the least of it. His wife had been strong, steady, a rock in a disintegrating world, but this woman was edgy, defensive, troubled, and he sensed that she needed him in a way that Noor never had.

The glass rattled on the table as he turned back to her. 'I'm sure you would enjoy some tea,' he said. 'Something light to eat?'

'Actually, right now, all I want is the bathroom. A shower. To wash my hair.'

Lucy Forrester shuffled herself slowly up against the pillows, obviously finding it painful to put weight on her bruised elbows, but determined to have her way.

He knew how she felt. He'd taken hard falls back in the youthful, carefree days when he'd thought himself indestructible. Had chafed impatiently through weeks laid up with a broken leg.

'That's a little ambitious for your first outing,' he suggested. 'Maybe if I brought a bowl of water, you could—'

'I'm not an invalid. I've just got a few bumps and bruises,' she said, then let out an involuntary cry as she jerked her shoulder.

'That hurt?' he enquired, with an edge to his voice he barely recognised, annoyed with her for being so obstinate.

'No,' she snapped. 'I always whimper when I move.' Then, 'Look, I know you're just trying to help, but if you'll point me in the direction of the bathroom I can manage. Or did you want to come along and finish what you started in the hospital?'

'I apologise that there are no women in my household to help you. If you think you can manage—'

'Too right, I can. I'll bet you wouldn't allow your wife to be washed by some strange man, would you? Probably not even a male nurse.'

There were men he knew, members of his family even, who would not allow their wives to be examined by a male doctor, let alone be touched by a male nurse. He had long since passed that kind of foolishness.

'I would willingly have let my wife be cared for by a Martian if I'd thought it would have helped her,' he said.

Would have? Past tense?

Oh, no, Lucy thought, she wasn't going there…

'Look, I know you're just trying to help and I'm grateful, but I'll be fine once I'm on my feet.'

He looked doubtful.

'Honestly! Besides, it's not just a wash I need and I'm telling you now, you can forget any ideas you might have about trying out your bedpan technique on me.'

'You are a headstrong woman, Lucy Forrester,' he said. 'If you fall, hurt yourself, you may end up back in the hospital.'

'If that happens, you have my full permission to say I told you so.'

'Very well.' He glanced around as if looking for something, and said, 'One moment.' And with that he swept from the room, dark robes flowing, the total autocrat.

Oh, right. As if she was planning to hang around so that

he could enjoy the spectacle of her backside hanging out of the hospital gown.

Sending encouraging little you-can-do-it messages to her limbs, she pushed the sheet down as far as she could reach. Actually it wasn't that far and, taking a moment to catch her breath, she had to admit that she might have been a bit hasty.

Ironic. All her life she'd been biting her tongue, keeping the peace, not doing anything to cause a fuss, but the minute she was left to her own devices she'd done what her grandmother had always warned her about and turned into her mother.

Impulsive, impetuous and in trouble...

If Hanif bin al-thingy hadn't been passing she'd have been toast, she knew, and it wasn't worth dying over.

Money.

She'd been broke all her life and when she'd had money she hadn't known what to do with it. At least Steve had given her a few weeks of believing herself to be desired, loved.

He might be a cheat, a liar, a con man, but he'd given value for money. Unfortunately there were some things that she couldn't just chalk up to experience and brush aside. Which was why she had to get out of here...

Everything was going fine until she swung her legs over the edge of the bed and tried to stand up. That was when she discovered what pain really was.

She didn't cry out as she crumpled up on the floor. She tried, but every bit of breath had been sucked out of her and she couldn't make a sound, not even when Hanif dropped whatever he was carrying with a clatter and gathered her up, murmuring soft words that she didn't understand; the meaning came through his voice, the tenderness with which he held her.

Idiot! Han could not believe he'd been so stupid. He was so used to total obedience, to having his orders obeyed without question, without explanation, it had never occurred to him that Lucy would ignore his command to stay put until he found the crutches, the ankle splint, which had been tidied away by someone as he'd dozed on the day bed in the sitting room.

Over and over he murmured his apologies and only when she let her head fall against his shoulder and he felt her relax, did he gently chide her.

'You could not wait two minutes, Lucy?'

'I thought I could manage. What have I done?' she asked into his shoulder. 'What's wrong with me?'

'You've torn a ligament in your ankle, that's all.'

'All?' She looked up.

'I know,' he sympathised. 'It is an extremely painful injury.'

She remembered.

At the time it had all happened so quickly that she'd felt nothing. It had been just one pain amongst many. Now, though, she was reliving the moment in slow motion...

He was holding her, supporting her, holding the sheet to her mouth before she even knew she was going to need it, but there was nothing to throw up except water...

By the time her stomach caught up with reality and gave up, she was sweaty and trembling with weakness. He continued to hold her, offering her water, wiping her forehead, her mouth—so gently that she knew her lips must look as bad as they felt.

'You're very good at this,' she said, angry with him, although she couldn't have said why. Angry with herself for having made such a mess of everything. 'Are you sure you're not a nurse?'

'Quite sure, but I took care of my wife when she was dying.'

His voice, his face, were wiped of all emotion. She wasn't fooled by that.

She'd become pretty good at hiding her feelings over the years, at least until Steve had walked into her life; he'd certainly cured her of that. But when you knew how it was done it was easy to spot.

'I'm so sorry…Han,' she said, trying out the name he'd offered, as near as she could get to an apology for behaving so badly, so thoughtlessly, when all he was doing was trying to help her. When he was clearly reliving all kinds of painful memories.

'Nausea is to be expected,' he said distantly.

That wasn't what she'd been apologising for and she was sure he knew it. Questions crowded into her mind, but she had no right to ask him any of them and she let it go. Better to keep to the practicalities.

'Didn't they explain your injuries to you at the hospital?'

'They tried. I didn't understand most of what they were saying. I was just so confused. By everything.' She looked up, appealing for understanding. 'I saw a mirage,' she said, trying to make him see. 'At least I thought I did. Then, after the crash there was an angel. He had gold wings and he was coming to get me and I thought I was dead—'

'Hush, don't distress yourself—'

'And then you were there and I thought… I thought…'

She couldn't say what she'd thought.

'You drifted in and out of consciousness for a while. The mind plays tricks. The memory becomes uncertain.'

'You're speaking from experience again?' she asked, trying a wry smile, but suspecting that it lost something of its subtlety in translation from her brain to her face.

'I'm afraid so.' Then, 'They did a scan at the hospital,' he said, wanting to reassure her. 'There was no head injury.'

'Just my ankle? Really? Is that it?' she asked. 'No more nasty surprises?'

'Lacerations and bruising.'

'Cracked ribs?'

'No one mentioned anything about cracked ribs,' he said, finally showing some emotion, if irritation counted as emotion, although not, she thought, with her. 'Are they sore?'

'Everything is sore. So, tell me, what's the prognosis?'

'The bruises, abrasions, will heal quickly enough and you'll need to wear a support on your ankle for a couple of weeks, use crutches. That's where I went. To fetch them for you.'

'Oh. I didn't know.'

'Of course you didn't. I should have explained.' His smile was a little creaky, as if it needed oiling, she thought. 'I'm so used to being obeyed without question.'

'Really? I hate to have to tell you this, Han, but western women don't do that any more.'

'No? Do you want to take a shower?'

'Please…'

'Then you're going to have to do as you are told.'

'What…?' Catching on, she laughed and said, 'Yes, sir!'

'Hold on,' he said and she didn't hesitate, but grabbed at his shoulders, bunching the heavy dark cloth of the robe he was wearing beneath her fingers as he lifted her back up on to the bed.

Her laughter caught at him, tore at him, and he did not know which was harder, taking her into his arms or letting her go so that he could fasten the support to her ankle. He reached out to stop her tipping forward when she was overcome by dizziness.

'I'm fine,' she assured him. 'Just pass me the crutches and give me some room.'

He didn't try to argue with her, but he didn't take any notice of her either, Lucy discovered. The minute she had the crutches in her hands, had settled them on the floor ready to push herself up, she found herself being lifted to her feet.

She would have complained, but it seemed such a waste of breath.

He didn't let go either, but just leaned back a little, spreading his hands across her back to support the shift in weight. Strong hands. Hands made to keep a woman safe.

He was, she thought, everything that Steve was not.

A rock, where the man she'd married in such haste was quicksand.

Light-headed, drowning in eyes as black as night, her limbs boneless, she knew that if she fell into Hanif al-Khatib's arms the world would turn full circle before she needed to breathe again.

'Lucy…'

It was a question. She thought it was a question, although she wasn't sure what he was asking.

She swallowed, shocked at the thoughts, feelings, that were racing through her body—struggled to break eye contact, ground herself.

'I'm all right.' Breathless, her words little more than a murmur, he was not convinced. 'You can let go.' Then, when he still didn't move, 'I won't fall.'

She looked down and slowly, carefully, felt for the floor beneath her one good leg, took her weight. Then she leaned on the crutches. Still he held her, forcing her to look up.

'Please,' she said.

Han could not let go. It was as if history was repeating itself, that if he stopped concentrating, even for a moment, she would fall, be lost to him.

Stupid.

She was nothing to him.

He was a man without feelings.

Yet from the moment her dust trail had caught his eye

his world had become a torrent of emotions. Irritation, anger, concern...

He refused to acknowledge anything deeper.

'We'll do it my way,' he said abruptly, taking a small step back, without removing his support. 'Or not at all.'

'It's that instant obedience thing again, isn't it?' she said.

'Try it. You might like it.'

She blew a strand of hair from her face, took the weight on her hands and swung forward a few inches, barely stopped herself from crying out in pain. For a moment his entire body was a prop for hers, her forehead against his cheek, her breast crushed against the hardness of his broad chest, her thighs, clad in nothing but a skimpy hospital gown, against the smooth, heavy cloth of his dark robes. And, as he held her, for one giddy moment she felt no pain.

'This is harder than it looks,' she admitted after a moment.

'You are not ready,' he said, tucking the loose strand of hair behind her ear, doing his best to ignore the silky feel of it.

'Thanks,' she said. 'I usually wear it tied back. I really must get it cut the minute I get home.'

'Why?' he asked, horrified. 'It's beautiful.'

'It's a damned nuisance. I meant to do it before...'

'Before?'

She shrugged. 'Before I came to Ramal Hamrah. Okay, I'm ready. You can let go now.'

Against his better judgement, he took another step back, still keeping a firm hold of her.

In this manner, her persistence wearing down his resistance, they crossed the room one step at a time until they were standing in the bathroom with the wall at his back. 'This is as far as we go.' Then, when she was slow to respond, 'Enough, Lucy,' he said impatiently. 'You've made it to the shower. You can drop the crutches. I have you. You won't fall.'

Lucy's leg was shaking from the effort, her hands, arms, shoulders, back, shrieking in agony. It wasn't that she wouldn't obey Han, it was because she couldn't. Her fingers were welded to the crutches and she was unable to straighten them.

'I can't,' she said.

Looking down, he saw her problem and, muttering something she did not understand, but was sure was not complimentary, he caught her around the waist and, propping her up against his body, eased the crutches from her grasp.

'You've done enough for today,' he said.

Lucy, the hot grittiness of her skin made all the more unbearable by the very nearness of relief, persisted. 'I'm not leaving here until I've had a shower.'

He shook his head, smiling despite himself. 'I have to give you ten out of ten for determination, Lucy Forrester.'

'Yes, well, no one ever accused me of being a quitter. And look, the shower has a seat. Easy. Just turn it on, give me back the crutches and leave me to it.'

He did as she'd said, testing the water until he was certain it was not too hot or cold, making sure that she had everything she needed to hand before turning to go. 'Do not,' he said, 'lock the door.'

'Got it,' she said—as if she had the energy to waste on that kind of nonsense. Then, clutching hold of a handrail, 'If I need you I'll scream. Deal?'

'Deal.'

'Oh, wait. Um, can you unfasten the bows at the back of this thing?'

Keeping his gaze fixed firmly above her head, he tugged the fastenings loose on her hospital gown. 'Anything else?'

'No. Thank you. I can manage.'

It was an exaggeration, but she did what she had to, then settled herself in the shower, keeping her splinted foot propped out of the way of the water as much as she could. The warm water seemed to bring her back to life, but washing her hair was more than she could manage and by the time she'd struggled into the towelling robe he'd laid out for her she was almost done.

'Han?'

He was there almost before the word was out of her mouth.

'Thanks,' she said, swinging herself through on willpower alone. 'I would have opened it myself, but I had my hands full.'

'You, Lucy Forrester, *are* a handful,' he said. 'Come, there is food, tea. Eat, then you can rest.'

Hanif had hoped for a few minutes alone walking the quiet paths of the ancient garden surrounding the pavilion where Lucy Forrester lay resting.

Fed by a precious natural spring that irrigated the orchards, guarded from the encroaching desert and wandering animals by thick, high walls, they had been laid out centuries earlier as an earthly reflection of heaven and he'd come here hoping to find some measure of peace.

In three years he hadn't found it but today it wasn't his own guilt and selfishness that disturbed him. He'd barely reached the reflecting pool before an agitated Zahir came hunting him down.

'Sir!'

Han stopped, drew a deep breath then turned, lifting his head as the tops of the trees stirred on a windless day. Knowing what Zahir was going to say before the words left his mouth.

'Sir, I've had a signal from the Emir's office.'

No one had been here in months so this was no coincidence; it had to be something to do with Lucy Forrester.

'Who is it?' he asked. 'Who is coming?'

Was it the man—he was certain it would be a man—she'd been so desperate to reach?

'It is the Princess Ameerah, sir.'

Not her lover, then, but nevertheless Lucy Forrester was the direct cause of this invasion.

'I am to have a chaperon, it would seem. You wasted no time in reporting last night's event to my father, Zahir.'

'Sir,' he protested. 'I did not. I would not…' Then, 'Your father is concerned for you. He understands your grief but he needs you, Han.'

'He has two other sons, Zahir. One to succeed him, one to hunt with him.'

'But you, Han…'

'He can spare me.'

Zahir stiffened. 'You were not recognised at the hospital, I would swear to it, but the removal of Miss Forrester by your staff would not have passed without comment. Sir,' he added, after a pause just long enough to indicate that he did not appreciate his loyalty being doubted. 'It was only a matter of time before news of it reached your father.'

'He will want to know why the news did not come from you.'

'You undertook a simple act of charity, Excellency. I did not believe the incident was of sufficient importance to interest His Highness.'

'Let us hope, for your sake, that His Highness takes the same view,' Hanif replied wryly, briefly touching the young man's shoulder in a gesture that they both understood was an apology. 'I would hate to see him replace you with someone less concerned about bothering him.'

Or was that what Zahir was banking on? Did he consider the chance of returning to the centre of things worth the risk of irritating the Emir?

'I think I should warn you, Zahir, that the arrival of the princess would suggest otherwise.'

'It may be a coincidence.'

'I don't believe in coincidence.' Undoubtedly his father was making the point that if he could take in and care for some unknown foreign woman, he could spare time for his own daughter. He turned away. 'Make the necessary arrangements to receive the princess.'

'It has been done, Excellency.' Zahir raised his voice as the helicopter appeared overhead, shaking a storm of blossom from the trees. 'Will you come and greet her?'

'Not now. She'll be tired from her journey. Maybe tomorrow,' he said when his cousin looked as if he might press the point.

He'd had three years of tomorrows. One more wouldn't make any difference.

CHAPTER THREE

Lucy had refused the painkillers Han offered, but he'd left the two capsules beside the bed with a glass of water in case she changed her mind, and a small hand bell that she was to ring if she needed anything, before leaving her to rest.

She was, she had to admit, feeling exhausted, but it wasn't just the effects of the accident. She hadn't slept since the second credit card statement had arrived. The first she'd assumed was a mistake, had emailed Steve and he'd said he'd sort it out. When the second one had arrived a couple of days later she'd known that the mistake was all hers.

Her body jabbed her with irritable reminders of what she'd put it through with every movement, but for the moment she'd chosen what passed for clear-headedness over relief.

She needed to think, try and work out what to do. How much to tell Hanif al-Khatib. She didn't want him to get into trouble, but neither did she relish the thought of being turned over to the authorities, which was what he would have to do once he knew the truth.

Her research on the Internet at the library had informed her that Ramal Hamrah was a modern state that paid due respect to human rights; what that meant in terms of punishment for car theft, justifiable or otherwise, she had no idea. And actually she was finding it hard to convince herself that her actions were justifiable.

Gran wouldn't have thought so, but then she'd taken an unshakeable Old Testament line when it came to sin. Thou shalt not...

The only certainty in her own life these days was that she'd behaved liked an idiot. If she'd gone to the police, instead of taking off after Steve like some avenging harpy, she wouldn't be in this mess. Now she'd lost the moral high ground, had put herself in the wrong.

Maybe a good lawyer could get her off on the grounds that the balance of her mind had been disturbed, she thought. Hold him responsible for everything. Make a counter-claim against him, at least for the fraud.

But what good would that do? Even if she could afford a lawyer, Steve wouldn't be able to repay her if he was in jail.

Besides, it was no longer just about the money.

That was what was so unfair. When she'd taken the 4x4 and set off to look for him it hadn't been herself she'd been thinking of. All she'd wanted was for him to put things right...

As if.

That was the point at which she decided that a clear head was not so very desirable after all but, as she reached for the painkillers, she realised that she was not alone.

'Hello.' Lucy forced her swollen face into a smile. The tiny girl, exotic in bright silks, half hiding behind the open door, didn't move, didn't speak, and she tried again, using her limited Arabic. '*Shes-mak?*' What's your name? At least she hoped that was what it meant since the child's only response was a little gasp of fright before she took off, tiny gold bangles tinkling as she ran away.

Her place in the doorway was immediately taken by a

breathless figure, a lightweight black *abbeyah* thrown over her dress, who paused only long enough to gasp her own quickly muffled shock before murmuring, 'Sorry, sorry…' before disappearing as fast as her charge.

Did she look that bad?

There must have been a mirror in the bathroom—there was always a mirror above the basin, even in her grandmother's house where vanity had been considered a sin.

Maybe some inner sense of self-preservation had kept her from examining the damage but now she wondered just how grotesque she looked. Was she going to be permanently scarred?

She raised her hands to her face, searching for serious damage. Everything was swollen—her lips, her eyes, the flesh around her nose. None of her features felt…right, familiar.

Han had moved the crutches, the plastic splint, had propped them up out of the way on the far side of the room. It didn't matter, she had to know the worst. Putting her sound foot down, she heaved herself upright, grabbing the night table for support.

For a moment every muscle, every sinew, every bone, complained and it was touch and go whether the table would fall or she would.

She didn't have a hand to spare to catch the painkillers as they spilled on to the floor, or the glass which followed them, toppling over, spilling water as it spun before falling on to the beautiful silk carpet. Then the bell succumbed to gravity, landing with a discordant clang, followed by the crash of the telephone.

There was nothing she could do about any of it; all she could do was hold on tight and pray.

Apparently that was enough.

After a moment the room stopped going round and, since she wasn't sure what would happen if she put her weight on her damaged ankle, she used her good one to hop across the room, hanging on to the table, the wall, the door, jarring every bone in her body, but gritting her teeth, refusing to give up.

Once she reached the door, however, she was on her own. It seemed an unbridgeable distance to the basin, but she wasn't about to give up now and, with desperate lurch, she reached her goal.

It was only when she finally recovered her breath sufficiently to turn and confront her reflection, that she realised all her effort had been for nothing.

There had once been a mirror over the basin—the fittings were there—but it had been removed.

Did she look that bad?

Without warning her legs buckled beneath her and, still hanging on to the basin, she crumpled up in a heap on the floor. For a moment she sat there in shock. Then, as she tried to move, haul herself back up, she discovered that she hadn't got the strength to do it, which left her with two choices.

She could shout for help or crawl back to bed on her hands and knees.

She was still trying to get herself up on to her knees when Han folded himself up beside her.

'Can I not leave you for a moment, Lucy Forrester?'

She shrugged, forced a smile—or more probably a grimace.

'I guess I'm not cut out for total obedience.' She forced a smile—or more likely a grimace—and said, 'I was doing okay until I was overcome by gravity.'

'Don't knock gravity. Without it we'd be in serious trouble.' Then, 'I thought we'd agreed that you would ring the bell if you needed anything.'

'Did we?' As a slave to her grandmother's bell, she was somewhat averse to them. 'You said I should; I don't recall agreeing to it. Besides, I thought you'd try to stop me.'

'Why would I do that?'

'I wanted to look at my face. I scared a little girl. She ran away when I spoke to her. I needed to know the worst.'

'Ameerah? She was here?'

'Is that her name? She looked really frightened, the poor child.'

'Poor child, nothing,' he said dismissively. 'She ran away because she was caught where she shouldn't have been.' He got up and offered her his hands. 'Come along, let me get you back to bed.'

It was a clear change of subject and, although she was curious, Lucy thought it wiser to leave it at that. But she made no move to accept his support.

'I still want to see the damage,' she said. 'If I look so bad that you took the mirror away—'

'No!' He seemed at a loss, she thought. 'No, it was nothing to do with you. The mirror was broken. A long time ago. You look…' Words failed him.

'That bad?'

He shook his head. 'You have some bruising, that's all. It looks worse than it is.'

'How much worse? Do I have a black eye?'

He hesitated. 'Not exactly.'

'Not exactly black?'

'Not exactly one,' he admitted with a wry smile. 'And really, they're more an interesting shade of purple. With yellow highlights.'

'An overrated colour scheme, I've always thought,' she replied, equally wry, but omitting the smile. 'Anything else?'

'There are a few minor cuts, nothing that will leave a scar. And your bottom lip is swollen.' He looked as if he was going to say more, but thought better of it.

'And?'

He gave the kind of shrug that suggested she'd be wiser to leave it at that.

'And?'

'It would seem that there was a bag loose in the car. It must have caught your cheek…' he touched a finger to her cheekbone '…here,' he said, lightly tracing a curve first one way, then the other.

'My Chanel bag?' she said, realising that it had gone up in flames with everything else.

Han glanced up, looked into her eyes. Then, suddenly distant, 'I'm sorry you lost it. I hope it was insured.'

'I hadn't got around to it,' she admitted. 'Don't worry, it was almost certainly a fake.'

'You don't know?'

'It was a gift.'

He frowned as if he didn't understand. Clearly he would never have given anyone a knock-off as a gift. Would certainly never have pretended it was the real thing.

'Maybe I'm being unkind,' she said, although in the light of recent events it seemed unlikely that Steve would have paid for the genuine article.

He didn't pursue it. 'I hope you're reassured that there's no permanent damage to your face, Lucy, but in any case I'll have the mirror replaced for you.'

'No rush,' she said, finally placing her hands in his, allowing him to help her to her feet, to put his arm around her waist and support her back to bed. 'Now you've given me a blow by blow description, I'm in no great hurry to see the reality for myself.'

Someone, she noticed, had picked up the pills she'd dropped. The water and broken glass had been cleaned up too, the bell and telephone were back in place.

'Han…' She had to tell him about the 4x4. He had to know that he was harbouring a criminal. A wanted woman. 'There's something I have to tell you—'

'Take the painkillers the doctor gave you, Lucy,' he said, cutting her short as he lowered her on to the bed. For a moment she sat there, his arm still around her, his cheek close enough to feel the warmth emanating from his skin. Then, abruptly, he moved, lifted her legs, turning her so that she could lie back in comfort. Covered her with the sheet. 'You need to rest, give your body a chance to recover. There is nothing you have to say that will not wait until tomorrow.'

Maybe he was right. He'd want to know why she had stolen the four-wheel drive, what she had been doing out in the desert on her own. To tell him would mean betraying Steve, with consequences beyond her control. She needed to think it through properly.

He'd picked up the capsules and offered them to her and, after a moment, she took them, swallowed them.

'If you need anything, please, just ring the bell. Someone is always near.'

Whatever was in the capsules had to be more than simple painkillers because within minutes she was sinking fast into sleep but, before she went under, her mind snagged on the one question she hadn't asked.

Who was the little girl?

And why had he said that there were no women in his house?

She might even have cried the words out loud as she was dragged under by the sedative because, far away, she was certain that he answered her.

Han watched Lucy slide into unconsciousness; she was troubled, tried to speak even as sleep claimed her, but trouble,

as he knew, did not go away. Whatever was on her mind
would wait until morning and he murmured some meaningless soothing words.

Apparently satisfied, she finally let go, slept and, dismissing the *faraish* who had been on duty in the adjoining sitting
room ready to find him at a moment's notice should Lucy need
him, he opened the doors to the balcony and sat watching as
night drew in and the stars began their journey across the night
sky. Breathing in air heavy with scent of jasmine.

A thin crescent moon rose and set. The darkness faded to
grey, then lilac. He was finally roused, cold and stiff, when
Lucy Forrester called from the inner room.

'Hello… Is there anyone there?'

'Is the bell not working?' he asked, opening the door from
the balcony into her room.

She scowled at it. 'Ringing a bell for attention is a bit prin-
cessy, don't you think?'

'You have no desire to be a princess?'

'I'll bet Cinderella had trouble making the leap,' she said.
'From ringee to ringer.'

'Quite possibly.' It had been his intention to tease her a little
for her reticence. Living in the company of men, his horses,
hawks, for so long, he'd clearly lost his touch. 'How do you
feel?' he asked, deciding that it was safer to stick to the basics.

'Better, thank you.' Then, glancing to the window where
the soft light that preceded dawn was filtering through the
shutters, throwing bars of coloured light across the room, 'I
thought I'd been asleep for longer.'

'You've slept the clock round, Lucy. That's not sunset,
it's dawn.'

Her long sleep had done its work, he thought. It would take
days for the swelling to go down, longer for the bruising to

fade, but she looked much brighter and seemed to be moving more easily too. And the colour in her face was not entirely the result of her accident.

'Would you like to join me for breakfast?' he asked. 'Outside on the balcony.'

The invitation came from nowhere; the private meals he'd shared there with Noor, with time running out for both of them, had been precious moments, hoarded in his memory. Breakfast had long since lost it charm, ceased to be a meal to linger over; it was a long time since food had been anything but a necessity. But once voiced, however much regretted, the invitation could not be withdrawn.

Besides, the cool morning air would be good for Lucy and over breakfast she would have a chance to unburden herself.

'I'll bring your crutches,' he said, without waiting for an answer.

'Right.' Despite the half-closed eye, a split lip, she somehow managed a smile. 'This comes under the heading of total obedience, does it?'

He should return her smile, reassure her, put her at her ease. He'd learned the art at his father's knee. As a diplomat he'd practised it in the highest circles. When was the last time he'd done it for real? Not simply a going-through-the-motions movement of facial muscles, a polite response, but really smiled?

He had, he found, no difficulty in pinpointing the exact day. The exact moment.

He didn't try the diplomatic variety on Lucy Forrester. She deserved better.

'On the contrary, Lucy. I am at your command.' He picked up the telephone receiver and pressed a button. 'Tell me what you would like to eat.' Then, when she hesitated, 'Please, just say.'

'Orange juice?'

She was so uncertain. How could such a woman lack the confidence to ask, demand what she wanted, needed?

'Orange juice,' he agreed. 'And tea? Coffee?'

'Tea. Thank you.'

'And to eat?'

'Anything. Really.'

At that point he gave up prompting her and ordered a selection of food for her to choose from.

'It will be a few minutes,' he said when it was done and, picking up the robe that he had found for her, holding it so that she could slip her arms into the sleeves, said, 'plenty of time for you to practice your new found skills.'

After her shower Han had produced a full length cream silk nightgown, the kind donned by glamorous film stars way back in the days when they'd worn more than a spray of scent to bed, and a matching robe. Not new, for which he'd apologised, but clearly something that had belonged to his wife.

She wrapped the robe about her, moved, under her own steam, to the bathroom and finally joined him outside on a broad balcony. Shaded by an ornate wooden roof, trailed by scented jasmine, it ran the entire length of the building.

Below them was a formal garden divided by long rills of water that opened up at regular intervals into pools, clustered with lilies. There were almond trees in blossom, twining around slender cypresses stretching into a wilder distance. It seemed to go on for ever. When she lifted her eyes to the horizon all she could see beyond the trees were dark mountains, peaks already turning golden as the sun rose behind them.

'How beautiful!' she said as he held a chair back for her, relieved her of the crutches. 'What is this place?'

'In ancient times the Persians called it a *pairidaeza*,' he said.

'It sounds like paradise,' she said. 'Actually it looks like paradise.'

'In modern Persian they use the same word for both paradise and garden, but a *pairidaeza* is simply a place with a wall around it. This is known as Rawdah al-'Arusah,' he said, pouring a glass of orange juice, handing it to her as she repeated the words, glanced at Hanif for a translation. 'The Garden of the Bride.'

'Oh…'

For one terrible moment she thought the bride was his, but even before he shook his head she realised her mistake. This was old. Centuries old. 'The original pavilion—' he indicated the building they occupied '—this garden, was built by one of my ancestors for his Persian bride, homesick for the garden she'd left behind.'

'All this for one woman? He must have loved her a great deal.'

'That surprises you?'

'Yes. No…' Confused, and not a little embarrassed, she said, 'I imagined that marriages among the wealthy would have been arranged. Alliances between great families. Just as they once were in England.'

'Of course. It is expected that suitable marriages will be arranged, to strengthen ties between allies, to unite those who were once enemies.'

She did not miss the present tense and said, 'It is still your custom?'

'Matters of such importance cannot be left to chance.'

She sipped the juice. Made no comment.

'You think it cold? Passionless?'

'You've just described a business transaction,' she pointed out.

'When a man and a woman come to an alliance with honour,

the knowledge that their future has been written for the benefit of family and state, love and duty are one,' he replied.

Love and duty.

Her life, until a few weeks ago, had been entirely a matter of duty. There had been precious little love in it.

Then, in an instant, everything had changed.

She put down the glass, flexing the fingers of her left hand which had, until yesterday—was it only yesterday?...no, the day before that—worn a plain gold band. Unused to wearing a ring of any kind, it had felt odd, uncomfortable, on her finger, yet now it was gone she missed its reassurance. That heady, unaccustomed status of being a woman who the world could see was loved.

Realising that he was watching her, a slight frown creasing his forehead, she asked, 'Is it that easy?'

'Nothing of worth is easy. All partnerships require effort, understanding, compromise, if they are to work.'

'You discount initial attraction? Did you meet your wife before your betrothal?'

'Not before the contract was signed.'

'And yet you loved her.'

'You doubt that happiness can be achieved between two people united in such a manner?'

'Actually, when you put it like that I can see that I would have been much better served by such a clearly understood arrangement.'

'You were married?' He sounded surprised and she remembered how carefully he'd washed each of her fingers; presumably he'd noted the absence of a wedding ring. Which was undoubtedly why he'd used the past tense.

'I am married,' she said with reluctance. 'I was married six weeks ago.'

'Six weeks?'

This time he was not simply surprised, he was openly astounded.

'Your husband can bear to let you out of his sight so soon?' He spoke as a man whose culture could not conceive of such a thing. With derision for a man who took so little care of that which was his. Or possibly for a woman could not keep her man close.

Whichever it was, his attitude was entirely alien and yet she would have welcomed a little of his honour, his notion of love bound to duty in her own ill-fated union.

If she'd been offered an old-fashioned alliance, a contract that laid out the terms in black and white, giving her the security of marriage, the glamour of being the wife of a man like Steve Mason in return for the inheritance that she had never expected anyway, she might still have thought herself luckier than she had any right to expect.

Instead Steve had tricked her, cheated her, taken everything and given nothing, which was why she'd thrown the ring that he'd put on her finger, that had chafed at her skin, into a Ramal Hamrah gutter.

Now, clinging to all that was left to her—pride—she lifted her head and said, 'My husband had urgent business to attend to.' That was what he'd told her; it was probably the only thing he had said that was the truth.

'So urgent that you have decided not to bother him with your accident?'

Belatedly, it occurred to Lucy how this must look to Han. That she was taking advantage of his generosity when she had a husband whose duty it was to care for her. Who might, for all he knew, take violent exception to the fact that another man had usurped his place, touched his wife, held her so intimately.

Or had she, as the wife of another man, somehow compromised him?

'I'm so sorry, I should have told you straight away. My presence must be a dreadful embarrassment to you. I'll leave—'

He reached out, catching her hand as she turned, reaching for the crutches.

'No,' she said. 'Really, you can see how much better I am—'

'On the contrary, Lucy Forrester,' he cut in, 'you need time to recover your strength. You are welcome to stay in my house for as long as you need sanctuary.'

'Sanctuary?' she repeated, staring at his hand, wrapped around hers. Strong, sinewy, without a trace of softness, yet he held her as gently as he would an injured bird.

'I have used the wrong word?' he asked. 'It means a place of refuge, does it not?'

'Well, yes. It's just...' She forced herself to look up, meet his gaze. 'Sanctuary is a word more usually used to describe a place of safety for someone on the run from danger, in fear of their life, even. Of asylum,' she added, when he made no comment.

'We are all running from something, Lucy, even if the demons at our heels are nothing but shadows.' Then, as if suddenly aware that he'd overstepped some invisible boundary, he let her go, picked up a dish—a diversion, she thought, to give them both time to recover.

'In my case they're not exactly shadows,' she said, still feeling the cool strength of his fingers against her skin. This was not a man to deceive. He deserved nothing less than the truth. 'You have a right to know that the vehicle I was driving, that I wrecked, did not belong to me.'

He paused in the act of spooning yoghurt into a dish, regarding her steadily. 'It was rented?' he enquired. 'Borrowed?'

A tiny prickle along her spine warned her that he already knew what she was going to say.

'Not rented. Not borrowed. Steve told me he owned Bouheira Tours, but he may have lied about that. He lied about everything else. If he did, then I stole it.'

He handed her the dish of yoghurt and said, 'This is very good. It is made from milk produced by our own goats. Can I offer you honey, fruit, to flavour it?'

She ignored his gesture towards a dish of fresh fruit. 'Didn't you understand what I said?'

'You took the 4x4 from Bouheira Tours without permission.'

'A fine distinction, but not one that would impress the courts, I imagine.'

'Possibly not.' He served himself yoghurt, took some dates from the dish, bit into one. 'I recognised their logo, of course, and naturally they were the first people we contacted. We assumed you were an employee or a client of theirs. That they would take care of you.'

'Then you knew all along. I should have realised. What did they say? Am I going to be charged with theft?' Her heart was beating like a drum. Was that why he'd bought her here, to keep her from running away?

'It may interest you to know that Bouheira Tours not only denied knowledge of anyone by the name of Lucy Forrester, but they were adamant that none of their vehicles is missing.'

'But I...' She sat back, frowned. 'But I took it from their yard. The keys were in it and I thought...' He waited, but she couldn't begin to explain exactly what she'd been thinking. 'You saw it, Han. You must have done. Their name was plastered all over it.'

'A clerical error, no doubt,' he said. 'But if they insist they aren't missing a vehicle, they can hardly make a fuss about its disappearance. And even if they belatedly realise their mistake, be assured that your shadows cannot penetrate my walls.'

Walls?

She glanced at the mountains, so close in the clear morning light. They had been nothing more than a shimmer through the heat haze when she'd landed at the airport.

'We are out in the desert, aren't we? This is where I crashed?' She turned to Han. 'I saw high walls…glimpsed green just before the accident. I told you, I thought it was a mirage.' She considered what that meant. What he'd said about a *pairidaeza,* the sheer scale of it. 'All this…' without taking her eyes off him she swept her arm in a wide gesture to take in the vastness of the gardens '…all this is behind walls? In the middle of nowhere?'

'The walls are necessary to protect the spring that waters the garden, to keep out wandering animals who would graze the garden back to desert in the blink of an eye.' Then, 'You would prefer to be in Rumaillah? The city.'

'No!' she said without thinking. 'No…'

'It can be arranged. My house there is closed up, but my mother or my sisters would, I'm sure, be happy to take you in.'

If he asked them. The fact that he hadn't asked suggested they wouldn't be exactly thrilled at the prospect. Which made his own concern for a stranger all the more worthy. Especially one who had committed a criminal act.

'No, really,' she assured him. 'I'll be fit in a day or two and once I have my tickets, a passport, I'll be out of your hair. No need to bother anyone else.'

'Take as long as you need to regain your strength before you confront whatever troubles you.'

'Why do you insist that I am troubled?'

'No one who is at peace steals a vehicle, or risks her life as you did.'

She had no answer to that.

'Eat,' he said. 'Try the figs; they have been picked especially for you.'

He picked up a purple fruit with a bloom on its skin, handed it to her. Then took another and bit into it. Obviously, the subject of the stolen vehicle, any discussion of her departure, had been dismissed and to pursue either seemed rude. Instead she looked at the heavy fruit filling her palm, so different from the dried figs that had been a feature of her grandmother's Christmas sideboard. She'd hated those chewy, pippy things, but this was nothing like them and, somewhat cautiously, she bit into it, uncertain quite what to expect.

As the fresh sweetness filled her mouth she gasped in surprise, catching the juice that trickled down her chin with her hand, staring at the red flesh with astonishment.

'That's amazing! So different!'

He laughed too, apparently delighted with her delight. Then, as if caught unawares by the sound and horrified by it, he got up and strode away from her, putting the length of the balcony between them, before gripping the ornate wood rail as if it was the only thing stopping him from throwing himself to the stone path twenty feet below.

He looked so alone that Lucy felt an almost overwhelming urge to follow him, wrap her arms around him and pull his head down on to her shoulder in a simple gesture of comfort. Reassure him that it was all right to go on living. That laughter was not a betrayal.

It was probably a good thing that crutches made any such gesture out of the question.

She didn't know what he was going through, how he was

suffering. She knew nothing of comfort, love, tenderness, and, having barely lived herself, she was in no position to offer advice to anyone else on how it should be done.

Unable to do anything useful and certain that he would rather she ignored his loss of control and left him to gather himself, she instead forced herself to give her complete attention to the breakfast that had been provided for her.

There were a great many covered dishes and lifting the lids she discovered scrambled eggs, goat's cheese, olives, tomatoes, slices of cold meat that she thought must be lamb.

Her pathetic inability to just say what she wanted, she realised, had meant extra work for Han's staff and a shocking waste of food.

She did what she could to make amends.

Keeping her eyes politely averted from the dark, motionless figure of her host, whose gaze seemed riveted to the far mountains, she took a little of the yoghurt, laced it with honey.

Han, she discovered, was difficult to ignore and, unable to help herself, she glanced up. He had not moved, yet the still, warm air seemed to vibrate with his presence and she saw at that moment how a woman could have looked at him for the first time and fallen in love with him.

Every line of his body was charged with power, strength, grace.

His eyes were fierce, his profile carved from granite, yet she was certain that when he had taken Noor's hand, held her for the first time, he would have been tender.

She could not have helped but love him.

Her throat tightened and her eyes stung. Would Steve have been tender too? If he hadn't been called away to some emergency, would he have made her feel like a queen? Her reward for being so gullible, so naïve?

She too found it necessary to spend a moment or two contemplating the peace of the garden before forcing herself to eat a spoonful of scrambled egg with a little thin crisp toast.

She was struggling to lift a heavy silver teapot when Han said, 'Leave it, I will do that.'

Her hand trembled slightly as he took it from her, held her fingers for a moment as if to reassure her that she would regain her strength quickly, before pouring tea into two cups.

'I apologise for abandoning you. I have black moments when memory overwhelms me and I am not fit company for man or beast,' he said, placing a cup before her.

She had no comprehension of such grief, but resisted the urge to offer spurious platitudes. Yet to say nothing, ignore his pain, change the subject to something bland and safe was not an option.

'How long is it, since you lost her?'

For a moment she thought he would not answer, but then he said, 'Three years. It has been three years since Noor died.'

He sank back into a high cane armchair and closed his eyes, whether to discourage her curiosity or to block out the memory she couldn't say, and it took courage to press on. 'Noor? I've heard the name before.'

'It was chosen by the American wife of the late King of Jordan.'

'Maybe that's what I was thinking of.'

'Maybe.' He opened his eyes, turned to look at her. 'Once we were married she was known as Umm Jamal. The mother of Jamal.'

Lucy knew that the best thing for him was to talk, that as a neutral listener, someone to whom he could tell anything, safe in the knowledge that she would be gone within days, she was the ideal person. But as if it was not difficult enough that this was an unfamiliar culture and the possibilities for insult were endless, Han seemed to be locked within a minefield of pain; her only way forward was to prompt his confidence with the questions that came to her and pray that they would not explode in her face. She owed him that much.

'The name of your son was chosen even before you were married?' she asked.

'I am the son of Jamal.' With a barest gesture with one of those long hands, he suggested that was explanation enough. Then, because obviously for her it was not, 'I will be the father of Jamal, *in sha'Allah*. It is our way.'

'I see.'

She sipped her tea.

'My wife died from leukaemia,' he said, after a seemingly endless silence in which she sought a way to phrase the impossible question.

'Leukaemia? But surely… I thought…' The words escaped her before she stopped them.

'You thought that this is a disease from which most people recover.'

There was something about the way he finished the sentence for her that made her wary about leaping in. An edge to his voice.

'You're right, Lucy; with prompt treatment most people do recover, but Noor was pregnant when she was diagnosed. She refused to accept the treatment that would have saved her in case it hurt the baby she was carrying.'

Lucy's hand flew to her mouth to block an anguished cry, but no sound could have made it through the painful lump in her throat.

To have cherished an unknown, unseen son or daughter so

much; to have made the conscious decision to put her precious baby's life before her own...

How pitiful her own problems seemed in comparison.

'I told her that there would be other babies,' he said, his voice distant, as if he was not talking to her, but to someone unseen. 'That even if there weren't it did not matter. That she would always be Umm Jamal.' He turned to her, his face an expressionless mask, nothing but skin over bones. 'Nothing would move her. She would not save herself. Not even for me.'

'And Jamal?' she asked. A son given at such cost must surely be the most cherished gift. Had the sacrifice been in vain?

'Her child was born, healthy and strong,' he assured her.

Her child?

And then she knew. There had not been a son, but a daughter. The little girl she'd frightened with her bruised and swollen face.

'Ameerah.' He did not deny it. 'She must give you such solace.'

A frown creased his wide brow, as if he did not under-stand. 'Solace?'

'She is Noor's gift to you. A part of herself. A precious daughter.'

'She knew. All the time she was telling me that she was sac-rificing herself for Jamal, she knew the baby she was carrying was a girl.'

'She was a mother protecting her unborn child,' she said. Surely he must see that?

'She lied to me!'

She flinched at the ferociousness of his response, let out an involuntary cry as all the aches that had settled to a low background hum were jerked back into life by the spasm.

'Lucy, I'm so sorry...' He reached out as if to comfort her.

'I'm fine,' she snapped, moving her arm before he could touch her.

How dared he talk of love? Of honour.

His anger was not directed at the disease that had killed his wife, but at the woman who had defied him to protect the baby she was carrying. If it had been a boy, she would have been celebrated, honoured. But his anger was eloquent testimony to the fact that a girl child was no compensation for the loss of his wife.

She'd thought him sympathetic, someone with whom she could converse on an equal footing, but her first terrified impression had been right. The man had the surface manners of a gentleman, but beneath the veneer his instincts were still those of a primitive tribal chieftain for whom women were no more than the expendable vessels who provided them with sons.

He grieved not for his wife, but for the son she had promised him.

CHAPTER FOUR

'LUCY?'

She forced herself to face him.

'Have you eaten well?' Unable to speak, she just nodded. 'Then I shall wash your hair.'

What?

How could he do that? One minute act like a relic of the Middle Ages, the next like some caring 'new' man?

Or had she misunderstood him? Misjudged him? Was his anger nothing more than a reflection of his pain that his wife had played on an Arab's desire for sons. Had not trusted him to accept her decision?

'If you'd rather not,' she said cautiously, 'perhaps Ameerah's nurse would help me.'

'Ameerah's nurse?'

'I saw her yesterday when she was chasing after your daughter.'

'I see.' His dark eyes glinted dangerously. 'You saw her and now you think I was lying to you when I told you there were no women in my house?'

She tried to deny it—the thought hadn't crossed her mind until he put it there—but the one word she needed seemed stuck in transit, somewhere between her brain and her mouth.

'Why would I do that?' he asked, taking her silence as affirmation.

She was not deceived by his reasonable tone, his bland expression. Too embarrassed to look at him, she simply shook her head. It was not enough and he reached across the table, hooked a finger beneath her chin, forcing her to meet his eyes.

Never had a touch been gentler or seemed more dangerous. The heat of it rippled through her. As a demonstration of her vulnerability, a warning of how totally she'd placed herself in his power, it had everything and, transfixed, she didn't move a muscle as his gaze drifted down to where the robe she was wearing over the nightgown had fallen open, unnoticed, as she'd eaten.

'You think that I am like some predator, perhaps, who takes a victim to his lair to feast upon at his leisure?'

'No!' She finally managed to deny it, released from stasis by the desperate need to reassure him that she'd never thought any such thing. The image he evoked was that of a leopard, or a bear. It did not suit him. If Hanif al-Khatib was a predator, he was a hawk, an eagle...

'No,' she repeated, but her denial was somewhat undermined by the nervous manner in which she clutched at the fragile silk, holding it together with one hand where it scooped low over her breast.

'Do you think that if I was the kind of man who preyed on helpless women,' he continued, the edge of his thumb so close to her cheek that she could feel the down rising to meet it, 'the presence of a dozen old women would stop me?'

'No! Yes!' At which point she realised that there wasn't a right answer to his question. That the only way to repair the unintended insult was to meet his gaze head on. Match his directness with a clear and unequivocal response.

'I assure you, Hanif bin Jamal bin Khatib al-Khatib, that you have done nothing to make me feel uncomfortable or awkward. On the contrary.' He did not move. 'You have done nothing that a much loved wife could have reproached you for.'

For a moment the only thing that moved was the blood rushing to her cheeks. Then, with the slightest of bows, Hanif let his hand fall to his side.

'You are right to be careful, Lucy Forrester. You know nothing about me.'

She knew enough. Enough to judge him by his deeds rather than his words. To regret the unworthy thoughts that had filled her head, be grateful that she had not given them voice.

'I know that you saved my life, Hanif. That I am nothing to you, yet you have not spared any expense, begrudged one moment of your time, to care for me. It must have been out of the goodness of your heart,' she said as, desperate to convince him, she made a gesture that framed her bruised and swollen face. 'It certainly couldn't have been because of my beauty.'

He did not protest, attempt meaningless flattery, but said, 'The arrival of Ameerah and Fathia, her nurse, was as unexpected as your own.' For unexpected read unwelcome, she thought. 'They did not arrive until yesterday afternoon and, as you have already noted, the old woman has her hands full.'

Hanif al-Khatib, she was almost certain, rarely felt the need to explain his actions. She understood instinctively that she had just been shown more than usual courtesy.

'She does not live with you?' she asked, as if they were having the most ordinary of conversations. Only the slightest tremble in her voice betrayed how intense the moment had been. 'Your daughter?'

'The garden offers no more than a pavilion for a pampered

wife, a hunting lodge for her lord. There is nothing here for a child,' he said dismissively. 'Ameerah lives in the capital with her grandmother.' He rose to his feet and she thought the subject was closed, but then his mouth twisted in a parody of a smile. 'I suspect that when she heard I had taken in a young foreign woman, my mother despatched Ameerah to Rawdah al-'Arusah as a hostage to my honour. Or yours. I leave it to you to decide which,' he added, and the parody came close to approaching the real thing.

'If your mother could see the state of me,' Lucy assured him, wincing as her own attempt at a smile—just to demonstrate how it should be done—pulled at a cut on her lip, 'she wouldn't give the matter a moment's thought.'

'You are right, of course. Let us hope that Fathia will make time to call and reassure her.'

Oh, nice!

About to point out that a gentleman wouldn't have agreed with her, she thought better of it.

'I'm afraid that what should have been a simple rescue mission has caused you far more trouble than you could ever have bargained for.'

'*Mash'Allah,*' he said, handing her the crutches. Keeping close in case she needed help. But not, she noticed, making any attempt to assist her.

'*Mash'Allah,*' she said, repeating the words to herself as she swung herself back in through the open French windows, then, looking up at him, 'God's will?'

'You have been learning Arabic?' he enquired with interest.

'I bought one of those teach yourself language CDs. I was…' She stopped. She had been planning to surprise Steve, determined to learn enough to help him run the business. 'I was hopeless,' she said.

'It's difficult to learn anything on your own, but in four weeks you can learn a great deal.'

'Four weeks?'

'Since you wanted to know how long it would take for your ankle to heal, I spoke with the doctor. He thought three or four weeks.'

'Oh, I see. Well, thank you, but I promise that I won't be imposing on your hospitality for more than a few days.'

'It is no imposition. And what will you do in England, alone in your cold, empty house? How will you manage to buy food, cook, take care of yourself?'

The one thing she wouldn't be doing was expecting help from the congregation of her grandmother's church. They had lost interest the minute they had discovered that there would be no more money. Besides, they all knew she was the devil's handmaid, born in wickedness, headed for hell.

'It's not cold,' she said.

'Everywhere in England is cold.' Apparently taking her silence for assent, he continued, 'You will stay here until you are fully recovered, Lucy.' Then, almost as an afterthought, 'Or until your husband comes to find you.'

He picked up a chair and took it through to the bathroom, setting it with its back to the sink.

'Sit,' he said. 'I will try not to get you too wet,' he said, lifting the shower head from its holder and turning on the water.

She remained on her feet. 'You don't have to do this. I'm sure I could manage.'

He clearly did not think her protest worthy of a reply, but instead ran the water, adjusting the temperature. Or maybe it was a test of her trust. Of her sincerity when she'd assured him that he'd done nothing to offend her.

She sat down, did her best to scoop up her hair, lift it over the edge of the basin.

'Leave it. I will do it.'

She ignored him. She was not helpless. Another day, two at the most, and she would be on her way, however tempting it was to stay and be treated like a princess.

She had debts to deal with, a living to earn, a husband to divorce.

Han tucked a towel around her shoulders, then said, 'That is not too hot?' She shook her head without thinking and barely felt a twinge as warm water began to soak into her hair.

The lack of fuss with which he washed, then combed through her long difficult hair while it was slick with conditioner, left her in no doubt that he'd done this many times for a wife grown too weak to do it for herself.

The man seemed a muddle of contradictions, but then what did she know? She hadn't needed her grandmother's exhortations to purity to keep her chaste. There had been nothing about her to attract a man, even if she'd had the chance to meet one, until she'd inherited her grandmother's house and Steve had turned up on the doorstep.

Hanif was a man so far outside her experience that she had no right to judge him, or the standards by which he lived his life. Only the manner in which he treated her.

'I used to hate this,' she said afterwards, when they'd gone back out on to the balcony so that her hair could dry in the sun.

'Having your hair washed?'

'The washing wasn't so bad, but when I was a child my grandmother had this horrid scratchy comb and very little patience with tangles.'

'I will not hurt you,' he said, refusing to surrender the comb he'd brought with him but, taking infinite care not to hurt her, continued what he'd begun. 'It is unusual to see such long hair on a European woman.'

'Gran belonged to a dogmatic religious sect which believes it's a sin for women to cut their hair. She used to make me wear it in painfully tight plaits when I was little.'

'Plaits?'

She took a piece of hair and demonstrated what she meant.

'Oh, yes.'

'I once hacked them off with her kitchen scissors.' She used her fingers to show how she'd cut them as short as she could.

'She was angry?'

'She wasn't pleased,' Lucy admitted. She'd never told anyone about the beating she'd been given. Ghastly as her hair had looked, it had been less painful than the weekly agony with the wet tangles. The bruises had long faded before her hair had grown enough for plaits again and by then she'd taught herself to do it herself, putting it into a single French plait that was tight enough, unflattering enough, to keep her grandmother happy, grown up enough not to provoke cruel teasing at school. 'I was not a good child,' she said.

'Children are not supposed to be good. They are supposed to be children. You had no mother?'

'Somewhere.'

The truth slipped out before she could stop it. It wasn't her usual response. She usually told people that her mother had died when she was a baby. So much less painful than the truth. But she couldn't bring herself to lie to Han, who had a truly motherless child.

'I had—have—a mother somewhere. She abandoned me. Left me with her mother, ran away.' She didn't blame her for running. Only for leaving her behind. 'She was sixteen. Unmarried.'

It occurred to her that this would probably shock him. Maybe it had been her intention to shock him, show him just how special Noor had been. If her mother had had an ounce of his wife's compassion, love…

'Girls in the west are not protected by their fathers,' he said, apparently missing the comparison, or perhaps choosing to ignore it. 'They dress provocatively, go out unaccompanied. It is bound to happen.'

'Perhaps. Her father, my grandfather, died when she was fourteen. Maybe if he'd lived things would have been different.' Her grandmother might not have been drawn to such an intense religious experience. Her mother would not have been driven to rebel…

'He had no brothers?'

'Brothers?'

'Here,' he explained, 'when a man dies, his brother will take his family into his house. Care for his children. Stand in his place as husband.'

She frowned, turned to look up at him. 'Do you mean that literally? The husband bit? Even if he already has a wife?'

'A woman has needs,' he said. 'To be held, to have the comfort of the marriage bed if it is her wish. It is his duty.'

'I've never thought of it in quite that way before,' she admitted.

'You're blinkered by your own cultural traditions,' he said, clearly picking up more than a touch of irony in her response.

He had finished combing her hair and he moved her chair round so that the sun could finish drying it. 'You believe a man who does this is simply thinking of his own pleasure. That it demeans the woman.'

'To be wife number two?' She was absolutely sure it didn't

raise her status, but thought she'd be well advised not to make comments on a subject she knew nothing about.

'The custom of taking more than one wife began as a way of caring for the widows of those fallen in battle,' he explained. 'It is not an easy thing for a man.'

'No?'

Maybe she didn't sound convinced.

'In the west you think of a man being served by two or three women. You find it salacious, titillating. The truth is that his responsibilities are onerous. Each wife has to be treated equally in all things. Give one woman a trinket, a dress, new furniture, and they must all have the same.'

'A man has to pay for his pleasure.'

'You are amused?'

'You expect me to feel sorry for a man who has three wives?'

'I was not seeking your sympathy, but your understanding of the reality. Have you any idea what would have happened to a woman left to fend for herself? To her children? There was no welfare state to care for them. They would have had to scrape a living any way they could. You need look no further than the evening news bulletin on your television to see the reality.'

'Oh.' She swallowed. 'I see.'

'It is rare for a man to take more than one wife now,' he said, as if to reassure her.

'Yes, well,' she said, rallying, 'I can see that in this consumer-led age it would be prohibitively expensive.'

'And physically exhausting.' And this time there was just a hint of a smile. 'Equality, as I said, in all things.'

'In England,' she said quickly, to cover her blushes, 'it has never been legal to have more than one wife at a time. Besides, my grandfather had no brothers. It was just me and my grandmother. And now she's dead too.'

'I am sorry to hear that.' Then, 'You have not looked for her?' he asked. 'Your mother?'

'Why would I do that?'

He shrugged.

'If she'd wanted to see me, Hanif, she knew where I was.' She'd dreamed of that. Of her mother swooping down to carry her off, taking her away to live with her in a warm house, dressing her in pretty clothes, giving her birthday parties at the local burger bar like the other kids. 'I was exactly where she left me.'

'Maybe she is too ashamed to come to you.'

'I don't believe she ever wasted a single thought on me,' she said.

He regarded her thoughtfully, but let it be. Her relief was a heartbeat too fast. 'And your husband?' he enquired. 'Does he not think of you? Wonder where you are?'

Even before the words left his mouth, Hanif wished them unsaid. He had offered her refuge without condition. Seeing her struggle to find some answer that would satisfy him only confirmed his opinion that she was in trouble. But while he would do whatever he could to extricate her from any legal problems she had in Ramal Hamran, any difficulty between Lucy Forrester and her new husband was none of his business.

'Enough,' he said, standing up. 'The sun is too hot for your fair skin. You need to be inside where it is cool, resting.'

'I thought it would be hotter,' she said, gratefully seizing on the change of subject. 'When I arrived at the airport it seemed worse.'

'The humidity at the coast can be unpleasant at this time of year. It is higher here and cooler, but you must still take care. The breeze from the mountains deceives. You do not need sunburn to add to your discomfort.'

The balcony was wide and shaded, but even so her skin was flushed with the heat. Or maybe, he thought, it was guilt.

It did not matter.

He handed her the crutches and said, 'Come, this way.' And forcing himself to turn away, leave her to it, he walked further along the balcony, opening the French windows into the sitting room.

'Zahir! I have a job for you.'

'Excellency?'

'You were given Lucy Forrester's belongings? At the hospital?'

'Yes, Excellency, but they were beyond saving. The nurses cut them off her.'

'Was there any jewellery?'

'I have the bag in my office.'

'This is everything?' Hanif asked, when the envelope containing only a wrist-watch, no longer working, had been opened.

'Was there something in particular you were looking for?'

'I want you to go back to the hospital and make sure nothing was missed. Find the nurse who admitted her if you can and ask if there was a ring.'

'Yes, sir.'

'And while you're in Rumaillah you can buy clothes to replace those she lost in the crash.'

'Me?' The word was little more than a squeak.

'You can take the sizes from these,' Hanif said, indicating the ruins of the clothes she'd been wearing.

'You're asking me to shop for women's clothes? Women's underwear?'

'The duties of an aide are onerous,' he agreed. Then, taking pity on him, he said, 'Maybe one of your female relatives would do it for you if you asked politely.'

'You are joking! Ask my sisters to help me buy underwear for a woman? I'd have my ears boxed.'

'Then it would appear that you are in for an uncomfortable time, either way.'

'On the other hand, if I explained it was a commission for you, they would fall over themselves to be helpful. In fact, that would work very well. They can shop while I take a closer look at this tour company. See what kind of an outfit they are.'

'How will you approach them?'

'There are sand-surfing trips run every day, with evening banquets in the desert to round things off. I've still got the clothes I wore when I was a student in the States so I can pass as a visitor and it will give me a chance to talk to the people who work there.' Zahir's eagerness suggested it was the chance to get away, be with young people, rather than the investigation that excited him. 'I'll arrange for the results of my sisters' raid on the mall to be sent back on the helicopter.'

'You seem to have it all worked out. Very well, Zahir, but be careful what you say and do not mention Lucy Forrester's name.'

Lucy thought she heard the sound of a helicopter flying low and peered out of the window, hoping to see whether it was leaving or landing.

As she reached for her crutches, determined, despite Han's order to rest, that she would go outside and take a closer look, she spotted Ameerah peeping round the door. The child immediately ducked out of sight, but didn't run, and when Lucy called, '*Marhaban,* Ameerah,' her response was a giggle.

'*Ismy,* Lucy,' she said. 'My name is Lucy.'

'Lucy,' the child repeated, still not showing herself.

Lucy did not respond and after a moment Ameerah's face edged around the door. Her eyes were bright with mischief, her hair an untidy tangle of long dark curls with ribbons that had once been tied in bows but were now trailing loose.

When she was sure that Lucy was not going to shout at her or reach for the hand bell to summon her nurse, she eased herself around the door and into the room.

Her feet were bare and muddy, but she was wearing an exquisite cream silk dress, the kind worn by small princesses in story books. Once pin-tucked and perfect, it was now a mess, the hem soaking wet and coated with green algae as if it had been trailed through a pond and sporting the kind of jagged tear that suggested it had got into a fight with the branch of a tree and lost.

She'd obviously given her nurse the slip again. A handful indeed. And, with no one of her own age to play with, probably bored out of her mind.

Trawling through what she could remember of the language CD, Lucy was unable to come up with anything to fit the occasion. Instead she shifted herself to make more room on the day bed and patted the space beside her.

Ameerah didn't take up the invitation, but instead pressed herself against the wall and edged herself along it until she reached the safety of an elegant loveseat, upholstered in rose silk. Perching herself on that, feet swinging, she regarded Lucy with an intense, unblinking stare.

Lucy made no effort to coax her nearer, nor did she smile. Her reward for her patience came when Ameerah lifted her skirt and pointed to a colourful bruise on her shin.

'Ouch!' Lucy said sympathetically.

Ameerah nodded, then pointed first to her own eye, then at Lucy and said. 'Ouch!'

Lucy laughed. '*Nam,* Ameerah,' she said. 'Yes. A very big ouch.'

Encouraged, Ameerah slid from the seat and came a little closer, her interest apparently snagged by the splint Lucy was wearing. She looked at it, touched it very gently, then held out one of her own slender little arms, pointing at a small scar.

Lucy responded with a sympathetic expression, sucking air through her teeth in an internationally understood message of sympathy before asking, somewhat helplessly, in English, 'How did you hurt yourself, Ameerah?'

The child responded in a rush of Arabic, speaking so quickly that Lucy couldn't pick out a single word. When she held up her hands and shook her head, Ameerah responded by miming a break so graphically, with sound effects, that Lucy clapped her hand over her mouth.

Apparently delighted with the effect she'd produced, the child laughed, then, turning as she heard her name being called, dropped to her knees and scuttled beneath the day bed.

CHAPTER FIVE

AMEERAH'S nurse paused in the doorway, looked at Lucy and said, 'Pardon, *assayyidah*. I am seeking the child. Ameerah.'

Lucy said, 'If I see her, *assayyidah,* I will ring the bell.' Then, lifting a finger to her lips, she indicated Ameerah's hiding place and, using the same signs—patting the space beside her—made it clear that she was welcome to stay for a while.

The woman smiled, nodded, indicated that she'd be within call and disappeared, presumably to have a much needed break.

Once she was gone, Lucy leaned down, lifted the drapes that hung to the floor and said, 'Okay, Ameerah, you can come out now.'

The child's head appeared; she looked around, up at Lucy, who nodded, then, with a huge smile on her face, she crawled out and bounced up beside her.

'Lucy,' she said, touching her hand.

'Ameerah,' Lucy replied, gently touching the child's cheek. And they both smiled.

Then Ameerah pointed to the jug on the table beside her. '*Mai,*' she said.

For a moment she thought the child was saying 'my', then realized she was asking for water. She poured some into the glass. '*Tafazzal…*' she said, offering it to her. Please have.

Ameerah giggled, repeating the word several times before taking the glass. Then, as soon as she'd finished her drink, she wriggled down, put the glass on the table and ran to the door.

'Oh, I see. Cupboard love, is it?' Lucy said, laughing.

Ameerah turned and, with a neat curtsey that belied her untidy appearance, said, '*Shukran,* Lucy.'

'*Afwan,* Ameerah. *Ma'as salamah.*'

The child laughed, calling something back to her as she ran off.

Lucy reran the words in her head until she could make sense of the sounds, match them to the CD she'd spent so much time listening to. 'Oh, right.' She laughed. 'See you later.'

She rang the bell and, when the nurse reappeared, indicated the direction her charge had taken.

Han heard Lucy's bell. The sound surprised him. He had come to the conclusion that she would do anything, even crawl on her hands and knees to the bathroom, rather than ring for help and in another five minutes he would have looked in on her to see if she needed anything.

Maybe, he thought with more than a touch of amusement, beneath that reticent exterior there was an unsuspected 'princess' trying to break free.

Or maybe she was in real trouble. He wasted no more time in speculation.

Lucy, however, was sitting quietly, a small wistful smile lifting the corners of her mouth. It disappeared the minute she caught sight of him.

'Oh… Han.'

'You seem surprised to see me, Lucy. You did ring?'

'Yes, but—'

'But?'

But she hadn't rung for him, that much was clear. He could almost see the cogs whirring around in her head as she struggled for some explanation.

'—but I didn't expect you to be so quick. You said someone would come and find you. I thought it would take longer.'

'This is not a palace, Lucy. It is, as I told you, nothing more than a small pavilion. A place to spend the hot summer months. What you would call a holiday cottage.'

'Only in the way that Balmoral or Camp David is a holiday cottage,' she replied. Then, apparently unsure whether he'd ever heard of either of them, she explained, 'Balmoral is Queen Elizabeth's Scottish home. Our royal family spend their holidays there.'

He didn't tell her that he'd not only heard of it, but had been a guest there on more than one occasion. Instead he said, 'You mock me, Lucy. Rawdah al-'Arusah has no more than twelve rooms.'

'Twelve. Is that all?'

Sarcasm, too. Lucy Forrester was recovering fast. 'Fifteen, at the most,' he assured her. He discounted all but the major rooms.

'It seems very grand to me.' She gestured around at the exquisite hand-painted tiles, the rugs, the furniture upholstered in rich silk. 'It is certainly beautiful.'

'It was built as a setting for a princess. The only man allowed within its walls would have been her husband.'

She blushed. 'Excuse me? Are you telling me that this was a harem?'

'I suspect what you mean by that word and the reality are so far apart as to render it meaningless. This was a citadel. A place apart where no one could come unless she permitted it.'

'Not even her husband?'

'Not even her husband.'

'Really?' Her surprise amused him. 'So where did he stay?'

'There is a lodge, out of sight of the pavilion, where he stayed with his men, as I did myself until Noor became ill and I took a suite of rooms for myself to be near her.'

Something knotted in Lucy's stomach, a feeling she could not describe. But in her head she saw the beautiful Noor summoning her husband to her. Dressed in silk, her hair polished and glowing, she would have prepared everything to please him. She would have offered him food, made him laugh, made him wait as she drove him wild with desire…

'Lucy? Are you all right?'

She came to with a start, swallowed. 'Yes. Fine. Really.' Then, 'You stayed here. Afterwards.'

'It is peaceful. I do not disturb my family.'

They worried about him, she thought. He stayed here so that they shouldn't see him grieve…

'What do you find to do all day?'

'I take my hawks into the desert to exercise them. Visit with local tribes to ensure they have everything they need. And the garden had been neglected for a long time. It needs care.'

'You're restoring it?'

'Returning it to what it was? It can never be that, but some of the irrigation systems are showing the signs of age; if they are left to crumble the garden will eventually die. And my library is here, so you see I have more than enough to keep me occupied.'

'Even without having the additional worry of stupid women doing their best to kill themselves on your doorstep.'

'The life of one woman is more important than a hundred gardens, a lifetime of study.'

'Study?' In a moment she was all remorse. 'You were working? Just now? I'm so sorry to have disturbed you—'

'I am translating the work of one of our poets into French and English. Scarcely a matter of urgency,' he said, dismissing what would be a life's work with a gesture.

'Then you too must be a poet.' Before he could deny it, she said, 'It is not just a matter of translating the words, but the meaning, the voice, the rhythm.'

'You speak as someone who knows the problems.'

'I was hoping to study French literature at university.'

'This did not happen?'

'My grandmother thought university was a haven of sin. That I would be corrupted by it. When I refused to obey her and stay at home she became so angry that she had a heart attack and then a stroke. There was no one but me to nurse her.'

'She paid a high price for getting her own way.'

'We both did.'

'Is there anything to prevent you from resuming your studies now?'

'I thought of it, but then Steve Mason turned up on my doorstep, so once again university has become the impossible dream it always was.'

'Because you are married? This Steve Mason is the man you married?'

'Yes. You know him?'

'No. I'm simply surprised that you do not use his name.'

'It's a long story, Han, and you have work to do.'

'Even poets take coffee breaks,' he said, but the last thing he wanted to talk about was her marriage, her husband. Instead he turned to the telephone beside a small love seat and immediately saw the wet, muddy smear on the edge of one of the cushions. So the mystery of the bell was explained. Ameerah had been here again and, protective of the child, Lucy had not been prepared to betray her.

He asked for coffee to be sent up, then turned and sat down facing his guest. 'So, you are rested, Lucy Forrester and impatient to see the garden?'

Startled by the abrupt change of subject, she said, 'I'm sorry?'

'I assume you summoned me to take you for a walk.'

Lucy had been wondering how she was going to save Ameerah from the consequences of her trespass into the forbidden area of the pavilion. She wasn't exactly keen to tell Han the sorry tale of her marriage either and, tossed a verbal lifeline, she seized it gratefully.

'You're right. I crave fresh air. A book. A shady seat.' Then, because it had been bothering her, she said, 'Can I ask you something?'

'What do you wish to know?'

'How did you find my address? In England. I know my memory, in the aftermath of the accident, became a little muddled, but I can't recall giving it at the hospital. Or insurance details, come to that.' He didn't immediately answer and, certain she was right to press it, she said, 'Everything was destroyed, you said.'

'It was,' he assured her, then turned to welcome the arrival of a servant with coffee. He dismissed the boy, served her himself and offered her a plate containing small sticky cakes. 'They are very good,' he said. 'The almonds are grown here.'

Lucy did not have a sweet tooth, but she took one and tasted it. 'Delicious,' she said politely. 'And the honey? Is that produced here too?'

He glanced at her a little sharply, as if suspecting that she was teasing him, then said, 'I did not say; I thought you might think me boastful.'

'On the contrary, I believe you to be the most modest of

men,' she said, resting the cake in the saucer of the coffee cup he'd placed beside her.

It was true. His robes were plain, dark, simply cut, without adornment, and the *keffiyeh* he'd been wearing when he'd rescued her was the kind worn by desert tribesmen rather than those made from fine white voile and worn with the elaborate gilded camel halters favoured by the rich.

Then, persisting, 'You didn't ask me for my address, Hanif. Yet you knew it.'

'You were in shock, in pain, when we arrived at the hospital and you were not making a great deal of sense. We needed to find your friends, so I had my aide make enquiries, first, as I told you, with the company whose vehicle you were driving and then, when that proved a dead end, he spoke to the immigration department. Fortunately the officers on duty when you arrived remembered you.'

'I find that hard to believe.'

'Your hair, I understand, made a considerable impression.'

'Oh.' She normally wore it in a French plait or coiled in a bun to keep it out of the way, but in her agitation, her rush to get to the airport, her fingers had refused to co-operate and she'd simply dragged it back from her face, fastened it at the nape with a clip, leaving it to hang loose down her back. Then, 'Your aide?'

'Zahir al-Khatib. A cousin. He's in Rumaillah this morning.'

'Making further enquiries?'

'Replacing your wardrobe. Or, rather, delegating the task to one of his sisters.'

Lucy suspected this was a distraction, tossed into the conversation to avoid more questions. No doubt she was supposed to exclaim with horror, tell him that he could not do that, but she didn't waste her breath. If he'd decided she needed clothes, then clothes she would have. And, unless she was prepared to travel home in his late wife's nightdress, she was going to have to accept them. But not as charity.

'I did have travel insurance,' she said. 'It will cover the replacement of my clothes.'

'Are you sure? I suspect that if they discover you were driving a stolen vehicle when you lost your possessions, you might find the company disinclined to pay out.'

Oh, good grief, she hadn't thought of that. 'If, as you say, Bouheira Tours deny all knowledge of the vehicle, that shouldn't prove a problem. I will pay for my clothes, Han.'

Lucy saw him bite back an instinctive response.

He must know that even in Britain it would be inappropriate to buy clothes for another man's wife. Here, she suspected, such liberties might get a man killed, although the truth was that he'd gone way beyond any such barrier even before he'd removed her from the hospital; the fact he hadn't known she was married would be no excuse.

But he was safe enough. She doubted Steve would come looking for satisfaction—not unless he thought there was money in it.

'There were traveller's cheques too,' she said. Not many. She could not afford to be extravagant. Actually she couldn't even afford to be cheap... 'And my return ticket. Will the airline issue a replacement?'

'If you give me what details you can remember, Zahir will deal with it for you.'

'The same Zahir who was able to bypass all red tape and get my address from immigration? He must be a handy man to have around.'

'The population of Ramal Hamrah is small,' Han said. 'The immigration officers will have known him.'

'Is that enough? I can't imagine being an acquaintance of an immigration officer would get you access to that kind of information in England.'

'This is not England. This is Ramal Hamrah.'

A country rich in oil, with a thriving offshore banking industry and a growing tourist sector. A very foreign country. One where marriages were arranged, where a man could take more than one wife if he had the wealth and the stamina, and where daughters had no value.

'So if they knew your cousin, it follows that they would know you.' His shrug was imperceptible. 'Why does the name Khatib seem so familiar?'

'The Khatibs are an old Ramal Hamrah family.'

That didn't explain it, so she came at it another way. She had already learned the importance of names. That a first-born son was named for his grandfather...

'You are not your father's oldest son,' she said, 'or your name would be Khatib bin Jamal bin whatever.'

'That is the name of my oldest brother,' he confirmed, but offering her nothing more.

He wasn't exactly hindering her, but she sensed a mystery, that she was missing something.

'If I were a Ramal Hamrah, if I lived here, your extended name would be enough to tell me who you are and your place within the family.'

'I am the third son of Jamal,' he said. Then, apparently taking pity on her, 'Perhaps, if I show you a photograph of my father, you will understand.'

Family photographs? Her heart skipped a beat... 'I should like to understand.'

He summoned the *farraish* who was sitting cross-legged in the hallway waiting to take away the tray when they were finished, gave him an order. It seemed for ever before he returned, not with a photograph, as she'd expected, not even a portrait, but with a small piece of coloured paper, folded in two. He offered it to Han, who indicated that he should give it to Lucy.

He offered it with both hands, bowing low, taking care not to look directly at her, before backing out of the room.

'It's a Ramal Hamrah bank note,' she said, confused. 'A hundred riyals.'

Han said nothing. Obviously she'd missed something. She turned it over and that was when she saw the engraving of the Emir.

'Oh,' she said, finally remembering where she'd seen the name before—on the website when she had been researching Ramal Hamrah. 'I rather wish I hadn't asked that question. Why didn't you tell me straight away?'

'Because it was not important. I've only told you now because you pressed the matter and I wished to reassure you. Zahir was only able to learn your name so easily because he was asking for me. No one else will find you.'

'No one else is looking,' she said. 'I'm sorry, Han, but Steve isn't about to turn up and take me off your hands.'

For a moment she thought he might question her about that. About Steve.

'In that case it is even more important to assure you that you are safe here. You will be cared for. As soon as you are ready, Zahir will take you to your embassy so that you can arrange for new papers and, when you are fit, able to manage on your own, he will make whatever arrangements for your return home or, if you wish, your continued stay.'

'Why? Why are you doing this?' She didn't wait for one of his enigmatic replies, waving it aside before he could tell her that it was traditional courtesy to a stranger in need. This was more than that. 'You could have sorted all that out at long distance, Han…' Her voice wobbled on his name. The man was the son of the Emir, local royalty, and she was talking to him as if he were someone she'd known all her life. 'You could have left it to Zahir. Or even handed me over to the embassy.'

'Yes,' he agreed, 'I could have done that.'

'So why did you bring me here? You did not have to take me in, look after me yourself.'

'Maybe,' he said, after a silence that seemed endless. 'Maybe I needed to do it.'

Lucy opened her mouth, then closed it again and not just because the question that had rushed to her lips—*Why?*—seemed insensitive, intrusive. As his forehead creased in a frown she sensed that his response had been in the nature of self-revelation and for once this desert lord—and her instincts, so lacking where Steve had been concerned, had not let her down this time—appeared almost vulnerable.

Instead of challenging him, she turned away to give him time to gather himself. Picking up the cake, she concentrated her entire attention on it.

Eventually he stood up and left the room and the breath she'd been holding left her body in a rush. Her hand was shaking as she let it drop to her lap.

'Ready?'

She looked up. Han had returned with a lightweight wheelchair.

'No,' she protested. 'I can walk.'

'It is too far. We will take your crutches and once we have reached the summer house you can explore the garden, if you wish.'

'Are you sure?' she asked, feeling horribly guilty, and not

just because she'd lied about wanting to sit in the garden, although actually, now the possibility was offered, she couldn't think of anything she'd like more. But she didn't believe he'd brought a wheelchair from the hospital for her convenience; this was a state-of-the-art machine and clearly it had been used by his wife when she'd become too sick to walk.

She knew that everything he was doing for her must be bringing back dreadful memories, but she couldn't say that.

'If you're sure,' she said feebly. 'I don't want to disrupt your work.'

'The west has waited four centuries to read the beauty of Abu Jafr's words—another hour or two will make no difference.'

To protest further would embarrass them both and she surrendered, accepting a hand so that she could move from the couch to the chair, sweeping her hair to one side as she sat down.

'I don't suppose Zahir will think to buy hairpins, will he?' she asked. 'I usually wear it tied back. Did the hospital give you my things? There should be a large clip amongst them.'

Han knew there was not, but even if he hadn't looked through her pitifully few belongings he would still have known. When he'd found her, Lucy's hair had been tumbled loose about her like a shawl.

'There was nothing salvageable.'

'Well, that's it,' she said, with the air of someone who had made an irrevocable decision. 'I'm going to get it cut the minute I get home. Really short.'

'But why?' he asked. He could understand why a child might cut off hated plaits, but for a grown woman to deprive herself of such glory seemed perverse.

'It gets in the way. It's a nuisance. I meant to have it cut right after my grandmother's funeral, in one of those flirty little bobs,' she said, flicking at it. She'd wanted to do it before

the funeral, to shock all those miserable old biddies who'd
helped make her life a misery until she'd been old enough to
refuse to do more than deliver her grandmother to the church
door and collect her after the service.

'Your grandmother could not have stopped you from doing
what you wanted with it these last ten years, surely?'

'No. She could not have stopped me; in fact, she expected
me to cut it.' Just as she'd expected to be abandoned, to have
revisited on her all the misery she'd dished out over the years.
'Was waiting for it. Instead, once I had control of the housekeeping money, I bought good shampoo, conditioner, a soft-
toothed comb. Wore it loose.'

'To torment her?'

'I told you I was not good.'

'So you did.' He lifted a handful of her hair and let it fall
slowly before her eyes in a shimmer of palest gold. 'I hope
you'll forgive me if I suggest that you did it a little for yourself
too.'

Her lips parted on a protest. He didn't know what he was
talking about.

The words didn't come.

'I will find some pins for you,' he said, tugging on the
leather cord tying his own hair back, looping it around hers
in a bow to keep it from falling over her face. 'In the meantime, perhaps this will help.'

Neither of them said a word as they descended in the small,
ornate lift that took them to the ground floor, or as he wheeled
her through blue-tiled cloistered arches and out into the
dappled shade of the willows and Judas trees that overhung the
sparkling rill of water. But as the warmth wrapped itself around
them like a comfort blanket, Lucy sighed with pleasure.

'You're right, Han,' she said, glancing up at him. 'In comparison with this, England does seem cold and uninviting. Did you spend much time there?'

'School, university,' he said. 'Do not misunderstand me. Your country is a place of great beauty and I loved it. But the rain...'

'I know, but I'm afraid all that greenery comes at a price.'

'At first it was a novelty,' he said, encouraged by her laughter. 'I ran outside just to feel it on my face.'

'I'll bet you soon got over that.'

He parked her in the shade of an extensive rose-covered summer house set beside a large informal pool and placed a small leather-bound book on the table beside her.

She picked it up, opened it.

'Some of the translated poems of the Persian poet, Hafiz,' he said. 'He uses the imagery of the garden to express love in all its forms.'

'I can't think of anything more perfect to read in such a place.' She glanced up from the page. 'You know you don't have to stay, Han.'

No. He did not have to stay, but for once in his life he was in no hurry to return to his study. To sit beside Lucy while she read the poems of Hafiz, share lunch with her, was a far more appealing prospect.

'I have your book, the garden,' she said. 'I've disturbed you enough. Please don't let me keep you from your work.'

She did more than disturb him. She stirred him.

Injured, unhappy, she still brought with her a breath of something rare, something forgotten. It was anger that had brought her flying to Ramal Hamrah on the heels of her husband, passion that had driven her to steal a vehicle, risk everything to chase him across the desert.

He almost thought that if he held her, touched his mouth

to hers, took in the breath as it left her body, he would feel it too, would begin to breathe again, feel again.

'Go,' she said, laughing, opening the book, glancing at the pages as she sought some word, some phrase to catch her eye. 'I promise I won't do anything stupid, like falling in the water.'

It was her laughter, the echo of other, infinitely precious days, that brought him to his senses. This was where he'd sat with Noor, reading to her as the child she loved more than him sucked the life out of her, knowing that with every breath she was slipping away from him, knowing that no amount of money, power, could save her...

'With that guarantee, I will leave you in peace,' he said abruptly.

Lucy waited until he was out of sight before she lifted her head from the book. She couldn't believe how hard it had been to send him away. How the presence of a man she barely knew could make her feel so precious, so special.

But, no matter what Steve had done, how he had betrayed her, she was not free to feel this way. Even so, she could not stop herself from looking back along the path he'd taken to the pavilion. The air was filled with the scents of herbs where he'd brushed past them as they spilled over on to the warm stones.

A dragonfly hovered, darted over the water, and still she looked, half expecting him to return.

Instead, after a while, a young servant came down the path, bringing jugs of water and juice. Her crutches too, in case she wanted to explore. He plugged in a telephone and set it beside her. Finally, he offered her a note written on thick cream paper.

The hand was bold, strong, the words brief.

Lucy, if you need to make calls home, please just lift the receiver and press 0 and you will have a line—the in-

ternational code for the United Kingdom is 44. Leave
out the first 0 in the number. If you need anything else,
just press 1. Han.

She sighed.

She really should call the estate agent she'd instructed to
sell the house. Tell them to put it back on the market.

It had been her intention to use the money to buy something small, modern, with central heating and hot water
whenever she wanted it.

She should have done it before she'd left on this wild goose
chase, but she'd still been fooling herself that it was all some
kind of mix-up. Some mistake.

Then she'd walked into the office of Bouheira Tours and
had come face to face with reality.

There had been no mistake. No point in putting off the inevitable. The money would be needed to pay off the debts
Steve had run up in her name and the sooner the better.

She should call her next door neighbour too. She had a key;
the estate agents would need that.

And the insurance company to make a claim for medical
expenses—there must have been medical expenses—and for
her luggage.

And the bank. She'd assured them she was sorting everything out. They wouldn't be patient.

Han sat at his desk, the translation he'd been working on
ignored. For a while he'd been in danger of forgetting the
torment of the days he'd spent with Noor, knowing that there
was nothing he could do, seeing the fear grow behind her
brave smile.

To even smile at another woman was a betrayal of her

courage. To hold Lucy, the way he'd held Noor, as he'd helped her walk to the shower, to wash and comb her hair, to feel the heat of her body through the finest silk, her curves yield to his hands, to respond to her closeness as a man, enclosed so intimately with a woman, must always respond.

He did not understand why he felt this way. There was nothing to attract him. Her face was bruised, her eyes half closed, her lips puffy and cracked...

Yet, even now, he was waiting for the phone to ring, longing for the phone to ring, wanting her to need him so that he could go to her.

Disgusted with himself, he abandoned his translation, deliberately walked away from his desk, determined to visit the stables, the mews. His animals were well looked after, but he should still have seen for himself that his horse had suffered no ill effects from the headlong rush down the *jebel* as he'd ridden to Lucy Forrester's aid. He should spend time with his hawks.

He had scarcely left the pavilion before the sound of laughter reached him, brought him to a halt. Who was she talking to? Who had she called? Was it the neglectful husband who brought such joy to her?

He couldn't get the picture out of his mind of the reckless way she'd been driving the 4x4, racing across the desert. Had she been flying to Steve Mason, or running away from him?

It shouldn't matter. She belonged to another man.

Then he heard the laughter again and, unable to help himself, he moved closer, standing in the deep shade of a gnarled and ancient cypress tree watching as, completely absorbed in each other, Lucy Forrester and the child he had never been able to bring himself to touch, hold, acknowledge, played the simplest of games together.

'…chin,' Lucy said, touching her chin, then taking Ameerah's hand and holding it there.

'Chin,' Ameerah repeated, then touched her own face, said the word in Arabic, before taking Lucy's hand to her own face and waiting for her to repeat it.

They moved on. Hair, hand, elbow—first in English, then in Arabic.

Ameerah made Lucy say 'elbow' over and over, repeating it herself with a long roll on the 'l'. There was much laughter.

It was a scene of such innocence, such simple joy, that he had to reach out and grasp one of the twisted trunks of the tree as raw pain threatened to overwhelm him.

CHAPTER SIX

LUCY wasn't sure when she first became aware of Hanif, of a deeper shadow beneath the ancient cypress tree. She sensed him before she saw him. Felt the air shimmer with some powerful emotion that swept over her, raising the hairs on the back of her neck.

It took every ounce of effort not to look up, stop herself from turning to include him in their game, keep her attention totally focused on Ameerah.

His little girl had sought her out, bored with her own company, with a nurse who could not keep up, and it should have been the most natural thing in the world for Hanif to join them, pick up the child, hug her, tease her a little.

She had never had that for herself, but had seen it outside school, had seen other children scooped up, cuddled, their pictures admired by loving parents. She'd been the one alone, then, outside; she knew how it felt and she wanted to turn to him, stretch out a hand, say, Come and play. But he wasn't a child. He had chosen to cut himself off from this scrap of a girl who, with her dark hair and eyes, shining smile, represented everything that he had lost.

It wasn't just grief that kept him here in Rawdah al-'Arusah, shut away from life. It was anger too. And perhaps more than a little guilt that, unable to save her mother, he could not find a place in his heart for the child for whom she'd sacrificed herself.

Despite the fact that this was his home, it was his dark and solitary figure which was standing on the outside, looking in, unable to make that first step, breach the barriers.

Hanif had implied that the child had been sent as some kind of chaperon, but it occurred to her that his desperate mother may have hoped that a woman, someone the lively and curious Ameerah would be drawn to, might, in some way, be the catalyst who would draw them together.

It would be small enough repayment for all he'd done for her, but Hanif al-Khatib was a complex and sophisticated man. He would see right through an invitation to Come and play.

'Are you hungry?' she asked Ameerah. '*Aakul?*' She caught the little girl to her, rubbed her tummy. 'What would you like to eat? Chicken? Hummus? Some of that good goat's cheese?'

The child giggled, wriggled around in her arms to face her, not to pull away.

'You know, what we really need is some paper and pencils,' Lucy said. 'Then you could draw me a picture of what you'd like.'

Han knew she'd seen him.

There had been no change in her manner and yet he sensed an awareness in her; Ameerah was no longer the sole focus of her attention. She was no longer entirely lost in the game.

And having been seen, he could not just walk away. He should have stuck to his original plan, gone to the stables; now he had no choice but to join them.

He crossed to the summer house, ready to send Ameerah back to her nurse, insist that Lucy return to her room to rest. But Fathia, the old woman who had once been his own nurse and as dear to him as his mother, was there too, dozing on a sofa, while Lucy occupied the child.

He didn't know what his mother had been thinking of, sending her out to al-'Arusah. She had long since retired and should be sitting in the shade of her own garden, being cared for by her own family, not chasing around after a three-year-old. Ameerah needed a young nanny, someone with the energy to keep up with her.

Someone to amuse her, play with her, as Lucy had been doing. But to say so would give his mother the opportunity to tell him it was time he did something about it.

Since Fathia was here, he had no option but to pick up the phone and, doing his best to ignore the way Ameerah shrank nervously back against Lucy, hiding herself in the folds of her robe, trying to make herself as inconspicuous as possible, he gave orders to the kitchen to send food out for the three of them.

'Lunch will be brought out here for you,' he said, turning to Lucy. Then, obliquely, 'Don't tire yourself.'

'I'm fine.' As he moved to leave, she said, 'Han? Won't you stay and join us?'

'No.' The sound of her laughter had drawn him here and if she'd been alone he would have been tempted. More than tempted. Ameerah's presence had worked a charm, serving to remind him of reality, but, aware that he had been abrupt, he gave the slightest of bows and said, 'I regret that I have things to see to in the stables.'

From the depths of the sofa Fathia snorted, her voice following him as he walked away. 'Going by the scenic route, were you?' she said, taking the kind of liberties permitted an old woman who'd held him as a helpless baby.

Since she spoke in Arabic, Lucy did not understand what she said or, worse, what she'd implied, while he took the only course open to him and resorted to diplomatic deafness. But, before he went to the stables, he returned to his study. Searching through a cupboard for coloured pencils, he found a box of pastels. He brushed the dust from the lid, opened it. They were old, worn from use. They had been given to him by his father one summer when he'd had to stay in the capital on affairs of state and couldn't come with them to al-'Arusah. He'd used them, had drawn pictures to send his father every day. Had kept and treasured them.

It was a small victory. Hanif had been listening. He hadn't stayed, but he had responded to his daughter's needs. They ate, played the finger games she'd learned when helping at summer play camps, used the paper and pastels he'd sent with a servant to draw pictures, while Fathia watched contentedly from the sofa.

But as the sun came round, grew too hot for comfort, Fathia summoned Ameerah, explaining, 'It is time for her to sleep. You, too, *assayyidah*. You must go inside now, rest until the evening.'

Lucy was flagging in the heat and she made no protest when Fathia insisted on wheeling her inside, settling her comfortably on the day bed, before dragging a reluctant Ameerah away for her afternoon nap.

'I'll see you later, sweetheart,' she said. *'Bashufak bahdain.'*

Ameerah broke away from Fathia to thrust one of the pictures she'd drawn into Lucy's hand, scampering shyly away before she could look at it.

It was a simple enough picture, the kind that any three-year-old might draw. Three stick people. A tall daddy with a straight mouth, a smaller smiling mummy and a little girl with a smile that reached from ear to ear.

As Lucy held it, certain for a moment that her heart would

break for the child, she heard someone coming and she quickly folded the drawing and tucked it inside the book of poems, out of sight. Then, heart beating so fast that she was sure he must hear, she waited. But it wasn't Hanif. It was a young servant bringing her fresh water, a small bowl of dates. He bowed himself out and, after a moment, when her heart had returned to something like its normal pace, she sank back against the pillow and closed her eyes.

When she woke the sun was low. She yawned, stretched, sat up and saw that every surface of the room appeared to be covered by pastel-coloured boxes with famous names upon them. The kind of glossy carriers that only came from the most expensive stores.

Hanif had been there while she'd slept, she realized, a Santa in Sheikh's clothing.

Excited by the prospect of new clothes, she picked up the crutches, got to her feet and began to explore the contents. Silk underwear, designer label shirts, beautifully cut trousers, as well as more traditional clothes. There was a *shalwar kameez,* embroidered kaftans and wide silk chiffon scarves. More shoes than she could wear in a year, exquisite handbags. She touched one that had a Chanel logo on the fastening and knew without having to be told that this was the real thing.

And it wasn't just clothes.

Whoever had been given the task of replacing her belongings had taken the job seriously. There was every kind of personal toiletry, make-up, a hairbrush, pins, combs to keep her hair in place.

She subsided on to the satin love seat, holding a wrought silver pin against her breast. Had he remembered? Called someone, asked them to be sure and bring something to hold her hair in place?

She looked about her in desperation. It was all so beautiful. So expensive.

She'd told him that she would pay for the clothes she needed, but she should have explained that her travel insurance would only cover the most basic of chain store buys. She wouldn't be able to pay for these if she worked for the rest of her life.

She had to explain. Tell him. Now. And she set the silver pin on the table, picked up her crutches and made her slow, careful way along the wide hallway to his study.

Hanif was sitting with his back to the open door, his gaze fixed on some distant horizon far beyond the darkening skyline. She hesitated in the doorway, unwilling to disturb his reverie.

'Will I never persuade you to ring the bell, Lucy Forrester?' he asked, without turning around.

'Not in a thousand years,' she assured him. 'I'm not an invalid. Besides, I need the exercise.'

'Always an answer.'

'That's what you get when you ask a question,' she pointed out.

He spun around in his chair. 'What is it? What do you want from me?'

To be back in her room, she thought, taking a step back, stumbling awkwardly.

'No...' The word escaped him as if, against his better judgement, he wanted her to stay and, before she could regain her balance, he was beside her, helping her towards a deep sofa. 'Please. Tell me what I can do for you.'

She regarded the sofa with misgiving. He was not going to be happy with her and at least while she was on her feet she could walk away. Sunk into the depths of those cushions, she would be trapped. But he waited, hand at her arm, until she lowered herself carefully on to the edge of the seat.

'Can I offer you something? Tea? Coffee?'

She shook her head. 'I just wanted to talk to you about the clothes you've bought me. They're going to have to go b-back…' she began, but his forbidding expression brought her stuttering to a halt.

'You are unhappy with them?'

'Unhappy?' She realized he thought she did not like the beautiful things he'd had sent from Rumaillah. 'No! They're lovely, but—'

'They do not fit?' He made a dismissive gesture. 'That is not a problem. They can be changed.'

'No!'

His eyes narrowed, but she refused to be intimidated. 'Just listen to me, will you? I don't know if they fit or not. There's no point in trying them on.' Now he was silent. 'I can't afford such expensive clothes.'

'The cost is immaterial,' he said evenly. 'I do not expect you to pay for them.'

She hadn't for one moment thought that he did. On reflection, even he must have realized that a basic travel policy wouldn't cover designer clothes. But that wasn't the point.

'I can't accept them as a gift.'

'I understand,' he said. 'Of course it would not be appropriate for a married woman to accept clothes from another man. I will send a full account to your husband.'

'Oh, right. I see. Well, take my advice, Han. Don't accept a cheque.'

She struggled to stand, but before she could organize her crutches to make her getaway, Hanif had taken them from her, put them out of reach. Was beside her.

'Why did you marry this man, Lucy?'

She did not move, did not answer. What could she say? That she had been a fool? That she'd craved love and he'd been there when she'd been adrift, alone. A life raft.

A leaky, rotten life raft...

She closed eyes that, without warning, began to sting and, unable to speak, simply shook her head.

'It is clear from everything you say that he has not shown you the respect, the honour, that you deserve,' he said more gently and somehow he was sitting beside her and she had a tissue in her hand. 'Why did you marry him?'

But she refused to break down and cry, instead managing a careless shrug. 'Because he made it so easy.'

'Easy?'

How could she make him understand?

'Gran was so afraid that I'd be like my mother, go off the rails. Maybe I should have fought harder, but by the time I was old enough for meaningful rebellion I'd worked out that my best way of escape would be university.' She looked up at him, hoping that he would understand. She hadn't wimped out. Her major asset had been her brains and she'd used them. 'Then she had the stroke and there was no escape.'

'When she died, you were alone?'

'Alone, completely lost. And suddenly Steve was there, a prop, taking away the need to think. It was just so easy.'

He frowned. 'You knew him?'

She nodded. 'His family lived around the corner from us. Steve was in the same year as me in school.'

'You had been in love with him since then?'

'In love?' She shrugged. 'There wasn't a girl in the school who wasn't a little in love with Steve Mason. He stood head and shoulders above everyone, you know?' She turned to him, unsure whether he would understand. 'He was a straight A student, great at sports, always wore the latest must-have clothes. He even had a motorbike.'

'Deadly,' he agreed, with the faintest of smiles, and she knew that he was speaking from personal experience. Of course even the oldest, grandest of British public schools took girls at sixth form level these days and she had no doubt that, in the hothouse atmosphere of a boarding school, Hanif would have been a danger to the heart of any girl.

But she raised her eyebrows and somewhat mischievously said, 'The motorbike?'

'What else?' he replied. 'Dangerous things.'

'I'll bet you had one.'

'My father forbade it,' he said. Then, when she lifted her brows a fraction higher, 'But yes, you are right. I had a motorbike. So, where did Steve Mason take you on this dangerous machine?'

'Me?'

'I assumed that there must have been a long-standing arrangement between you. Something of which your grandmother would not have approved.'

'She'd have locked me up in the cellar rather than let me out with Steve Mason,' she assured him. 'With or without the motorbike. But the situation never arose. He never even knew I existed back then.'

'I find that hard to believe.'

'You wouldn't, not if you'd seen me. I wore the most unattractive charity shop clothes my grandmother could find, my hair scragged back in a plait. Not a scrap of make-up.'

'A woman does not need make-up to be beautiful. It is in the bones, in the character, in the heart.'

'You might think that. I might like to believe that. But

when you're in the sixth form and the object of desire is an eighteen-year-old boy with a soul as deep as an August puddle, you need make-up. The works. Believe me. Not even the cool girls wanted to be seen with me.'

'Then I do not understand. If you had not been kept apart by your grandmother, how did you meet, marry, so quickly after her death? It is a matter of months, you said.'

'I think the official term is "swept off your feet".'

Actually, it hadn't been so much 'swept' as gently lifted on a tide of yearning to belong. To be like other women. To come in from the cold.

'I hadn't seen him for years, not since I left school. He went off to university, never came home to live after that. Then, when Gran died, I found out that she'd left me the house.' She glanced at him, but it was impossible to tell what he was thinking. 'She'd always told me that she was going to leave it to her church, but at the last minute she relented, or perhaps she was afraid my mother would turn up and challenge the will, demand what was rightfully hers.'

'And then this man appeared, magically, on your doorstep. Prince Charming to your Cinderella.'

'That's almost scary.'

'What is?'

'The Cinderella thing. I was wearing an apron, my hair tied up in a scarf, sweeping the path...'

'Oh.'

'He stopped, looked up at the For Sale sign, then at me, then he said, "Lucy Forrester..."' She gave a little shrug. 'I couldn't believe he remembered my name.'

Han forced himself to get up, walk away, using the excuse of pouring a glass of water for her.

From the outside it was so easy to see what had happened.

She had been left property and, alone, with no one to advise her, she had been a gift for a man who had no doubt been using women since he'd been a youth.

Add to that the disappearance of the burned out 4x4, the denial that she'd ever been to the Bouheira Tours office, and it occurred to him that her disappearance might suit her husband extremely well. That she might, in fact, be in very real danger.

There was no way that he could allow Lucy to leave his protection until he'd talked to the man, made it plain that Lucy was under his personal protection. That if anything bad happened to her he would find himself removed from society—not comfortably ensconced in a well-lit cell in a modern prison, but dropped in the darkest oubliette in one of those long-forgotten mountain-top forts that would never make any list of tourist attractions.

He forced his mouth into a smile before turning to Lucy, handing her the glass. 'So, there you were,' he said, 'Prince Charming himself ready to sweep you away on his Harley. What happened next?'

'Nothing dramatic. He said he'd heard about my grand-mother. How sorry he was. How tough it was that I'd missed out on university…'

She lifted her hand in an unconscious gesture that said more than the words she couldn't manage about how hard that must have been for her.

She sipped the water, put down the glass and said, 'I asked him, as you do, what he was doing now. He told me that he'd got a job with an offshore bank here in Ramal Hamrah, but had immediately seen the potential for tourism, not just the standard dune-surfing operations that were opening up in other states, but for longer trips out into the desert to oasis camps, to archaeological sites. As soon as he'd managed to scrape together the capital, he set up Bouheira Tours.'

'Zahir is always telling me of the possibilities,' Han said. Then, 'What was he doing looking at houses in the UK if he was so busy building up his business?'

'Property prices were rocketing and he thought he ought to get a foothold in the market. Somewhere he could let while he was away. He wanted it near to his mother so that she could keep an eye on it for him.'

'Did he make an offer? For the house?'

'Well, no. He'd just been looking around the neighbour-hood to see what was available. As soon as he said it was a buy-to-let I knew my house was wrong for him. It needs a lot of work and he would want somewhere modern, ready to go. He didn't even come in, but as he turned to go he stopped and asked me if I'd have dinner with him that evening.' She smiled. 'And no, he wasn't riding a Harley, he was driving his mother's old Ford. Far from sweeping me off my feet, Han, it was pretty clear that everyone he knew had moved on and I was the only person saving him from a night in front of the television with his mother.'

'Good dinner?'

'I can't remember. We talked about Ramal Hamrah, mostly. He made it sound magical. Encouraged me to come and visit once I'd sold the house. I didn't actually believe he meant it.'

'Why not?'

'It's just the sort of thing people say, isn't it? I just said it sounded lovely and I'd think about it and then he took me home, thanked me for a lovely evening and drove away. I didn't expect to see him again.'

'How long before he was back?'

'I was on my way upstairs to bed when he phoned, asked

me if I'd spend the next day looking at houses with him.' She looked down at her hands as if embarrassed by her gullibility. 'He made it all so easy,' she said again. 'I'd never been on a date, didn't know what a man would expect, but Steve never did anything to make me feel uncomfortable. He was just so different from what I'd expected. From the way he'd been at school.' She looked at him, pulled a face. 'Still as gorgeous, still the kind of man who turned heads in the street, but Prince Charming himself couldn't have been more circumspect.'

'Never trust a man...' he began, then stopped.

'Never trust a man who doesn't want to get into your knickers?' she said, completing the sentence for him and doing it with a smile, more because of his reluctance to embarrass her, than because she found it amusing. 'Because if he doesn't want sex, you have to ask yourself what he does want.'

'I'm sorry. I shouldn't have implied—'

'It's okay, Han. Life is a steep learning curve and I started later than most, but I'm getting there.'

'How long did he wait before he asked you to marry him?'

She really didn't want to talk about it any more, but Han had been patient. He had a right to know what he'd got himself into.

'Not long. He said...'

No. She really, really didn't want to think about the soft, sweet lies Steve had told her and waved her hand as if pushing the words away.

Han caught it and, before she knew how it had happened, her face was in his shoulder, her cheek against the smooth cloth of his robe.

'I shouldn't have asked,' he said. 'It doesn't matter.'

'He was so sweet.' She lifted her head, looked up at him. 'He said I should take the house off the market, that when he

came back from Ramal Hamrah we'd do it up together so that
I could sell it for what it was really worth.'

'A friend in need.'

'For the first time in my life I thought someone actually
cared about me,' she admitted. 'But there was a problem. I had
no training, no job, no money. It had taken every bit of Gran's
old-age pension and my carer's allowance to keep us alive and
now she was dead I had no income of any kind.'

She didn't bother to mention the much larger private pension
that her grandfather had provided, that could have made their life
so much easier. She hadn't known about that until afterwards,
when she had to sort out her grandmother's papers, and had discovered that it had been paid direct to the church each month.

'The house was my only asset. I was nearly twenty-eight
years old and had never worked; the only jobs open to me paid
the minimum wage. There was no way I could afford even the
most basic running costs. That's when Steve said we should
get married right away. So that he could take care of me.'

'That's when he swept you off your feet.'

'He brought all these forms from banks, credit card companies, changing the address on them to mine, adding my
name to his accounts, not even waiting until we were married.'

She couldn't look at him, but he cradled her cheek and
gently turned her face so that she had no choice.

'He borrowed money on them?'

'Oh, yes…' her laughter was mirthless '…and don't those
banks love to lend money?'

'And the cards, of course, were not his, but new ones he'd
applied for in your name.'

'You see? You got it straight away. Why was I so dumb?'

'Because it never occurred to you that he would do
anything so wicked.'

'Pretty naïve, in retrospect. I mean this was Steve Mason. Why would he look at me twice?'

'I've had a new mirror fitted in the bathroom, Lucy. Maybe you should take a look in it.'

'Oh, *please.*' Then, because she didn't want him to think she was totally stupid, she said, 'I did actually read all the forms he brought me to sign. Even the small print. They were all what he said they were. I guess it must have been the ones underneath, the ones he said were copies and just lifted the top copy for me to sign in duplicate, that he sent to the banks.'

'I imagine that if he'd worked in a bank he must have known all the ways to work a fraud. Is that it?'

She wished.

'He made me a partner in Bouheira Tours as a wedding present. I imagine the papers that I signed, in quadruplicate, are fakes. At least some of them. Somewhere in amongst them was the big one. The guarantee for a loan against the house.'

'I'm not surprised you were in such a breakneck speed to catch up with him.'

'Yes,' she said. Then, not quite meeting his eyes, 'I think it's just as well I rolled the 4x4. At least this way I'm not languishing in a Ramal Hamrah jail on a charge of grievous bodily harm or worse.'

'You would not have hurt him,' Han began, but hesitated and she knew he was wondering if Steve would have hurt her. 'But you might easily have killed yourself.'

'I know. What I did was stupid. I just wanted...' She stopped. 'It doesn't matter. All I have to do is sell the house, pay my debts and learn my lesson.'

'All?'

'Yes, Han. That's all. Since I never expected to inherit it, I'm exactly where I expected to be when my grandmother died. The pity of it is that she changed her mind about leaving the house to the church. That way she'd have saved everyone a great deal of trouble.'

CHAPTER SEVEN

HAN could not believe Lucy was going to allow this man to get away with stealing from her.

She was shivering just from the memory and he held her closer, wanting to warm her with his own heat. He'd told Zahir that having saved her life he was responsible for her but they both knew that he could have done everything that needed to be done from a distance.

It went deeper than duty, deeper than the care of a stranger in need. From the moment he'd set eyes on her, it had always been more personal than that.

He'd saved her life and now he wanted to save…her life.

'You really need to take legal advice before you do anything, Lucy,' he said, keeping it as businesslike as it could be with his arms around her.

'Good money after bad,' she said. 'There's nothing anyone can do.'

'There is always something.' But he was speaking to himself rather than her.

'I talked to the card companies, explained what had happened. They produced the forms I'd signed and what could I say? They had paid up in good faith. They didn't do anything wrong, Han. It was my responsibility to read what I was signing.'

'You trusted him. He took advantage of that. And what about the mortgage? You knew nothing about that. He tricked you into signing the papers. I'm no lawyer, but that sounds like a clear case of fraud to me.'

'They explained it very clearly. It's my house and he is…'

'Your husband,' he said, filling the gap when she faltered. He had to remind himself of that. Keep reminding himself.

'That was why he married me.' She shuddered.

'You make your mistakes, Han, and you have to pay for them.'

He knew that was true. And that some debts could not be paid with money…

As if suddenly aware just how close they were, how tightly he was holding her, Lucy eased herself away from him, out of his arms.

'I'm sorry,' she said carefully. 'I didn't intend to burden you with my problems.' Her smile did a good job of masking everything she must be feeling—the rage, utter helplessness in the face of such treachery. 'You shouldn't have been so stubborn about sending back the clothes. If you'd agreed with me, you wouldn't have been forced to listen to me wittering on like this.'

It was harder than it should have been to let her go, but then he shouldn't have been holding her in the first place.

'I'll remember for next time,' he assured her. He'd remember that disregarding her wishes brought her close, opened her up. Encouraged her to talk.

'Then you will send them back?'

'If you insist,' he said, standing up, a hand ready to help her to her feet if she needed it, but she used the arm of the sofa to lever herself up. 'I must, of course, do as you ask.'

'Thank you.'

He handed her the crutches, let her reach the door before he said, 'There is just one small problem.'

She didn't turn around, didn't ask him what the small problem was, but waited for him to tell her; he could tell from the way she kept her eyes facing forward, lifted her a head a little, that she knew she wasn't going to like it, whatever it was.

She was probably right, but there was no way in this world that he was going to ask Zahir's sister, or his own for that matter, to return the clothes they'd bought and replace them with chain store versions.

'If I return these clothes what are you going to wear?'

That got her.

'I...' She glanced back over her shoulder and, as her eyes met his, she thought better of whatever she'd been about to say. 'If you could replace them with something more in line with my financial situation, I would be most grateful. Just a few things to keep me going until I can get home.'

Back to the charity shops, no doubt.

'Of course. I understand. That will mean a delay, of course. I will have to find someone who is prepared to undertake such a task. While Zahir's sister was happy to spend time choosing clothes for you from her favourite designers, she would, I think, baulk at visiting the *souk*.'

'I'm not totally helpless,' she said. 'Take me to Rumaillah and I'll do it myself.'

'Of course. Whatever you wish.' He waited until he saw the tension drain from her shoulders, then said, 'But first you will need something to wear.' He let his gaze travel the length of her body before meeting her gaze head on. 'Unless, of course, it is your intention to cause a riot in the streets?'

Her mouth opened, but nothing emerged and after a moment or two she closed it again.

'It will mean waiting another day, maybe two,' he continued, since she appeared to have lost the power of speech, or perhaps had chosen discretion over candour. 'And of course another trip for the helicopter. Will your insurance company pay for that, do you think? Will you ask them?' Not waiting for her to reply—the question was outrageous, unworthy—he went on, 'While we are waiting, you're going to need to borrow some basics to tide you over.'

Her eyes remained fixed on his, defiant to the last, but her shoulders had slumped in defeat and it was difficult to keep up the act. But if that was what it took to make her accept the clothes, that was what he would have to do.

'You will find a walk-in closet off your room,' he continued, with a dismissive gesture that under normal circumstances came as naturally to him as breathing. These were not normal circumstances and he had to force himself to treat the matter as if it was of no consequence. 'Noor was not as tall as you, nor as slender, but I'm sure you'll find something you can wear. Take what you need.'

'You don't mean that.' She gave up on looking over her shoulder and, carefully balancing herself on her crutches, she turned around so that she was confronting him head on. 'You're just making a point, aren't you?'

Of course he was. He knew she would not wear Noor's clothes, not because she had a problem with used clothes—she'd already told him that she'd been dressed in charity shop donations all her life—but because she believed it would distress him.

He wasn't about to disabuse her of that idea.

'And if I am,' he replied, 'are you getting it?'

'The point being,' she said slowly, 'that you have gone out of your way to provide me with everything I need. That

I'm being a pain in the backside. That I should quit while I'm ahead.'

'You appear to have mastered the essentials.' Then, because he could not resist it, 'Of course I would not have been so un-gallant as to comment on your backside, no matter how pain-ful.'

'I believe the colloquialism refers to your backside rather than mine,' she said, scowling, he suspected, to prevent herself from laughing.

'I stand corrected. English is such a complex language; I fear the finer points occasionally escape me.'

That did it. 'You are so full of it, Han,' she said, finally breaking down and letting a bubble of laughter escape. 'I don't appear to have much choice, do I?'

'There is always a choice, Lucy, but believe me when I tell you that the simple pleasure you gave two young women today,' he said, magnanimous in victory, 'and the goodwill I have accrued by providing my sister with enough speculative gossip to keep the females in my family entertained for weeks, far outweighs the small cost involved.'

'Gossip? You mean…' She clearly did not want to voice what she thought he meant and instead said, '*Your* sister? I thought it was Zahir's sister who had drawn the short straw. Or would that be the long one?'

'For the pleasure of spending money without having to account for it to their husbands? What do you think?'

'I think I'd better say thank you and shut up before you award me some Ramal Hamrah decoration for services to entertainment.'

Beaten, struggling between laughter and rage, Lucy retreated to her sitting room and sat amongst the piles of bags and boxes, touching fabrics she'd only thought of wearing in her wildest teenage dreams. Wallowing guiltily in the luxury of it all, she discovered that it was tears that threatened to overwhelm her as she touched the softest silk to her cheek.

'Lucy…'

Ameerah's voice jerked her back to the present. The child was standing in the doorway, her expression anxious.

'Hello, sweetheart,' she said, sniffing back the threatening tears, smiling as she reached out a hand, inviting her to come and play. 'Do you want to help me unpack?'

She needed no further encouragement and together they dived into the boxes, spreading clothes over every surface. They exclaimed over the colours, sprayed scent on each other, laughed, talked—the words didn't matter. Two females exclaiming over clothes were always going to be talking the same language.

'What shall I wear?' Lucy finally asked, her gestures, making the meaning clear. Then, 'What would *you* wear?'

Ameerah went straight for a raw silk *shalwar kameez* in a deep glowing red, holding the top up against her small body.

'Good choice!' she exclaimed, clapping. The outfit was stunning, sophisticated, exotic. She might be only three years old, but this little girl clearly knew what she wanted, what was due to her. 'Well, that's you sorted,' she said, helping the child into it, laughing as she paraded with all the haughty air of a catwalk model. Then she looked around a little desperately for something ordinary that she would feel at home in. Everything was so beautiful. So stylish.

Nothing was *her*.

But she had to wear something and, in the absence of anything as plain as a white cotton shirt, she chose the nearest alternative in amber silk, teaming it with a pair of beautifully cut black linen trousers that amongst the jewel-bright colours were positively understated.

Unfortunately, the legs of the trousers proved too narrow to accommodate the splint. Ameerah, who had not been impressed with the trousers, offered her a rich blue kaftan as an alternative.

The style was practical, but Lucy picked out one in silvery grey, with black embroidery around the hem, at the wrists, the neck. It was not exactly plain, but it was more in keeping with her Anglo-Saxon need to blend into the surroundings.

Ameerah pulled a face but accepted her decision and set about finding a scarf to go with it while Lucy confronted the piles of sexy underwear.

For a girl, woman, who'd never worn anything but plain white and practical, the underwear was a revelation, but since it quickly became clear that every outfit had been teamed with its own matching bra and pants, choice was not a problem. Grey silk it was.

Han was right. Those two women had really enjoyed themselves at his expense.

Lucy, anxious now to shower and get into some real clothes, sent Ameerah to show herself to Fathia, then braced herself to face her reflection in the bathroom mirror.

The bruising was shocking, it was true, but her eye was open now and the swelling was nowhere near as bad as she'd imagined.

She unfastened her hair and, for just a moment, held the thin leather cord that Han had used to tie it back, touched it to her cheek as she had the silk. Then, about to place it on top of the nightdress and robe that had once belonged to his wife, knowing that as soon as she left the room someone would come and clear them away, she tucked it into the pocket of the bathrobe.

She managed the shower more easily this time, even washed her hair without too much difficulty. She was recovering, she thought. Regaining her strength. Regaining her life. She was even getting about on her crutches without help. In a day or two she'd be able to leave Rawdah al-'Arusah, return to the real world.

And tried to feel a little happier about that.

She'd half expected to find Ameerah waiting for her when she emerged in her new bathrobe, her hair wrapped in a towel, but the sitting room was empty, although someone had folded the clothes, had brought them through to the bedroom and taken away all the empty packaging.

The toiletries had been neatly arranged on the dressing table, along with combs, brushes, hairpins. There was a hairdryer, too. Not a new one, though.

She didn't bother with make-up; there was, after all, nothing that could cover up the interesting colour effects. She just dried her hair, trying not to think about the way Han had done it for her. Then, rejecting the pull of the leather cord in her pocket, she pinned it at the nape with the intricate silver clip.

When she was done, she slipped her feet into a pair of grey ballet-style pumps made from butter-soft suede, picked up the long palest primrose scarf that Ameerah had selected for her and stepped out onto the balcony to cool herself in the breeze from the mountains.

Han saw Lucy long before she saw him.

Jamilla, his youngest sister, had called him from Rumaillah, wanting details of Lucy's colouring. Zahir, she'd said, had been no use whatever. On reflection, he wondered if that was true or whether Milly had made an excuse to find out if he'd noticed the colour of his guest's eyes.

Whatever her reason, he had to admit that she'd chosen well. The light grey silk, caught by the breeze, moulded itself to Lucy's figure. With a pale scarf draped loosely over her hair and floating over her shoulders to the ground, she looked more like a fairy tale princess from a tale woven by Scheherazade than some modern western woman with the troubles of the world on her shoulders.

Then, as if suddenly aware that she was not alone, she turned, saw him, smiled, and something deep inside him warmed and smiled back.

'You look stronger, Lucy Forrester.'

'I feel stronger. There's something about wearing night-clothes in the day that makes one feel like an invalid. Just getting dressed has made me feel better,' she said, and then she turned away quickly, but not before he saw that her cheeks burned.

'You must not do too much too quickly,' he said, and he burned too, thinking, as she must have, that she was dressed, as a wife or mistress would be, wrapped at his insistence, in clothes it pleased him to see her wear. Knew that every time the breeze caught the silk, brushed it against her skin, she would remember that.

For a woman to wear the clothes that a man had bought her was to feel his touch with every movement. For a man to hear the whisper of cloth as she walked, was to feel her response to him, the throb of her pulse as it intensified, the silky heat between her thighs as she waited for him to unwrap her.

It hadn't occurred to him that she would feel this. She had not been brought up to think in that way, not taught that her role was to please her husband. But neither was she like the western women he had met in his youth, at university, in the free and easy days before he'd buckled down to duty, accepted the bride his family had chosen for him. Spirited women who took life head-on, denied themselves nothing, knew everything, or thought they did.

He had enjoyed their company, had taken pleasure in their freedom, admired their directness. Lucy had something of their spirit in her character, but she had an innocence too, like a girl before she had been touched by a man. Knowing but unknowing. Afraid and yet trembling with eagerness.

And he was clearly losing his mind.

'I was wondering, Han, would it be acceptable for me to write notes to your sister, to Zahir's sister, to thank them for taking such trouble on my behalf today? I accept your assurance that they enjoyed themselves, but even so.'

'I know that Jamilla would be touched by the thought.'

'Thank you. And I'd like to see more of the garden before I leave,' she said, as the silence between them stretched to breaking point. 'If I may? Are there places where I should not go?'

'You are free to wander where you will, Lucy. No one will bother you.'

'I was thinking that I might be the one causing a disturbance. You said there is a hunting lodge. I'd hate to blunder into some men-only territory, make anyone uncomfortable.'

She had the courage to hunt down a fraudster in his own territory, yet she retained the air of a virgin, had all the instincts of a princess. She would grace the garden with her presence.

'You need not concern yourself,' he said.

His men, those who came to hunt, those who worked here, would melt away at her approach. She would never suspect they were there unless she needed help and, unless it was urgent, they would summon him to provide it.

She was under his protection and they would treat her with

the same respect as they would any woman in his family. The same respect they would show towards his wife.

About to offer to show her the hidden beauties of the garden, he instead inclined his head and said, 'The garden is yours, *sitti.*'

Sitti? It was a word Lucy was unfamiliar with and she wished she had her language CDs, her phrase book. Already her ear was becoming accustomed to the sounds and this would have been the perfect place to continue with her studies of the language.

Sitti. My lady…

Han stepped back within the safety of his study, crossed to his desk, hunted desperately amongst the drawers for the photograph of Noor that he had put away, unable to bear the love in her eyes.

He set it where it belonged, where he would see it every time he looked up. Touched her face with his fingers as he had done a thousand times before, as if he could somehow call her back, as he'd tried to hold her in this world when all she wanted to do was leave it.

'I did everything I could to keep her alive,' he said, aware that Lucy had followed him, was standing in the doorway. He didn't turn. Already she was filling the places in his home, in his head, that belonged to Noor.

If he turned from the photograph to look at Lucy, the image, already fading, would become fainter. Her voice, her laughter, dimmed to nothing more than a distant rustle in the memory.

'She wanted to come back here, spend some time with her baby. Die in peace,' he said, jabbing himself with the words. 'I couldn't let her go, wouldn't let her go, and to please me she spent the end of her days in the hospital, having the treatment that was too late to do anything but cause her pain.'

Lucy propped her crutches against his desk, took the photograph from him, looked at it for a while.

'She was very beautiful.'

'It was Noor who broke the mirror,' he said. 'In the bathroom. She threw a bottle of scent at her reflection, unable to bear what was happening to her. She thought she had become ugly.'

'How could she have believed herself ugly when she only had to see herself reflected in your eyes to know how you loved her?'

He frowned, looking at Lucy, not the photograph she was holding out to him.

'I've seen the way your eyes soften as you speak of her, Han. Appearances may alter, but love is constant.'

'Is it? If I'd loved her, I'd have let her die as she wished—at home, with her baby in her arms.' He'd never voiced his guilt before, had never said the words out loud. He'd kept them locked up inside him, afraid that if the pain of it escaped it would devour him. He didn't know why he was doing it now. Only that since Lucy's accident everything inside him felt shaken up, disturbed. Like a numb limb coming back to painful life. He looked at her now, as if it was her fault, and demanded, 'How can I forgive myself for that?'

'You're human, Han. You couldn't bear to lose her. She knew that.'

'Being human is an excuse?'

'It's why she broke the mirror. Her reflection was a constant reminder to her that she was never going to see her baby grow into a young woman, have children of her own. That she wasn't going to grow old with you in this garden.'

Lucy had followed him on pure instinct. Nothing in his expression, his voice, had indicated that she had said or done anything to offend him, yet the abruptness with which he'd left her was so at odds with his usual manner that she had barely been able to stop herself from reaching out to him, holding him beside her.

She'd left it a few moments, telling herself that she was wrong, giving herself time to think.

But it had been no good. Something had disturbed him. While self-preservation had suggested it would be wiser to take advantage of his invitation to make free with his garden and leave him to get over it, she had found she could not simply walk away.

She'd had the excuse of asking him for paper, a pen, to write her thank you letters while the moment was fresh, should she need it.

Too late she wished she had chosen the garden option, not because she didn't have the answer to his question, but because she did. From the outside, looking in, it was easy to see that he was angry with Noor, angry with Ameerah, and he hated himself for it.

Easy to tell him that he would not find self-forgiveness in a photograph, that he must look to the living, to his daughter, for that. To tell him that only when he'd forgiven her for living when Noor was dead, to find it in his heart to love her as a father should, would he be able to forgive himself.

Move on.

Easy, but impossible. Besides, she was certain that at some untapped, deeper level of consciousness he already knew it. If it was that easy, he would have done it long ago.

All she could do, would do, in the limited time available to her, was to make herself a bridge between them. Hope that he could find the way across.

'You loved her, Han.' She set the photograph carefully on the desk. 'She submitted to the treatment because she loved you, wanted you to be able to feel that you had done every-thing possible.'

'How do you know that?'

'Because it is what I would have done,' she said truthfully. 'She did it because she chose to, not because you insisted.'

He stared at her.

'You could not make her hurt her child, Han. Do you truly believe that she would have let you hurt her?'

She might be so far out on a limb here that she was about to drop off the end, but she could only say what she believed. And she believed—no, she knew—that Noor would have been willing to suffer anything to save Han from what must have been desperate feelings of helplessness.

She gave a little shake of her head.

There was no point in telling him that the last thing his wife would have wanted was for him to spend the rest of his life beating himself up with guilt. He was right, he should have accepted Noor's decision, but desperation made fools of us all, and maybe Noor, human and afraid, had hoped a little too, that somehow, against all the odds, he might in the end save her.

Instead she briefly rested her hand on his sleeve, an instinc-tive gesture of reassurance, then lowering her head in the slightest of bows, she said, 'I'm sorry. I have disturbed you.'

As she turned away Han half reached for her, then, as if burned, he snatched his hand back, let it drop. 'What did you want, Lucy?'

'Nothing. It does not matter.' Then, 'Just some notepaper. And a pen.'

'You were brought up to write your thank you letters before you enjoyed your gifts?'

He was, she thought, mocking her. In truth, thank you

letters hadn't featured much in her childhood, but she smiled and said, 'It's just good manners.'

He took notepaper and envelopes from a stand on his desk, found a pen. Handed them to her.

'And their names? Jamilla al-Khatib?'

She spelled it out and he nodded, clearly impatient for her to be gone. 'I'll have to ask her which of Zahir's sisters accompanied her.'

Han watched her swing easily away from him on her crutches, her name already filling his mouth, to call her back, before he caught himself, tightening his hand into a fist, rubbing it against the place on his sleeve where she had touched him as if to capture her essence, to hold it fast.

Her own life was in turmoil and yet she'd brought him a glimpse of peace, as if she had opened the door a crack and shown him a way through to warmth and light.

He took a step after her, pulled himself up, confused, turning to snatch up the telephone as if it was an anchor holding him in place, punched the button on the fast dial.

'Hanif. How good to hear your voice.'

Milly's voice was warm, but he caught the subtext. That it had been too long since he'd called her.

'I wanted to thank you for your time today. I realise how onerous a task it must have been.'

She tutted at his sarcasm. 'Did your guest have everything she needs?'

'Everything and more, I suspect.'

'She may have needs she is too shy to mention to a man who is not her husband.'

If her husband was any kind of a man, he thought, it wouldn't be necessary.

He said, 'I doubt it.'

Lucy might blush like a maiden, but she didn't seem to have any problems communicating with him. On the contrary, the insight she'd given him into Noor's state of mind in those last weeks had been like hearing her speak from the grave.

A superstitious man might have believed her to be a *Peri*, one of those fair spirits, endowed with grace and beauty, who inhabited the empty places, a genie, sent to guide him from the wilderness.

'Hanif?'

'I'm sure you covered every possibility. She will be writing to thank you herself. In fact that was my reason for calling you; I need the name of your partner in retail therapy.'

She laughed. 'It was Dira. I'm so glad she called me. We had a wonderful time.'

'Will you please find her some suitable gift? A token, from the family, of our appreciation for her help.'

'Of course.'

'And when Lucy's fit enough to come down to Rumaillah to sort out her passport, can you find time to take her to stores where she can buy the sort of clothes she would normally wear in England? Nothing too expensive. She can't afford designer labels and she'll insist on paying for it herself.'

'An independent woman.'

'Yes,' he agreed. But not independent enough for the totally inappropriate responses she stirred in him.

He needed to distance himself a little from Lucy.

Distance himself a lot.

With that in mind, he put through a call to Fathia, suggesting she ask Lucy to spend the evening with her, to eat with her, then he wrote Dira's name on a sheet of paper, planning to leave it for her before he took himself to the lodge to eat with men whose conversation would consist of nothing more disturbing than the speed of their horses, the superiority of their falcons, the stamina of their camels.

Lucy's room, however, was empty. No doubt she was taking advantage of the cool evening air to enjoy the garden. Which was good.

He crossed to the table to leave the note, saw the book of poems he'd given her lying open. Unable to help himself, he picked it up to see what had caught her attention—

'...In the Garden of Paradise vainly thou'lt seek
The lip of the fountain of Roknabad
And the bowers of Musalla where roses twine...'

As he snapped it shut a piece of paper, folded in two, flew out from between the pages and fell to the floor. He'd had no intention of looking at it, but as he picked it up it fell open and he found himself looking at a childish drawing of three people.

A family. A father, a mother and a child.

The detail was minimal but even so there was no mistaking who they were meant to represent.

And when he looked up Lucy was in the doorway, hand in hand with the traitorous little artist.

While he had been struggling with feelings that threatened to overwhelm him, threatened to obliterate Noor from his memory, his life, her precious daughter had abandoned her without thought for the more immediate gratification of having someone with arms to hug her.

Someone living, breathing, with a heart that could love her back.

CHAPTER EIGHT

'HAN…'

Lucy flinched as he crushed the paper in his hand and flung it into the corner, putting her arm protectively around Ameerah as she turned to hide herself in the folds of her dress.

'Han, it doesn't mean anything,' she protested. 'She's a little girl. She doesn't understand.'

'But you do. You sat and watched her, encouraged her…' He stormed towards the door, but she stood her ground. 'Let me pass, Lucy.'

'Where are you going?' she demanded. Demanded! She had no right to ask him what time of day it was…

'Nowhere. To the desert. A place as empty as I am. A place where the air smells of nothing. Where each day the sand is wiped clean. Where there are no memories.'

Then, somehow he was by her, striding away down the wide corridor, the fine camel-hair cloak thrown over his shoulders flying behind him, shining like gold in the light. It hadn't been a hallucination, she thought.

He was her angel…

'It isn't true,' she called after him. 'You carry your memories with you.' He made no indication that he'd heard. 'Good and bad. They become part of you, make you what you are.' She lifted her voice, insisting on being heard. 'You have to live with them, Han. You have to live…'

But he was gone.

She sighed, wishing she could have made him listen, but he was hurting and, however unintentionally, she was the cause of his pain.

She knelt beside Ameerah, holding her close. 'It'll be all right, sweetheart,' she said softly. 'He doesn't mean it. Your daddy loves you; he just can't allow himself to feel anything right now because it hurts too much. One day he'll come and take your hand. He'll pick you up, hug you so hard you'll think you might die of happiness.'

And she kept on saying it until she wasn't sure whether it was Ameerah or the desperate, motherless little girl she had once been she was talking to.

Hanif did not return for days.

As the reality of what that meant gradually sank in, she looked at the beauty, the luxury around her in a different way. It had seemed like a refuge, but now… Well, she was the one who'd suggested this was a harem and, despite Han's suggestion that it was a place of power, she caught a closer glimpse of the truth. He wasn't keeping her against her will, but without him to authorise it no one seemed capable of doing anything to get her home.

Short of embarrassing the British Ambassador—and she had enough problems without appealing to the Foreign Office to extricate her from the home of the Emir's youngest son—she was stuck at al-'Arusah for the foreseeable future. And when she asked Fathia—the only other person around who spoke any English—when he was likely to return, her only response was a shrug and, *'Bukra, insha'Allah.'*

Tomorrow. If God wills.

She suspected she should have been more agitated, upset, even angrier than she was, but actually it seemed pointless, a waste of energy. He would return. She would go home.

In the meantime she'd done everything possible to sort out her finances. Had instructed the solicitor who'd handled her grandmother's affairs to begin procedures to extricate her with the utmost speed from her marriage.

All she could do now was search for a job so that she could take her own advice and 'live' and, aware that she was unlikely to impress prospective employers with her black eyes and crutches, she did what Hanif had insisted she do—before he'd lost his temper and stormed out.

She relaxed, spent time exploring both the pavilion and the garden. Helped herself to the books in Hanif's library.

Oh, and she wrote to Jamilla and Dira.

Jamilla phoned her, encouraging her to ask for anything else she needed and inviting her to come and stay when she returned to Rumaillah. She'd been so chatty, informal, charming that Lucy had been bold enough to ask not only for a replacement for her lost Arabic language CD, but for books, toys, anything likely to amuse Ameerah, keep her occupied.

She hadn't anticipated the difference between her vision of what a three-year-old needed and what a Ramal Hamrah princess might consider appropriate for a tiny princess in waiting.

It wasn't all bad.

The tricycle, for instance, was a huge hit. The books and jigsaw puzzles filled quiet afternoons, although Ameerah ignored the brightly coloured crayons, clinging instead to the pastels Hanif had provided for her artwork.

The pair of Siamese kittens were, perhaps, a gift too far for a rather wild three-year-old, but Lucy was enchanted with the way they curled up together by her feet as she practised her

Arabic, followed her as she walked in the garden with Fathia, listening to her stories about Han. How wild he'd been as a boy. How fearless.

How like him Ameerah was.

She suffered the most painful lurch of her stomach when she heard how he'd nearly killed himself playing polo. Felt a disturbing mixture of sympathy and relief when assured that he'd given up the sport for his mother's sake, turned to more serious things, taking on the role of diplomat to please his father.

Learned how this man who'd touched her so deeply, had been the adored youngest son, a golden boy who could do no wrong and had, in a few short years of manhood, become a credit to his family and his country.

Which, Lucy thought, explained a lot. When you lived your life in the sun, perfect in every way, it must be cold in the shadows. Impossible to forgive yourself the smallest of mistakes.

They were sitting in the summer house, keeping an eye on Ameerah, who was chasing butterflies around the pool.

Lucy, who suspected that she was supposed to join in the breast-beating at the harshness of fate, at Hanif's grief, thought there was more than enough of that to go around, but was saved from saying so by the predictable becoming reality.

'Ameerah!'

Too late. As the child's attention was caught by the shimmer of a dragonfly, she swivelled on one toe and, as she made a wild lunge towards it, lost her balance and toppled dramatically into the water lilies.

Before Fathia could move, Lucy had waded in, caught hold of the billowing silk of her dress and hauled her out of the water.

'Brat!' she said. 'You did that on purpose.' Then, 'Look at your gorgeous dress! If you're going to behave like a boy you should be wearing shorts and a T-shirt.'

Ameerah, while not understanding every word, certainly got the meaning, just giggled, wriggled free and turned, planning to wade further in.

Lucy, who'd acted without thinking, was standing up to her thighs in water and realised, too late, that she'd run without a thought for her ankle, that she had nothing to hold on to, that both her feet were sinking into the slippery mud at the bottom of the pond.

Everything that followed seemed to happen in slow motion, as if to someone else. She saw herself open her mouth, cry out as the pain caught up with her. Saw herself crumple as her ankle gave way, the soft billow of rich blue silk swelling around her as she sank into the water.

Then suddenly it was all too real and very loud.

The pain, the cold water, the mud. Only the shrieking wasn't coming from her but from Ameerah, who'd flung her arms around her neck and, no longer laughing, was instead crying, 'Sorry, sorry, sorry…'

'Hush, it's all right,' she said, turning to Fathia to rescue them both, but it was Hanif wading through the water towards her. Hanif in dark and dusty clothes, a *keffiyeh* wound around his head as if he'd come straight from the stables to find her…

Breathe, she reminded herself. Breathe…

She knew the theory, the in-out, in-out basics of staying alive, but somehow the mechanics of it were beyond her and for a moment she thought she might faint.

'Don't move,' he said, catching her around the shoulders, hunkering down to steady her, but this time his voice was gentle. This time she was not afraid. 'Don't even think about trying to move.'

'No,' she finally managed. 'I'm not going anywhere.'

And for a second it seemed the world stood still.

Then Fathia's anxious voice shattered the silence and Lucy, suspecting that she'd been calling for some time, said, 'If you could just take Ameerah?'

It seemed for ever before he straightened, a lifetime before he bent and took the child from her, holding her, dripping, at arm's length.

No! Not like that! Lucy thought fiercely. *Hold her close to you. Hold her against your heart...*

As if he heard her, he slowly drew the child to him, tucking her against his shoulder. Then, with his arm protectively around her, he waded to the edge of pool.

Fathia said something to him, reached out to take her.

It seemed for ever before he surrendered her. Lucy heard him murmur something, whether to the woman or child she had no way of knowing.

She released a long slow breath as he turned back to her and thought *Yes!* but all she said was, 'Rescuing me is getting to be a full-time occupation.'

'Am I complaining?' Before she could reply, he bent, scooped her up as easily as he'd picked up Ameerah and said, 'This is nothing.'

'Believe me,' she said, trying to ignore the closeness, the fact that the silk of her dress had soaked up the water and that it was now clinging tightly to every curve, 'the alternative, crawling back to the side of the pool on my knees, would not be nothing.'

'But you could have done it. Rescuing me is another matter. A miracle...'

Was he talking about Ameerah? About the fact that he'd held her the way a father should?

Then, realising that he was carrying her into the summer house, 'Han! No, I'm soaking! The mud... The carpets...'

Ignoring her protestations, he laid her on the sofa, propping her up with pillows at her back before kneeling beside her to unfasten and discard the ankle splint and its soggy lining. Then, having eased off her ruined sandals, he unwound his *keffiyeh* and carefully wiped the worst of the mud from her feet, her ankles, before tossing that too aside.

Only then did he sit back on his haunches, look at her and, on the point of scolding him for ruining the cushions, she held her tongue. Without the sun at his back, she could see how gaunt and hollow-eyed he looked, as if he hadn't slept or eaten in days.

Her fault, she thought, her fault and, without thinking, she reached out, wanting to comfort him, tell him how sorry she was, as he would have comforted her. For everything.

He caught her wrist before she could touch his face, held it in a grip of steel.

For what seemed like a year he held her there, an inch away from him. It was not enough. Heat fried the air between them, sucked Lucy's breath from her body, licked along her limbs, reducing to ash all the hellfire lectures she'd been read about what happened to girls who succumbed to their wanton desires.

There was no defence against the power of such feelings, no barrier made that was strong enough to withstand this yearning to be held, kissed, possessed.

She hadn't understood, until this moment, what all the fuss was about.

She felt her mouth soften, her lips part, as his hand loosened its grip on her wrist, slid along the length of her arm until his fingers reached her hair, pulled loose the pin that held it back from her face, slid his hand beneath her hair to hold her, his willing prisoner.

The moment stretched endlessly as he lowered his mouth

to hers. Then, as he brushed his lips against hers, she felt something deep inside her dissolve, melt.

All pain was forgotten as he leaned into the kiss, deepening it as a thirsty man might drink at a well and Lucy, blown away, matched his need with a passion, a desperate need, beyond her wildest imaginings and she rose to meet him, wanting to feel the heat, the strength of his body against hers.

As if he knew, felt it too, he caught her at the waist, lifting her, holding her to him as if she were the last woman on earth, while his mouth—hard, almost desperate—obliterated everything but the sensory seduction of his body—the silky sweep of his hair against her cheek, the touch of his fingers at her nape, the salty, dusty taste of his skin.

And finally she understood the force that drove men and women to cross continents, conquer nations, give up their lives.

It ended.

It had to end; the fervour of it was too intense, too powerful to be sustained.

He eased back, broke contact despite the fact that her mouth refused to let go, shamelessly caught at his lower lip, reaching out with her tongue, greedy for more of him.

Eyes closed, he rested his forehead against hers, said, 'You were right, Lucy.'

'R-right?'

'We cannot pick and choose from our memories. Cannot erase them like files from a computer, no matter how profoundly we wish it. They make us what we are.'

It took a moment for his words to sink in. Memories could not be erased. And then, as if someone had turned on a light in her brain, she understood what he'd meant by 'rescue'. He'd turned to her in desperation, hoping that, by some miracle, she could overwrite the memory of his dead wife with her mouth, her body. Drive her from his head.

Rescue him…

The pain that swept through her was a revelation. Until that moment she hadn't realised just how much she felt for this tortured man. How could she have known? She knew nothing of love, of tenderness, of passion.

Steve had romanced her but she'd had no yardstick by which to measure him as a man. She'd mistaken his easy charm for genuine feeling, had mistaken her gratitude, relief at having someone take responsibility for her future, for love.

In one touch, one brief moment of conflagration, she had learned the difference.

This might not be love—how could she know?—but these raw emotions were real enough. She knew that because they touched her, hurt her in a way that her ankle never could. That Steve never could. He'd stolen money from her, but that was nothing. He hadn't changed her life in any way that mattered.

Hanif al-Khatib had stolen her heart and, whatever happened, nothing for her would ever be the same.

Except, of course, she had to act as if the world hadn't just exploded in a rainbow of bright colours. As if the scent of the roses, the cypress trees wasn't suddenly richer, more intense. As if her skin didn't sing with his touch.

She had to pretend it was exactly the same.

'M-memories…' She struggled to speak, had to speak. 'Memories make us what we are, Han.' She did a reasonable job of keeping her voice steady. Not perfect, but under the circumstances, not bad. 'We cannot escape our past. All we can do is use our experience to make a better future.' And, summoning up every fibre of willpower, all the hard-learned self-restraint of her upbringing, she pressed her lips against his forehead, letting them linger a second more than she should have, before, with her hands on his shoulders, she gently pushed him away.

For a moment he continued to hold her, look at her. Then, as if suddenly aware of what he was doing, what he had done, he pulled back, stood up, walked away from her, keeping his back to her until he had himself under control.

When he turned his face was once again expressionless. 'I'm sorry...' he began, stopped. 'I cannot find the words; there are no words—'

'Please...don't. I understand.'

She understood that he was apologising for kissing her. Could not decide whether it made things better or worse.

No.

She knew.

Worse. Infinitely worse.

'I will, of course, make immediate arrangements to have you moved to the protection of my mother's—'

'No! Thank you, Han.'

Oh, right. That made sense. Now he was back and ready to do as she'd asked, to send her to Rumaillah so that she could sort out her documents, leave Ramal Hamrah, leave him in peace, she was resisting it.

She would go. Of course she would. She had no choice. But not like this.

Not with Hanif feeling yet more guilt for having kissed her. Besides, if she left, she had no doubt that he'd use the excuse to send his daughter away too, which was the last thing she wanted.

He'd held her, made a start. He mustn't be allowed to step back now.

'I don't need protection from you,' she said. He neither confirmed nor denied it and, emboldened, she said, 'And I'd rather stay here, where it's cooler, until Zahir has sorted out my papers.' Lying back like a princess against silk pillows, it seemed perfectly natural to make the kind of imperious gesture she'd seen him use a dozen times. 'He is sorting them out, isn't he?'

Han considered mentioning that his family had installed air conditioning some time ago, but discovered a hitherto unsuspected selfish streak in his nature.

Here the air was warm, sultry, laden with the scent of roses. In another world, he would lie here with this woman, they would end what they had begun, make love by moonlight, read poetry, share food and the world would, once again, be a place of promise. Something he had never imagined possible.

In this world, however, Lucy Forrester belonged to another man.

He'd ridden out into the desert, certain that it was Noor's memory he was running from. But alone, with only the stars for company, he'd discovered that it was Lucy who filled his thoughts.

No matter how hard he'd ridden, she had been at his back and he'd found no peace in sleep, but woke from disturbed dreams, his body hard, throbbing with raw desire, completely focused on a living, breathing woman for the first time since his world had fallen apart.

He'd come back determined to do what he should have done from the first—to move her to his mother's house or maybe ask Jamilla to take care of her until Zahir could organise her departure.

But he'd brought her here to appease some deep-seated need of his own. To help her and, in doing so, assuage his own desperate yearning for atonement.

How could he send her away now, because her presence disturbed his peace of mind? His mind deserved no peace…

'I'm sure Zahir is doing everything required,' he said. Although he was sure of nothing of the sort. He had not spoken to Zahir since he'd left for Rumaillah.

'If you could pass me my crutches?' Lucy prompted, sitting up, trying hard not to wince as her foot dragged on her ankle. 'Your lily pool is a joy to look at, but the mud is something else. I really need to go and wash it off.'

'Your sandals are ruined. I will fetch the wheelchair.'

'Okay, I'll reach them myself,' she said, pushing her good foot into a wet and muddy sandal and lifting herself using the arm of the sofa, swaying unsteadily as she kept one foot clear of the ground.

He reached out to steady her. Then, with his arm around her waist, he looked down at her and said, 'I should not have kissed you.'

'No,' she agreed, but her voice, as she continued, did not match her apparent carelessness. 'But then I really shouldn't have kissed you back. Why don't we forget it ever happened?'

As she turned to move away from the support of his arm, Han tried to imagine a world in which he could forget a kiss which, for one perfect moment, like the garden itself, had seemed to promise heaven on earth.

Lucy might, in law, belong to someone else, but she had kissed him as if he were the man she had been waiting for all her life and, in doing so, had delivered him from the past.

This was her place, her citadel, and he made a silent vow to himself that if Steve Mason had plans to reclaim his wife, he would have to wait on her convenience, her pleasure, make reparation for all the harm he'd done her, get on his knees and grovel for forgiveness before he would be allowed to cross the threshold. And then only to offer her the freedom to choose whether she left with him or stayed here, where she belonged.

Lucy had to force herself to move away from Han, from the support of his arm, even though all she wanted to do was lean against him, feel his arm at her back as she faced the future, but as she tried to ease clear, he tightened his grip.

'Han—'

Her voice rose in a cry of alarm as he bent and caught her behind the knees, lifting her into his arms and, dropping her crutches, she made a wild grab for his shoulders.

'I will do my best to forget that I kissed you, Luçy Forrester,' he said. 'That you kissed me.'

She was clutching at the cloth of his robe, bunching it beneath her hands, struggling for breath.

'Good,' she managed. 'Now, if you'll just put me down—'

'But as you told me so forcefully just a few days ago, memories become a part of us, make us what we are. Good and bad, we have to live with them.' He looked down at her, she thought, as if he was seeing her for the first time. 'We have to *live*.'

'I said that?' He did not reply. 'I said that,' she confirmed. 'Did you mean it?'

'Of course I meant it.' As if to demonstrate her sincerity, she stopped fighting the longing to let her arms wind themselves around his neck and let them have their way. 'I didn't think you were listening.'

'I did my best not to hear you,' he said, setting off with her, carrying her towards the pavilion. 'I rode like the wind, but your words kept pace with me. I tried to lose them, but there was nowhere to hide. Your words, your face when you want to be angry but you can't stop yourself from smiling, the scent of your skin as I washed you in the hospital—'

'Antiseptic,' she said, reliving a memory of her own. His irritation, his gentleness, his care…

'Antiseptic,' he agreed. 'Petrol fumes. Dust. The shampoo you'd used to wash your hair. Something else. Not scent…'

'Soap,' she said. 'I have this thing about really good soap. Gran used carbolic and it stung my face. I could never get away from the smell of it.' Even now, just to think of it brought back the smell, the roughness of the washcloth, and she buried her face in his shoulder. 'The first time I earned some money of my own, babysitting for a neighbour, I used it to buy good soap.'

'Your grandmother was harsh.'

'She did what she thought was right. She thought she'd failed with her daughter, wanted to save me from following in her footsteps. From the temptations of the flesh. The fact that I wanted expensive soap only proved to her how weak I was, strengthened her determination.'

He stopped. 'What did she do?'

'Nothing terrible. She just made me put it in a bowl of water, watch until it had completely dissolved and there was nothing left.'

'And yet you stayed, took care of her for all those years.'

'My teachers thought I was a fool. They wanted me to put her in a home, take my place at university. But she didn't do that to me, Han, even though it must have been hard for her to be left all on her own to bring up a baby. How could I leave when she needed me?'

'When you love someone you let them go, even when you need them more than life itself.'

That sounded, she thought, as if he was finally coming to terms with his loss. But despite the warmth of his body, of his arms, she shivered a little as he carried her out of the sunlight and into the blue shade of the arched walk.

* * *

Han picked up the phone, hit the fast dial for Zahir's cellphone. He should have returned days ago. He'd expected messages to be waiting for him. But there had been nothing.

The voice mail prompt cut in, asking him to leave a message. On the point of leaving one that was brief and to the point, he found himself distracted by the sight of a kitten scampering past the French window.

There were feral cats that lived wild around the stables, feeding off mice, but this was a pretty pedigree kitten, cream with a smudge on its nose and ears that would darken to chocolate and, if memory served him right, it would have blue eyes.

Abandoning the telephone, he followed the creature—creatures, there were two of them, he discovered—along the balcony, scooping up the pair of them in one hand before they could enter Lucy's sitting room.

She was lying back, her feet up, headphones in place, oblivious to everything but the Arabic lessons she was repeating. He stood there, listening for a while, enjoying the sound of her cool English voice grappling with the unfamiliar sounds.

There was nothing half-hearted about her efforts. She was trying really hard and was clearly well along with her lessons. Determined, it seemed, to play a full part in the business she apparently half-owned.

He set one of the kittens down on the floor and watched as it ran to her, using its tiny claws to pull itself up on to her lap. She paused the CD player and, even though he couldn't see her face, he knew that she was smiling as she said, 'Hello, sweetie, where's your brother?' She turned to look for the kitten and saw Hanif.

She pulled off the headphones and said, 'Ah.'

The second kitten was wriggling desperately and he set it free to join its brother.

'I was going to tell you about the kittens.'

He didn't care about the kittens, but he envied them their freedom to rub against her, to demand her attention.

'Where did they come from?'

'Your sister. She phoned me and I asked if she could send some things to amuse Ameerah.'

'Did they?'

'Amuse her?' Her smile was rueful. 'For about five minutes. Then they wanted to sleep and when she wouldn't let them they scratched her.'

'Predictable, I would have thought. What else did she send?'

'A tricycle. Books. Games. Puzzles.'

'You seem to have kept yourself busy.' Then, because he knew his sister and because he had come to know Lucy too, he said, 'What else?'

'What makes you think there's something else?'

'Because, Lucy Forrester, your face gives away your every thought.'

'No…'

'It is true. You look at me and I know what you are thinking.' Even when her face was still, all expression blanked out, her eyes spoke volumes for those with the heart to read them. He should not be telling her that, but he could not help himself. He wanted her to know. To understand. 'Today,' he said, 'even when you were in pain, your only thought was for Ameerah. In your heart you were begging me to hold her close.'

She swallowed, gave a little shake of her head as if she found it disturbing to be so open to him, said, 'It was your own heart you were listening to, Han.' She quickly changed the subject. 'A Shetland pony arrived in a horsebox this morning, along with all the tack, riding clothes and a hard hat.' When he didn't say anything, she said, 'I'm sorry.'

'Don't be. You could have had no idea what forces you were unleashing.' Then, 'So, tell me, why is Ameerah chasing dragonflies instead of trotting around the garden on this fat little pony, giving Fathia palpitations and keeping a groom from his work?'

'I told Ameerah that the pony was tired from his journey.' Then, 'As you know, the Shetland Islands are a very, very long way from here.'

'And here I was thinking that Milly had offloaded one of the ponies her own children had grown out of.'

'She might have done that,' Lucy said. 'I wasn't prepared to take the risk.'

He laughed. Laughed out loud. The sound was rich and full and warmed Lucy's heart in a rush of joy. She had made him laugh and it was the most precious sound.

Then he reached for her hand and said, 'Don't go, Lucy.'

CHAPTER NINE

'DON'T go, Lucy. Stay here.'

Han was on his knees beside her, clasping her hands, and she could have no doubt what he was asking. He was offering her the citadel and she yearned to say yes, to take it, take him and all that he was offering.

When he'd kissed her, her response had been instinctive, without thought, without consideration of right or wrong, of what would follow. In his arms there had been no need to think.

Even the touch of his hands as they held hers was enough to drive all rational thought from her mind, tempt her in ways she could never have begun to imagine.

But she must think.

Not just for her own sake, but for his.

She had already made one terrible mistake, reaching back for the life she should have had when she was eighteen, desperately grabbing at a schoolgirl fantasy when she was a grown woman who should have long ago learned that life was not a fairy tale. But she'd learned nothing. She'd had no life. No chance to measure herself, make judgements, make mistakes, grow up.

How could she know whether this was real or just another fantasy, another crutch, so that she wouldn't have to face the reality of the life she'd been handed on the day her mother had abandoned her?

And maybe that was all she was for Hanif too. A crutch. Forced into such heightened intimacy, it was not surprising that he'd found himself responding to needs that he'd denied since Noor's death.

They'd both been living half lives for so long that they couldn't begin to know if what they felt was true emotion or simply the tingling of pins and needles as the blood began to flow back into unused muscles.

The heart, after all, was nothing more than a muscle. Wasn't it?

Unable to look at him, knowing that to look up into his face was to signal surrender, she stared at their hands, linked together. His so strong, so beautiful. The hands of a horseman, a poet, a prince. Hers were the practical hands of a woman who had spent her life doing the kind of chores for which nails had to be kept short, that no amount of hand cream could ever keep soft.

Maybe Han had been right when he'd suggested she'd kept her hair long for herself. The one symbol of her femininity that no one could take from her.

He seemed to understand her instinctively, to know her every thought. Was that love?

Unable to help herself, she looked up, meeting eyes that seemed to assure her that it was. Found herself floundering, falling into their depths.

The kittens saved her, their needle-like claws jabbing her back to reality as they kneaded themselves a comfortable bed on her stomach.

'Ouch! Stop that!' she said, flustered, hot, confused.

Han, with his ability to read her thoughts, plainly understood that she had seized this excuse to avoid answering him.

Before she could say another word, he raised her hands to his lips, stepped back, bowed—not with the barest inclination of his head this time, but with his shoulders, his body, his hand to his heart—then, without uttering another word, he was gone.

She was right. Despite everything, Han thought—she was tied to another man and until she was free she could not pledge herself to him.

He might regret that, but he must honour her for doing what was right. Maybe it was time he did that too. Found Lucy's husband.

He called Zahir again and this time responded to the voice mail prompt. 'Find Mason. Bring him to me.'

Then, because he could not stay in the pavilion, because he did not want to go to the lodge, because he was restless and needed some distraction for a burning need that was in danger of consuming him, he went to the stables to see for himself what horror his sister had visited upon him.

And that was a mistake too.

Ameerah was there, grooming the already glossy little pony under the eye of one of the grooms. With a silent gesture he sent the man away, took his place. She was so engrossed, chatting away happily to the pony as she brushed his thick cream mane, that she did not know he was there.

She was so like her mother that it hurt to look at her. Her gestures, the way she held her head to one side, the way her hair grew in soft curls.

She moved to the pony's forelock but, unable to reach, she turned to the groom for help. Froze as she saw him.

He could not speak, did not know what to say, but the pony snorted, nudged her in the back, and as she stumbled forward he caught her, picked her up. Knelt with her so that she was at the right height to finish grooming him.

'Tomorrow,' he said, before he set her down so that she could run to find Fathia, 'tomorrow I will teach you to ride.'

'Lucy! Lucy!'

It was early, the sun had barely risen above the mountains, but she was dressed as plainly as possible in a linen skirt that skimmed her ankles, a long-sleeved silk blouse.

Today she was leaving Rawdah al'-Arusah. It would, she thought, break her heart to leave, but it was impossible for her to stay.

After Han had left her she'd chosen to eat alone in her room shutting all the doors to keep out temptation. Closing herself away so he could not tempt her with a look that burned into her soul, or read her thoughts and know that she was lying when she said she wanted to leave.

Ameerah took no notice of closed doors. She burst in, a tiny dynamo in jodhpurs, ankle boots, a crisp white shirt and with her hair fastened up in a net under her velvet-covered hard hat.

'Come and watch me,' she begged, her eyes alight with happiness. 'I'm going to ride Moonlight!' The words came out in a jumble of Arabic and English but Lucy understood her perfectly. Then, as if sensing her hesitation, 'Pleeeease!'

How could she refuse? Besides, it was the one place she could guarantee not to meet Hanif. When she spoke to him she would have to be in total command of every one of her senses.

She followed Ameerah, moving swiftly now on her crutches. The extent of the stables should not have surprised her, but it did. There were boxes for dozens of horses around a paved yard as well as garaging for horseboxes and the powerful four-wheel drive vehicles required for desert travel.

'This way!'

Smiling, despite a sleepless night, a heavy heart, she allowed Ameerah to tug her in the direction of Moonlight's loose box. He was being saddled before being led out into the yard, a groom crouched low on his haunches so that he could tighten the girth.

Except that it wasn't a groom. As he straightened, towering over the tiny pony, she saw that it was Hanif and when he saw her he smiled.

'If I said that I can read your thoughts right now, Lucy Forrester, would you believe me?'

Shaking, weak with a confused mixture of feelings, she said, 'Believe me, at this moment even I do not know what I'm thinking.'

'Then I will tell you—'

'No!' The sting of tears that were both of joy and sadness cleared her mind as nothing else could have. 'I will not be responsible for any delay.' She tore herself away from the power of his gaze and turned to Ameerah. 'Your daughter will explode with excitement if she has to wait another moment.'

'She and I have that in common.'

Before she could respond, he turned to Ameerah, lifting his little girl into the saddle, adjusting the stirrups for her, showing her how to hold the reins. Then, because the attention span of a three-year-old was limited, he led her slowly around the yard so that everyone could see how wonderful she looked, before taking the pony for a walk down a shady path.

Lucy did not follow—this was a time for father and daughter. Turning to go, she found herself confronted by Fathia.

'You really are leaving today, Lucy?'

'I have to.'

'Hanif will miss you.'

'He has his daughter. In a few weeks he will rediscover his life.'

The woman took her hand and patted it, whether with sympathy or gratitude, she could not have said. 'Go to the summer house, Lucy. I will send him to you so that you can say goodbye.'

A light breeze was blowing across the pool, cooling the summer house. A servant brought coffee, freshly baked croissants, a bowl of fresh figs.

After a while Hanif joined her and she poured coffee for them both, handed a cup to him. He took it, capturing her fingers so that she could not let go.

'So, Lucy, you have decided to leave us?'

'Is that what you read in my thoughts?'

'Not just that.'

No. Caught off guard her thoughts must have blazed like a beacon. 'You no longer need me, Hanif.'

He smiled at that. 'You stayed for my sake?'

'I asked to leave days ago,' she reminded him. She'd spent a long and sleepless night thinking about what she would say to him. 'I have to go, Hanif.' She swallowed, forced herself to continue. 'But there are some things I have to ask you before I leave.'

He released her hand, put down the cup.

'Do not ask anything for this man you married—'

'No! Not for him.' He waited. 'Steve was living with a woman in Rumaillah. Jenny Sanderson. She's the office manager of Bouheira Tours. She's expecting a baby very soon...'

Lucy struggled to continue, remembering that moment when she'd walked into the office, introduced herself, said, 'Hi, I'm Lucy Mason. I'm looking for my husband...'

She hadn't needed the 'couple' photographs pinned to the notice-board to warn her. The look on Jenny Sanderson's face had been enough to tell her whose baby she was carrying.

Han said something beneath his breath, but it was not anything she was meant to hear or understand and she didn't ask him to repeat it.

'How long ago did he marry you, Lucy? Weeks? How many months has this woman been carrying his child?'

'He must have been desperate for money, in real trouble, Hanif, but she and her baby have done nothing.'

He didn't leap to agree, but he let it go, said, 'What do you want me to do for her?'

'She may need support and I'm not sure that Steve can provide it. Maybe money to get home. I don't know if the company is worth anything, or if the papers that give me a half share in it are valid, but if a buyer can be found I'd like to use that money to give her a fresh start.'

'Let me tell you something, Lucy. This woman, for whom you feel such empathy, is the person who denied you existed. If I had not been near, if you had run out of fuel so far from the track, you could have died.'

'What do you mean, far from the track?'

'You were headed to Mason's camp in the foothills of the mountains?'

'Well, yes…'

'You were miles off track, headed into empty wilderness. The satellite navigation system on the 4x4 was malfunctioning.'

He saw her take in what he'd told her, the colour leave her face. 'How do you know that?'

'Zahir has spent the last few days piecing together exactly what happened. He called me last night. Jenny Sanderson thought you were dead and to cover for this man she had someone drive out and collect the burnt out 4x4, take it away to be crushed.'

Lucy gripped the arm of the chair for a moment, then forced herself to say, 'She was protecting her baby, Han. A woman will do anything...'

She stopped. The air was as fragile as glass. One word, the wrong word, could shatter it.

'You would forgive her anything?' Han said.

'Please, Han.'

Han had known from the moment he had stood up and seen her in the stable that she was ready to leave. She had convinced herself that it was the right thing to do. And seeing him with Ameerah had only made it easier for her.

If the pain of losing her was not enough to convince him that he loved her, the compassion she could show for another of Mason's victims left him in no doubt. He did not believe the woman deserved a second thought, but he could deny her nothing.

'Very well, Lucy. If you can forgive, then I must too. I'll see that she comes to no harm.' He regarded her for a moment. 'What about Mason?'

'What about him?'

'He is your husband. Having disposed of the pregnant girlfriend, is it your intention to return to him?'

The question had to be faced; he knew she was the kind of woman who would always honour a promise, keep a vow.

'Is that what a good Ramal Hamrah girl would do?' she asked, surprising him.

'A good Ramal Hamrah girl would hunt him down and cut out his treacherous heart,' he assured her. 'But your marriage was not arranged, it was a love match. As you have just proved, a woman in love will forgive anything...'

'Hanif…'

She said his name and he saw a reflection of what she must see in his eyes.

'Lucy…'

If he did not look away, if he could hold her, like this, locked in his eyes, she could not leave him…

'Lucy…' The voice became more insistent and with a sigh she turned away from him to look at the man she'd married. The man who'd so cruelly cheated not only her but the woman who was carrying his child.

'Oh, my God, look at the state of you! Your face…'

Mason reached out as if to touch her and it was all Hanif could do to stop himself from slamming him back against the trunk of the nearest tree.

'My apologies, Excellency,' Zahir said quickly. 'I was told you were here. I assumed you were alone.'

Hanif rose to his feet, waving away his apology. 'I did not hear the helicopter.'

'There is a *shamal* blowing down the coast. We had to come by road.'

He nodded, turned to confront the man. 'You have something to say, Mason?'

'Your Highness,' he said, bowing, 'Thou who hast long life. I can do nothing but offer the humblest of thanks for rescuing Lucy. For taking care of her.'

His contempt for the man knew no bounds. Did he think to charm him with formal greetings, smooth words?

'Not to me. To your wife.'

Lucy stared, first at Hanif who had, before her eyes, it seemed, morphed from the gentlest of lovers into the most aloof of autocrats, then at Steve, blathering nonsense in an attempt to ingratiate himself with Hanif.

Embarrassed for him, she said, 'Save the apologies.' Then, as he opened his mouth to say something, no doubt some well rehearsed story that was meant to melt her heart, but she'd had enough of his lies, 'Just tell me why you did it.'

It was strange. Now she knew he was lying she could see what he was doing, recognised the exact moment when he realised that the truth would serve him better. The subtle rearrangement of his expression from humble penitent to frankness and honesty.

'You're right. You deserve an explanation.'

Lucy made no comment on what she deserved, simply waited for him to continue.

'I came to England to try and raise some finance for the business. I needed capital, but no one here would back me. My last hope was that my parents would raise a loan on their house. It's a brilliant business, Luce—'

'Lucy,' she snapped, cringing at the familiarity of a diminutive that she'd once thought meant something. 'My name is Lucy.'

'Lucy,' he repeated.

She waved him on and Han found himself having to hide a smile. Not one of his sisters could have done it with more authority, more disdain, he thought.

'It's a brilliant business,' Mason repeated, now less certain of himself. 'There are endless possibilities. The desert is the last great tourist destination...'

'But you are not a great credit risk, are you?' Zahir said, cutting him short. 'This isn't the first business you've tried. You take short cuts. You have no staying power.'

Mason looked for a moment as if he was going to protest, but finally he shook his head.

'No. Even my parents turned me down. I was going into town to book my flight back when I saw the For Sale sign up outside your house, Lucy. My mother had mentioned that your gran had died and I realised that she must have left you the house.'

'I was surprised you remembered me. School was a long time ago.'

'Oh, please. All those brains. All that hair. It was a matter of considerable debate whether, if you cut your hair, you'd lose the power of thought. The way that Samson lost his strength.'

'And no one thought to corner me somewhere, cut it off, to find out?'

He looked embarrassed. Probably a first, Han thought.

'You had something about you, even then, Lucy. We were all a bit in awe, to be honest.'

Han saw her eyes, felt the loneliness of the girl she'd been, saw her rally as she realised that this was no more than a ploy to gain her sympathy.

'Not that much in awe, obviously,' she said. 'You let me keep my hair, but my money was something else.'

'I always meant to pay you back. You have to believe that. I thought I'd be able to pay off the cards, or at least some of them, before you ever knew.'

'And the bank loan?' Han interjected, growing impatient. 'When were you going to repay that?'

'I intended to pay off the first instalment. Once I'd done that I was going to explain everything,' he said, turning to Lucy with all the natural confidence of a man who believed all he had to do was smile. That something would always turn up to save him. 'Cash flow is the killer.'

'Not quite as deadly as a malfunctioning satellite navigation system in the desert,' Zahir suggested.

'Look, Jenny didn't know Lucy had taken the 4x4. She'd left it for the garage to pick up. It was only when you called that she realised what had happened. She called me in the most terrible state. She thought Lucy was dead.'

'So you told her to collect the burned out vehicle, have it crushed and no one would ever be able to prove anything.'

He drew a breath. 'No. I organised that. I panicked…'

'She told Zahir that she had done it.'

'She was protecting me.'

'More fool her,' he said.

Lucy caught his eye. *A woman will do anything…*

'I did give you half the company, Lucy, and there are bookings. Zahir will tell you. He's seen the books. Seen everything. I was desperate for capital. I needed more equipment, better transport, a decent website. Time. Give me a chance and I will repay you every penny and more.'

'It is true, Excellency. The money he took has certainly been ploughed into the business and there appears to be no shortage of people who want what Bouheira Tours is offering.'

Han could almost feel Zahir's excitement, enthusiasm.

'Han?' Lucy prompted.

He had thought it a blessing, a treasure, to be able to read Lucy's thoughts, but now he saw all too clearly what she wanted. Mercy.

He didn't want to breathe the same air as this man and yet he appeared to expect to be treated as a businessman rather than the criminal he undoubtedly was.

'You plead for him? When he has betrayed you in every way a man can betray a woman?'

'I'm not pleading for him.' She reached out, didn't quite touch his hand. 'I ask your mercy for the girl who loves him, her unborn baby.'

'You ask me to allow this man to remain in Ramal Hamrah? Polluting my country with his presence?'

'If he is ever to repay me, the company has to be made to pay.'

'Pay? You believe he will repay you?'

'If I have to stand over him with a whip.'

'You will stay? Work with him?'

Live with him?

Never, while he had breath in his body and, recalling her compassion for a wife who had to share her husband, he used it shamelessly.

'You are prepared to share him?' he demanded. 'Play the role of the second wife? Counting the baubles. Keeping watch to make sure he does not visit his girlfriend more often than he visits you.'

He turned away before he saw her answer in her eyes.

Why wouldn't she? Hadn't Lucy told him, over and over, that a woman would do anything, not just for her child, but for the man she loved? He recognised that he was being given a second chance to prove that he could do as much for a woman who had given him back the capacity not just to love, but to live, no matter how much it cost him.

'Actually…'

They all turned to Mason.

'The thing is that Jenny…' All the colour had leached from his skin, leaving him looking yellow rather than fit and tanned and his voice was less than steady. 'I'm sorry, Lucy, but she's not my girlfriend, she's my wife.' He looked terrible, but even so he seemed to be standing a little taller, looking more of a man. 'The thing is I love her. I'd do anything for her.' Shrugged. 'Have done just about anything…'

Lucy's face was expressionless and, for the first time since their eyes had met in the split second before she'd passed out on him, Han didn't have the slightest idea what she was thinking.

No one prompted Mason, demanded answers. They all simply waited.

'The emergency that called me back here straight after the wedding ceremony was a fake, Lucy. All that flap about getting a seat on a plane was just so much window-dressing. I already had my flight booked.'

'Am I supposed to thank you for that?'

'No. It wasn't that you aren't lovely, Lucy. Any man would be proud…'

'But you loved Jenny too much to be unfaithful to her?'

He nodded. 'I sort of surprised myself. I guess I must have some standards—'

'Standards?' Han demanded, quite certain that this was nothing more than a ploy for sympathy. 'Isn't bigamy a criminal offence?'

'Not one that gets taken very seriously these days. The worst I'm likely to get is a caution.'

'You checked it out, did you? I think you might be just a little optimistic; I've no idea what we do with bigamists in Ramal Hamrah, but we do take fraud very seriously.'

'He has a wife, Han, and a baby on the way. I'd already talked to a lawyer about a divorce, but now I can get an annulment. That's all I want.' Lucy's voice was trembling a little, as if she'd been under a tremendous strain and suddenly it was over.

'Divorce?'

She gave an awkward little shrug. 'I'm sorry, Han, you're going to have a heck of a telephone bill and it appears that I haven't, after all, got a husband for you to send it to.'

Her words, her face were solemn enough, but her eyes… Her lovely silver eyes were smiling.

'If you say one word about paying for it yourself,' he warned, 'I shall have to insist that you marry me.'

He'd thought he'd been losing his mind, but even when he'd thought her married he'd seen the innocence shining from her. He hadn't needed Mason to tell him that he had not touched this wife, had not stolen from her the one thing that he could never return.

It occurred to him that everyone was staring at him and he turned to Zahir.

'Miss Forrester wishes to sell her half of Bouheira Tours, Zahir. As a graduate of Harvard Business School and a keen advocate of our burgeoning tourist industry, it seems to me that you might be interested in investing in such a venture.'

'I would be delighted to have such a partner,' Mason began.

'I'm sure you would,' Han said, cutting him short. 'However, the State of Ramal Hamrah does not allow felons to profit from their crimes. Your assets will be confiscated and sold to repay your creditors, of whom, I'm sure, there are many.'

'You're going to deport me?'

He looked, Han thought, almost indignant.

'Deport you? On the contrary. We will deport your wife. Pregnant or not, she was a party to your crime. A willing accomplice—'

'Han! You promised!'

'—but you, Mason, will remain in Ramal Hamrah until our courts decide what to do with you.'

'Han, please!'

'Do not plead for him, Lucy. This man stole your money, very nearly stole your life. He's full of remorse now, but if I let him walk away, how long do you think it will be before he's cruelly abusing the trust of some other vulnerable woman, stealing her money and destroying her life in the process, now that he knows how easy it is? How reluctant she would be to press charges. Are you prepared to take the responsibility for that?'

Her eyes blazed at him. 'You promised me that you would take care of Jenny Sanderson.'

'I will. She'll be repatriated at my expense, which is rather more than she was prepared to do for you.' She turned away, furious with him. Or more probably furious with herself. The fact that she somehow felt guilty for their crimes was one of the nastiest things about this. 'Zahir, after you've delivered Mr Mason to the relevant authorities, I suggest you take immediate control of Bouheira Tours. We can't have our tourists left stranded.'

'Excellency…' The boy seemed unable to speak. Totally overcome. 'His Highness the Emir, your father…'

'I will be returning to Rumaillah, Zahir. Your duty here is done.'

CHAPTER TEN

LUCY stared out of the window at an aircraft taxiing towards the terminal building. Anywhere but at Han.

She'd stayed with Milly while her papers had been organised, been introduced to Hanif's mother, his grandmother, and received with the utmost courtesy.

Did they have any idea of the trouble she'd been in? How much Hanif had done for her? She couldn't ask him. She hadn't seen him since she'd been left in Milly's care. According to his sister, he was spending all his time with his father.

'They're discussing Han's future,' she said.

'Future?' It was none of her business, she knew, but she couldn't stop herself.

'He's resuming his diplomatic career, going to the UN as a special envoy to the commission on world poverty.'

'The UN?' New York? That was so far away... 'And Ameerah?' she managed.

Milly smiled. 'He's taking her with him.'

Relief swept through her. It would have been so easy for him to leave her behind. 'She must be so happy.'

'Yes.' Milly's smile faded. 'Noor was brought up in an old-fashioned household where girls were not valued. She didn't understand that our father, our brothers...' She shook her head. 'Every time that Hanif looked at Ameerah he remembered that Noor had lied to him, that she couldn't bring herself to totally trust him. We are all so grateful for what you've done, Lucy.'

'It was nothing. He saved my life.'

Milly reached out, took her hand, squeezed it.

'I think the honours are about even.' She turned at the sound of footsteps crossing the hall, 'It's time to go. Have you got everything?'

'Yes…' And without warning she found herself looking at Hanif for the first time since they'd parted in anger. 'I'm just leaving,' she said stupidly.

'I know. Ameerah and I have come to take you to the airport.'

'Oh.'

Of course. How foolish to think that he had come to ask her to stay. He was leaving too. Reclaiming his life, as she must reclaim hers.

The little girl grabbed her attention in the car, chatting all the way to the airport, telling her about going to New York.

It was only after they had been ushered through to the luxury of a private lounge, when Ameerah had been distracted by the planes, that they had a chance to speak.

'You are still angry with me, Lucy?'

'Angry?'

'You believe I treated Mason harshly?' She gave an awkward little shrug. 'He has to learn that his actions have consequences, Lucy.'

'Then maybe I should be in prison too.' She turned and regarded him levelly. 'I wanted the fantasy. To be the kind of girl that a boy like Steve Mason would notice. If I hadn't been so needy, so pathetic, he wouldn't have been able to fool me. He wouldn't be in jail.'

'You are not needy, Lucy. No one has a more giving or warmer nature than you.' He took her hands. 'Too good for the world, maybe. I do not think I should let you go back to the world. I should keep you in my garden with the other flowers, where you will be safe.'

She shook her head, tried to pull away, but he would not let her go.

Han wanted to hold her, keep her safe, offer her all the fantasies she'd ever dreamed of. But she had taught him that when you loved someone, you had to let them fly. Take the risk that they might not ever return.

'I'm not a flower,' she said.

'Are you sure? You have all the attributes of the rose, including the thorns.'

'What will happen to that poor woman and her baby?'

'Jenny Sanderson? Why do you care more about her than yourself?' he demanded. He did not want to talk about them, or the past. He wanted to talk about the future.

'It could have been me,' she said desperately, wanting him to understand. 'I feel responsible.'

'No, Lucy. They are responsible for what they did. They must face the consequences of their actions, as we all must.'

'You once said that you could refuse me nothing.'

And, God help him, he had meant it.

'Not this. On this I am adamant.' Then, because he could not help himself. 'Do you have to go?'

'I have to sell the house, Han. Settle my debts. Find a life that's my own. Not a prison, not some fantasy, but something real.'

This is real, he wanted to say. What I feel, what I know you feel...

She lifted her head a little. 'I'm going to try and get a university place as a mature student.'

'You want to take your degree in French literature?'

'No, I'm not that girl any more. I've been thinking about what I'll do…'

She seemed about to say something, but changed her mind about sharing it with him. He didn't press her, but said, 'What about your mother? Will you look for her?'

She nodded, apparently unable to speak.

'If there is anything I can do to help, Lucy…' Before he could say what was in his heart, a steward arrived to inform them that Lucy's flight was boarding.

'One moment.'

But Lucy had already detached herself, was on her feet, burying her face in Ameerah's hair. 'Goodbye, my darling. Have a lovely life.'

Then, having composed herself, she turned to him.

'Thank you, Han.' She offered him her hand. 'For my life. For everything. I will never forget you.'

He recognised the gesture for what it was. It was how the British said goodbye. Not just goodbye for now, but goodbye for ever.

He ignored it, taking not one, but both of her hands, holding them against his chest, willing her to understand that while he'd learned the lesson about letting go, for him this was not goodbye, only a necessary pause while they put what had happened into the perspective of their everyday lives. Time for him to rebuild his life, for her to reach out for the life she'd never had.

There were a thousand things he wanted to say to her, but he recognised that she wasn't ready to trust herself with the kind of decisions, commitments, such declarations would demand. Instead he kissed both of her cheeks before raising her hands to his lips.

'*Ma'as salamah,* Lucy. Go, in the safety of Allah.'

'*Ma'as salamah,* Han…'

Lucy wanted to say more. To let him see that she understood that this was an end. That they came from different worlds and that whatever he'd said, done, she understood that once he had returned to his real life she would become nothing more than a memory. A sweet memory, she hoped, a memory to raise a smile long after he'd forgotten what she looked like, struggled to remember her name.

But her throat was constricted and the words wouldn't come. It didn't matter. A week, a month, from now and he would discover it for himself.

All she could do was grab her crutches and follow the steward assigned to take her to her seat, but as she reached the door Ameerah raced after her to give her a last hug, clutching at her legs, holding her there.

Han said something to the child and she let go, ran back to him, lifted her arms. There was no hesitation now as he bent, picked her up. No uncertainty as Ameerah wrapped her arms about his neck and buried her head in his shoulder.

She had done that.

If she did nothing else in her life, Lucy would always cherish the thought that she had once managed to unite a little girl with her father.

Their eyes met one last time over Ameerah's head. His lips moved but a tannoy announcement drowned out his words. It didn't matter, there was nothing left to say, and with a brief nod she turned, boarded the truck that was waiting to carry her to the aircraft.

She'd had a lifetime of keeping her feelings hidden, kept tightly locked away. Her throat was tight, aching, she could barely speak to thank the steward after he'd carried her flight bag upstairs, installed her in the luxury of the royal suite on the upper deck of the Ramal Hamrah airliner.

It was the last word in luxury. It had armchairs, a fully functioning office with every communications device known to man, even a bedroom, should she choose to sleep.

But it was the book waiting by her seat that really undid her.

Han's own volume of the poems of Hafiz, inscribed on the flyleaf—'So that you will not forget'. He had signed it, not in English, but in looping Arabic script.

Any girl would cry.

As Han watched the airliner lift off from the runway, he felt for one desperate moment as if he was losing his heart for the second time.

'Where has Lucy gone, Daddy?'

He looked down at the child in his arms.

No.

It wasn't like that. A heart that was fully functioning, beating soundly, had an infinite capacity to expand, to fill many places, many time zones.

It might be lifting at that moment with Lucy, being torn from him as the plane lifted her six miles above the earth, but it was here too, on the ground with his daughter.

It resided, he realised in a sudden flash of insight, with everyone one had ever loved.

In the past with those who had gone to paradise. In the present with family, friends, all those who cared for you, who you cared for in return. With all the possibilities of the future.

Lucy, whose boundless love had been constrained and cramped in a joyless life, had nevertheless endless compassion for a woman who had not loved her as she deserved.

Empathy for two people who would have stolen her life if she had not had the courage to come and take it back.

She'd had love to spare for a small motherless child and even a little left over for a lonely, half-dead man.

Now she was going to find the mother who'd abandoned her and he had no doubt that she would find it in her heart to forgive her, love her too if she had the courage to cherish the gift of a daughter.

'Where has she *gone,* Daddy?' Ameerah persisted.

'She's gone to a place called England. It's very green. Very beautiful.'

'Why has she gone there?'

'She has some things she has to do.' As he did. A life to resurrect, a family to spend time with, a country that needed him. He owed his father three years of duty. He'd asked only for three months.

'Will she come and see us soon?'

'*In sha'Allah,* my sweet.' If God wills.

Life, Lucy quickly discovered, was not as difficult as she'd imagined.

For the best part of twenty-eight years she'd clung to a small core of resistance, keeping a part of herself inviolate from the buffeting of a life that hadn't handed her any easy options. At school she'd learned to keep her head down, avoid trouble and reach the goals she'd set herself. Since then, she'd had ten years of dealing with Social Services, the medical profession, her increasingly frail grandmother.

Steve had caught her at the one moment when she'd had her guard down; when she'd stopped fighting; when it had seemed that, finally, it was to be her turn and he'd taken pitiless advantage of her at a vulnerable moment. Han had been right; once he'd realised just how easy it was he'd do it again in a heartbeat.

She wished she could tell him.

Explain that once she was back in England and faced with sorting out the mess, confronting the true horror of what Steve had done, she'd understood why he'd acted the way he had.

As for Jenny Sanderson, Zahir had forwarded a letter from her, telling her how sorry she was for what she'd done. That she felt as if she'd been woken up from some drugged dream in which she'd been sleepwalking into danger. How grateful she was to be back home with parents who loved her, were eagerly looking forward to the arrival of a grandchild. The chance to make a fresh start.

It was a fresh start all round, it seemed. Having put the house back on the market, she'd wasted no time in taking herself to an employment agency to see what kind of job she might get. A bit of an eye-opener, that one.

'What qualifications do you have, Lucy?'

'None. I'm not expecting anything more than the basic wage,' she admitted. 'I've no experience, you see. I've never had anything but holiday jobs. I've been caring for my grandmother for the last ten years…'

Even as she said the words she realised that she was simply repeating what Steve had told her, using her insecurities to bind her to him.

'Scrub that. I've got twelve O levels, four A levels, I've spent the last ten years running a house on a pittance and dealing with Social Services in all its forms. I speak passable French, can get by in Italian and I'm learning Arabic. Oh, and I can drive.'

'French?' The woman smiled. 'How are your computer skills?'

Computer skills… Her confidence ebbed. 'I haven't used a computer since I was at school.'

'Don't worry, we'll give you a crash course on the latest software this afternoon. That's if you're free to start a temp job tomorrow?' She smiled. 'At considerably more than the basic rate.'

After a couple of days, when she discovered that common sense and the ability to knuckle down and get the work done were just as valuable as her ability to answer the telephone confidently in French—and not panic when the caller replied in the same language—made her a very valuable commodity indeed. The only thing that she lacked was someone to tell.

There was, she discovered, a great big Han-shaped void at the centre of her life. Just how big a hole that was she'd only discovered when she got home from work one day and turned on the little television set she'd bought herself, to catch the end of the evening news.

She'd switched on in the middle of a report from the UN on international aid and, without warning, she was looking at the impressive figure of Sheikh Hanif al-Khatib as he addressed the Assembly. He looked, she thought, like a man who had the world by the throat. Strong. Passionate. Alive in every sense of the word.

Alive and so far away.

She'd pressed her hand against the screen, faint with longing to be near him. In the same room as him. In the same country…

She relived every moment of the time they'd spent together, her anger, that last moment when his words had been drowned out by the speaker system. And suddenly she knew what he'd said. *'Call me…'*

And say what? *I miss you. I love you...*

Or was that simply *I need you?*

Was she still looking for a prop?

She did miss him, she did love him, but she had to prove to them both that the only person she *needed* was herself.

She applied for a place at the School of Oriental and African Studies in London. The temporary job at the international finance company had become permanent but she had bigger ambitions. With her languages and a degree in Arabic Cultural Studies she could aspire to a post at the Foreign Office, join the Diplomatic Service. Get a job at the United Nations...

That would be a Life.

Then, to stop herself thinking about Han, she turned to the one thing she'd been putting off and searched out the name of the agency where she could register to find her mother.

'I'll take the details, Lucy,' the counsellor told her. 'But I don't hold out much hope that we can help. You weren't adopted so there won't be any records.'

'No. I understand.' And she understood the unspoken sub-text—that if her mother had wanted to find her, all she had to do was go back to where she'd left her.

'Maybe you could try an Internet search? There is a website where families can get in touch. It's basically for genealogy, but it would be a start and if that doesn't come up with anything, well, you could just type her name into a search engine and see what you come up with.'

She did both. The Internet came back with 654,000 hits for Elizabeth Forrester.

After a quick look at some of them, she realised that she'd got every Elizabeth and every Forrester in the entire world. And that the Elizabeths were not necessarily connected to the Forresters.

She refined her search details and tried again. And again. When she'd reduced the number of hits to three, she sent each of them the same email.

Are you Elizabeth Forrester, the daughter of Jessica Forrester, who once lived in Maybridge? Lucy.

She didn't give a street address. Her mother would know it. A fake would not.

Her job, the discovery that she had skills people were willing to pay for, that she could make friends—Deena, the Jordanian student she'd found through the university who was teaching her Arabic script, people she worked with—was giving her confidence.

Life was teaching her caution.

Parties, concerts, diplomatic functions… Han stripped off and stood beneath the shower to wash away the latest round of polite and meaningless conversation.

Three months…

After yet another reception fending off the attentions of women who hoped to bag themselves a sheikh to add to the notches on their bedposts, of forcing himself to be polite to the front men of dictators who let their people starve while they lined their pockets at the expense of the poor, a day without Lucy was beginning to feel like a lifetime.

If she had been with him to share the horrors, make him laugh at the foolishness of it all, make it all go away with the sweetness of her mouth, the tenderness of her touch…

He wrapped a towel around his waist, crossed the bedroom to the telephone, picked up the receiver, wanting more than anything in the world to hear her voice.

He held it for a moment, then quietly replaced it. He had told her to call him. When she was ready, when nothing else was possible, he had to believe she would, trust her to do that.

Lucy heard from her solicitor that her marriage had been officially annulled. Was as if it had never happened. Which, in every way that counted, it never had.

To celebrate she took her nails, growing strongly now, to have them manicured in a new nail bar in town and after that, she paid a long delayed visit to the hairdresser.

'How much do you want me to take off?' the girl asked.

Lucy thought about it. Thought about all the times she'd dreamed of this moment, then, realising that she had nothing to prove, no one to please but herself, said, 'Just as much as it takes to straighten up the ends, please.'

The family genealogy Internet site, on which she'd carefully entered her limited family tree, had not produced any results. She'd two negative replies to her emails, both of them wishing her luck with her search, which left just one Elizabeth Forrester to answer. Was it her mother? Was she some respectable woman who had wiped out the past and was even now living in fear and trembling that her daughter was about to turn up and destroy her neatly ordered life?

She wrote again.

If you are Elizabeth Forrester, formerly of Maybridge, if you are my mother, all I want is...

She stopped. She didn't know what she wanted. Everything. Nothing. To hear her voice. Look her in the eyes and see... What?

She deleted the message.

A month passed and still there was no answer from Elizabeth Forrester number three.

Suppose her email had not arrived? Was it still buzzing around somewhere in cyberspace? It had happened at work only the other day and a deal had nearly fallen through…

She wrote again.

I am looking for my mother, Elizabeth Forrester, daughter of Jessica Forrester of Maybridge. Please, if it's not you, will you let me know so that I can cross you off my list? Lucy Forrester.

She hit 'send', then stared at the screen as if expecting a reply to drop into her mailbox.

'A watched computer never delivers mail,' Deena told her. 'Come on, let's go to the supermarket, I'll make you some *khoushaf*.'

The distraction worked until Lucy saw the fresh figs on display, cold, hard, a world away from the soft, sweet fruit she'd shared with Han. She told an unconvinced Deena that she had a headache, went home and took out the kaftans Han had bought for her, rubbing the silk against her cheek, imagining some faint lingering scent of roses, remembering Ameerah's face as she'd paraded herself in the *shalwar kameez*.

Picked up the poetry book he'd given her and held it against her heart, wondering what he'd be doing at that moment in New York.

Was he at some diplomatic cocktail party surrounded by countless women, all of them cleverer than her, prettier, dressed in the kind of clothes that a man like Han would expect a woman worth his attention to wear?

Then she realised that she was still doing it. Despite her good job, the place she'd won at SOAS, the friends she'd made, she hadn't moved on where it mattered. In her head she knew that she was a strong, bright woman who deserved everything that life had to offer, but in her heart she still believed that because her mother hadn't wanted her, she wasn't worth anything.

The next day she placed advertisements in the personal columns of all the national newspapers, appealing for information. Contacted the local radio station and used their 'find a friend' request programme. She was even interviewed by the local newspaper.

She hated every minute of it. It was like exposing herself in public. Walking naked down the street in slow motion.

And it was all for nothing. Worse than nothing. The only responses she had were from desperate women looking for their own children, desperate children looking for their mothers, all of them wanting to share their own stories.

At least she'd finally managed to sell the house, get that burden off her back, clear her debts.

She moved into a flat share with one of her colleagues from work, learned how to head off the invitations to drinks, dinner, the movies from the men she met. Not because they weren't decent men, not because she didn't trust her own judgement, but because they weren't Han.

Then one evening when she got home from work there was a woman standing on the pavement looking up at the first floor windows as if she'd knocked, had got no answer, but still hoped that there might be someone home.

'Can I help?' Lucy asked. 'Who are you looking for?' But even before the words were out of her mouth, she knew.

She'd seen photographs of her grandmother as a young

woman. Had seen her own face in the mirror countless times. This woman was both of them, neither of them, unknown and yet recognised in ways that went to the deepest part of the soul.

Lucy just stood there, unable to move, to speak…

'I went to the house,' her mother said. 'The woman who lives there gave me the name of the estate agent who sold it to her. I thought they might know where you were. I was going to ask them to send on a letter.' She made a vague wordless gesture. 'One of the women there told me where to find you. She said you'd want her to…'

Someone else arrived, opened the door, held it for a moment and then, when neither of them moved, let it swing shut.

Still Lucy stood there.

'Maybe she was wrong. I'll understand if you don't want to see me, talk to me…' She turned, began to move, but Lucy reached out, laid her hand on her mother's arm, kept her from walking away, finally managed to say, 'No. Please. I've been looking for you.'

'Looking for me?'

Lucy saw hope in her mother's face and all the years fell away.

'For months. I used local radio, newspapers, the Internet…'

'I've been living abroad. New Zealand. My husband knew nothing about you until a few months ago when I had a bit of a scare. A lump in my breast.' She shook her head. 'No. It wasn't, but for a while I thought I might die and that I'd never have known you… I told Michael everything and he brought me home to confront my mother, to demand to know where she'd placed you so that I could begin to look for you.'

'Placed me?'

Her mother struggled to speak. 'She took you away from the hospital, told me you'd been given to a good God-fearing couple who couldn't have children, that they were going to adopt you, take you away, that I'd never see you again. That it was best.' Tears were pouring down her cheeks. 'Everyone said it was for the best.'

'But she didn't,' Lucy said. 'She raised me herself.'

'She kept you?' Her mother stifled a cry of anguish with her hand. It was a cry, Lucy realised with an overwhelming sense of her loss, that she'd been stifling all her life. 'I never went back. I walked out of the hospital and never went back. I never wanted to see or speak to her ever again. I couldn't forgive her. Bear to be in the same house, the same room…'

She put out a hand as if to touch Lucy, but couldn't quite bring herself to bridge the gap in case she was not real, only some figment of her imagination.

'If I'd come back, just once, I could have been with you. I could have borne anything to be with you…'

'Don't,' Lucy said, reaching out as her mother had. Not quite touching. 'Please, Mum…'

And then, somehow, without either of them knowing how it happened, they were in each other's arms, holding each other, weeping and laughing.

It was being with her mother, discovering that she had a wonderful stepfather, a sixteen-year-old half-sister, had been given the family she'd always longed for, that made her realise that finding a life was nowhere near as important as living the life you'd been handed. Being with the people you loved. That the risk of looking a fool was nowhere near as bad as being one and losing something unbelievably precious.

On a Monday afternoon, a month after she'd been reunited with her mother, she picked up her cellphone and called the

United Nations building in New York, asked to speak to Sheikh Hanif al-Khatib.

She was put through to his office. His secretary was polite. 'Sheikh Hanif is not expected in the office today, Miss Forrester. Do you wish to leave a message?'

Having screwed herself up to make the call, disappointment flooded through her.

'Tell him I called, will you?'

Then, even before she'd hung up, she was summoned to the Chairman's office and, before she knew it, she was on a plane to Paris.

'Are you doing anything tonight, Lucy?' one of her colleagues asked as they went down in the lift.

'Forget it, Jamie. After that Paris trip, she's holding out for the boss.'

'I think she's got bigger ambitions than that,' someone else chipped in as the doors opened and they headed for the door.

'Bigger? What's bigger than that?'

'Royalty.'

Lucy, who had until that moment ignored the usual banter, turned and stared at the girl who'd spoken.

'What are you talking about?'

'I took a phone call for you from some bloke who said he was a sheikh. While you were away.'

Lucy felt her knees buckle. She'd come back from Paris hoping that Hanif would have called back. When she found out he hadn't...

'I didn't get any message. When did he ring?'

'Come on, it was a wind-up,' the girl said. Then, 'Tuesday, Wednesday. I left a note on your desk.'

'It wasn't there when I got back this morning.'

'Hey, don't fret,' Jamie said. 'I'm short a white stallion but I can whisk you away in a BMW coupé—'

'Black,' she said, cutting him short as she punched the lift button to call it back so that she could go and search for the message. 'The stallion has to be black.'

'Black. Right.' Then, 'Is that your way of telling me that there's no point in asking you out for a drink?'

'No point whatever,' she assured him, but none of the men were listening. They were all too busy crowding through the door to drool over the black Aston Martin parked in front of the entrance.

From her place by the lift Lucy saw the door open, the driver step out. He was dressed casually enough in well cut trousers with a cashmere sweater over an open-neck shirt, but no one would have mistaken him for anything but what he was. A man who commanded vast empty spaces that ordinary men would find daunting.

His eyes held hers as the lift doors opened in front of her. People filed out but she didn't move and a pathway seemed to open up as he walked towards her.

'Hanif…'

Lucy felt as if the air had been knocked from her body and he caught her shoulders as if afraid she might fall. He was always catching her before she fell, she thought.

'You called,' he said.

'I only just got the message that you rang back,' she managed. 'I was in Paris…'

'Paris?' He smiled. 'You are living life with a capital L…'

'No. It's my job… What are you doing here? Is Ameerah with you? When did you arrive?'

She was gabbling, talking too quickly, asking too many questions, but not the important one. The one that mattered.

Why are you here?

'You called and I came,' he said in response to her thought. 'I would have been here earlier but I had to present my credentials at the Court of St James's this morning.'

She frowned. 'But doesn't that mean…'

'That I've delivered my report to the UN, that my new post is in London. I'm here as my country's Ambassador.'

'Don't tell me,' she said. 'You miss the rain…'

'I miss you. And since you are here, this is where I must be too.'

He'd had his hair cut, she realised. It lay in thick, soft, dark layers, shining under the street light, and she reached without thinking for the leather tie that she'd used to hold back her own hair.

The one he'd used to tie it back for her. The one that she shouldn't be wearing. Like the amber silk blouse. The black linen trousers…

'And yet you put the Queen before me?' she demanded.

He smiled as if no words could have pleased him more.

'When Her Majesty finds ten minutes in a busy schedule, it's a brave man who is prepared to ask her to wait, to tell her that he has someone more important to see. Besides, now that's done, I can concentrate my whole mind on you.'

'Oh…' Then, 'Your *mind?*'

'My mind, my body, take whatever part of me you want.'

She swallowed. 'Is Ameerah with you?'

'In London, safe in the care of her nanny. She cannot wait to see you.'

'I've missed her so much.'

'Just Ameerah?'

No. Not just Ameerah.

'Can it be,' he said, glancing at the men standing slack-jawed behind her, then slipping into Arabic, 'Can it be that you have found the life you were looking for and have no time to spare for me?'

'No! I will always have time for you, Hanif. I owe you my life.' She smiled up at him. 'It's finally on a path forward, thanks to you. I've found my mother—at least she found me. I'm starting university next autumn—'

'I'm glad for you, Lucy,' he said softly and at that moment she realised that her path forward had begun not when she'd walked away from him, but at the very instant she had met him, when he had scared her witless with his knife, had saved her from a fiery death.

'Have you found somewhere to live yet?'

'What?'

'In London.'

'No. I haven't even begun to look—'

'The embassy is conveniently close to the School of Oriental and African Studies.'

She did not ask him how he knew. He could read her mind... If only she could read his.

'The rooms are large. Fully furnished. There is every comfort.'

Her breath caught in her throat. For a man of Hanif's traditions, beliefs, there would be only one reason he would ask her to move into his embassy.

'Have you come all this way simply to offer me accommodation, Your Highness?'

'You begin to read my mind, as I read yours, Lucy. There is, however, one small problem. You will have to share.'

'A room?'

His hands slid from her shoulder to her hands. He clasped them in his, drew them close to his chest, to his heart. 'Share my life, my world. You called and I have flown from New York with my heart in my hands, Lucy. My future. I have come to beg you for yours. To ask you to be my only wife, my one princess, to be the honoured mother to Ameerah. To the children that may come.'

She bent to kiss his hands and when she looked up at him her eyes were misted with tears.

'You are my life, Hanif. My one love. You are my prince and the husband of my heart. My life is yours.'

EPILOGUE

'ARE you sure about this?'

Lucy straightened, refusing to give into the backache that had kept her awake all night, had been plaguing her all morning. Nothing, not even the imminent arrival of her first baby, was going to deprive her of the magic moment when she received her degree.

'You can't make it through dinner without a dash to the bathroom,' Han said. 'You'll never be able to make it through the entire ceremony.'

'They've given me a seat on the aisle so that I can take comfort breaks. Honestly, I'll be fine, Han.' Her darling looked so anxious that she reached out, rubbed her hand reassuringly against his arm. 'Just tell me that this ridiculous hat is on straight and then go and sit down.'

'It's perfect. You're perfect.' Then, 'If it's too much, just get up and walk out. Everyone will understand.'

'Han!'

He kissed her and then, because there was nothing else he could do, he joined her mother and all the other proud family members waiting to see their loved ones receive their degrees.

The wait seemed endless for him as name after name was called. For Lucy, he suspected, it felt like an eternity.

'Her Highness Princess Lucy al-Khatib…'

He let out a sigh of relief. Another few minutes and they could leave.

She made it up the steps, graceful as a galleon in full sail, crossed to the Chancellor, the daughter of another royal house, who kissed her cheek as she offered her congratulations.

Then, as Lucy reached for the certificate, he saw her face change.

He didn't wait for her to turn to him. He was out of his seat and running towards her before she found him amongst the crowd.

Two hours later, Lucy, exhausted, watched as he took this newest member of the al-Khatib family from the midwife.

'Well?' she asked.

There had been an unspoken pact between them; neither of them had wanted to know whether the child they were expecting was a boy or a girl, but there was a wobble in her voice now, an uncertainty, a fear that he would be disappointed if this baby was not the son he had so longed for.

'Do we have Jamal or Elyssa?'

He looked at her, took her hand and raised it to his lips, before laying their newborn against her breast.

'We have a baby, my love. A beautiful, healthy baby.'

THE ICE
MAIDEN'S SHEIKH

ALEXANDRA SELLERS

Alexandra Sellers is the author of over twenty-five novels and a feline language text published in 1997 and still selling. Born and raised in Canada, Alexandra first came to London as a drama student. Now she lives near Hampstead Heath with her husband, Nick. They share housekeeping with Monsieur, who jumped through the window one day and announced, as cats do, that he was moving in. What she would miss most on a desert island is shared laughter. Readers can write to Alexandra at PO Box 9449, London NW3 2WH.

**Alexandra Sellers' fabulous new novel,
The Untamed Sheikh, will be published in the
Summer Sheikhs collection from
M&B™ in August 2010.**

The author would like to express her grateful
thanks to the publisher for the permission to
use the following stories:

"*There is more Light here*," the story of Mulla
Nasrudin and the lost key, has been retold from
THE EXPLOITS OF THE INCOMPARABLE
MULLA NASRUDIN by Idries Shah (Octagon
Press, London, 1983). Used by permission.

"*Hospitality*," the story of Anwar Beg and the horse,
has been retold from CARAVAN OF DREAMS
by Idries Shah (Octagon Press Ltd., London, 1968).
Used by permission.

One

The bride was missing.

Jalia ran along the balcony, anxiety beating in her temples. The soft green silk of the bridesmaid's veil fell forward yet again to cover her face, half blinding her, adding to the helpless confusion she felt. But she had no time now to struggle with it.

What was wrong? Where had Noor gone, and why?

Oh, please let it be just one of her games. Let her not have changed her mind like this, in the most embarrassing possible way....

"Noor!" she called softly. "Noor, where are you?"

A confused, murmuring silence was replacing the earlier sounds of celebration coming from the large central courtyard of the palatial house, and Jalia's heart sank. Hopeless now to think she might find

Noor quickly so that the wedding could proceed without an obvious delay.

This balcony overlooked a smaller courtyard. If Noor had come out here, surely she would have realized at once that she had gone the wrong way?

"Noor?" She leaned over the railing. Below, the courtyard was empty. A fountain played with the sunlight, creating an endless spray of diamonds; flowers danced in the breeze; but no human shadow moved across the beautiful tiles.

Ahead of her, in a breathtaking series of arches and columns, stretched the shadowed balcony, leading to an ancient arched door like the secret door of childhood dreams. No one.

"Noor?" A bead of sweat dropped from under the veil onto her hand. Half heat, half nerves. Was the bride's flight her—Jalia's—fault? People would think so. Jalia would be blamed, by some more fiercely than by others.

Latif Abd al Razzaq Shahin, for one, would condemn Jalia's interference in her cousin's sudden engagement to his friend Bari. He already had, and Jalia was still smarting from the contact.

"Noor!" she cried more loudly, because secrecy was impossible now. Oh, how like Noor to create a melodramatic, self-centred, eleventh-hour panic, instead of taking the calm, rational course Jalia had advised. All the princess bride had had to do was insist on taking a little more time before committing herself irrevocably to a stranger in a strange land!

And how like Noor, too, to leave her cousin to pick up the pieces. Thanks to Noor's open-mouth policy, Jalia's opposition to the hasty wedding was well-known in the family. People would blame her for this outcome.

He would blame her. Not that she cared a damn for Latif Abd al Razzaq's opinion, but his criticism could be biting and cruel, and he disliked Jalia almost as much as she disliked him. He would probably relish this opportunity to put her so drastically in the wrong.

As if the thought had given rise to the devil—or the devil to the thought?—the man himself appeared before her on the balcony a few yards away. He was wearing the magnificent ceremonial costume of a Cup Companion, but she shivered as if at the approach of menace and dodged behind one of the columns of worn, sand-coloured brick.

But she had been mesmerized a second too long, and he struck fast, like the falcon he was named for. The next moment he was before her, blocking her path.

"Where has your cousin gone?" demanded Latif Abd al Razzaq Shahin, Cup Companion to the new Sultan, in a commanding voice.

Jalia's skin twitched all the way to her scalp. She shrank against the pillar in instinctive animal alarm, then forced herself to stand straight. Her face was totally covered. How could he know who she was, behind the veil? He was only guessing.

"I dant now vot you are tawkeen abowt," she said in a deep, breathy voice. "You are made a meestek."

He shook his head with the unconscious, bone-deep arrogance she so hated. Whatever Latif Abd al Razzaq decided to own was his, whatever he decided to do was right, and everyone else—life itself—had to submit. That was the message.

Anger sang through her blood and nerves. How she detested the man! He was everything she most disliked about the East.

"The game is over, Jalia," he said through his teeth. "Where did she go?"

She wanted to walk away, but her path was blocked by his body. She would have to push past him, and she discovered that she was deeply reluctant to do so.

"I am not who you sink. Lit me pess," she commanded, with icy disdain.

He raised a hand, his teeth flashing as she instinctively flinched. Slowly and deliberately he caught a corner of the scarf that covered her to draw it back over her head.

Her thick, ash-coloured hair lay over one side of her face, a heavy wave curving in against the high, delicate cheek, half masking one slate-green eye as she lifted her chin with a cool, haughty look.

His hand remained tangled in the scarf, the pale hair brushing his knuckles as Latif and the Princess gazed at each other. Deep mutual hostility seemed to warp the air between them.

After a curious, frozen moment, his fingers released the supple silk and his hand withdrew. With the breaking of the connection the air could move again.

"Where has your cousin gone?" he asked in a harsh, low voice.

Her chin went up another notch, and her jade eyes flashed cool fire. She showed no embarrassment at having been caught in a lie.

"Don't speak to me in that tone of voice, Excellency."

"Where?"

"I have no idea where Noor is. Perhaps in a bathroom somewhere, being sick. I am looking for her. You waste time by keeping me here. Let me pass, please."

"If you are looking for her in the house, it is you who waste time. She has fled."

Jalia's heart dropped like a diving seabird. "*Fled?* I don't believe you! Fled where?"

"That is the question Bari sent me to ask you. Where has the Princess gone?"

"Are you telling me she's left the house?"

"Don't you know it?"

Involuntarily she glanced down at her own closed fist. "No! How would I know? I was waiting with the other bridesmaids...."

His eyes followed hers. Her fist was clenched tight on something. In a move that was almost possessive, his hand closed on her wrist. Calmly he forced her hand over, so that the fingertips were uppermost.

"What is it?" His eyes flicked from her hand to her face and rested there, with a grimly determined look.

"None of your bloody business! Let go of me!"

"Open your hand, Princess Jalia."

She struggled, but his strength was firmly turned against her now, and she could not get free. After a moment in which they stared at each other, she had the humiliation of feeling the pressure of his finger between her knuckles, forcing her hand open.

On her open palm a diamond solitaire glittered with painful brilliance.

Again his green eyes moved to her face, and the expression she saw in them made her stiffen.

"What is this?" he demanded as, with long, strong fingers, he ignored her struggles and plucked the ring from her palm. He let her wrist go so suddenly she staggered.

He held it up in a shaft of sunlight that found its way into the shadows of the balcony through some chink in the ancient arched roof. It glowed and flashed, but even the fabulous al Khalid Diamond couldn't match Latif Abd al Razzaq's eyes for glitter.

"What is this?" he repeated accusingly.

"A cheap imitation?" Jalia drawled with exaggerated irony, because Noor's engagement diamond was unmistakable. The al Khalid Diamond was probably worth about a thousand times what had been paid for the modest engagement band of opals encircling Jalia's own finger.

The ring's value, as much as its stark, flashing beauty, had delighted Noor, but it didn't tempt Jalia one bit. She knew too well what came with a ring like that—a man like Bari al Khalid...or Latif Abd al Razzaq.

"Tell me where your cousin has gone."

"What makes you so damned sure *I* know? Back to the palace, I suppose! Where else would she go?"

Her scarf was slipping forward over her face again. Jalia began irritably tearing at the pins that held it. What a stupid bloody custom it was, the bride having to be chosen from among a group of bridesmaids, all with scarves draped over their heads, to test the groom's perspicacity! Everyone knew the groom was always tipped off as to exactly what his bride would be wearing, and today anyway Noor had infuriated all the diehards by wearing Western white. Bari would have had to be blind and ignorant to miss her, even under the yards of enveloping tulle.

But everyone had insisted on playing the ancient ritual out, nevertheless. It was just one of many reasons why Jalia was grateful that her parents had fled Bagestan years before she was born, and why she was not happy about their plans for coming back.

Latif Abd al Razzaq was another.

He gazed at her, incredulous. Jalia knew he would never believe that, as opposed as she had been to Noor's hasty, ill-conceived wedding, Jalia had had absolutely nothing to do with this last-minute sabotage.

But what did she care? What Latif Abd al Razzaq thought of her mattered precisely nothing to her.

She flung the beautifully embroidered scarf away from her, not caring that it caught on a rosebush bristling with thorns.

"You have her ring."

"Yes," Jalia admitted coolly.

"How did you get it?"

"What makes it your business to ask me that question, Excellency? And in that particular tone of voice?"

His voice shifted to a deep growl. "What tone of voice do you want from me, Princess?" he asked abruptly.

Jalia's skin twitched, but she brushed aside her nervous discomfort.

''I would be quite happy never to hear your voice at all.''

Jalia was glad of Latif Abd al Razzaq's dislike, of the fierce disapproval that he didn't bother to hide. A man like him could only be an enemy—she knew that much—and it was safer to have the enmity in the open. Then no one was fooled.

Looking up at him now, in the deep green silk jacket that intensified the dangerous depths of his emerald eyes, a thickly ornamented ceremonial sword slung from one hip, she felt the antipathy like a powerful current between them.

She didn't know why he should dislike her, though she understood her own deep dislike of him clearly enough: he embodied everything she least liked in a man. Autocratic, overbearing, sure of himself, supermasculine, proud of it.

''Did Noor speak to you before she fled?''

She sighed her outrage. ''What do you hope to gain by this?''

''Did she drop any hint? Did she say she was heading to the palace?''

''Will you stop imagining I stage-managed this? Whatever Noor is doing, and whoever is helping her, I had nothing to do with it! Has it occurred to you *at all* that this may not be what it looks like? For all you or I know, Noor was enticed out of the house by some threat—''

''Ah! She did not leave of her own accord?'' The emerald eyes glinted with mocking admiration.

''I don't know! Can't you get it past your rigid mind-set that I have no idea why Noor has left—if she has?''

"If?"

"Well, I only have your word for it, Excellency, and you have now and then shown a predisposition to wanting to see me put in the wrong!"

His Excellency gazed at her without speaking for a moment.

"We must talk to the others. Come."

He turned on his heel and started along the wide, roofed terrace, then entered the arched passageway that led into the main courtyard of the house.

Jalia's jaw clenched, but she had to talk to Noor's parents, and that meant apparently obeying Latif's command. Besides, she reminded herself, he had the ring, and if she wasn't present he would be sure to put some damning interpretation on the fact that he had found it in Jalia's own hand.

TWO

They descended the magnificent worn marble staircase to the main courtyard, where an air of subdued confusion hung over the wedding party. People were milling around, wondering and speculating, or simply looking bewildered.

Only the Sultan and Sultana looked unruffled, serenely chatting to whoever approached them, so that a tiny island of calm was created in the sea of unhappy excitement.

''What happened?''

''Where is the Princess?''

''Has someone been taken ill?''

''Is the wedding called off?''

The cloud of questions billowed her way, but Jalia didn't stop; Latif was striding along as though the people were so many trees, and she was grateful to have the excuse to keep going. She had nothing to tell.

In the spacious, pillared reception hall, the families were grouped together on the low platform at one end of the room, talking in quiet, distressed voices. Everywhere the rich carpets were spread with tablecloths laid with china, crystal and silver, as if a thousand people had decided to picnic at once.

"Jalia!" Her mother and aunt, both looking tearful and confused, ran to her. "Did she say anything to you before she went? Where is she going? What happened?"

"H-has she really left the house?" Jalia stammered. She had never seen the two princesses so deeply distressed. Oh, how she wished she had been a little more reasoned in her opposition to Noor's wedding! If her interference had contributed to this unhappiness…

"Didn't you know? She has gone! She took the limousine! Still wearing her dress and veil!"

"She didn't even change?" Jalia gasped. "But where could she go in her dress and veil, except back to the palace? Did she take any luggage?"

"The servants say it is all still stacked in the forecourt, nothing taken. There's no sign of her at the palace. They will phone if she turns up, but if she had been heading there, surely she would have arrived by now! Tell us what happened!" her aunt begged.

"Aunt, I have no idea what happened! I wasn't with her."

But any information, she knew, was better than nothing at a time like this. "I went up with the other bridesmaids to collect her at the right time. The hairdresser said she'd gone into the bathroom. We waited. After about five minutes, I followed her in. She wasn't there.

"I'm sorry, Aunt Zaynab, I should have raised the alarm right away, but I thought it was just nerves or she'd gone out to the wrong balcony or—" She bit her lip. "So I went to look for her. I suppose that wasted time, but I thought…"

Her aunt patted her hand. "Yes, you thought it was just one of Noor's little games, Jalia. Anyone would have. But it's more serious than that. It must be, for her to leave the house. Did she say anything to anyone? When I was with her she was fine, laughing, so happy and excited…."

"Aunt, she—I found her ring. It was on the floor in the room I am using. She must have gone out that way to avoid being seen."

Latif produced the al Khalid Diamond. Her aunt all but snatched it from him, moaning with horror.

"She must have panicked," someone offered. "Bridal jitters."

All around the room, eyes dark with blame rested on Jalia. She was saved from whatever might have been said next when Bari al Khalid's uncle came into the room, looking harassed and bewildered.

"Bari has gone, too! The guards say he drove out a few minutes after Noor!"

"*Barakullah!*" Princess Zaynab wailed. "What is going on?"

Latif Abd al Razzaq spoke, his calm voice stilling the rustle of horrified panic. "One of the guards saw her drive away and came to tell Bari. He went after her to bring her back."

Where Latif stood was suddenly the centre of the room. Everyone turned to gaze at him.

"He asked me to find Jalia and ask her what she knew."

Again, as one, they all turned more or less accusing eyes on Jalia.

"I don't know anything about it!" she wailed. "She didn't say a word to me." She flicked a glance at Latif. She was sure he had deliberately dropped her in it. "Is it possible she got a phone call—?"

"The maids say not." Princess Muna answered her daughter.

"Where's her mobile? Did she phone someone?"

"In her handbag, in the bedroom. She didn't even take money, Jalia!"

"Oh, my daughter! What is to be done now?" Princess Zaynab cried. "If Bari finds her, so angry as he must be…"

"I will go after them," Latif announced.

"Ah, Your Excellency, thank you! But if you find Noor—"

"Jalia will come with me."

Jalia looked up in startled indignation. "Me? What good can—"

Her mother hurried into the breach. "Yes, go with His Excellency, Jalia. You might be able to help."

Go with Latif Abd al Razzaq? The words had a kind of premonitory electricity that made her skin shiver into gooseflesh. Why was he asking for her company, when he clearly thought her poison?

"Help how? I don't know where she's gone!" she protested, but not one face relaxed. She glared at Latif. "I have absolutely no idea what she's…"

He only lifted an eyebrow, but it was a comment that she was protesting too much. She could see in their faces that most people saw his point. Damn the man!

"Of course you don't, Jalia," Princess Zaynab murmured, patting her hand again, her soft dark eyes liquid with worry. "But Bari will be so angry. Please go with Latif. She may be...calm her down and bring her back. Tell her it's not too late. We will wait here."

Outside, a hot, dry wind smacked her, blowing her wedding finery against her body and dust into her eyes.

The hem of her flowing skirt and the bodice of her tunic were encrusted with gold embroidery, sequins and gold coins. How stupid to go searching for Noor dressed like this! As if she were one of the mountain tribeswomen she had seen in the bazaar, who even seemed to go shopping dressed in magnificently decorated clothes. Some of them were blond, with green eyes, like Jalia, though she had always believed that her own colouring came from her French grandmother.

By the time Latif's car arrived from the parking area, her skin was glowing with sweat and she realized she had taken nothing to protect herself from the sun.

The Cup Companion's ceremonial sword in its jewelled scabbard had been tossed into the back seat. He watched her silently as she slipped into the seat beside him.

"I can't imagine why you feel you need me!" she remarked.

Sheikh Latif Abd al Razzaq gave her a long unreadable look.

"Need you?" he repeated with arrogant disdain, and she felt a strange, dry heat from him, like invisible fire deep under dry grass that hadn't yet burst into open flame. "I was getting you out of the way before they all turned on you. Not that you don't richly deserve it."

As the big gates opened the car crept forward, and two men and a woman flung themselves towards it. One man had a camera on his shoulder, and the woman was thrusting a tape recorder towards Latif's face as she banged on the window.

"Excellency, may we have a word, please?"

"Can you tell us what happened? Did the wedding take place?"

"Why did Princess Noor drive off?"

More reporters were now surging around the car, forcing Latif to drive very slowly to avoid running them down. The questions continued nonstop, shouted through the windows at them, while rapid-fire flashes burst against the glass. Several little red eyes gazed hotly into the car, as if the cameras themselves took a fevered interest in the occupants.

"Damn, oh damn!" Jalia cried.

"Don't give them an opening," he advised flatly.

Jalia had to admire Latif's cool. Although forced to drive at a speed of inches per hour, he gave no sign that he heard or saw the media people. She, meanwhile, found her temper rising as the reporters deliberately blocked their path, banging on the car as if somehow they might not have been noticed.

The fact that the air-conditioning hadn't kicked in and the car was like an oven didn't help her mood.

"Princess! Your Highness!" someone called, and she turned in dismay as another flash went off right in her face. How did they know? She had been so careful!

"Can you tell us why Noor ran?"

"Where did she go?"

"Was she escaping a forced marriage, Princess?"

Forced? Noor had been laughing all the way to the altar. Jalia couldn't prevent a slight outraged shake of her head. Instantly someone leaped on this sign.

"The marriage was her own free choice? Are you surprised by the turn of events?"

But she had learned her lesson, and stared straight ahead. "Damn, damn, damn!" she muttered.

Latif put his foot down on both brake and gas, spinning the tires on the unpaved road. Immediately the car was enveloped in a cloud of dust that blinded the cameras.

Coughing, frantically waving their hands in front of their noses, the journalists backed away. Latif lifted his foot off the brake and, belching dust, the car spurted away.

For a moment they laughed together, like children who have escaped tyranny. Jalia flicked Latif a look of half-grudging admiration. She would have congratulated anyone else, but with Latif there was an ever-present constraint.

"I've been so careful to avoid being identified!" she wailed. "How did they know who I was?"

Unlike Noor, who had reacted with delight, Jalia

had greeted the news that she was a princess of Bagestan with reticence, and was determined to avoid any public discovery of the fact. She hadn't told even her close friends back home.

Who could have given her away, and why?

Latif's dark gaze flicked her and she twitched in a kind of animal alarm. It was just the effect he had on her; there was no reason for it. But it annoyed her, every time.

"They just took an educated guess, probably. Your reaction gave you away."

The truth of that was instantly obvious.

"Oh, *damn* it!" cried Jalia. "Why did I ever take off my veil?"

Three

Laughter burst from his throat, a roar of amusement that made the windows ring. But it wasn't friendly amusement, she knew. He was laughing at her.

"Does it matter so much—a photo in a few papers?"

Jalia shrugged irritably. "You're a Cup Companion—the press attention is part of your job. And anyway, you're one of twelve. I'm a university lecturer in a small city in Scotland, where princesses are not numbered in the dozens. I don't want anyone at home to know."

He slowed at the approach to the paved road and turned the car towards the city. Two journalists' cars were now following them.

"Aren't you exaggerating? You aren't a member

of the British royal family, after all. Just a small Middle Eastern state."

"I hope you're right." She chewed her lip. "But the media in Europe have had an ongoing obsession with the royal family of the Barakat Emirates for the past five years—and it jumped to Bagestan like wildfire over a ditch the moment Ghasib's dictatorship fell and Ashraf al Jawadi was crowned. If I'm outed as a princess of Bagestan, my privacy is—" Blowing a small raspberry she made a sign of cutting her throat.

"Only if you continue to live abroad," he pointed out. "Why not come home?"

Jalia stiffened. "Because Bagestan is not 'home' to me," she said coldly. "I am English, as you well know."

The black gaze flicked her again, unreadable. "That can be overcome," he offered, as if her Englishness were some kind of disability, and Jalia clenched her teeth. "You would soon fit in. There are many posts available in the universities here. Ash is working hard to—"

"I teach classical Arabic to English speakers, Latif," Jalia reminded him dryly. "I don't even speak Bagestani Arabic."

She felt a sudden longing for the cool of an English autumn, rain against the windows, the smell of books and cheap carpet and coffee in her tiny university office, the easy, unemotional chatter of her colleagues.

"I am sure you know that educated Bagestani Arabic is close to the classical Quranic language. You would soon pick it up." He showed his white teeth in a smile, and her stomach tightened. "The bazaar might take you a little longer."

The big souk in Medinat al Bostan was a clamour on a busy day, and the clash between country and city dialects had over the years spontaneously produced the bazaar's very own dialect, called by everyone *shaerashouk*—"bazaar poetry."

Jalia looked at him steadily, refusing to share the joke. She had heard the argument from her mother too often to laugh now. And his motives were certainly suspect.

"And I'd be even more in the public eye, wouldn't I?" she observed with a wide-eyed, you-don't-fool-me-for-a-minute look.

"Here you would be one of many, and your activities would rarely come under the spotlight unless you wished it. The palace machine would protect you."

"It would also dictate to me," she said coolly. "No, thank you! I prefer independence and anonymity."

He didn't answer, but she saw his jaw clench with suppressed annoyance. For a moment she was on the brink of asking him why it should mean anything to him, but Jalia, too, suppressed the instinct. With Latif Abd al Razzaq, it was better to avoid the personal.

Silence fell between them. Latif concentrated on his driving. One of the press cars passed, a camera trained on them, and then roared off in a cloud of exhaust.

She couldn't stop irritably turning the conversation over in her head. Why was he pushing her? What business was it of Latif Abd al Razzaq's where she lived?

"Why are you carrying my mother's banner?" she demanded after a short struggle. "From her it's just about understandable. What's your angle? Why do you care what I do with my life?"

In the silence that fell, Jalia watched a muscle leap in his jaw. She had the impression that he was struggling for words.

"Do you not care about this country?" he demanded at last, his voice harsh and grating on her. "Bagestan has suffered serious loss to its professional and academic class over the past thirty years—too many educated people fled abroad. If its citizens who were born abroad do not return... You are an al Jawadi by birth, granddaughter of the deposed Sultan. Do you not feel that the al Jawadi should show the way?"

Jalia felt a curious, indefinable sense of letdown.

"You've already convinced my parents to return," she said coolly, for Latif's efforts on their behalf, tracking down titles to her family's expropriated property and tracing lost art treasures grabbed by Ghasib's favourites, had been largely successful, paving the way for them to make the shift.

"And my younger sister is considering it. Why can't you be satisfied with that?"

"Your parents are retirement age. Your sister is a schoolgirl."

Jalia was now feeling the pressure. "Nice to have a captive audience!" she snapped. "Is this why you decided I should come with you on this wild-goose chase? You wanted to deliver a lecture? Do you enjoy preaching duty to people? You should have been a mullah, Latif! Maybe it's not too late even now!''

He flashed her a look. ''My opinion would not anger you if you did not, in your heart, accept what I say. It is yourself you are angry with—the part that tells you you have a duty that is larger than your personal life.''

She was, oddly, lost for an answer to this ridiculous charge. It simply wasn't true. Neither in her heart nor her head did she feel any obligation to return to Bagestan to nurture its recovery from thirty years of misrule. Until a few weeks ago she hadn't spent one day in the country of her parents' birth—why should she now be expected to treat it as her own homeland?

In spite of her parents' best efforts to prevent it, England was home to her.

''Look—I've got a life to live, and I've paid a price for the choices I've made. Why should I now throw away the sense of belonging I've struggled for all my life, and reach for another to put in its place? I don't belong here, however deeply my parents do. I never will.''

He didn't answer, and another long silence fell, during which he watched the road and she gazed out at the vast stretch of desert, thinking.

Her parents had tried to keep her from feeling she belonged in England, the land of her birth, and she was resentfully aware that to some extent they had succeeded. Her sense of place was less rooted than her friends'—she had always known that.

Maybe that was why she clung so firmly to what

she did feel. She knew how difficult it was to find a
sense of belonging. Such things didn't come at will.

At the time of the coup some three decades ago,
her parents had been newly married. Her mother, one
of the daughters of the Sultan's French wife, Sonia,
and her father, scion of a tribal chief allied by blood
and marriage to the al Jawadi for generations past,
had both been in grave danger from Ghasib's squad
of assassins. They had fled to Parvan and taken new
identities, and the then King of Parvan, Kavad Panj,
had put the couple on the staff of the Parvan Embassy
in London.

Jalia had passed her childhood in a country that
was not "her own," raised on dreams of the land that
was. As she grew older, she began to fear the power
of those dreams that gripped her parents so inescap-
ably, and to resent that distant homeland from which
she was forever banished. From a child who had
thrived on the tales of another landscape, another people, another way of being, she had grown into a scep-
tical, wary teenager determined to avoid the trap her
parents had set for her.

When she turned sixteen they had told her the great
secret of their lives—they were not ordinary Bagestani exiles, but members of the royal family. Sultan
Hafzuddin, the deposed monarch who had figured so
largely in her bedtime stories, was her own grandfather.

Jalia had been sworn to secrecy, but the torch had
to be passed to her hands: one day the monarchy
would be restored, and if her parents did not live to
see that day, Jalia must go to the new Sultan....

Her parents had lived to see the day. And now Jalia's life was threatened with total disruption. Her parents, thrilled to join the great Return, were urgent that their elder daughter should do the same. But Jalia knew that in Bagestan something mysterious and powerful threatened her, the thing that had obsessed her parents from her earliest memories.

And she did not want to foster the empty dream that she "belonged" in an alien land that she neither knew nor understood. That way lay lifelong unhappiness.

Attending the Coronation had been an inescapable necessity, but it had been a brief visit, no more—until her foolish cousin Noor had undertaken to fall madly in lust with Bari al Khalid, one of the Sultan's new Cup Companions, and promised to marry him.

"Showing the way for us all!" Jalia's mother declared, wiping from her eye a tear which in no way clouded its beady gaze on her elder daughter.

Her mother had been convinced then that Jalia had only to flutter her lashes to similarly knock Latif Abd al Razzaq to his knees, and was almost desperate for her daughter to make the attempt.

Princess Muna had wasted no time in checking out the handsome Cup Companion's marital status and background: not merely the Sultan's Cup Companion, but since the death of his father two years ago, the leader of his tribe.

"He's called the *Shahin*, Jalia. No one's sure whether the word is an ancient word for king or really does mean *falcon*, as the myth says, but the holder of that title is traditionally one of the most respected voices on the Tribal Council. Not that Ghasib ever consulted the council, but the Sultan will.''

Although Jalia hadn't believed for a minute that the fierce-eyed sheikh was attracted to her, the mere thought of what complications would ensue if he or any Bagestani should declare himself had terrified her. She had gone home as soon as politeness allowed.

Of course she couldn't refuse to return to Bagestan for the wedding, but this time she had come with insurance—Michael's engagement ring on her finger. Now when she was asked whether she intended to make the Return, Jalia could dutifully murmur that she had her future husband to consider. No one could argue with that.

''Why do you say this is a wild-goose chase?''

The Cup Companion's voice broke in on her thoughts. Jalia jolted back into the here and now and gazed at him for a moment.

''You think Noor ran of her own accord, do you?'' she said at last.

''She was seen driving the car herself.''

''And if that's so, it means she's changed her mind about the wedding?''

''Do you doubt it?''

Jalia shrugged. That wasn't her point. ''That being the case, do you honestly imagine that, even assuming we find her, we're just going to bring her meekly back to marry Bari?''

''Women do not always know their own minds,'' Latif said with comfortable masculine arrogance.

It was the kind of thing that made her want to hit him. Jalia sat with her fists clenching in her lap.

"Is that so?"

"Your powers of persuasion may have undermined her. But she will return to her senses when she realizes what she has done. Then she will be glad to know that there is a way back."

"Or perhaps she's come to her senses!" Jalia countered sharply. "That's why she ran. It's a pity it took her so long, that's all."

"But of course—she did not come to her senses until she agreed with you!"

The sarcasm burned like acid.

"She was rushing into marriage with a complete stranger, which would entail a total transformation of her life, and on the basis of what? Nothing more than sex! Would you *encourage* someone to do what Noor was doing?"

He turned and gave her a look of such black emotion she almost quailed. "Why not?" he demanded grimly.

If Noor *had* simply bolted, it was going to cause hideous embarrassment all around, but surely anything was better than to marry in haste? Noor had been totally swept away by Bari's looks and wealth and sex appeal, but that was no foundation for a marriage, still less for uprooting from everything she knew and transplanting to Bagestan.

"For a start, because she's not in love with him! She's blinded by—"

"If she does not love him yet, it will not be long coming. Bari will see to that, once they are married."

Jalia's mouth fell open, angry irritation skittering along her spine. "Oh, a man can make a woman love him, just like that?"

"What kind of man cannot make his own wife love him?"

Her eyes popped with reaction to the arrogance; her mouth opened.

"And how exactly does a man go about it?"

At the look in his eyes now she gasped as if she'd been punched in the stomach.

"Who is your fiancé, that you do not understand a man's power over a woman?" asked the Cup Companion.

Four

Jalia sat up with a jerk. A chasm seemed to be opening up before her, and without having any idea what it represented, she knew it was dangerous.

"What *are* you talking about?" she said mockingly.

The car stopped at a traffic light on the outskirts of Medinat al Bostan. Below them, in the magnificent tapestry that was the city, sunlight gleamed from the golden dome and minarets of the great Shah Jawad mosque and glittered on the sea. It was a heart-stopping sight, she couldn't deny that. Talk about your dreaming spires!

Latif turned and gazed at her for an unnerving few seconds.

"You know what I am talking about," he accused through his teeth.

She didn't, if he meant from personal experience. No man had ever reduced her to adoration on sheer sexual expertise alone, and what he said was just so much masculine arrogance!

"So sex is a crucible in which to melt your wife's independence?"

"Her independence? No. Her dissatisfaction."

"And how many wives are you keeping happy?" she asked sweetly.

"You know that I am not married."

"But when you are, your wife will love you? Oooh, I almost envy her!" she twittered, while a kind of nervous fear zinged up and down her back and she knew that the last woman in the world she'd envy would be Latif Abd al Razzaq's wife. "I *don't* think!"

His eyes burned her.

"So what is the secret of eternal wedded bliss?" Jalia pressed, against the small, wise voice that was advising her to back off.

His jaw tightened at her tone, and he turned with such a look she suddenly found herself breathing through her mouth.

"Do you wish me to show you such secrets in the open road?" he asked, and she was half convinced that if she said yes he would stop the car where it was and reach for her....

"Not me!" she denied hastily, and a smile, or some other emotion, twisted the corner of his mouth. "But if you look around—well, it can't be well-known, or there'd be more happy marriages, wouldn't there? I can't help feeling you could make your fortune marketing this secret."

She was getting under his skin, she could see that, and she pressed her lips together to keep from grinning her triumph at him.

He looked at her again, a narrow, dangerous look, and Jalia's eyes seemed to stretch as she watched him. ''In the West, perhaps. But I think even a How To book would not help your fiancé.''

''I—what—?'' Jalia babbled furiously.

Latif moved his hand from the wheel to where her hand lay on the armrest between them, and with one long, square forefinger fiercely stroked the three opals of her ring.

Jalia snatched her hand away in violent overreaction.

''Do you intend to marry this man?''

''What do you think?''

''I think you would be a fool.''

The light changed and he let out the brake and turned his attention to the road. Fury swept over her like a wave. Though he spoke perfect truth, *he* could not know it. She laughed false, angry, deliberately mocking laughter.

''How kind of you to have my interests at heart! But you don't know anything about Michael.''

''Yes.''

''What, exactly, do you profess to know? You've never even seen him!''

''I have seen you.''

''And you don't know anything about me, either!''

''All I need to know for such a judgement.''

''And what have you learned about me that allows you to prescribe for my future?'' she couldn't stop herself asking, though a moment's thought would have told her she would not come out of the encounter the winner.

He deliberately kept his eyes on the road.

"Your fiancé has never aroused real passion in you," he said grimly.

Jalia jerked back as if he had slapped her. A rage of unfamiliar feeling burned in her abdomen, almost too deep to reach. She felt a primitive, uncharacteristic urge to leap at him, biting and clawing, and teach *him* a lesson in the power of woman.

"How dare you!" she snapped instead, her Western upbringing overruling her wild Eastern blood. She was half aware of her dissatisfaction that it should be so.

His laughter underlined the feebleness of her reply.

"This is what you say to your English boyfriend, I think! Do you expect it to affect such as me?"

"And what would it take to stop *you?* A juggernaut?"

"Ah, if I taught you about love, you would not want me to stop," he declared, a mocking smile lifting one corner of his mouth, and outrage thrilled through her. She knew the last thing on his mind was making love to her. He didn't even like her!

"It'll be a cold day in hell before you teach me about love!" Jalia snapped, as something like panic suddenly choked her. "Suppose we agree that you'll mind your own business when it comes to the intimate details of my love life?"

He was silent. She looked up at his profile and saw that his face was closed, his jaw clamped tight. Disdain was in the very tilt of his jaw as he nodded formally.

''Tell me instead where your cousin will have gone.''

She didn't know how she knew, but she did: the words were a struggle. They were not what he wanted to say.

''I have told you I don't know.''

Although she had demanded it, Jalia was disconcerted by the abrupt change of subject. She had more to say, plenty more, but to go back now and start ranting would look childish.

They were approaching the city centre now: the golden dome appeared only in the gaps between other buildings as they passed.

''You must have some idea.''

''If you're thinking I'm a mind reader, you overestimate me. If you imagine I had prior knowledge, go to hell.''

His eyelids drooped to veil his response to that.

''I am thinking that if your cousin had made friends in al Bostan you would know who they are. Or if she had found a favourite place—a garden or a restaurant—she might have shown it to you.''

My manner is biting off heads. The line of poetry sounded in her head, and he really did look like a roosting hawk now, with his cold green eyes, his beaked nose, his hands on the wheel like talons on a branch. A brilliantly feathered, glittering hawk, owner of his world.

And exerting, for some reason she couldn't fathom, every atom of his self-control.

''She is wearing a white wedding dress and veil, you know. She's not going to be able to just disappear. In a restaurant or any public place she'd attract comment.''

''Where would she go, then?''

Her imagination failed. Where could you hide wearing a staggeringly beautiful pearl-embroidered silk wedding dress with a skirt big enough to cover a football field and a tulle veil five yards long?

Latif put his foot on the brake and drew in to the side of the road, where, under a ragged striped umbrella, a child was selling pomegranates from a battered crate. At the Cup Companion's summons the boy jumped up to thrust a half dozen pomegranates into a much-used plastic bag, and carried it to the car.

As Latif passed over the money he asked a question, which Jalia could just about follow. The urchin's response she couldn't understand at all, but from his excited hand signals she guessed that he had seen Noor pass.

Latif set the bag of fruit into the back seat beside his sword and put the car in motion.

''What did he say?''

''He saw a big white car go past with a woman at the wheel and a white flag streaming from the roof,'' he reported with a smile twitching at the corner of his mouth. ''About half an hour ago. Another man in a car asked him the same question soon after. The white car hasn't come back. He's not sure about the other.''

''A white flag!'' Jalia exclaimed. ''Why would she be flying a white flag?''

''To signal her surrender?''

His dry voice made her want to laugh, but she suppressed the desire. She had no intention of getting pally with the man.

They were in the city centre now. Latif began cruising the streets, turning here and there at random. As best she could, Jalia monitored passing cars as well as those parked at the side of the road. She glanced down each side street as they passed.

Jalia sighed.

"Oh, if this isn't just Noor all over!" she muttered. "Turn a deaf ear to everything until it suits her! If she'd listened to me when I was talking to her—if she'd actually sat down and considered what I was saying, she would have come to this conclusion long ago. Instead she waits until it's almost too late and will cause the maximum chaos!"

Latif threw her a look. "Or you might say that if you hadn't tried to force your views on her so unnecessarily, there would have been no fear suddenly erupting in her and taking over."

"You say unnecessarily, I say necessarily…" Jalia sang in bright mockery, then glowered at him. "Why are you right and I'm wrong?"

"I?" he demanded sharply. "It is Bari and Noor's judgement that you challenged, not mine! I have no opinion, except that when two people decide to get married they should be left to make their own fate!"

She whooped with outrage.

"And what were you saying to me not twenty minutes ago?" she shrieked. "Were you advising me not to marry Michael, or was I hallucinating? *You would be a fool to marry this man!*" she cited sharply. "Was that what you said, or do I misquote you?"

His eyes met hers, and she sensed a kind of shock in his gaze. A muscle in his cheek twitched, but whether with annoyance or an impulse to laugh she couldn't tell. It *was* funny, but she was too annoyed to find it so.

"You blame your cousin for not giving serious consideration to your doubts about her engagement, but you do not listen to my doubts about yours. Who has the double standard now?" he said, with the air of a man pulling a brand from the burning.

Laughter trembled in her throat, but she was afraid of letting her guard down with him. Jalia bit her lip.

"Great! We're both hypocrites," she said, shaking her head.

Instead of making a reply to that, Latif jerked forward to stare out the window.

"*Barakullah!*" he breathed.

He had turned into the wide boulevard that led down to the seafront. At the bottom was the broad, sparkling expanse of the Gulf of Barakat, and miles of bright sky.

Jalia narrowed her eyes against the glitter. Off to the right a forest of silver masts marked the yacht basin.

"A yacht!" she cried. "Of course! I'll bet she knows someone on a boat—maybe some friend even sailed over for the wedding. The perfect hide—"

"Look up," Latif interrupted. He stretched an arm past her head, pointing into the sky, where a little plane glinted in the sun as it headed up the coast towards the mountains.

"That plane? What, do you think—?"

"It is Bari's plane."

Jalia gasped hoarsely. "Are you sure?"

"We can confirm it soon enough."

"But what—?" Jalia fell silent; there was no point

babbling questions to which neither of them had answers.

Latif turned the car along the shore highway. After a few minutes he turned in under an arched gateway in a high wall, and she saw a small brick-and-glass building and a sign announcing the Island Air Taxi service to the Gulf Eden Resort.

Out on the water several small planes were moored, bouncing gently in the swell. Latif stepped on the brakes and pointed again. Ahead of them on the tarmac, carelessly taking up three parking spaces, as if the driver had been in too much of a hurry to care, sat a large white limousine, parked and empty.

They slipped out of the car.

"Is that it? Is that the al Khalids' limousine?" she asked.

He nodded thoughtfully.

"My God," Jalia breathed. She felt completely stunned. She stared up at the glinting silver bird in the distance. "Is Noor at the controls, do you think? Why? Where can she be going? And where's Bari?"

Latif turned his head to run his eyes over the half dozen other cars in the lot, then shook his head.

"His car is not here."

She stared up at the plane as if the sight of it would tell her something. A gust of wind struck her, blowing the green silk tunic wildly against her body. She felt a blast of fine sand against her cheek.

Latif stiffened to attention beside her. He was still looking into the sky, but not at the plane. Frowning, Jalia turned her head to follow his gaze.

In the past few minutes a mass of cloud had boiled from behind the mountains, and even as she watched it was growing, rushing to shroud the sky over the city.

Over the water the sky was still a clear, hot blue, but that couldn't last. Jalia turned her head again to stare at the plane, watching anxiously for some sign that it was banking, turning, that the pilot had seen the clouds building and made the decision to put down again.

But the little plane, the sun glinting from its fat wings, sailed serenely on.

FIVE

Five

There was little sleep for anyone in the palace that night. The phones rang constantly, with family and friends in the country and abroad calling for news, calls from officials organizing the search team, and journalists around the world clogging up the line asking for details of Princess Noor's Fatal Peril.

Everybody felt worse when the couple's disappearance began to be announced on repeated television news bulletins in the early evening and the announcer's voice resonated with the kind of gravity that meant he thought Princess Noor was probably dead.

But they couldn't just turn it off. It was entirely possible that some reporter would get wind of a search team discovery and broadcast the news before the family was notified. The regular announcements became a horrible kind of compulsive listening for them all as more and more journalists joined the fray.

On the breakfast terrace early the next morning, bleary-eyed but unable to sleep, and fed up with the constant insensitive badgering, Jalia delivered herself of a few blistering comments to one journalist and hung up the phone to find Latif watching her.

He was silhouetted against the morning sun, and she couldn't see his expression. She dropped her eyes and picked up her coffee.

"Is there any news?" she asked. The question had taken on the impact of ritual. They were all constantly asking it of each other.

"Have you heard that the Barakat Emirates have sent a couple of planes to join the search this morning?"

Jalia nodded.

Latif set something on the ground, then moved over to pour himself a cup of coffee. "Then there's no news."

"God, how I hate sitting here doing nothing more productive than fielding calls from the media. If only there was something to *do!*" she exploded. Part of the emptiness she felt was the letdown after the blizzard of wedding preparations, of course. But Jalia was also missing the hard, rewarding work of her university life.

Latif remained standing, resting his hips back against the table, gazing out over the courtyard. He swirled the coffee in his cup.

"Well, why not?"

Jalia looked up, and his eyes turned to her with a hooded expression she couldn't fathom. "What do

you mean, why not?'' Suddenly her eye fell on the
case he had set down by a column. She frowned in
sudden dismay.

"Are you leaving?" How could he go when they
were in such trouble? Bari was one of his closest
friends!

He took another sip of coffee. "I'm going to drive
up into the mountains to ask in the villages whether
anyone saw or heard a plane coming down in the
storm.''

She stared at him, the fog of a sleepless night
abruptly clearing from her brain. "What a brilliant
idea!'' she breathed. "I wish I could do something
useful like that!''

Latif shrugged as if she impressed him not at all.
''Why don't you?''

"It would take me a week to decipher the answers." The mountain dialects of both Bagestani Arabic and Parvani, Bagestan's two languages, were
very different from what was spoken in the cities, and
Jalia had trouble enough even in the city.

Latif said nothing, merely turned, set down his cup,
and rang the bell. A servant came out and asked what
he would eat. Latif shook his head.

"I don't want food, thanks, Mansour," he began
in Arabic. "You have a son named Shafi."

"God be thanked. Fifteen years old, a strong
healthy boy. A very good son."

"I am going into the mountains to help the
search," Latif explained. "I will need another pair of
eyes. Would you allow Shafi to accompany and assist
me? I may be gone several days."

Mansour's expression was pained as he clasped his

fist to his chest. "Willingly, Lord! But alas, he is not at home! As you know, he—"

"Thank you, Mansour," Latif interrupted him.

The servant turned to go, but Jalia called him back.

"I beg that thou be so good as to bring His Excellency some food wherewith to break his fast, if it please thee," she said in her formal, antiquated Arabic. And to Latif, "You ought to eat something if you're going on the road."

Latif laughed aloud and turned to the servant. "An omelette, then, Mansour."

Mansour bowed and went back inside. In the tree a bird sang entrancingly, but could not lighten the gloom and worry in Jalia's heart.

"What are you going to do?" Jalia asked.

Latif pulled out a chair. "I have no specific plan," he said, sitting down opposite her. He reached for the warmed bread left on her plate with a kind of intimate assumption of her permission, and tore a bite-sized piece off with long, strong fingers. "The mountain villages don't get television and they don't have phones. So the only way to—"

"I meant, who will you take with you to be the extra pair of eyes?"

He shrugged. "It's not important."

But of course it was. How could his search be effective if he had to watch the road the whole time?

"I'm not doing anything. I should have been going home tomorrow, but I can't leave with Noor missing," she offered hesitantly. "I could go with you, if you liked."

Latif's mouth tightened. "I expect to search v

something definite turns up," he said stiffly. "I may be away several days."

"Where will you sleep at night?"

"Sometimes in village rest houses, sometimes under the stars. Whatever comes. It won't be comfortable. And there may be fleas in the rest houses."

Maybe it was his obvious reluctance that hardened the momentary impulse into determination. This was her chance to get away from the media, the phone and the helpless speculation and do something actively useful.

"Better fleas with a chance to help," she said, who had never had a fleabite in her life, "than sitting with my mother and aunt, worrying uselessly."

She could see that Latif didn't like the idea, and of course she didn't relish being with him, but what would that matter if they found Noor and Bari?

"Don't you think you'll do better with another pair of eyes?" she pressed.

His eyes rested on her face with an unreadable expression.

"She's my cousin, Latif."

"And he's my friend. But conditions will be primitive."

"What gave you the idea I expect to be pampered?"

"There's a lot of ground between primitive and pampered, Princess."

A glint in his eyes made her think he was deliberately baiting her as a way of resisting her suggestion, but his resistance only fuelled her determination. She stifled her irritation, always so quick to ignite in his presence.

"You won't be able to look around for signs of the plane as you drive if you go alone. You'll need your concentration for the road—especially those twisty, rugged mountain roads," she argued. "And even supposing you did find them, how would you cope with…"

She trailed off. In a sudden moment of clarity, as if she had come out of a trance, or lifted her head out of water, the thought appeared in her head: *Travel around the countryside with only Latif Abd al Razzaq for company? Are you crazy?*

What demon had possessed her?

"Oh, never m—" she began. But she had come to her senses too late.

"No, you are right. Two will be much more effective than one. Thank you, I will be glad of your help. Pack something warm. It gets cold in the mountains at night," said Latif Abd al Razzaq as the trap closed on her. "We will leave in an hour."

"Do you have a plan in mind?" Jalia asked as the road began to climb and the mountains rose over them, dangerous and seductive, like Latif himself.

Jalia was lying in the bed she had made, though she had done her best to unmake it. She had rushed to tell her mother about the trip, hoping for a reprise of the old *this is not the West, this is Bagestan, and we must not offend people by violating their customs* argument. But when she had gently hinted that people might be shocked if she drove around with a man not related to her, her mother had only shrugged.

"Ghasib ran a secular government for over thirty years, and people here have more casual attitudes now. If you meet someone disapproving, just say Latif is your husband.''

"Thanks, Mother!" Jalia snapped. "And then they'll put us in the same bed! I don't think so!"

Her mother lifted her hands. "Then say he is your bodyguard. For goodness' sake, Jalia, who would have guessed you would be so old-fashioned? Noor is missing. Your aunt is out of her mind with worry! If you have to put up with the company of a man you don't like for a few days to help find your cousin, surely that's a small price to pay?''

Which was quite true. Noor's parents had been hugely kind to Jalia all her life, giving her fabulous holidays in Australia every year since she was a child. They had always treated her very kindly on those long childhood visits.

Of course she was grateful to them. Noor was like a sister to her—spoiled and exasperating, but nevertheless loving and loved.

And yet, it was with a feeling of somehow having been outmanoeuvred that Jalia had joined Latif and tossed her pack into the four-wheel drive.

"Plan?" Latif responded now. "My plan is to follow the advice of Mulla Nasruddin.''

The name was familiar: it signified a joke figure in folktales, but Jalia hadn't paid much attention to the ancient stories since she was a teenager.

She frowned a question, and Latif explained,

"One day one of his neighbours discovered the Mulla on his hands and knees under a street lamp near his house and stopped to ask what the problem was.

"'I am looking for my house key, which I have dropped,' said the Mulla.

"The helpful neighbour immediately dropped to his knees and joined the Mulla in the search. After some time, the key had not turned up.

"'Where exactly were you when you dropped your key?' the neighbour asked at last.

"'Standing at my front door,' said Mulla.

"The neighbour stared. 'But in that case why are you searching here in the street, yards from your house?'

"Mulla Nasruddin drew himself up. 'Have you not noticed,' he said, 'that *this* is where the *light* is?'"

One corner of Latif's mouth curved up as he finished the tale, and Jalia laughed. He told the story well.

"But I'm not sure I get the point," she confessed.

Latif flicked her a smile. "We don't know where the plane went down. But we will look for it where we *can* look."

Jalia laughed softly; they exchanged a look; and suddenly a powerful connection was flowing between them that was very different from the suppressed hostility she usually felt.

A jolt of awareness socked through her. For the first time she realized how deeply attractive a man Latif was—not just physically, with his black hair, his falcon's looks and his smoothly muscled body, but mentally.

But what did that matter? She wasn't attracted to him, and even if she were, nothing would induce her to turn her back on the life she had created for herself and come to Bagestan.

She knew without asking that Latif Abd al Razzaq was inextricably bound to Bagestan. He had worked and struggled for years to assist the Sultan to the throne.

So there was no need for her heart to start beating as if she had discovered danger.

The woman moved smilingly around her simple house, dressed in one of the most gorgeous outfits Jalia had ever seen anyone make mint tea in—a wine-red velvet skirt and long tunic trimmed around neck, hem and cuffs with gold braid and shimmering gold medallions, almost as elaborately beautiful as the bridesmaids' outfits at Noor's wedding.

Over her waist-length black hair a gauzy black scarf glinted with more medallions. Her arms were circled with dozens of bracelets; black, kohl-rimmed eyes breathed the power and mystery of the feminine.

The mountain tribeswomen were known for the luxury of their daily dress, and Jalia couldn't help wondering what effect it would have on the psyche to get up every morning and dress in such finery. In front of the house a young girl, similarly dressed, expertly kept her veil in check as she pounded spice in a stone mortar. The sharp, pungent odour filled the air.

"It is well that the Sultan has come back," the woman was saying, and either this village dialect was extremely pure, or her own ear was acclimatizing after a few days, because Jalia could understand her with little problem. "Please tell him that whenever he wishes to call he, too, will be an honoured guest in our house."

She was laying out a huge meal for them, on the traditional cloth spread on the ground under a tree.

Jalia was horrified by the amount of food being prepared for them, for these were obviously poor people. The woman's husband, she had told them, gathered firewood and sold it in the village to eke out the living from their farm.

"But what will they eat tomorrow if we eat all their food today?" she demanded of Latif when the woman left them alone.

He lifted his eyebrows at her. "God will provide."

"After three years of drought," she pointed out dryly.

"You are too Western," Latif said. "Do you think we have adopted Western generosity here—to give only what does not cost us? Here in the mountains, generosity is generosity. Do you not know the story of Anwar Beg?"

She sometimes felt with him that she was in a book.

"Tell me."

"He had a magnificent horse, which a friend of his wished to buy. But however high the price, however hard he negotiated, Anwar Beg would not part with his prize beast, and at last the man was forced to give up.

"Then one day he heard that Anwar Beg had fallen on hard times, and hardly had food to put on the table. He said to himself, now he will have to sell that wonderful horse of his, and he went to Anwar Beg's house.

"Anwar Beg invited him in, and his friend sat down and tried to open negotiations. But Anwar Beg stopped him. 'You are my guest. First there is the matter of hospitality,' he insisted.

"So the two men waited while the meal Anwar Beg ordered to be prepared for him was cooked and served. Scarcely containing his impatience, his friend ate the delicious meat stew that was brought, complimenting his host on the meal.

"'Friend,' said the man when the meal was finished, 'I wish to make you an offer again on that magnificent horse which you have always refused to sell.'

"Anwar Beg shook his head. 'Impossible,' he said.

"'But surely, with things with you as they now are,'' the neighbour cried, 'you must listen to reason! Sell me the horse! I will give you a good price for it so that you can provide for your family.'

"'It is impossible,' repeated Anwar Beg. 'You came to me as a guest, and it was necessary to show you hospitality. Having no other food to offer you, I ordered that the horse be slaughtered to make the stew you have just eaten.'''

Jalia gazed at Latif a long time when the story was finished, and predominant among her feelings was guilt. "I could never live up to a standard like that," she said quietly.

"Yes," he contradicted her. "This story describes not what is, but what we strive towards. You have a more generous spirit than you know—it is in your eyes. And in your blood. The al Jawadi have a tradition of great generosity.

"Think of your grandfather's generous treatment of the young orphan boy, Ghasib, who grew up to betray him. This is the blood you have inherited, Jalia, whether you know it or not. And when you stop being afraid, then you will find your generosity."

He was always saying things like that, what she called his "gnomic utterances."

"When I stop being afraid of what?" she asked, indignant.

"I cannot do all the work for you. Some things you must discover for yourself," he said, and in his voice was an urgency that frightened her.

Six

Latif kept his eyes on the road. It was all he could do not to shout at her, so angry was he—at her wilful blindness, at fate, at himself.

Himself. Why should he blame her, or fate, when his trouble was of his own making? Fate had put her in his way; he had doubted fate's wisdom, as fools do. He had been too cautious in embracing the way fate showed him, and now he could never embrace her as his wife....

"Princess Muna, Sheikh Ihsan," Ashraf had said, "here is my trusted Cup Companion, my ally and support throughout our struggle. Latif Abd al Razzaq Shahin will aid you and your family...."

The rest of what the new Sultan said was lost in the clamour in Latif's head. For, standing beside Princess Muna and her husband, watching him with a clear, level gaze, was the woman he had been waiting for since that moment his soul had been plucked from its nest beside her in the heavens and sent into the cruel, testing world.

A stern nobility, which must have told anyone who looked at her that she was of royal blood, was evident in the set of her mouth, the lift of her head.

In addition she had an unusual, harsh beauty, proud and unapproachable. Her eyes were coolly intelligent as she gazed at him, and he felt that only he could see through to the secret of a passionately generous heart.

All that he saw between one painful heartbeat and another.

The thick fair hair had seemed like a fall of honey against her cheek, the promise of sweetness so tangible he had to clench his fists not to wrap his hand in its silky strands, bend closer to inhale the odour, bury his mouth in the taste.

"…Jalia…" he heard through the drumming of his heart, and with a fist at his breast, he bowed.

"Princess Jalia," he said. His voice must have told her what he felt, how he took her name into himself, took her, possessed her self and her name forever by speaking two words that changed his life….

"I don't use that title," she had responded with chilly disdain, cutting through the haze that enveloped his brain with the frosted blade of hauteur. "My name is Jalia Shahbazi, Your Excellency."

Like a man on a journey faced with an ice-topped mountain in his path, he had advised caution to his heart. She was hostile and guarded, and he couldn't guess why.

Logic told him that nothing would be gained by a direct assault. He must give her time.

Weak, cowardly thought that it was, his heart had given it room, had considered it, had bowed to the dictates of logic when deep instinct told him that he must challenge her, that his own passion's fire would melt the ice in which her heart was encased.

He had given her time, but time was not his to give. Within days she had fled back to the cold northern country of her birth.

She had given no warning of her departure. Merely the next time he had met her parents and asked for her, he learned that she had gone "home" that morning.

For the next few weeks, carrying out his duties for the Sultan, advising Jalia's parents about their lost properties and treasures, helping them in their plans to return to Bagestan, he had called himself a fool. To be so blinded by a woman's beauty, to be so challenged by a cold demeanour—it was no more than a fool's obsession, a child seeing what it can't have and wanting it because of that.

Angry with her for her coldness, angry with himself for his heat, telling himself his heart was not truly engaged—so he had passed the time until the day of her cousin's wedding to his friend had approached, and Jalia had reluctantly returned to Bagestan.

And now she was wearing a ring. Another man's ring.

The first time he had seen her he had been deafened by the thunder and rushing of his own blood. This time he had been blinded—by a haze of anguished fury that ripped at him. Broken heart? he remembered thinking dimly. Whoever felt so weak a torment had never known love: Latif's heart had been set upon by wild dogs and torn to pieces. He would never put it together again.

It waved at her from the top of a ridge, a soft silver hand catching the sunlight with a syncopated rhythm of glimmer under the bright sun, a liquid mirror. The breath hissed between her teeth as she groped for the binoculars against her chest.

"Something?"

The truck slowed, and she nodded once as she fitted the glasses to her eyes. "Something large and metallic. Moving in the wind."

Latif Abd al Razzaq pulled the four-wheel drive off the road and stopped, and Jalia combed the ridge with the binoculars to find it again.

"There," she said. It was a chunk of aluminum, perhaps, silver but not necessarily with the glitter of newly ripped-apart metal, not necessarily part of a plane that has crashed taking two young and vital human beings to a wasteful death.

"I can't tell what it is."

But he had already turned off the engine and now stepped out on the grey-and-brown mountainside. Jalia scrambled to follow.

A familiar sense of dread dragged at her. In the past few days there had been a half dozen times when she had seen something that might have marked wreckage from a downed plane, and each time her heart beat a frantic, anxious message in her temples, weighted down her stomach so that she felt old.

She clambered after him across the rugged, half

breathtaking, half terrifying landscape, towards the ridge of rock overlooking a crevasse. Behind it the mountainside rose sheer and raw, making her dizzy.

If the plane had crashed here and gone over the edge…how far down was the floor of the crevasse behind that ridge?

The last few yards were difficult, and she was panting with fear and exertion as she approached the edge. Above her, Latif reached the object she had seen and knelt down to examine it.

"A cargo door," he said as she came up, and her hand flew to her mouth.

"Oh, God!" It lay broken and torn where it had been caught on a sharp rock and prevented from falling over the edge. A thin strip of torn shiny metal attached to a hinge waved in the air. "Was there—is it part of Bari's plane?"

A sudden breeze caught the glittering aluminum, and her heart fluttered in time with it. Jalia dropped flat on her stomach and peered over the rocky ridge.

"No, it is too big. Part of a commercial or military aircraft, lost in flight. It has been here for a long time," Latif said.

"Oh, thank God! Are you sure?" Her constricted lungs opened again, her heart calmed. She believed him, but still she put the binoculars to her eyes and peered over the ridge to get a view of the bottom.

She wasn't sure what hope there could be, if the plane had come down anywhere in the mountains. But she hated to imagine it pitching down into terrain like this.

"There's a *valley!*" she cried. Nestling down among the crags was a wide green oval, thriving with life. She took the glasses from her eyes and peered down, half disbelieving.

"From the road you'd never guess it was there!" At either end of the valley two thrusting formations of rock created a kind of optical illusion when she looked up, seeming much closer together than they were.

"Look at those two peaks at either end! From this angle, don't they look like falcons or hawks or something? What a beautiful place."

"Royal falcons," he said. "They are called the *Shahins*."

She became aware of a sense of peace surrounding her. In the far distance Mount Shir presided over all, a brooding presence, dangerous and protective at the same time, the powerful mother-father of the lands that pressed against her like suckling infants.

Jalia lifted her head and gazed up at the rich blue sky. Suddenly she understood that her defensive attitude towards this country had prevented her truly seeing it.

Now, for once, she allowed herself to see what she was looking at, to feel the air that surrounded her. It was so fresh, so pure. And it seemed charged with energy, as if the great mountain were a generator.

"This really is a wonderful place," she murmured and, turning to share it with Latif, she smiled at him. "I'm beginning to understand why my mother and father never lost their hope of returning home."

She gazed down at the valley again. There weren't words to describe the calm and beauty that lay over the scene.

"I can see goats! And farms—how can it be so

green after such a long drought, I wonder? So many trees. Do you know the name of the valley?" she demanded, thinking she would not be surprised to hear him say *Shangri-La*.

"We call it Sey-Shahin," he said. "Three Falcons."

She turned to look into his face, her eyebrows climbing with surprised enquiry.

"Yes, this is my home," said Latif Abd al Razzaq Shahin. "Outsiders give us, and the valley, the name Marzuqi."

"Marzuqi," Jalia repeated softly. *The Blessed.* She could see how the valley had achieved the name. It looked fertile and protected, and as old as time.

"It's so green," she said, feeling how inadequate the word was to describe what she saw and felt.

"The drought did not affect us so badly here, so when the rains came, the fields recovered quickly."

Jalia glanced around. "Can we go down? Where is the road?"

The valley looked at first glance to be completely surrounded by impenetrable, unyielding rock. But Latif pointed across the valley to where a grey line emerged from a dark circle like an egg under the feet of the falcon-shaped rock, and slanted slowly down to the valley floor.

"That is the tunnel. The road has been badly damaged by the heavy rains since the drought ended. At the moment the way in and out is on foot, or by mule."

"My God, how will people manage?"

A pebble was dislodged under her elbow and went over the edge to bounce down and down. She watched it with a curious feeling that the movement had significance.

"We are used to it. The road is only a few years old, and was badly made. Ghasib finally forced the tunnel through because every time he sent his administrators to the valley they lost their way in the passes. Some say that Genghis Khan had the same difficulty."

Jalia laughed and clapped her hands together in delight. "So this is the valley that was never conquered?"

"Even Islam came to Sey-Shahin very late. There are many ancient rituals among our people that exist nowhere else in the world. Western scholars sometimes wish to come here to study what they call 'living tradition'—hoping to find a mirror of the past in the present practices of the Marzuqi people."

She frowned in thought. "I remember someone in the department coming on a field trip here a few years ago with very high hopes. But I don't think—"

She stopped because of his expression. "What happened? Do you know?"

"Possibly he got lost in the passes," Latif said guilelessly, and Jalia erupted in a burst of laughter, then clapped her hands over her mouth and sat gazing up at him, her eyes alight.

His eyes met hers in shared amusement, and she felt a treacherous prickle along her spine that said it was not only the land her prejudices had prevented her seeing clearly.

"The only experienced guides in this area are Sey-Shahini tribesmen. Sometimes a bribe is high enough, and someone slips through. That encourages others to think that such bribes work. Guides used to make a living in summer from failing to find the valley.''

She was laughing, though God alone knew why. Being an academic herself, she ought to have regretted the thwarting of scholarship.

But the valley looked so enchanting that something in her did not want to think of its people being analysed and ''published.''

Her blood was stronger than her academic loyalties, maybe. Certainly as she gazed down at the flourishing little valley, her heart was drawn there.

''Suppose *I* wanted to—''

The expression on Latif's face struck her a blow that left her breathless, and choked the words in her throat. He was looking at her as if that was exactly the question he wanted to hear.

A chasm opened in front of her, without warning, dangerous and deep, as Jalia understood that she had been mistaken in his feelings all this time. Latif Abd al Razzaq might be angry, he might be impatient, but it wasn't dislike that was motivating him.

He wanted her. It was there in the fierce emerald eyes, in the set of his jaw, in the way his hand gripped the rock he leaned against—as if he held it to prevent himself from reaching for her. Every muscle and ligament now shouted the truth that she should have heard weeks ago—had heard, perhaps, and had run from.

But blindly. Like a terrified fool in the dark she had run straight into danger, straight into the falcon's nest.

Suddenly she saw it—the whole process by which he had brought her here, out into the starkly beautiful land of her ancestors, to the heart of his own existence, to a state of mind where she could no longer deny the land's deep and abiding hold over her heart and blood. It was a trap, baited with the simplest psychological techniques.

This was what her parents had hoped for—that the country would somehow get to her. That the land and the people would convince her where words could not.

What a fool she had been, playing with so potent a danger as a man like Latif Abd al Razzaq. Her first instinct had been right—to run. She should never have come back to Bagestan, ring or no ring. What good would a ring do if her own heart betrayed her?

The silence extended while he watched the play of emotion on her stern, beautiful face.

"What did you want to say?"

"Nothing," said Jalia. "We'd better get going."

She was under threat. She knew it. Back in the little truck she watched Latif's profile surreptitiously, and reminded herself that she didn't go for the dark, eagle-eyed look.

And yet...oh, how his masculinity emanated from him, reaching out and touching her with an aura that said, *I am a man. You are a woman.*

She might not go for his type, but from the beginning she had instinctively felt that there was something about Latif that spelled danger for her. She should have done anything rather than let herself get into this vehicle with him and head off into a country of stark beauty with no time limit and no destination.

But she knew it too late.

They got lost in the passes. Jalia looked around her as they drove over the rough stony road. My God, and well they might! she thought. The road itself was sometimes hardly discernible to an untrained eye; could she be sure of following it even five miles?

If she tried to get away from Latif up here she'd be the Woman Who Never Returned. They'd find her skeleton in twenty-five years…

She was stuck with him. Because she knew without asking that he would not turn around and take her back home. And she was afraid to ask, for fear of what the asking would tell him.

She was watching him, hardly aware of her own focus, in a state near panic. He was so attractive, so vital, like a healthy wild animal. His blood seemed to pulse with life just under his skin.

And he was getting under hers. He always had, if only she'd had the wit to realize it. *This* was why she'd run home after the Coronation. It was why she was wearing Michael's engagement ring right now.

Not because of some nameless threat from her parents, but because she was on a precipice with Latif Abd al Razzaq, as surely as the pebble she had knocked over the ridge to the valley.

Seven

Night closed in quickly in the mountains. As darkness fell Jalia sat by their campfire on a plateau, watching the sunset.

In the broad rugged pass they were travelling through, the villages were few and far between. Below, a boy followed a couple of skinny goats along a sloping path, his lazy switch urging them home. In the little village on the edge of the valley, a white cloth hung on a line, flapping in the breeze. Smoke trickled up from a hearth fire.

She wondered who was tending that fire, and whether that woman's life was anything like her own.

It was Sey-Shahin Valley again, but from a different vantage point, for the road had twisted away from the valley for the past few days as it fought its way through the passes.

Last night they had stayed in a small village clinging to a rugged slope. It was the last village they had seen.

Today they had travelled a whole day through bleak, empty passes, in a large erratic circle around the base of one giant falcon-shaped peak.

The road had finally led down into the tunnel hewn through the living rock. An hour ago they had emerged onto a narrow plateau, with the valley spread out below them.

To one side, a tiny waterfall showed where a mountain stream tentatively flowed again after the years of drought. There they had found a level, lightly wooded spot to pitch their tent.

The haunting sound of goats' bells and a distant *muezzin* mingled on the clear air. The sun was going down in flames behind the mountains, and in the long, lonely shadows all around her lay a starkly beautiful landscape dominated by the two rocky sentinels, one towering above her, one on the opposite side of the green valley.

Over all brooded the ever-present, distant white peak now bathed in liquid gold, Mount Shir.

Jalia wished it were not so beautiful. Out here, face-to-face with the land, she found that it pulled at her heart with a feeling that was almost pain. From the beginning of the adventure this yearning for the might-have-been had been aching in her, just beyond the reach of consciousness.

Since her first view of Sey-Shahin Valley, though, she had been sharply aware of it: if Ghasib had never betrayed her grandfather, this would have been her country. She would have been familiar with these crags and passes, with the magical green valleys, with the handsome and courageous people who lived here, where life held such different values than those she had grown up among.

And where she might have thrilled with delight when Latif Abd al Razzaq took command of every situation and of her, looked at her with possessive eyes, told her what a man could do to make his wife love him....

The memory of that conversation in the car on the day of Noor's disappearance had been called up again since her moment of enlightenment overlooking his valley home, and now, with the birds in the valley singing the sun down, the air crisp and clear all around, and water set for boiling in the fire she tended, it summoned up in her a fierce longing.

What Latif had spoken of was part of the mountain warrior's code in the land that should have been the land of her birth—bravery in battle, generosity to friends, hospitality to strangers, and for your wife...virile lovemaking.

At the time, sitting in the car beside him, feeling so attacked by his disapproval, she had been sure Latif had said what he had merely to be provocative. But after that strange silent exchange on the crag overlooking the valley, something had changed between them.

Now her imagination kept revisiting earlier moments, reassessing what she had seen and felt from him. And now, when it was too late to do her any good, the truth of that conversation in the car seemed so wildly obvious she could hardly believe she'd missed it—Latif had spoken the way he did because he was attracted to her. Because, in spite of his denial, he *had* imagined teaching her—what had he said?— *a man's power over a woman*. Even then.

And the attraction had not lessened with proximity. What a fool she had been to come with him on this fruitless search! Instead of saving Noor, she had put herself in danger.

She could feel the intensity of his desire, as if the air thickened around them, whenever he approached, and it was getting more powerful and impossible to ignore by the hour.

She could feel it now, when he was out there in the shadows somewhere, hunting. It was over her like a cloak, a blanket of sexual heat, stroking her hair, kissing her skin with a hunger unlike anything she had dreamed possible.

How had she not understood it from the beginning? How had she been so blind?

Need burned like honey in her muscles as she remembered his eyes, his deep voice, making her stretch slowly and lift the heavy fall of hair from the back of her neck while an unfamiliar sensuousness warmed her, and she heard his voice again in her head.

Who is your fiancé, that you do not understand a man's power over a woman?

She raised her head, and Latif was there, standing in the black shadows on the other side of the fire, watching her with a face like a brigand's, the face of a man who sees what he wants and means to take it.

Jalia's eyes widened as she stared up at him, double flames leaping in her half entranced, half frightened gaze, her hands frozen in her own hair, sensual need making all her movements languid with unconscious erotic temptation.

He could take her now—the truth was there in her eyes. For one night he could make her his.

This night.

Latif's gaze licked around her with flame hotter than the fire. His lips parted for a moment, then closed resolutely. She saw how passionately full his mouth was, and how iron control held it firm. If a man like him ever let go...

If the mountain beneath her cracked from side to side...

Without a word he turned away and bent to drive a notched stake at one side of the fire with neat blows from his axe. Then a second, on the other side. He set a third, thinner stick to rest on the notches. On it was a small animal carcass, neatly skinned. The flesh began to hiss and blacken as the fire licked it.

Later they lay side by side in their sleeping bags with the night all around them. Overhead the stars gleamed against the lush black fabric of the sky, dense and rich, and so far away.

She was bone tired, she was well fed, but still she couldn't sleep. Jalia lay gazing up at the stars, wondering which of the thousands of sparkles she saw were still alive, and which had died before the earth gave birth to life, yet still sent their light through the void to thrill her.

She felt Latif stir beside her, and turned her gaze. He was lying on his back, his hands crossed under his head. She saw starlight reflected in his eyes. He couldn't sleep either, and she knew why.

It would be dangerous, oh so dangerous, to let him love her. And yet, for one night, just one night…

"Tell me a story," she begged softly.

He turned his head towards her, so that the light was lost from his eyes and she only sensed the way his gaze touched her, dark and probing, almost angry.

"A story?"

"You always have some story that's relevant to whatever situation we're in. Haven't you got a relevant story now?"

"Relevant to what part of this situation, Jalia?" his voice asked softly, and she suddenly felt that where softness was, there lurked danger. "To our search for your runaway cousin, who may have died for a foolish fear? Or to our desire for each other, which we pretend not to be consumed by even though it burns us like a drought every minute, every second we are alive?"

Jalia gasped. Need flamed over her, burning and desperate, because he had put it into words.

"Latif—" she protested. Whether she would have begged him to love her, or to leave her alone, she really didn't know. But whatever she might have said was lost when he spoke.

"A story, you say. Shall I tell you the story of how my desire grew, Jalia? But it did not grow. It was born a giant. In the first moment that I looked at you it was already too big, too powerful, too overwhelming to kill.

"I could only trap it, like a tiger in a net of ropes, hampered, bedevilled, unable to run, made mad by its confinement. Is this the story I should tell you? And what will you tell me in return?"

He paused, and she licked her lips, but no word came.

"You came to this country determined to hate it, to resist it, to reject its claim on you and your mind and heart. I saw this and still I could not stop my heart's knowing that you are mine. You belong to me, Jalia—my heart, my mind, my body, my soul...all that I am says that it is so."

She was shivering with reaction, with fear and dismay. This was more, so much more than she had imagined. This, then, was what she had protected herself against when she put Michael's ring on her finger.

"No," she said, her heart fluttering with panic.

"No," he agreed harshly. "I know it. You have said it every way you can. After the Coronation, before I could try to tell you, to make you see, you fled me. Didn't you? You ran from me because you knew without my telling you.

"I would have hidden it, I would have played the slow game, the Western game, where a man pretends he does not want a woman—or maybe it is not a pretence. How does a man see what his whole life depends on and then pretend he does not need it?

"You knew how it was with me. But I did not know you knew until you had run away from me.

"I could not chase after you, to that cold country where you live, not when there was so much for me here, so much work that every day, every hour counts. And even if I had gone to bring you back—you are a woman who does not love this country. Was it right that I should go after you, bring you home, make you mine, when your whole heart could not be here?

"I said to myself, I will let her go. A man does not love forever in one moment."

Chills coursed over and through her, of an emotion so powerful it was like drowning.

"That was my foolishness, to think so," he went on, his deep voice beating with emotion like a drum. "You are mine, and it has been so since the first moment. Nothing changes that, whether you stay or go, whether you admit it or not.

"You are mine because my heart bound itself to yours before you were born. Because fate made us one heart and then divided it, and now I have found you again."

She tasted salt on her lips, and discovered that she was crying. Tears of grief because of who she was, because she couldn't be the woman she might once have been, that woman whose heart could go to him freely, who could see her fate, her whole life, in a man's words.

"Oh, Latif," she whispered desperately.

"No," he said, "I must tell you the story you asked for. Here in the land that is mine, I must tell you. You came back, but not to me. You were next to me, but out of reach. You came back with a ring that tells me you belong to another man. That is our story, Jalia."

Eight

He raised himself on one elbow beside her, and his head blotted out the rising moon. It was a welcome darkness, a darkness in which anything was possible, and without conscious thought, driven by a hunger too strong to resist or to name, she reached for him.

With the cry of a soul stretched beyond its limits he wrapped his arms around her, dragged her bodily across the little distance that separated them, so that she was pulled half out of her sleeping bag. Then with a muttered word of protest—against her? against his own weakness?—he bent and smothered her mouth with his kiss.

Jalia's heart leaped like a wild animal, twisting and writing against the cage of her ribs, straining to get into his hand, the strong, hard hand that gripped her ruthlessly and pulled her against him, as if his hands understood her heart's call, were trying to free her heart to love him.

His mouth was fierce against her lips, pressing, chewing, his tongue seeking, his hunger harsh against the soft flesh he desired. With a moan Jalia gave herself up to the assault, her arms clinging, her mouth opening wide to receive his kiss, to give whatever he asked.

Her body raged with a passionate need that distantly amazed her, her blood hot, melted gold, a rich, slow river delivering glowing desire to every part of her, body and soul.

Her breasts sang with delight at the pain of being crushed against his warm chest, at the joy of feeling his heart's wild beating against her body. Her skin shivered and burned as his hands pressed and owned her back, her arms, her neck and face.

His mouth lifted from her mouth and traced over her cheek and chin, then, as her head fell obediently back, down the long line of her throat to the wild pulse at its base.

Then he lifted his head and his hand gripped her upper arm and held her away.

"But my story does not end here," Latif said ruthlessly, and his voice grated with the effort he was now exerting over his own flesh, his blood, his heart, his soul.

"Latif." Jalia moaned her loss in the syllables of his name, a pleading that had never been in her voice before. "Latif, love me, please love me."

He raised his chest, and cool air brushed her. She felt how real the bonds that linked them were, now, because they were being torn as he drew away from her.

"Latif!" She lifted her hands to his face, feeling she would die if she could not hold him and love him.

He caught her wrist and held it tight, too tight, lifting her hand into moonlight.

"Do you ask me to love you with this on your finger?"

The breath rasped in her throat. She had forgotten Michael, forgotten the ring, forgotten everything in the mad sweetness that flooded her.

"Yes!" she cried, for the sweetness still beckoned her on. "Latif, please!" She reached for him again.

"Take it off," he growled, as the tendrils of belonging took advantage of their closeness to enwrap them.

"What?" Jalia pressed a kiss into the little hollow in his shoulder that had been designed for her lips. Drunkenly she thought that she would give anything for the right to kiss his skin just here, all the rest of her life.

"Take off this man's ring. You will marry me. Swear it, and I will love you and you will be mine forever."

So the serpent entered paradise; and she felt its cool silkiness shiver up her heated body, and trembled under the sudden chill of its whispered reasoning.

"What do you mean?" she faltered.

"Do you think I want you for one night, one week, one year, even? You are mine, Jalia. In your heart already you belong to me. Only say it, and I will love you."

An emerald sparkled in a stray moonbeam as his

eyes burned her from the mysterious darkness where his face was. His hands held her tightly, and a part of her thought that she would always be safe in a hold such as this.

"I can't marry you," she protested, and inexplicable tears burned her cheeks.

"Can't?" He repeated the word in a harsh, grating voice, and she saw a flash of white teeth.

"You know I can't. You said it yourself," she accused. "I don't belong here, Latif. It's not my home."

"A woman belongs with her husband. His home is her home. You belong with me. You are Bagestani. Your blood is here. Your heart is here. Your people call to you. I call to you."

His hands tightened on her as the words rained down on her, as if he knew that he had lost. He bent and kissed her again, and fire swept out from the contact of his mouth into her body and soul.

"Answer me," he commanded.

"I want to be your lover," she sobbed. "Please take me as a lover, Latif, and don't ask me for more."

He sat up, his sleeping bag falling down to his hips, exposing his hard-muscled torso to the sharp light and shade of moonlight.

"Are you such a fool as this?" he rasped. "Do you think we can be lovers, and then you will go back and marry that man, and forget what love we had, forget how my body has branded you?

"If I love you, I make you mine! You will be closer to me than my own heart! What shall I do when my heart wishes to leave my body? Do you ask this of me?"

His eyes were black hollows in the harsh shadow

now, his face angled and sharply defined in the moonlight, making him more like a bird of prey than ever.

Her heart twisting with hurt, she drew back from him into the comfortless warmth of her own sleeping bag.

But fear was more powerful than the pain. She knew this was not a question of heart, or even of love: she hadn't known him long enough for that. This was powerful sexual passion, masquerading as love, and she would be ten times worse than a fool to be swayed by it.

Like Noor. Who was now in a downed plane somewhere, paying, perhaps with her life, for a too-long toying with dangerous magic. Was she, who had seen the truth so clearly in Noor's case, going to be blind in her own?

"I'm not Bagestani, Latif," she said, her voice hoarse. "I'm English. We can't change the past. I can't live by your rules."

The look on his star-shadowed face then she knew she would remember all her life long. His jaw clenched and, deft as a wild animal, he slipped away from her side and into the night.

She awoke to sunlight and the sound of cracking wood and turned her head to see Latif on his haunches, the long line of his naked back tucking down into lean hips and thighs as he tended the fire.

He must have hamstrings like elastic bands: he sat easily on the flat of his feet, his butt resting down on his calves, as if the difficult posture were second nature to him.

Watching him now she sensed something that surprised her, because he had always seemed at ease in the city and palace environment: here he was in his true element.

Now she could understand what people meant when they said he was a mountain man. The Sultan had told her that during the long years of working for Ghasib's overthrow, Latif had been his chief liaison with the mountain tribes. The nomadic mountain tribes could not be policed and respected no borders; Latif had slipped in and out of Ghasib's Bagestan at will.

Here she became aware of something she couldn't have named before—his inner silence. He had a capacity for stillness, as if he had learned patience from the mountains. It was deeply attractive.

He was quiet, concentrated, open, like an animal drinking at a spring—as if the mountains were a source of sustenance to him.

And like an animal at a spring, he became aware of her regard, and turned his head. Their eyes met for the first time since he had gone off into the darkness last night. She had fallen asleep without hearing him return.

"*Sabah al kheir,*" he said, in the poetic greeting that was still used in the mountains. *A morning of joy.*

"*Sabahan noor,*" she replied with a smile. *A morning of light.*

And it was. The air was fresh and clear and invigorating, and Jalia accepted the now-familiar jolt of longing for a simpler life, slithered out of her sleeping bag, got up to stretch and yawn luxuriously.

When she recovered, he was watching her with unreadable eyes.

"Yes, you are very beautiful," he said. His voice was a rough, possessive caress, and her flesh moved with that heavy awareness that seemed to be associated with him.

She felt fully in her body now, felt how her breasts sat against her rib cage, felt the mobility of her hips, the length of her own legs. Her skin felt every spot where the cotton of her pyjamas brushed her, felt the elastic snug around her slim waist. How her bare feet were planted on the ground, as if she drew her aliveness from the rock, as much as from the air.

She brought her arms across her breasts, her right hand clasping the opposite shoulder, the left hand under her chin, as she stood looking down at him. Unconsciously she stroked the opals with her thumb.

"Yes," he said, taking the gesture as a protest, "and you are mine, and you do not know it. You do not wish me to say it, but I only tell the truth. You are mine. If you wear another man's ring, even if you marry him, does it change the truth? If it is the truth, nothing can change it.

"We belong together. It is better to say it. My silence was not right. I should have told you in the first moment, when I knew it. Then there would not be this engagement. The fault is mine."

Jalia would have denied everything, if only she could have trusted herself to speak. Sensation was running over and through her, half indignation, half melting response. If she opened her mouth to speak, could she know which half would get the microphone?

The mountain man turned back to his task with the fire, and Jalia picked up her toiletry bag, towel and clothes and slipped off up the slope to her morning scrub.

So there were going to be no reproaches over what had happened last night. Latif was, apparently, a man not inclined to sulking when he didn't get what he wanted, and as she washed in the icy little mountain stream, gasping with the shock, she thought of how it would be to have such a man for a husband.

Most of the men she dated sulked, one way or another, if they didn't get their own way. As if they had never quite got over some disappointment with their mothers.

Latif was a man who could, it seemed, accept setback as a part of life, not—as with so many of the men she knew, including Michael—as something someone had done to him.

Her father had always said the mountain men of Bagestan were a breed apart. Maybe you had to come to the mountains to get a real man. If you wanted one. Jalia didn't. Anyway, it was too late for her. To have a man like Latif as husband, she should have been here from birth, for how could she ever fit in to this culture and life, growing up the way she had in the bustle and freedom of a world-class city?

She wasn't sorry, not really. She belonged in another world, when if history had been different she might have belonged in this one, and that, too, was just life.

But a part of her, she realized as she rubbed herself down with the rough towel, trying to get warm again after her chilly dip—a little part of her was sorry to think that she would never experience Latif's real passion.

And she did wonder if she would always remember Latif's passionate proposal as the moment of wildest romantic thrill of her life. How could any Western man match it?

She dressed and returned down the slope to the evocative smell of coffee and wood smoke.

Latif had draped two round flat pieces of *naan* over the spit, and when he handed one to her it was toasted and deliciously flavoured with the fat of last night's meat it had absorbed from the spit.

She spread some goat's cheese on the bread and rolled it up for a simple, succulent breakfast.

"Where to this morning?" she asked, for something to say.

"I want to go down into the valley. It is a journey on foot, since the road has been washed out in many places. Do you want to come with me, or wait for me here?"

Jalia hesitated. "How long will it take?"

"If I go alone, a few hours. If you come with me, longer."

Maybe it was his arrogant assumption that she would slow him down, or maybe just a reluctance to sit here doing nothing, she wasn't sure. But with a little flick of her head that made him smile, Jalia opted to accompany him.

Nine

Arrogant or not, he had been speaking nothing but the truth. Latif went over the deep gullies the rains had gouged into the road with an ease and a balance that terrified her, while Jalia could only inch her way with his help.

When they came to a terrifying drop, an ugly, massive gouge in the road that fell away to nothing, he took her piggyback, and the sheer power and strength beneath her knees had a rhythmic, muscled beauty that carried to her animal brain a deep, pure erotic message, so that her legs' sudden tightening around him caused him to lose his hold for a second, almost pulling them to their doom.

On the road again her body was lazily reluctant to get down.

Panting with the aftermath of sharp fear and sudden

desire, Jalia straightened her clothes fussily, irritated with herself for that uncontrolled response. If she didn't get a grip, she'd find herself married to the man, for no better reason than to experience his love-making.

A truth suddenly dawned on her, as stunning as a clap of thunder—every time she had argued with Noor about her foolish attraction to Bari, she had been talking to herself. She might not have allowed the information into conscious awareness, but unconsciously she had recognized how wildly attracted she was to Latif.

What a fool she had been, blind and smug: because if she had allowed herself to see the real problem, she could have taken much smarter action to avoid Latif.

And she wouldn't be where she was right now—dependent on him for her survival, and hoping against hope that he would crack and make love to her before she cracked and promised him whatever price he asked.

"Why won't you make love to me?" she asked, before she could stop herself, as they picked their way past the boulders strewn in the road.

Latif glanced at her without surprise, so he must have felt that deep connection, too. "I will," he said.

"Oh!" She couldn't stop the smile that played over her mouth, nor the delighted surge of anticipation in her blood, and as if he were powerless in the face of such evidence of her desire, his arms went around her and he pulled her against him.

Fire burned up around her, and with a gasp she parted her lips and tilted her chin to invite his kiss.

"When you have my ring on your finger instead

of the one you now wear," he continued, and then his lips came down on hers with a power of masculine demand that sent sensation whipping into every nerve.

Her arms wrapped him, her body fitted against his as he bent her back over his arm, twined his fingers into her hair, and the hard, pushing response of his arousal pressed against her to produce a fierce melting that buckled her knees like butter on a stove.

Her head was caught in the crook of one arm, his other hand was hot and hard against the back of her waist, and she felt how easy it would be for him to overwhelm her, because he was strong, much stronger than she had guessed, and her blood soared with the knowledge.

He lifted his mouth and stared at her from green eyes almost black with need. She had never seen so deep a green, and she could have stayed there all day just exploring the magic of that emerald pitch, that glinting hunger, feeling her danger and her safety in his hold, feeling how the world held its breath.

"It will be difficult," he admitted, with a hoarse exhalation. "Which of us will be the winner?"

Jalia took a deep, calming breath. It was impossible to make love here on the road, but she had lost track of time and place while his mouth was on hers.

Around the next mound of fallen rock they met a team working to mend the road. With only manpower and a couple of donkeys they were gathering up the rocks that had come down from the ridge above and were packing them into the gullies that the rains had gouged: backbreaking, dangerous work, but the men and boys seemed cheerful enough.

When Latif and Jalia appeared suddenly on the

road they all looked up and gave the Bagestani greeting of a fist to the heart. A moment later someone recognized Latif.

"You come in a good time, Lord!" they cried in formal greeting.

"May your shadow never grow less!"

"You come to sit on the council, Lord?" said another anxiously. "I have a petition...."

No one kowtowed to him, Jalia saw, though he was the man they called their *Shahin*: they had too much self-respect, it seemed. Between Latif and the men there was a mutual exchange of respect. And yet it was clear they would accept his judgement.

After a few moments Latif said, "I escort the Princess Jalia on a search for her cousin, Princess Noor," and explained about the downed plane for the fiftieth time since they had begun this quest.

She exchanged nods with the men. In her jeans and desert boots and shirt, she must have been a somewhat unusual sight, but none of them stared at her, a fact she was getting used to after so many days in the mountains.

As her father had told her in endless stories during her childhood, the mountain people of Bagestan were a ferociously proud people, but they were also hospitable and polite, and they would never stare at a strange woman.

Some of the conversation that now ensued was too quick for her to follow, more so since several people were talking at once, but she understood that no one had seen or heard anything resembling a plane in trouble or crashing.

Then it seemed they were urging Latif to remain

in the valley for a day or two to sit with the village council for some important cases. After a while, one man left the team and accompanied Latif and Jalia down the mountain.

The man led them to his own house, where his wife and daughters smilingly produced lunch for them. As usual, they ate in silence, and it wasn't till after the meal was over that Latif said, "There are several urgent matters before the council. It's important that I sit to hear them. But it means that we will not leave the valley tonight."

Jalia nodded her acceptance of the situation.

"Some of the younger boys will go and bring what you need from the truck. What do you need?"

"Only my backpack."

Later, while the members of the council gathered at one of the houses in the village, greeting Latif with loud welcome, the women led Jalia up the hillside to an isolated house set in a walled, terraced garden, whose profusion of flowers and greenery she had noticed from their campsite this morning.

"What house be this?" she asked in her archaic, textbook Bagestani.

"Lady Jalia, this is the home of your future husband." The women smiled. "If you do not know it now, you will soon be familiar with it, if God wills!"

Jalia's smile stiffened a little. This was a dilemma, for if she denied being Latif's fiancée, she would have to be housed somewhere else. She knew enough of the country traditions to understand that.

And she didn't want to sleep anywhere else; she wanted to sleep with Latif. Was she going to turn her back on the possibility that he had cracked, that he had decided to make love to her?

Not a chance. And if this arrangement left Latif in future explaining to his tribe just why Princess Jalia did not return to the valley as his bride, that was his problem, wasn't it?

So in the split second she had to choose, Jalia chose to say nothing. The women smiled and nodded and led her inside.

"The ways of the outside world are strange," one of them observed on a note of laughter. "Here in the valley no man takes his bride to his home before the ceremony has been concluded. How will you negotiate a good dowry, Lady Jalia, if you give up your jewel to his keeping before he pays for it?"

"Even a noble lord like Lord Latif—do not all men dream of capturing a woman's prize, giving nothing in return?"

"For shame, Amina! When a man like Lord Latif declares himself before witnesses, that is as good as a marriage contract!"

They were laughing the way women laugh who are leading the bride to her new husband's bed, and to her amazed dismay, Jalia felt her cheeks growing warm.

"When the time comes, Lady Jalia, will you come to the valley, and let us marry you?" asked one young, pretty woman who, it was obvious from certain joking comments, was only recently married herself.

"Foolish Parvana! The ceremony will take place in the palace, of course...."

So the laughter and banter went on, while the

women showed her around the pleasant house and garden that was Latif's family home. It was bigger than many in the village, but not out of scale: it had two domes, when many of the houses it overlooked had only one, and a very large enclosed garden, and a high wall.

"Because in times of trouble the women and children of the valley came here with the animals," someone explained. "Then the chief and the men would ride out to fight."

"When Ghasib's men came, we did not fight. We had heard that it was more dangerous to fight. Once the tunnel was built, we knew, he could bring as many soldiers as he needed...."

"Many of the treasures of this house were buried, Lady Jalia," someone explained, pointing to the bare walls and floors and niches. "That is how we protected ourselves from Ghasib's looting. We knew that his men would steal all our treasures if they saw them. We hid and buried many, and left out only a few, so that they would not be suspicious. That is why the house is so empty. Do not fear that Ghasib got the treasures of our Shahin."

"No, the earth holds them!"

That seemed to be a joke, too, but no one explained, and with so much going on, and the language so difficult for her, Jalia let it go.

"We had word that Lord Latif would come, but not that he brought his bride! Look how the chamber is not decorated, Lady Jalia, but we will bring perfumes and lamps...."

She didn't protest. Why shouldn't they set up the bedroom for seduction, though they completely misunderstood who would be seduced and who seducer?

Ten

The women, young and old, began the ritual decoration of the bedchamber.

It seemed as if, in order to cope with this invasion of outside moral laxity, they had simply decided to rewrite the agenda. Lord Latif had said that he intended to marry the Princess—therefore he had married her. This was their wedding night.

So the afternoon was spent preparing and bringing special foods for the couple, and creating a bed of flowers and scented boughs, in the ancient tradition, and enacting a few other little rituals that Jalia knew her colleague at university, whose field was the early history of the area, would give his eyeteeth to watch.

Someone gave her beautifully embroidered pyjamas to wear, in soft jade silk, the trousers caught at the ankles, the jacket closed over the breasts with one delicate embroidery frog. Jalia knew it must be something that had been worked on and treasured up for the girl's own wedding, but they insisted, and it was impossible to refuse the gift. All she could do was make a mental promise to herself to find something as beautiful to send back to the valley as soon as she returned to al Bostan.

They bathed her, and rubbed her skin with a curious perfumed salve, and plaited special love knots into her hair, though grieving that it wasn't long enough, not even to the shoulders!—how strange things must be in the outside world, if a woman voluntarily cut off her own glory!

They marvelled at the paleness of her hair, straight and almost white, when every woman in the valley had black, thick curls. Just so, they had sometimes heard, was the hair of the Kamrangi tribeswomen, a marvel someone's grandfather had seen many years ago, when he had accompanied some foreigner as guide into many strange places…

Jalia was falling more and more under the spell of the women and their beautiful valley. Their values were plain and true, their laughter infectious, their collective beauty and wisdom astounding. Whenever she tried to claw back a sense of her own world, it rang false in this pure environment, like a toxin in the fresh mountain air.

She mentioned, for example, the village council that was sitting—weren't the women annoyed that they were not members, that they didn't decide such matters along with the men?

There were smiles and shrugs all around the circle—yes, it was true that in the ancient days in the

valley the council had been all women instead of all
men, and that was as it should be, for women were
much better judges of human nature than men, and
everyone knew it.

But men were good judges of the law. Most peti-
tions to the council now were legal matters—who
owned a piece of land, who was entitled to inherit—
and were both uninteresting and unimportant, though
of course the men could not be expected to think so.

The serious work of the tribe—who should marry
whom, for example, and when, decisions about planting and harvest and festivals—was still carried on by
the women.

And eventually Jalia simply gave up trying to con-
nect the two worlds, and enjoyed being with the
women and seeing life from their point of view.

When the sun was setting beyond the walls of the
beautiful but neglected garden, their work finished,
the women declared that the council would have broken up by now. They left Jalia in the lamp-lighted,
sweet-scented bedroom, wearing the silky jade tunic
and trousers, and went off, promising to send Latif to
her.

And within the hour he was there, bathed, oiled and
perfumed in his turn, and wearing a white outfit,
beautifully embroidered, whose flowing silk only underlined his powerful masculinity.

He was unbelievably gorgeous as he entered the
room, a bemused smile playing over his dark falcon's
face.

He stood for a moment looking down at her in the
soft shadows cast by the candle lamps, and Jalia's

heart leaped at the expression that came into his eyes—possessive and hungry and determined.

With a curious shifting the atmosphere grew thick around them, and he gazed at her with green eyes gone black, a signal her body already understood directly. It responded with melting hunger, and she tossed her head in the way he knew so well, pressed her lips together, and let her eyes smile at him.

"The…the women left food for you," she murmured.

But he didn't hear. He was gazing at her, smelling her, almost tasting her across the room.

She was hauntingly beautiful now, in the traditional bridal robes of his tribe, which breathed across her body, hiding and revealing the curve and length, the softness and strength of her. Her hair was woven with flowers and shimmer, her skin oiled and scented, so that the least move announced itself to his desperately hungry senses.

His woman, prepared as a bride is prepared, in silks and perfumes, her eyes kohled and inviting, prepared as he had longed to see her since that first moment of glancing into cool slate-green eyes…

In two strides he was across the room, and he lifted his hands to cup her head and hold her face up, a flower, a perfect flower with two wide green centres so full of sweetness that his heart stopped.

"You are mine," he said, his voice rough with feeling. "You have promised. You have told the women."

Before she could protest that it was not so, he bent his head, and tenderly, tastingly, his mouth stroked hers, as a man might kiss a delicate bloom, to absorb its perfume through his lips.

The touch trembled against her mouth, and a thousand nerve endings sent shimmers of delight all through her. She shivered, and her lips parted. Her hands pressed his shoulders, and his mouth moved more and more hungrily against her, seeking the sweetness it tasted, as if the more he tasted, the more his need was fed.

Then his hand slipped under the silken shirt she wore, and she felt its heat and strength push along the length of her back, drawing her slowly, determinedly in against his body in a curving arc as he bent over her, lifting her almost off her feet. Her head he wrapped in the crook of his other arm, and she lay supported in his embrace, breast to breast, mouth to mouth.

With the flick of his thumb her jacket fell open, and he stroked her stomach, her chest, her breasts.

From every contact honeyed electricity poured through her, body and soul, setting fire to her mind, igniting her blood. Fever burned her, the fever of a deep hunger that was all new to her. When he lifted his mouth, his eyes, black with passion and intent, devoured her with answering hunger, and her throat of its own accord murmured its need.

With a directness that shook her, his hand left her back and moved between her thighs, and the million nerve endings there leaped to obedient awareness, and she swooned.

She lay helplessly arced in the air, supported between her feet on the floor and her head in his arm, and his mouth kissed her lips, her ear, her throat, while his other hand slid to her waist and unerringly found the tie of the pyjama trousers. Then she felt the whisper of silk over her stomach and down her thighs, and a moment later her lower body was naked and exposed. A sense of her own vulnerability charged through her.

He lifted his mouth from its exploration of her throat to look down at her body, and the expression on his face poured fuel on the fire of her hunger so that she gasped, and when his hand cupped her mound with possessive firmness, the small gasp was overtaken by a hoarse cry of surprise, hunger, and anticipation. Then she submitted to her own openness, to her vulnerable nakedness, to her admission of sexual hunger.

His hand moved unerringly against her thighs, drawing them apart to give him better access, and then returned to the soft nest of his intent. His hand clasped her again, and his eyes burned into hers, as if to declare his right to do so. Then, hot and sensuously tormenting, it began to move against the nested, humming nerves that waited there.

Under his rhythmic stroking a burning heat quickly built up in her, and she pressed hungrily against him, arching, tensing and seeking, until the pleasure burst under his touch, like a rivulet of lava whispering down a mountain slope.

Her thighs trembled, her breasts tightened, all her body awoke to song.

"Oh!" she cried softly. "Thank you!"

She sighed and tried to straighten, but he kept her there, kept his hand where it was, still moving, so that the burst of pleasure was overtaken by the promise of more.

"Do you thank me for so little?" he asked hoarsely. His eyes glowed the deepest green she had ever seen, and he smiled his falcon smile, hungry and intent. "There is more than this, I think."

A moment later, more pleasure zinged out from under his touch, shivering through her so that her back arched, and her hands gripped his shoulders. Her eyes squeezed shut, as if to concentrate on the path the liquid heat was taking through her blood.

Now her legs opened wider of their own accord, her feet planting on the floor, and he saw what he had wanted to see—an unashamed demand for her body's delight. He bent his head and devoured her mouth with his kiss, the better to taste the pleasure as it sang through her again.

"Oh!" Jalia whispered when he lifted his mouth again. "Doesn't it stop?"

He smiled. "No, Beloved. It doesn't stop."

He watched her face for the marks of the delight he gave her as he stroked her body, and sometimes he watched her body, and she saw the marks of her pleasure on his own face.

She had never before met such blatant determination to create sexual satisfaction for her, such open intent. Never had she felt so free to demand and enjoy her body's bliss. Never had she been so lost to her surroundings, her awareness limited to her body, his touch. Never had she felt she might faint with sheer sexual joy.

Her cries shuddered to the ceiling again, and then for a moment the stroking stopped and her hand was drawn into the light to expose the trio of opals on her finger.

Dark, dark eyes came close to hers, and even that was somehow lost in the haze. As was his voice.

You still wear his ring?

"Oh!" she cried softly.

She felt his fingers clasp her finger, felt electricity jolting through her.

Tell me to take it off. Tell me you break this engagement.

She half smiled, her mind reeling, for he had truly made her drunk with pleasure. "I can't do that," she murmured.

His dark frown came between her and the light. *Not? Shall I stop loving you, my Jalia, my woman, my wife? Shall I let you go to this man, my perfect bride?*

"Because we were never engaged," she continued dreamily, only dimly aware that she was throwing away her most potent armour and now nothing would protect her from the fierce wind of his love. "We just pretended, so I'd be safe. Michael's a friend at the university."

She felt the ring leave her finger, felt it in the burning stroke of his fingers as they drew it off her supersensitized skin, heard it bounce from a carpet and skitter across the tiled floor, and then she was falling.

Down, down he dragged her, to that sweet-smelling bed of boughs and blossoms so lovingly created by the women. His kisses grew wild and wilder, over her face, her throat, her ear, back to her swollen, starving mouth.

Now he stripped off her shirt, exposing her breasts

to the warm lamplight, and slipped out of the white silk that hid his dark body from her hungry gaze. He knelt between her thighs, his eyes moving over her beautiful body as his hands did, creating burning delight in their wake; and where he stroked, he knew her, and where he knew, he owned.

She shuddered as desire abruptly made the leap to passion in her, and groaning, she reached hungrily to pull him into the hot, moist nest of need between her thighs.

He resisted for a moment, and placed his mouth there instead, and as his strong tongue drove her higher up the peak of pleasure, with a last release of the invisible bonds that had constrained her, Jalia twined her fingers into his hair and pressed him against her flesh. His mouth obeyed, a rush of paralysing pleasure engulfed her, and she cried out with utter abandon and fell back against the bower spent and exhausted.

Then he knelt between her legs again, and she saw the engine of his own pleasure, hugely engorged, push its way into her body. Dimly she felt there was nothing more to give or to feel. But her throat opened on a high wild cry, for a deeper pleasure invaded her being now, and the promise of yet more.

She never afterwards knew how much time passed in that scented ecstasy of passion, with Latif's hands and mouth and body stroking her, body and soul, and calling up the deepest, most charged pleasure of all her life. There was a thrilling passion in every part of her being, a yearning and a delight, so that she lost track not merely of time, but of herself, not knowing where she ended and lamplight began, where she ended and pleasure began, where she ended and Latif began....

It was passion, and joy, and soaring, utter perfection. And now a roaring, burning pleasure began to build in her, unlike anything that had come before. She cried and whimpered, and moaned and called to him, as it built to a crescendo in them both, and his voice crying out his own hot urgency added to her delight.

Then she understood that the trickles and rivulets and rivers of heat and delight that came before had been only the foretaste of a deeper, richer, unimagined joy. And now it erupted in and through them both, as if they two—body and soul—were the conduit by which joy and delight and happiness and perfect union burst into the world to feed the starving multitudes.

And so Latif Abd al Razzaq Shahin took his beloved and made her his wife.

Eleven

Later she lay across his dark, damp chest and felt how right it was that she should be there. The memory of pleasure still coursed through her, so that small aftershocks shook her from time to time.

She lifted her head and gazed down into eyes that glowed back at her with satisfied fulfillment at having given and received so much deep pleasure.

After a moment, he picked up her left hand. His thumb stroked her ring finger.

"You were not really engaged to this man?"

"Michael was my insurance policy. My armour against—my parents," she admitted. She couldn't say *against you.*

"How does a man pretend to be engaged to a woman like you, and not wish to make it real?" he wondered softly. "It is not possible. This was a tactic he used. He will want to hold you to it."

She smiled, because the look in his eyes was in-toxicating, and shook her head.

"No, it's not like that. Michael's gay. He hasn't come out to his parents yet. I sometimes go to their family parties and things as his date, because he says he likes to keep his mother happy. So when I needed the return favour..."

He looked as though he hardly believed her, but the smile on his face betokened ill for Michael if what she said was not the truth. Jalia's voice faded into silence as she suddenly realized she might have taken powerful forces too lightly.

"I hope what you say is true," Latif said in a rough whisper.

She faltered. "Wh-what?"

"I will hold you, Jalia," he promised. "I will keep you. You are my woman, and so it has always been."

Just for one treacherous second she half wished this moment *could* seal her fate, the way he intended, the way it would have done if life had been different. Just here, and just now, she half believed it might.

It couldn't, but she wasn't going to let reality in yet. Tonight was dreamtime. Tomorrow was soon enough to awaken.

"There's some really delicious food over there," she murmured. "Are you hungry?"

One dark hand stroked her, and, exhausted as she was, her body sang another chorus for him. "For the food of my valley I am always hungry," he said. "Just as I shall always be hungry for you, as long as I live."

Her heart kicked a response so deep she felt tears burn her eyelids, but she smiled and lifted herself away from him. She stood naked in the soft, gentle light, and his gaze in its golden glow felt like honey on her skin—sweet, warm, sensuous.

"Come, then," she said, for the food was laid out to keep warm on a brazier beside piles of embroidered cushions, artfully arranged by the experts of the valley's wedding team.

They both pulled on the silk trousers of their outfits, and sank down again on the cushions, he looking like a genie sprung from one of the antique lamps, she like a dancing girl, her bare breasts glowing with the mix of oil and love-sweat.

Roasted eggplant in olive oil, spiced meats, yogurt and garlic, fresh herbs with goat's cheese, and a delicious pan-fried bread…nothing in her life had ever tasted so delicious, or so potently aphrodisiac, as this meal.

With smiles and lazy eyes they ate, and murmured appreciation both of this feast and of the one just past, fed each other morsels and tidbits, and, mouths shiny with spiced oil, licked each other's lips, and their own.

"The women around here certainly know how to cook," Jalia exclaimed once, a little breathlessly, as one such lip licking turned into a spice-flavoured kiss.

"The dishes of the Marzuqi are known through all the countries bordering the Gulf of Barakat," he said. They talked a little about the food they ate, while their eyes carried other messages, some lazy and slow, some electric with promise.

Once she gestured to the empty walls and niches of the room.

"One of the women—Golnesar, I think—said

something about the treasures of the valley having been hidden from Ghasib's men, and they all laughed, as if that was a joke. But no one explained.''

He smiled. ''You know what a taste Ghasib had for ancient art treasures.''

Jalia nodded. One of Latif's tasks had been to help her parents trace and reclaim family heirlooms grabbed by Ghasib or his minions in the years of the republic. They had looted in the name of the country's museums, but most of the treasures went into Ghasib's personal treasury.

''We all knew what it meant when the tunnel was being blasted through the rock to make way for Ghasib's road—first through would be Ghasib's acquisition team. There were many treasures decorating the homes of the valley, some of inestimable historical value.

''My father made the decision to prevent the stripping of the valley. He instructed the people to bring their treasures to him, and said that he would personally hide them all in a secret location.''

''Wouldn't it have been safer to have dozens of hiding places, so if they found one the others would still be safe?''

''Recollect that Ghasib had ways to extract information from people. Once he learned that one village or family had hidden something, no one in the valley would have been safe. This way, if Ghasib's men suspected a trick, under duress everyone could honestly say that they had been ordered to give up their treasures to the Shahin, and knew nothing more.''

''And your father would be the one who was tortured,'' Jalia suggested.

"Exactly. But he believed that the secret would be better kept if all knew that their Shahin's life hung in the balance, and he was right. Ghasib's men took the valuables that had been left in a few homes to allay suspicion, and never got a hint of the truth."

Jalia frowned. "And why haven't the treasures been brought out of hiding since the Sultan's return?"

"Because my father hid the treasures too well. Only he and a very old and trusted servant knew the location. He deliberately chose an old man—*If they torture us, we will die quickly,* he said. Pir Gholam died soon after, and my father, sadly, also died before Ash's plans succeeded. Just before his death he told me he had left directions for me, but I haven't found those directions."

Jalia laughed. "Have you any idea where the hiding place might be?"

"None. But I have been absent so much, there has been little time to conduct a search, even through my father's papers. When work with Ash eases off, and there is more time for the valley's concerns, I will embark on a systematic search."

His expression was completely open and true, and Jalia experienced a sharp jolt of culture shock. In the West, she thought, his father would have come under immediate suspicion of having stolen or sold off his people's treasures, and his son would be anxious to avert that suspicion.

But in Latif's face there was no awareness that such a suspicion might enter her mind or anyone else's. He trusted in his father's probity, and therefore in his own. And so, clearly, did his people.

"Now I see why they call your family the Third Shahin," she murmured.

He frowned quizzically. "Yes?"

"This afternoon I asked the women how the valley got its name," Jalia explained.

"And what did they tell you?"

"Sey-Shahin. Three Royal Falcons," Jalia said, unconsciously settling into the role of storyteller, as if she had been born in the valley herself.

"They said that in very ancient times, this valley was a plain. It was fertile, but because it was so flat, the wind used to blow over it, taking their seed before it had rooted, and carrying off the rich soil.

"So the people sent a messenger to the Great King—some say to God—and in reply the Great King sent his favourite royal falcon to stand guard over the valley, and protect it from the winds.

"And the falcon stood so long, and guarded them so loyally, that he became a mountain, and still stands guard now.

"But the people were still troubled, for the flood-waters came down from the mountains in spring, and because there was nothing to stop them, they flowed through the valley, carrying with them the seed before it could sprout, and the rich soil.

"So the people sent another messenger to the Great King, and he sent a second of his royal falcons, to guard the valley against the floodwaters. And the falcon stood guard so loyally that he became rock, and he is the mountain on the south.

"And the valley prospered with its two mountain guardians, but the people began to worry, for there was trouble in the lands, and a great conqueror was on the move.

"Then the people sent to God a third time, begging for protection from the invader, and God sent a third royal falcon—a great leader. And the leader reigned a long time, and protected them so well that his family became a rock for the people of the valley, and every generation produces a strong, able leader to protect them.

"They are called the Shahini, The People of the Falcon, and they will be leaders in the valley till the time comes for the valley to be destroyed. That's you, and they are so proud of you and your family, Latif."

Latif watched her from under drooping eyelids. "And what else?"

"So the valley was protected from the winds, and the floods, and from foreign conquerors, but there was still one thing that was not protected, and that was the hearts of the people.

"So the people asked God for protection for their hearts, and God sent the fourth and last protection—he sent them Islam. And now the valley is protected in all four directions, and no harm can come to the people, and that's why they are now called al Marzuqi, the Blessed, the Provided For," she finished, smiling.

"Did I get it right? It's a lovely story."

"You tell it well. One day, if God wills, you will tell it to our children."

She could only press her lips together and shake her head.

When they had finished the meal with fresh fruit, they washed hands and mouths with rose-scented water poured each for the other from the intricately moulded silver ewer with its matching bowl.

Then Latif lifted the trays and brazier to one side and Jalia lay back on the cushions, feeling crazily free and unlike herself in bare breasts and harem pants.

He lay down again and rested on one elbow beside her, gazing into her eyes in a way that made her body remember delight.

He drew out a tiny white flower that still lurked in a twist of her hair, lazily touched it to the end of his nose, inhaled like a man tasting fine wine, and, watching her with a look in his eyes that she would never forget, thoughtfully caught it on the end of his tongue, drew it into his mouth, and ate it.

Jalia's throat gave a little involuntary whimper of reaction and she lost track of what she was saying.

Latif lay back on the cushions and drew her onto his chest. Her breasts brushed hungrily against the mat of hair, and her hips melted with renewed yearning as his strong hand stroked down her back and over the swell of her bottom, lightly, possessively.

"Why did the women do all this?" she asked, nodding at the now empty trays and the room. "They know we aren't married."

"They tell me that the date is very auspicious for the wedding of the Shahin. There won't be another such beneficial day for months, or maybe years, according to the old way of reckoning such things."

Jalia frowned curiously. "What is the old way of reckoning such things?"

"Only the women know."

"Do you believe them?"

He shrugged. "It was predicted to me last year that

this year would be beneficial for our attempts to put Ash on the throne. They also said that if the Sultan returned the drought would end.''

''Pretty impressive. But we aren't married, so how can it be beneficial just to decorate a bedroom?''

Latif smiled. ''By the rules of the old, pre-Islamic tradition, we are married. This is all it takes, that bride and groom should be bathed and perfumed and led to bed by the women.''

''What?'' She leaped as if from an electric shock, and Latif laughed.

''The ritual allowed the women of the tribe to make sure that bride and groom had the necessary parts in good working order. Some parts of the ritual have been abandoned since Islam came to the valley—the groom used to be put through his paces by the women, they say.

''But the practice itself has never been wholly abandoned. Tradition is a powerful thing, and most people here would not feel married without this.''

He toyed with another lock of hair, twirled another flower, smiled at her. ''They didn't explain this to you?''

''No. They just—started stripping me off. Latif…what will you say when you come back to the valley and I'm not with you?''

He didn't move, didn't flinch. But she saw something hit him, all the same.

''What does man do when he loses what is most precious to him?'' he asked, his voice raw. ''I will tell them the truth. That I could not hold my woman, even though the world is black for me without her.''

Twelve

In the morning the council sat again, while Jalia was taken around all the houses in the village and introduced to children and pet goats. The women began to tell her of their lives and their problems, laughing with delight to hear her formal, archaic speech.

Bagestani Arabic was not the first language of the mountain tribes, and most people still spoke Parvani by preference, but even so they were all—even the oldest women—a whole lot more fluent than Jalia.

It didn't take Jalia long to understand what was going on—they were petitioning her interest as the wife of the Shahin. In this way they hoped to bring their problems to his attention.

Jalia began to deeply regret that she hadn't told the villagers at once that she was not going to marry their leader.

But she was also a cousin of the Sultan, she reflected after a moment. She could still be of use. So she listened as patiently as if she had been Latif's bride, after all.

Late in the morning, when she had been offered tea and a plateful of delicious little delicacies she couldn't resist, she was invited to visit the village's "carpet room."

"Indeed, it would honour me to make such a visit," the Princess said, making the young girls giggle again, and repeat her archaic speech. But there was no malice in their delight, and no one scolded them.

So they took her to a house where she was surprised to see a circle of hand looms. In honour of Latif and Jalia's visit, no one was working at them, but that it was a busy place when it got going was evident in the beautiful carpets partly finished on many looms and the stacks of coloured thread around the room.

Predominant among the clusters of wool and silk was a mountain of beautiful purple-blue thread, rich and luxurious, a unique colour; and with a gasp Jalia bent over the nearest loom.

"Marzuqi carpets!" she exclaimed in English. She hadn't made the connection before, but anyone with an interest in Eastern carpets would have recognized the distinctive colour and design at once.

Marzuqi carpets were extremely sought after, very expensive, and hard to come by, and Princess Muna had treasured the one she owned all of Jalia's life. But Jalia had simply not made the connection until it was right before her eyes.

"My honoured mother, the Princess Muna, hath of such carpets as these one carpet which she treasures greatly," she told them. "They are carpets among the most beautiful carpets in the world."

Of course this pleased them, but like a fool Jalia hadn't thought of the consequences. She was immediately presented with a silk carpet just finished, the result of at least a year's work on the part of one of the women, she knew: far too costly a gift.

She was sure that the carpet had been made to order for some client, yet it would be impossible to refuse without offence.

With a sinking heart totally at variance with her delight in the carpet, Jalia examined the intricate design, the beautifully woven pattern a mix of several intensities of the blue, accented with black, white, pink and green.

"This is a sacred pattern, Lady," she was told. "It is designed to draw Truth into the space. These are secrets handed down to us from our mothers since The Days Before the Law of Men."

The Days Before the Law of Men. It was a strange phrase, one she had never heard before, and yet it had the ring of common usage. She bent over the gorgeous carpet, listening while they explained how the meaning of the signs and markings had a deep mystery that could not be explained in words.

Afterwards, they folded the carpet up and tied it for her. Jalia made her thanks, but tried to protest that the client for whom this carpet had been intended would be angry.

"But it has been made for Lord Latif, against the day when he would appear!" they exclaimed. "Razan is the valley's best weaver—who else to weave a carpet for your husband? We are honoured to give it to you. You will take it to the city, so that there you and Lord Latif will be always reminded of your true home.''

Jalia didn't understand why that brought tears to her eyes. The valley was not her home, and it never could be. She had gone too far away from such roots. But still, some part of her yearned for the might-have-been.

After lunch, some of the men escorted Latif and Jalia back up the slowly mending road to their truck, loaded it with the carpet and fresh supplies, and waved them on their way.

As they drove, Jalia did not wait long before broaching the chief subject of concern that the women had raised with her: a problem that threatened their livelihood and the future of the entire valley.

''They've got two problems,'' she explained. ''The first is, the exporter of their carpets, with whom they have a contract to sell everything they produce, has started having cheap, production-line copies made in Kaljukistan, and is trying to pass them off as genuine.

''He says the women aren't producing fast enough to fulfill demand, but the truth is, he wants cheap carpets to sell to people who can't afford the genuine thing.

''But he's got a problem—he can't achieve the colour with chemical dyes, and you know the colour is half the beauty of a Marzuqi carpet. So now he's trying to force them to give him the secret of that wonderful purple-blue dye. It really beggars belief. It's just ruthless profiteering without any—''

Latif interrupted. ''But this could be a good thing for the women. Tastes change. Maybe they should profit from the demand for their designs while they can.''

Jalia turned to stare at him. ''Latif—handwoven Marzuqi carpets have been hot in the West for the past hundred years at least. That's not going to change as long as they keep it small and exclusive. It will certainly change if the market gets flooded with cheap copies and it becomes the latest craze.''

''They aren't going to lose their skill in making carpets. All they have to do is find new designs.''

She couldn't believe it. She had been so certain of being able to enlist his help.

''I thought these were your people, Latif,'' she cried. ''They need help!''

''Do they?''

''In the last contract the exporter tied them up without their realizing it. They can't sell to anyone but him, but he's not obliged to buy what they produce if there's no market.

''He's saying the carpets are too expensive, and take too long to make. He says there's no market beyond the carpets already ordered. Those carpets will all be finished within six months.

''After that—the prices they are being offered are less than half of what they now get, which is already obscenely exploitative. And the agent wants to bring in a designer, so that instead of creating their own variations on their designs as they go, the women just execute a preexisting design. That's supposed to make the work go faster.

"The women all hate the idea. Each carpet is unique, an individual work of art. With a preset design they'll be just technicians. They'll have no creative input at all."

"What help do they want?"

"Isn't it obvious? They want to break the contract with the exporter, and they want to prevent him flooding the market with cheap imitations. But after three years of drought no one has the money for a lawyer. And anyway, they don't know how to get one."

Latif shook his head. "It's not going to be as easy to stop him as you think. I was told of many problems this morning. This one will have to take its place on the list."

"Oh, the men's issues come first, do they?" She sat up straighter, outraged.

"I'll do what I can, Jalia. It just won't happen instantly."

Suddenly she was furious. How dare he care so little for his own people? The women had talked to her about their concerns till her head was ringing, and she had been so sure of his interest!

"I suppose there's no point telling you about all the plans and ideas those women and I talked over? With your head so full of priority masculine stuff?"

"I am sure they asked you to pass such things on to me, thinking as they did that you had agreed to be my wife."

She ignored the thread of steely anger. "They did. But then, they thought you were *their* Shahin as well as their husbands'."

"No, that is not what they think. What they think is that I love you and that I will give my wife anything she asks. That is why they appealed to you."

"But they were wrong," she suggested.

His eyes flicked away from the perilous road for one burning moment. "They were right. But you are not my wife. Ask me as my wife and I will do what you ask."

"That's outrageous!" she snapped. "Why don't you do it for them? They are your people!"

"They are your people, too, Jalia. All Bagestanis are your people. And what are you doing for them? Do not preach to me, when you yourself will turn your back on me and on your country to live abroad as soon as we return!"

"Are you going to punish the Marzuqi women because I won't do what you want?"

"Look at it another way. You have the power to help these women by marrying me."

Electricity shivered her skin as his hand left the wheel and he clasped the back of her head, turning her to face him.

"Marry me, Jalia!" he said urgently. "Don't you see it? You are my woman. My home calls to you, my people touch your heart! This tells you something, if you are listening."

She broke from his hold and turned away.

"Answer me!"

"I've already answered you, Latif. I'm English, for God's sake! I can't do it."

The road hung over a precipice so sheer and stony her heart leaped into her mouth.

"Can't? What does that mean—can't?" he demanded, as a magnificent panorama opened out before them. The road now passed through a three-sided cavity in the side of the mountain. The fourth side was open onto vastness.

"Do you really expect someone born and raised in a city like London to be able to make this kind of transition? I can't just take up a completely new way of life! I'd go mad after a month!"

Far, far below, a ribbon of river wound its way along a rugged chasm of green trees and rust-red rock.

Jalia gasped hoarsely. She'd never seen anything so powerfully moving as this country, with its alternating rugged mountains and green valleys. But this vista staggered her with its lonely magnificence.

"You can!" he growled.

"My whole life is elsewhere, Latif."

"Don't talk like a Westerner who understands nothing but money. Your heart is here—how can your life be elsewhere?"

"My God, will you watch the road? Do you know how steep this drop is?"

"I know this road as I know your heart—better than you do yourself."

"I know my *mind* extremely well. That is what counts."

"Do not be such a fool."

"What's your definition of fool? A woman who disagrees with you?"

Two angry emeralds blazed wrath at her.

"Last night you learned that you love me. Why can you not hold to this? It is weakness, what you do now!"

"Last night we made love, Latif. That's all. Wonderful as it was, and I'm not denying that—"

"You insult me. Am I a technician, to be complimented so?"

"Oh, there's no pleasing you!" she snapped.

"But yes, I am easy to please. You know the way."

Thirteen

After the night in the valley, the relationship between her and Latif grew progressively more edgy. Their exchanges were barbed, and neither seemed able to say anything that didn't have a double meaning.

At night, though everything in him said he was digging his grave deeper with every moment they spent in loving, he could not resist her. However harsh their daily conversation, however determined he became not to succumb this time, when night fell in the tent and her soft breathing filled the silence, his voice called to her of its own accord, and his hands, driven by unbearable hunger, reached for her, found her.

And for Jalia it was the same. Whatever he said in the day to anger or upset her, however resentful her heart when she climbed into her sleeping bag, at the first touch of Latif's hands all resistance melted, and she turned into his embrace with a sigh of need that always blasted the last of his control.

His lovemaking was fierce but tender, as if he never forgot that he was making love to his wife, the mother of his children. The deep respect, the reverence, almost, in his body's embrace meant that her whole being opened to him, and the trusting openness drove his passion to the wildest heights.

Then he called to her soul with terms of endearment he had never before used to any woman. Then he was like a man who has inherited a most precious jewel—touching it, stroking it, admiring its unmatchable beauty, and always his heart breaking a little with the knowledge that it could never be truly his own.

During the days, he punished her for that, for the way her beauty of soul and face and body remained remote and unattainable, for the fact that however deep his own knowledge that their love was the destiny of both of them, she could withhold a part of herself even in the depths of loving.

"You love me," he would accuse her, as his body moved in hers, provoking her to a throaty song of gratitude. And *yes,* she would reply.

"You are mine—say it, Jalia! Tell me you are mine forever!" *Latif, please don't ask me that,* she would say, driving him to a frenzy of passionate lovemaking, his body certain that the way to break down this last resistance was through pleasure that maddened her.

Sometimes his body was right. Sometimes he heard her say, *yes, Latif, yes, whatever you want, oh, God, I've never felt anything like this....*

Later, when the pleasure had faded, she always reneged. Then she would blame him for trying to hold her to promises extracted under duress.

"Duress?" he had rasped the first time she used the word. *"Duress?"*

"The duress of pleasure," she said unapologetically. He laughed angrily, but she stuck to her guns. "It's not fair to ask me to change my mind when I'm actually out of my mind. Of course I'll say anything you want to hear, when I'm effectively drunk with sex.

"I've never felt before what I feel with you. I have no defences. So whatever you make me say in the heat of the moment, Latif, I reserve the right to retract it when I'm sane and sober again."

Of course he was torn—between the satisfaction of knowing he gave her such unequalled pleasure, and the grief of that pleasure not carrying the conviction for her that it did for him, that through it they were united for all time.

Nowhere during the long journey did they hear news of a plane in trouble during the last big storm.

As they proceeded the task became really thankless, for as the mountains got steeper and more rugged, Jalia could no longer see very far from the road. They might be missing a wreckage that was only yards away behind a ridge or an outcrop.

And they could explore only so far on foot. The binoculars were virtually useless now, and though she still carried them around her neck, there was rarely any point in raising them to her eyes.

"When we reach Matar Filkoh airport, we'll turn around and start back," Jalia heard Latif say one day.

"There is no real reason even to continue to the airport—if the plane had passed anywhere close, they'd have picked it up on radar. But we need to radio for news."

Jalia heaved a sigh, and felt tears threaten. She knew in her heart Latif was right. They had covered all the territory they could by road. Either the plane had gone down in an area so remote that only search planes or climbers could hope to find it, or Noor and Bari hadn't flown this way.

And she couldn't be more glad to get out of this truck and away from Latif Abd al Razzaq Shahin if he were a real falcon daily tearing at the liver of her resolve. And yet...

"No!" she protested.

A wave of doubt and denial washed over her. What if the plane's wreckage was just one crag further on? It wasn't stretching hope too far that Noor and Bari could have survived a crash, might be waiting just beyond the next rise, praying for rescue.

Latif turned an emerald-chip gaze her way. "What are you saying?" he asked disbelievingly.

"We can't just give up!"

His jaw tightened, and she understood how much he wanted this to be over. Well, whose fault was it that they couldn't stand being in close confines together? Who had started the trouble?

"The road ends at the airport. After that it is little better than a trail leading to Joharistan."

Joharistan was the tiny country whose name was practically synonymous with remote inaccessibility and tribal unrest.

But Jalia had become too guilt ridden, too sharply

aware of how much her own stupidity must be to blame for Noor's flight. She couldn't give up till the last ditch. Her heart quailed at the thought of having to face her family without having some news to give them.

And if staying longer with Latif was her penance—well, it was a just one, wasn't it?

"There must be something more we can do," she said.

"Do you mean go on foot? What a futile exercise that would be."

Latif waved his hand at the mountains beyond the windscreen. "Where would you go? What direction? You might only succeed in getting hurt yourself, and provoking another air search."

Jalia gazed out the window at the rugged rock face above, and knew defeat.

"There must be something we can do!" she protested anyway.

"Not here."

"I don't believe you! You don't like being with me. You want out of the situation, that's all it is!"

Latif slammed on the brakes and turned to her, showing his teeth.

"Of course I want out of it!" he shouted, as if goaded past his self-control at last. "Do you think I like the torment—every night believing that I have convinced you, and every morning learning that you are a woman who can be confused by my lovemaking, but never convinced by my love? Knowing all the day long that I will not be able to resist the compulsion to try again, learning to half accept that all I will have in the end is the memory of what one day you will remember as a wild affair, and I as the crossroads of my life? Of course I want out!

"You are my future, one way or the other, Jalia—either as the memory of what I could not make mine, or as my wife and the mother of my children. Do you think I don't know that the longer I am with you now, not resisting what I should resist, the harder the memory of the loss will be? Do you think it makes me happy to feed on scraps, constantly hoping for a meal, knowing that after this, any other food will be tasteless to me?"

She gasped under the assault, while feeling charged through her like hot tears in her blood. Without another word he turned and put the vehicle in gear.

"I'm sorry," she faltered. "I didn't—"

He gestured once with an angry hand. "Do not tell me you—"

The truck's wheels slid dangerously into the massive rain-ruts he had been avoiding, and in the next instant he was totally absorbed with preventing the truck from sliding backwards into a gully.

Jalia watched his hands on the wheel, hard and expert, and felt a thrill of remembered delight. Just so did he guide her body when it was at the edge of an abyss of soaring pleasure.

For a crazy moment she wished that he would stop struggling and let them go over the edge now, and relieve her of the daily torture of not knowing her own mind. Sometimes it did seem to her that only death would resolve the dilemma in her heart.

It was tearing her in two. At night, in his arms, she was secure in the conviction his loving closeness induced in her—that love could conquer all. Then she was filled with a divine certainty that her true future lay not in England, but here in the land of her fore-bears, side by side with this strong, loving man, strug-gling to make a new life for herself and him and the country.

In the bright light of morning, all the opposing cer-tainty came rushing back, and she called herself a fool for imagining that she could forget all her life to date, make a new self of herself, pretend she belonged in this rugged land.

Then she felt he cheated, took advantage of her sexual susceptibility, gave her the wild pleasure she experienced in his arms only as the means to an end.

And yet, now that he was offering to end the or-deal, she had refused. Did that mean she secretly wanted this torment to go on?

Jalia wasn't at all used to second-guessing herself like this; it made her uncomfortable in her own skin. Until now she had always felt a measure of certainty over her choices, a certainty that was unassailable.

Or, perhaps, had never been deeply challenged. When she had made up her mind to reject her parents' life map, they had given in with sadness but little argument.

When she had made her life-directing decisions—to be an academic, for example—life had given in without much fuss. She hadn't found a position at the prestigious university of her choice, but she had been hired at a small, reputable university, a post that could easily lead to the greater things she still envisioned.

Life hadn't ever really fought back. Now that it was doing so, Jalia made the discovery that self-doubt is an enemy so potent and crippling no other may be necessary.

So for a moment now, watching with fascinated detachment as Latif brought the truck under control, she didn't reject the thought of oblivion as an end to her disquiet.

Or perhaps it was just that she was now dealing with almost unbearable guilt—the guilt of having tried so hard to convince Noor that she was making a dangerous, foolhardy leap in marrying Bari al Khalid. As long as she was here, searching, she didn't have to face what perhaps they had faced days ago at home—that hope diminished with every passing day.

If she had recognized what was really frightening her, if she had faced her own dangerous weakness relative to Latif instead of transferring it...Noor might never have had the second thoughts that had caused her flight.

"There is another road from Matar Filkoh that leads down to the plain and takes a different route back to al Bostan. It is not a good road, but I will ask at the airport if it is still passable after the rains. If it is, we can return that way. But it is futile to talk of going further into the mountains."

Jalia nodded, not trusting herself to speak. Never had she been so filled with guilt and self-doubt. Never had she been so unsure of her course.

They radioed home from the airport, but learned nothing new. The air search hadn't yet been abandoned, but only because of who was missing. For less high profile people, the search would have been given up long ago. Latif and Jalia reported their own lack of success, and both sides were more depressed after the call than before.

The road down was terrifyingly rugged, with the truck bouncing and jolting and threatening to pitch over the edge every five miles.

If she had had to drive it herself, Jalia would have turned tail (if there had been any room to do so) and fled back up to Matar Filkoh and the other road home.

Worse, the terrain made it impossible to pitch the tent, or even to find a comfortable spot for a sleeping bag. They spent their nights cramped and uncomfortable in the truck, while a wolfish wind howled around outside, battering their tiny haven and screeching into every crevice.

Jalia, lying on the back seat while Latif slept half-sitting in the front passenger seat, listened to the wind for hours in the night, where guilt and doubt took renewed strength from the darkness.

Each night she wrestled with the urgent need to sit up, bend over Latif, kiss him awake, and beg him to comfort her, to love her, to decide her terrible dilemma for her.

It was a massive relief when they finally found themselves back on the plain, with brown and gold and green stretching flat for miles ahead. And how glad she was to see villages again, and discover that for other people, ordinary life had gone on during her ordeal.

Still they got no news of Bari's plane.

Every day was making it more likely that the plane had headed out over the sea, for in not one village anywhere did Jalia and Latif find anyone who had heard or seen any sign of a distressed plane on the day of the storm.

"If they did come down over water..." Jalia began hesitantly, when at yet another village they had drawn a blank. She broke off, and Latif glanced at her.

"There is no way to say. It depends on how they came down. If they were hit by lightning, or they broke up in the air, then it is as God wills. But if Bari was able to bring it down with some kind of control—there is a life raft aboard the plane."

"But then why wouldn't they have activated the plane's EPIRB?" she pointed out sadly. "Or at least set off some flares."

The signalling device from Bari's plane, which would have allowed survivors to be found within hours, had never been activated, which was the single biggest argument against the couple's survival. If they had both been so hurt they couldn't find and activate the EPIRB, how long could they have lasted without rescue?

Jalia had begun this search full of hope and the determination that two such vibrant people as Noor and Bari couldn't just die like that, just disappearing into nothing. They would have had to leave some trace.

But as the days stretched into weeks, her hopes had begun to dim. Now she just wanted to get home, to the comfort of the family and familiar surroundings, where perhaps the grieving process had already begun.

They both greeted the approach to Medinat al Bostan with relief.

As they caught sight of the great golden dome of

the mosque and its picturesque minarets glowing in the hot, bright sunshine, Jalia was suddenly sharply aware of how grubby she was, and began to yearn for a long, warm bath, and her comfortable bed, with a power that had never assailed her on the road.

It was just before lunch when they drove between the gates into the great palace that now housed the Sultan again, after thirty years as a museum.

Jalia clambered out of the car, too tired to be anything but grateful when one of the servants who materialized dived for her backpack as she tried to shoulder it.

"Is there any news of the Princess, Massoud?" she asked, and as she expected, the man sighed gloomily.

"Nothing at all, Your Highness. And you—?"

"We found nothing." With Latif close behind, she followed Massoud under the arched passageway into the beautiful private courtyard, where she stood for a moment looking around her.

All around the courtyard arches and columns presented the eye with the comfort of perfection. With a delicious babble the fountain tossed diamonds up to be kissed by sunshine in endlessly repeated beauty; trees waved patterns of shadow against the worn tile over which her ancestors' feet had passed for generations; and ripe pomegranates weighted the branches of the tall shrubs, presenting their rich redness invitingly close.

Jalia reached out to stroke the dimpled fruit with a luxurious sigh. Would she ever get used to such beauty? "*Allah,* it's good to be—"

The look in Latif's green eyes made her suddenly conscious, and she choked the word back.

"Home?" he prompted.

"Jalia!" She heard the urgent voice overhead and looked up to see her mother anxiously leaning over a balcony. "Thank heaven you're back!"

Jalia's heart kicked hard. "Has there been news, Mother?"

"Yes—*no,* not about Noor," her mother cried. She flicked a glance at Latif. "But…"

"For heaven's sake, what is it?" Jalia called anxiously. "Mother, what's happened?"

"Well, darling—Michael rang yesterday."

So far from her thoughts was her previous life that Jalia only blinked. "Michael?"

Princess Muna cleared her throat. "Your fiancé, Jalia. He's flying out today."

"Flying out where?" she asked blankly.

"Here. He's coming…"

Latif's eyes were the precise green of jealous fury. She thought she had never seen anything more coldly beautiful, or more compellingly frightening, in her life.

"Here?" she almost shrieked. "Why?"

Her mother's eyebrows went up. "He said something about your hour of need."

"What?"

"His flight arrives in two hours," said her mother.

Fourteen

———

"**T**here is absolutely no reason for you to come with me!"

In dark glasses and with a scarf hiding her hair like a fifties Hollywood starlet, Jalia hissed her continuing protest as she strode into the concourse to wait for Michael's plane. Latif followed as close as her shadow.

"But yes," Latif Abd al Razzaq contradicted calmly.

"You'll only draw attention to us both. People know who you are, Latif. They're bound to start wondering who I am!"

"I wish to meet Michael," he said, with an immovability that made her want to sink her nails into something.

"And why can't you wait to meet him at the pal—

at home? This is ridiculous! All we need is for some damned journalist to be here, casting around…''

''I want to meet your fiancé,'' Latif repeated.

''He is *not* my fiancé,'' she hissed furiously.

''And then I wonder why he has come here.''

''I wonder, too, Latif. But can we get one thing straight? You do not have the right to this little show of jealous possessiveness!'' Her hand flattened the air. ''I made it clear from the outset that—''

''Do you talk about rights? I talk about love. There are no rights and wrongs. There is only—I want to see this man you tell me is not your fiancé. If you have told me the truth about him, why do you fear my meeting him?''

''I do not fear your meeting him!'' she lied fervently, though she didn't know herself why she feared a meeting. Perhaps because she didn't understand Michael's motives in coming here.

The Arrivals doors opened into the small waiting area and in ones and twos the people from the latest flight started trickling out. Jalia licked her lips and nervously began to watch their faces.

''Jalia!'' Michael's voice cried, and she turned to see him break away from a small group just emerging through the door, to stride towards her. He had lost none of the attention-seeking flair that made Michael a star amongst the staid university lecturers.

People turned to look, and Jalia instinctively lifted a hand to adjust her sunglasses and dropped her head.

A moment later Michael grabbed her close for a warm, enthusiastic hug.

''Darling, how good of you to meet me yourself

when you must be nearly exhausted. Desperately sorry I couldn't get here sooner!''

''Hello, Michael. This is a surprise! I—''

His arms still tight around her, he gave her a firm peck on her mouth that effectively silenced her, kissed her on each cheek, and lifted his head to smile a warning down into her startled face.

''I'm surprised, too! I certainly wasn't expecting to see you! Your mother said you were out scouring the mountains! When did you get back?''

She was acutely, uncomfortably aware of Latif standing behind her, watching with unblinking attention and restrained fury, a falcon choosing his moment to strike.

''A couple of hours ago. Michael, why on earth—''

''Not a word now, darling!'' Michael hushed her with another little kiss, and she sensed his discomfort. He really was not happy that she had met him. ''Plenty of time to talk.''

''Yes. Michael, this is Latif Abd al Razzaq,'' she said, easing out of the embrace. ''He—''

Michael didn't go for the dark, hawklike type, and he scarcely looked at Latif. ''Great!'' he said, grabbing his hand. ''Great to meet you! You look after the Princess, I imagine.''

Latif stood unmoving as a rock, so obviously dangerous that Jalia cowered for Michael. But he was oblivious.

''I take good care of her, as you will see,'' Latif murmured.

''Great!'' Michael said again. ''Any news about Noor, darling?''

''No, nothing new. Let's go, Michael. Is that the

only luggage you brought?'' She could see nothing but a leather carry-on bag slung over his shoulder. It looked new and very expensive. Too expensive for an underpaid university lecturer.

''I had no idea what clothes I'd need at the palace,'' he explained breezily. ''For all I knew I might need a *djellaba!*''

''Michael, could you lower your voice, please?'' she murmured. ''There might be journalists around. Latif—''

Michael's laughter was long, loud and false. ''But of course there are journalists around!'' He turned and held out a conjuror's hand towards a sharp-faced young blond woman standing nearby.

''Meet Ellin Black—from the *Evening Herald.* You probably know her name. Ellin, my very own Princess Bride!''

''Great to meet you, Princess,'' said Ellin Black, smiling at her with cool, self-possessed assessment. Her eyes flicked to Latif and widened with such an expression of curiosity, interest and female intent that Jalia would have laughed, except that she didn't feel like laughing. ''And who are you?''

''I look after the Princess,'' Latif said smoothly.

''And John is the *Herald* photographer,'' said Ellin, quickly disowning any closer relationship with a fair, heavyset, middle-aged man a few feet away.

John Bentinck lifted his hand away from his face and genially nodded at them before fitting the video camera to his eye again.

''Sit down, Michael,'' Jalia said crisply, leading the way into her private apartment at the palace an hour later. She was absolutely furious, and not hiding it well. ''What would you like to drink?''

''I'm absolutely gasping for a cup of tea,'' he said.

They had driven from the airport in silence, Jalia furious with his betrayal, and Michael almost equally angry because she had refused to let the journalists into the car. At first he had tried to explain how brilliant a coup it had been for him to sign an exclusive with the *Herald,* then had descended into sullen silence.

In the front seat beside the driver Latif might as well have been carved in stone—not that Michael spared a thought for her ''bodyguard.'' But Jalia had been nervous and edgy all the way, wondering when and how he would pounce.

He never did. On their arrival at the palace, he simply bowed and disappeared, leaving Jalia even more anxious, and faintly disappointed.

Of course she would have to sort this out with Michael privately, and yet—it would have been so much easier if Latif had insisted on staking his claim.

Jalia reminded herself that Latif had no claim. She had told him so herself. What had she been expecting? That he would knock Michael down? Send him packing?

Belatedly, very belatedly, she saw that she should have forced the showdown at the airport before Ellin Black got the wrong idea. Michael had found some way to cash in on the situation, that was clear. And it was going to involve publicity. By not denying their engagement instantly, she had given him a credibility that might now be harder to dislodge.

Why hadn't she seen things so clearly an hour ago?

But she had been so obsessed with avoiding notice, with not causing any kind of public scene that might get into the papers, that she had missed the chance to deliver a short, sharp shock.

It was all Latif's fault! If she hadn't been so worried about what he was thinking, she might have dealt with this better. And if only *he* had said something, Michael might have realized...

She brought herself up short. How could she have such ridiculously contradictory thoughts?

In a cool voice Jalia dispatched the ever-attentive servant for tea and fruit juice, then settled in a chair.

Michael stood in the doorway to the balcony under the arched framework of stained glass, gazing out at the courtyard. Across the way the rows of similar arches lay in picturesque light and shade. The music of the fountain and birdsong were the only sounds that met the ear.

"This is fabulous!" he exclaimed after a few minutes of silent appreciation. "Beats the new palaces all to hell, doesn't it? Look at that tiling—I've been on digs where we've found floors just like that dating from eight hundred years ago! The place must be—"

"Yes, Ghasib had some justification for turning the palace into a museum," she agreed. "It's still open to the public, of course, except for this wing, where the family live."

"The family!" Michael said, laughing and shaking his head. "You know, no one was all that surprised. In the Senior Common Room people were joking about how they used to call you the Ice Princess. Did you know that? They were walking around saying, 'Well, we always knew!'"

He laughed, but Jalia didn't. The servant returned with a tray, and when he had set it down she quietly dismissed him.

"No, I never knew it," she said, with a calm she didn't feel. "Come and have your tea."

He left his admiration of the courtyard from another age and sank onto the sofa opposite her as the door closed behind the servant.

Jalia poured out the amber liquid, passed him the small gold-traced crystal cup and said, "What exactly do you hope to get out of this, Michael?"

He laughed a little anxiously. "Come on, Jalia! There's no need to take that tone! You're getting what you want out of the engagement. Why shouldn't I benefit, too?"

"That's what you call it? You've come here without warning, at a hugely difficult moment for me and my entire family, with a sleazy tabloid journalist in tow—"

"Ellin is hardly *sleazy!*" he said. "And how was I to know you'd take it so hard? What's so terrible if our engagement is publicly known? How does it affect your life, Jalia?"

"I think the point is, how does it affect *yours?*"

He carefully chose a lump of sugar, set it between his teeth, and sipped his tea like an expert.

"A huge difference. You would not believe." He leaned forward earnestly, the cup held loosely between his knees, but looked down at it instead of at her.

"Listen, Jalia—you know I've been trying for

years for the chance to examine the private antique
art collections of the Princes of the Barakat Emirates—and Ghasib's, too, before the Sultan's return.

"You know what a boost it would be for my academic prospects if I succeeded. And do I have to remind you that these are difficult times in the academic
world?"

"No, you don't have to remind me," she said ston-
ily.

Sudden animation lit his features. "Do you remember that Mithra plate forgery Jasmin Shaw published
a few years ago, suggesting that the theme had been
copied from a genuine original? Do you know there's
a rumour making the rounds now that, during the Par-
van-Kaljuk War, when he was selling off his treasures, the King of Parvan actually sold King Daud of
the Barakat Emirates a Mithra plate? And it's now
hidden away in Prince Rafi's private collection? If I
could—"

"Michael. What has this got to do with our engagement?"

"Oh, don't be naive," he challenged irritably.
"You're related to these families now, Jalia! Engaged
to you, I'm not just an ordinary academic anymore,
am I? I'm inside the charmed circle."

He paused to drain his cup, and set it down.

"The *Herald* has contracted with me for a regular
column discussing the antique treasures of the Gulf
of Barakat—but it has to include some never-before-
seen pieces from the palace collections.

"It's going to put Middle Eastern antiquities on the
map, Jalia, and there's talk about my hosting a tele-

vision series if it's a success. This represents a huge forward step for my career.''

She stared at him in disbelief. *''Tabloids? Television?* I didn't realize you had ambitions to become a popular art historian.''

Michael, in common with many academics, had always sneered at colleagues who took their wisdom to the *hoi polloi*. Stooping to inform the general public wasn't an occupation for the true scholar. Not even for ready money.

''I didn't realize it myself, till the *Herald* put it to me. But beggars can't be choosers, Jalia. And university budgets are only getting tighter, aren't they?''

Jalia set her glass down with a little *chink*. ''And you thought that a fake engagement with me would open all those doors for you?''

''Why not?''

''Because it is *fake,* Michael. It was wrong of me to lie to my parents like that, though I thought I had good reason. But to go on lying and extend it to the Princes of the Barakat Emirates and Ashraf and everyone else would be worse than wrong. It would be an appalling abuse.''

''It doesn't have to be a lie.'' She saw the shadow of a haunted desperation in his eyes. ''We could get married.''

''What?''

''Just for a short time. What difference would it make to you, Jalia? We could get divorced in a year, say, no hard feelings. We've been good friends, haven't we? This could make me, Jalia. There's such a lot riding on it. More than you know,'' he added unhappily.

She stared at him in appalled silence.

"Michael, do you know what you're saying?" she whispered. "What has put the idea into your head?"

"You did, Jalia."

"But it's out of the question! You must see that it's impossible! I want to end this engagement farce immediately. If you hadn't been on your way here when I got back to al Bostan, I'd have phoned you to tell you so."

"But why, if it's serving your purpose? Jalia, please consider!"

"It's over, Michael. I'm sorry if it now puts you in the embarrassing position of being publicly dumped, but there's no one to blame but yourself for that. We agreed to tell no one but my parents. And in your heart you *know* you shouldn't have done this without checking with me first."

There was a long silence while Michael stared at her, stricken.

"Jalia," he said. "I'm really, really sorry. I really had no idea that you'd react like this. I just didn't know. And I've done something so stupid—it's not going to be as easy as that, I'm afraid."

She gazed at him in mounting anxiety. He was so white he looked sick.

"My God, what is it? What can you possibly have done?"

Michael leaned forward, clearing his throat.

"Ellin took me out after I'd cut the deal with the features editor. To the Savoy. We got into celebrating my new future…Jalia, I've never had so much Moët et Chandon poured down me in my life. I got pissed, and I mean completely pissed."

Premonitory dread shivered her skin. "Oh, Michael!"

He sat shaking his head, white and desperate. "She got the truth out of me. I'm sorry, Jalia. When I sobered up I was just—"

"The truth?" Jalia whispered, but she knew. "The truth about what?"

"That Princess Jalia was so terrified of being forced into marriage by her parents here in Bagestan that she begged her gay friend to pretend to an engagement."

"Oh, *God!*"

"Ellin really wants to use it, but because the deal I've cut depends on our engagement being real, she can't. She says that's a story that's really got legs—with Princess Noor missing, you know, and pretty well presumed dead.

"People are already suggesting maybe Noor ran to avoid a forced marriage, and Ellin says the story would really give that rumour weight. 'Imagine how the world would condemn Princess Noor's parents for putting her into the position where she chose death over an unhappy marriage,' she said to me."

Jalia felt as if all the oxygen had suddenly been sucked from the room.

"So we've got to go on with the engagement, Jalia. I'm sorry, but unless you want the truth blasted all over the front page, we have to go on with it. I'm sorry, love. Sorrier than I can say. You can kick me black and blue if you want, but no blacker than I've already kicked myself."

Jalia gazed at him, not really focusing on Michael at all. She was thinking how strange it was that she should choose such a moment as this to understand at last that she was in love with Latif Abd al Razzaq.

Fifteen

ENGAGED TO A PRINCESS!
  A *Herald* Exclusive
  Dr. Michael Wickliffe, 32, collector and Middle Eastern art history lecturer at Scotland's small but prestigious King James VI University, has particular reason to smile. Not only has his marriage proposal been accepted by the beautiful woman he knew only as Jalia Shahbazi, a fellow lecturer at the university, but she's also recently been revealed as a princess! Jalia is a first cousin of Sultan Ashraf al Jawadi, recently crowned in Bagestan....

At one end of the private courtyard an arched terrace caught the early sun, and since Noor's and Bari's disappearance a communal breakfast had been regularly served there.

Newspapers from around the world were on offer with the coffee, and in addition a radio, television and telephones had been set up.

Knowing what the morning papers would say, Jalia had come down early—but, she saw with dismay, not early enough. Latif was sitting alone at the table, an English paper open in front of him.

At the sound of footsteps, he lifted his head from the newsprint. Jalia's steps stopped abruptly as she saw his face, white and cold and harsh as a judge.

"Latif!" she whispered, her voice catching so that she had to stop and cough.

She had hoped to see him first, to try and explain, but last night there had been yet another reported sighting of Noor, this time on a French ferry. It had taken hours to confirm what they all instinctively guessed, that it was false, and she could not get him alone.

He tossed the paper and his table napkin down, every movement measured and deliberate, and stood. His chair squealed a protest against the tiles.

"So you did not deny your fiancé's story."

"No, because—I mean, he's not…"

His emerald eyes narrowed with ferocious feeling. "He is not your fiancé?"

His voice was terrible, raw and harsh and angrily contemptuous. Jalia flinched. "Well…"

"The journalist has printed a lie?"

She began to stammer. "Yes. Well, not exactly, but—"

She swallowed and pressed her lips together. She

did not know him. He was an angry, frightening stranger now, his fury lashing around her.

"Make up your mind," he said, and she had never heard such coldness in Latif's voice before.

"We have to go on pretending for the moment," she said in a gulp, and under his fierce gaze she stammered out the explanation.

Latif stood looking down at her, his face as unmoved and unmoving as rock, and she realized even before he said it that she was too late. Her understanding had come too late. Her love was too late.

"You use the engagement now as you used it before—to make yourself safe from me," he rasped. "But you no longer need this fiction. You are safe from me, Jalia."

"No! Why won't you believe me? It's the truth!"

He shrugged. "It is the truth, then. And what do you want now?"

Her heart beat with dread. She hadn't guessed it would be so hard, that she would have to spell it all out. She hadn't allowed herself to imagine that when she finally told her love Latif would no longer be interested.

"Nothing," she faltered. "I just wanted you to know how it had happened."

"Why?"

"Perhaps you've forgotten you once declared an interest in the matter. You said you loved me."

She lifted her head and forced herself to meet his eyes.

"Well, I love you, too, Latif. I'm sorry I found out so late, but I have found out. I love you, and I—I want to be with you, and if that means coming to Bagestan…"

His emerald gaze fixed hers, and for a moment her heart beat with hope so powerful she was almost suffocated.

"You will move to Bagestan for my sake?"

"Yes, if that's what you want. Yes."

"Jalia, you speak to me as the fiancée of another man," he said coldly. "Are you not ashamed of such betrayal?"

"I told you, this is being forced on me! I told you what the journalist told Michael…."

"And why did you not come to me before letting this story be printed?"

"What could you have done?"

His eyes narrowed suddenly, so that she gave an involuntary little gasp.

"That is no longer important. Now you have admitted to the engagement, and refuse to deny it. What do you expect me to do now?"

"Nothing! I'm waiting for things to sort themselves out with Noor and Bari first, and we'll find a way to get out of the engagement without a fuss."

"It is as I said. He wants to marry you. Doesn't he?"

She shifted uncomfortably. "Not really."

He stared at her from unreadable eyes.

She swallowed. "It's not what you think." Everything was backwards and upside down—how could she explain that Michael's reasons for wanting to marry her were so unlike Latif's? "We'll announce that the engagement's over as soon as—"

"And what shall I do in the meantime?" he demanded contemptuously. "Watch you as the promised wife of another man, and smile, and wait my turn? Or shall we cheat your fiancé as before?''

''Latif, I love you!'' How could it all go so wrong? Why couldn't she explain? Why couldn't he understand?

''A weak love, Jalia, if you can be happy to be engaged to someone else.''

''It isn't like that!''

She flung herself against him, her arms reaching around his neck, her face pressing against his throat, her tears hot and wet on her lashes, sobs shaking her. But he stood unresponsive under the embrace, until, utterly shamed, she released him and stood back.

''No, Jalia. I have had enough of humiliation and lies. I have learned my lesson. Now you learn yours.''

His face then she would never forget, not if she made a hundred.

ALL THAT GLITTERS...

And while we're on the subject of the al Jawadi—is the recently announced engagement of Princess Jalia and Dr. Michael Wickliffe all it appears? It seems that on her first visit to Bagestan, the woman they call the Ice Princess melted in a big way for one of the Sultan's handsome Cup Companions. Yet as soon as she returned to the U.K., she and Wickliffe privately announced their engagement. According to close friends, the move was a big surprise. Is there something the beaming fiancé should know?

''I hope you'll consider taking a position in one of the universities here,'' the Sultana was saying to Michael. "Under Ghasib, of course, the universities suffered from chronic poor funding—he knew good universities would be a source of dissent. Everyone who could studied abroad. But I'm sure you know Ash is very determined to improve the standards."

On Friday nights, the Sultan and Sultana hosted a family dinner, either in their private apartments or in the private courtyard of the palace. Members of the family and Cup Companions had a standing invitation.

Tonight the traditional *sofreh* was spread on the grass by the tumbling fountain. The first such gathering Jalia had attended had been soon after she and her family arrived in Bagestan, and then her heart had thrilled to the sight of her restored family, so numerous, sitting and lying on the grass while they put away vast quantities of perfectly cooked rice and lamb, bean stew, chicken with pomegranate sauce, and bowlfuls of pomegranate seeds so red and delicious she had felt she was eating rubies.

Tonight she wasn't enjoying herself. Not with Michael here, being welcomed and treated as her fiancé—for they were all in enough grief and turmoil over Noor without Jalia giving everyone more cause for concern.

"Thank you, Sultana. It's an option we'll certainly consider," Michael said, preening a little under the implied flattery, then went for broke. "I wonder if anything is planned about cataloguing the remains of the old royal collections? I might be very helpful there."

Jalia had told the Sultana the truth, just a few

minutes ago, when at Dana's suggestion the two women had gone walking together in the garden. It was clear the Sultana had sensed something, and even though the timing couldn't have been worse, Jalia had submitted to temptation.

"I think you're making the right choice," Dana had said, after hearing her out. "The engagement's public now—there's nothing to be gained from rushing headlong into breaking it. Your image wouldn't be improved by the move, and we can definitely do without another media feeding frenzy right now."

Jalia sighed. It had been a huge relief to confide in the Sultana. And an even bigger one to know the Sultana didn't think she was *too* much of a fool.

"That being said, however, we have to find a way out of this as soon as possible. I don't know how the gossip about the engagement got going, but it puts you in a very awkward position," the Sultana had murmured, her eyes wandering towards where Latif sat on the grass. "But we have to talk more another time. Let's get back, or God knows the next story will be about how concerned the Sultana is over the rumours. Not that I think the staff is suspect, but who *is* leaking the rumours?"

Now the Sultana was drawing Michael out, like anyone taking the trouble to get to know her cousin's new fiancé. Latif was sitting at the other end of the spread cloth, an irresistible magnet. Jalia couldn't stop her gaze unconsciously gluing to him.

And as if aware of it, his gaze rose and met hers. Jalia's heart leaped into her eyes. Then she gasped and drew back, like someone who has been unexpectedly stung.

His expression was totally indifferent. There was in his gaze no memory of anything between them, no desire, no condemnation, no interest. He didn't even seem to notice that she was a living creature. His glance wandered past, leaving her chilled and shaken.

Oh, how different from that first evening, when the brilliant emerald gaze had been a physical touch on her skin, potent, full of promise and intent. Then it had unnerved her, then she had felt anxious and unsettled, and under threat—not least from her own unrecognized feelings.

Well, Latif's passionate love had had all the staying power of cigarette smoke, and now it was safe to discover what her own real feelings were. Now that she no longer had it, she could admit that his passionate wooing, his approval, the hot possessiveness of his glance had felt like everything she needed to live.

Of course she would never marry Michael, and she had been doubly grateful to hear Dana say the engagement had to be ended soon. But now she saw what filled her with grief—that, whenever that happened, there would be no rekindling Latif's interest.

It was best this way. If she could not resist him— and Jalia was becoming daily more aware how deeply she had been fooling herself about her ability to do that—then thank God he had been made to resist her. She had almost started to believe she could make a go of things in this country.

"I suppose the cataloguing will have to be done sooner or later," Dana was saying, and Jalia came to with no idea of how long she had been in her trance. "But I doubt if it's high on Ash's list of priorities."

"It should be," Michael said, smiling. "The ancient history of Bagestan is enshrined in such treasures, after all. Sultan Hafzuddin's private collection was legendary. It's terribly important to learn what has survived Ghasib's depredations, don't you think?"

The Sultana smiled. "Not quite as important as reestablishing the damaged irrigation system in the villages which had the bad luck to get on the wrong side of Ghasib's agents, I'm sure you'll agree."

"But I wouldn't be of any use there," Michael pointed out with a winning smile.

The Sultana inclined her head.

"No, I see that," she said. Her eyes flicked to Jalia. "I do see."

"Princess!" Latif said, and in her sleep she whimpered his name and instinctively reached for him. "Princess! Wake up!"

The voice was urgent. Jalia came suddenly awake, sitting up almost before her eyes were open. Her bedside lamp threw a soft glow into the shadows. Outside, the first rays of sunrise were lighting the sky.

In the first sleepy moment she could think of only one reason for him to come to her like this.

"Latif!" she sobbed with tearing relief, and reached for him again.

"There's news," he said harshly, stepping back.

She saw that he was dressed, in jeans and a shirt and thin bomber jacket, and she snapped alert. Her heart pounded, closing her throat.

"Is it Noor? What have they found? Is she alive? Is Bari?"

His eyes ran over her as if involuntarily, making her sharply aware of her sleep-ruffled hair, her bare limbs, how incompletely the silk night-slip covered her breasts.

It was only a moment's weakness. He brought his gaze back to her wide-stretched eyes, her white face.

"The EPIRB of Bari's plane has suddenly started sending a signal," he said. "From the area of the Gulf Islands."

"Oh, *alhamdolillah!*" she cried, bursting into tears. "The islands! Oh, Latif, does it mean—they're alive?"

"I hope so, Princess. But we can know nothing till we get to the scene. Two helicopters have been scrambled. Ashraf has asked me to go. Please tell—"

She tossed back the coverlet and slipped to her feet. "I'm coming with you."

"No," he said. "Ash asks that you help break the news to Noor's parents and your own. Dana will meet you in her sitting room in a few minutes."

Jalia grabbed his arm. "Dana can do it without me. It'll only take me two seconds to put some clothes on. Wait for me. I want—"

Latif's jaw tightened, his eyes flashed. "You are not coming with me! Don't be such a fool! It is no place for you!"

"If Noor is hurt—"

"We will have medics aboard. Do you think the Sultan is a fool?"

She put out a pleading hand. "Latif—"

He caught her wrist in a hold that hurt. "Do you listen to nothing and no one? Go and—"

But it had been a mistake to touch her. He dragged

her closer and his other hand, of its own volition, buried itself in her tousled hair. Jalia melted against him with a yearning cry that scorched his blood, and his mouth clamped hers.

Hunger and need flooded her, but even as her arm reached up around his neck he dragged it down again, and stepped back. For one long moment they stared at each other, chests heaving, sharply aware of the bed behind her in the golden, inviting lampglow.

The indifference of the past few days had been stripped from him like the mask it was, and her heart was bursting at what she saw in his eyes.

But only for a moment, and then he was back in control.

''Wake her parents. I will be in contact as soon as we have learned anything.''

Sixteen

It always seemed strange to Jalia afterwards that it should be in that anxious hour when the family clung together, pacing and praying, waiting for the news, that she should have understood so much at last. About herself and life. About family and blood and tradition and duty.

About love.

Noor might be alive, she might be dead, or terribly wounded, and whichever it was, she, Jalia, could do nothing to change her cousin's fate.

Life was short and so precious, and was she going to live hers without love? Was she going to run from the challenge life was offering her—the challenge to do some real good in the world? The challenge to love and be loved from the most passionate depths of her soul, and another's?

She had two countries—the land of her birth, and the land of her ancestors, her blood. Each called to her, but only one really needed her. Needed everything that she was and would be. Needed her heart, her mind, her love, her education, her commitment, the life she would live, the children she would have.

In return it offered her its rich history, its beauty, a deep sense of blood connection and belonging, and the heart of a strong, noble lover, a one-of-a-kind man—if she could win him back.

Even if she could not, her future would be in this land, where everything she was and could be would be needed for as long as she cared to give it. Where her contribution would be unique, where her people needed her. Whether he loved her or not…her home was here.

She had seen the truth in Latif's eyes—he did love her. His indifference had been a disguise. But that didn't mean she could make him change his mind.

Their prayers were answered as the sun climbed brilliantly into the blue sky, when Latif phoned with the news that Noor and Bari were alive and well.

They had come down in the storm near one of the smallest of the Gulf Islands and had been marooned there the whole time.

Crooning and wailing with joy, Princess Zaynab spoke to her daughter first, and then it was the turn of each of them, father, cousins, aunts, uncles. Jalia was nearly dissolved in the flooding tears that poured out of her eyes as she took her turn and spoke to her cousin and childhood friend.

"Alhamdolillah rabilalamin!" Noor's father began

when they hung up, and the family softly, gratefully, slipped into the recital. *"Al rahman, al raheem."* Praise be to God, the Lord of the World, the Compassionate, the Merciful...

Miracles do happen, however unfashionable it may be in some quarters to think so.

"Please stop punishing yourself," Noor advised gently. "For a start, when I bolted it had nothing to do with anything you said. And anyway, as it turned out, it could be the best thing that's ever happened to me."

Noor had stepped off the helicopter a stranger—thin, bony, her hair a sun-bleached mess, her skin burned and rough...and with an expression in her eyes Jalia had never seen there before.

Jalia burst into overwrought tears. These days she couldn't seem to get any kind of handle on her emotions. "I'm sorry, but it was so awful!" she wept. "Not knowing anything about why you'd gone, where you were. Everyone was secretly blaming me, but not as much as I blamed myself. It was so wrong of me—"

"Wrong?" Noor protested. "You couldn't have been more right! Bari doesn't love me. He never did."

"Oh, Noor," Jalia objected sadly.

Noor lifted her hand from the bathwater, and absently studied her ravaged nails. She had eaten an enormous meal and then slept the clock around. After that the first thing she'd opted for was a bath. The cousins had drained and refilled the tub twice as Noor soaked out the accumulated grime of the island.

"Funny, isn't it, all that newspaper gossip about a forced marriage?" Noor said. "It *was* a forced marriage, but the other way around. I wonder why the media don't get hot and bothered when *men* are the ones being dragged down the aisle as a sacrifice on the altar of family duty?"

"I think Bari is in love with you. He told me…"

"I don't care what he told you."

"He says he should have realized before how he felt, and he fell truly in love with you on the island."

"Really!" Noor said brightly. "Well, he had a funny way of showing it!"

"Noor, can't you just talk to him?"

"And actually, I don't care when he fell in love with me, if he did. He woke up too late. If he did."

"I guess that's how Latif feels about me," Jalia said. "That I woke up too late."

"Oh, Jay!" Noor exclaimed remorsefully, reaching a damp hand out to her. "Oh, what a mess it's all turned out to be, this princess business!"

"Yes, in some ways."

Jalia picked up the little rag doll Noor had brought back with her from the island and absently wiggled its arms. It smelled of smoke and mildew, and a child's distress.

"But not a complete mess." Jalia paused. "Some things are much clearer than they were. I can see my way now, which I never could before. I've lost a big blind spot about Bagestan. I know how much I love this country now. I know I do belong here in spite of everything. I'm going to dig in and help…people like the women of the Sey-Shahin tribe, for example. They're really at a disadvantage trying to deal with the West. They need help. That's really important to me now. And I guess I've got Latif to thank for that, whatever happens.''

She held out the doll, and touched a finger to the pearl necklace around its neck.

''In some refugee camp somewhere in the world, the child who owned this doll is...suffering who knows what torments. I want to do something about that. And I guess that'll have to be enough for me for now.''

She was perilously near tears again.

Noor's eyes were bright.

''Latif loves you, you know. He still loves you. I was watching last night at dinner, and if you could have seen his face, Jalia!''

''Maybe. I don't think he cares whether he loves me or not. I think he's made up his mind that I'm not worth it. That's the problem I'm facing—that he can love me but still not want anything to do with me.''

''You have absolutely got to get out of this engagement thing with Michael!'' Noor said urgently, standing up and beginning to rinse under the shower. ''We've got to find a way. Maybe you should just bite the bullet, Jay.''

''Now's not the right time. Not with my parents back in England—they'd get mobbed if the *Herald* ran that story without warning now.''

Noor reached for the fluffy towelling robe and wrapped herself in it with a bone-deep appreciation of its soft luxury that was completely different from the take-it-for-granted attitude Jalia remembered.

''Well, from a purely selfish point of view it's sure easier not having to deal with stories about my supposed forced marriage in addition to everything that's going on now, Jalia, but don't you think our rescue gives you the perfect opportunity to bury the news?''

''I don't think I could stand the media attention right now. Those little smears about Michael and me and the mysterious sheikh I'm after are awful enough without that added. Thank God no one's managed to get Latif's name! That would just kill me! If I ever find out who—'' She broke off, because Noor stared at her, her hand to her mouth.

''Jalia, haven't you seen it?''

''Oh, *no!* What now?''

''On the table in the other room. The *Blatt.*''

Jalia leaped up and ran to the table, scrabbling through the newspapers lying there. Each one had photos of the rescued couple getting out of the helicopter, and happy headlines.

''It's that gossip-column thing opposite the op ed page,'' Noor told her as she came back into the bathroom. ''There.''

A water-shrivelled fingertip pointed to a small news item of the kind Jalia had come to dread.

The Gadfly can now reveal the name of the mysteriously impervious Cup Companion who's apparently captured Princess Jalia's heart: it's the dashing Latif Abd al Razzaq Shahin, chief of the Sey-Shahin tribe.

His title, *Shahin,* can be translated as *royal falcon,* and there *is* a certain bird-of-prey air about the Princess's reputed heartthrob.

A source very close to the palace has revealed that the Cup Companion and the Princess were alone together in the mountains, searching for her cousin, Princess Noor, and his friend, Bari al Khalid, throughout the time the couple were missing. A romantic opportunity, you might think, but whatever happened between them, it doesn't seem to have altered the Princess's status.

Nor did it arouse obvious jealous feeling in the heart of Jalia's supposed fiancé, fellow professor Dr. Michael Wickliffe. Could it be that his real love is the antique silver plate in the Sultan's private collection?

"Who did this?" Jalia wailed. "Who told them?" She closed her eyes to squeeze back the hot, bursting tears. "If they start asking me about Latif I'll go mad. Do you think it was Latif who told them? Is it his revenge, making a fool of me, proving something?"

"No, oh no!" Noor protested, shocked. "Oh, honey, I had no idea it would hit you so hard! I'm sorry I told you like that!"

Jalia sobbed, and Noor comforted her and began to weep, too, so that in the end they comforted each other. They both felt better for it.

"You've really changed, too, you know that?" Noor said, as they sat out on the balcony watching the fountain, drinking delicious juice. "You never used to talk about your feelings at all."

"Oh, I absorbed the English virtue of self-control, and like all converts, I took it to extremes," Jalia said with a watery smile.

"And maybe I was never really interested," Noor admitted softly. "Too self-centred, as Bari said."

"Did he say that? That's pretty hard. I guess you can get pretty close to the bone in a situation like that, face-to-face with the struggle to survive."

"When one of you is intent on breaking the other into little pieces, you get very close to the bone, yes," Noor said, with quiet bitterness.

"He didn't break you, though. Maybe he…"

"What?" Noor demanded.

"Well, cut you—like a diamond or something. So that your real self would be revealed."

"Thanks," Noor replied, with a snort of laughter that threatened to turn into a sob. "It was a bloody uncomfortable operation, let me tell you. And come to think of it, I could say the same of you. Latif cut you, but not like a diamond, like a person. Now I can see you bleed."

"It was a bloody uncomfortable operation, let me tell you," Jalia repeated.

The two cousins laughed together, ignoring the tears burning the cheeks of them both.

Seventeen

Creeping along a magical moonlit hallway that belonged to another age, Jalia wondered if she was merely following the trail blazed by her ancestresses in centuries gone by.

Because whoever had designed this wing of the palace had certainly not been unaware of the needs of midnight ramblers—the number of human-sized niches available for ducking into was testament to that. Not that she'd ever noticed that fact until she slipped into one to avoid a passing servant.

The only problem was that most of the niches were home to antique lamps or brass trays or ancient flint-lock rifles, their silver mountings decorated with ruby and emerald.

In the past, had it meant death to a woman if she tripped over one and brought the guards?

Her ancestors. Maybe this was simply in her blood—the urge that had suddenly overwhelmed her in the dead of another sleepless night to find her lover's door....

Except that he was not her lover anymore. From the day Michael had arrived, her nights had been filled with loneliness and heartache instead of Latif Abd al Razzaq.

How desperate love could make a person! Jalia thought back to those distant days when she had accused her cousin of falling for Bari based on sexual attraction alone, as if that were nothing much.

Well, she had learned.

She counted the doors again. Oh, let the count be the same on the inside as it was from the balcony side! One broom cupboard would throw her calculations adrift, and how unbelievably embarrassing if she ended up in some other Cup Companion's bed....

Her faint shadow on the moonlit floor wavered and darkened, and she frowned for a moment before she understood. Then with a stifled cry she whirled, to find one of the palace servants in an open doorway behind her.

"Good evening, my Lady," he whispered, showing no surprise. His voice sounded oddly familiar, though she could not recall ever having seen his face before.

"Good evening," Jalia said, and stood gazing blankly at him, unable to come up with any comment that would cover her presence in this corridor at this hour of the night.

Smiling, the man moved past her to a carved wooden door. "Allow me, my Lady," he murmured, opening it softly, and stood waiting for her to enter.

My Lady! Suddenly the strange title registered, and she realized why his voice was familiar—it was the accent she had heard in Sey-Shahin Valley. This man must be one of Latif's personal servants. And what was more, he wouldn't be calling her My Lady unless he had heard about that wedding night in the mountains....

Fire burned in her cheeks, but in the mountain custom he was not looking into her face. Jalia stood for a moment of dreadful, gnawing immobility.

Then she thought of her ancestresses and the niches so artfully created for them and their lovers by the palace architect. Clearly some would have risked death to be with someone they loved. Was she, who had so much less to lose, going to give up because she'd received encouragement?

"Thank you," she whispered, and stepped into the room. He closed the door softly behind her.

She was in a small anteroom lighted only by the moonlight filtering through from another door ahead. She could feel the faint breeze that said the door to the balcony was also open.

A moment later she was standing beside the bed, listening to Latif's deep breathing.

The black moonshadow of a tree in the courtyard danced in the pale blue-white light that played over the balcony, the tiled floor, the silk carpet, the beautifully carved fireplace...Latif's bed.

That was spread on the floor, in the Eastern way, a thick mattress strewn with pillows and cushions and covered with a coverlet like a miniature painting, blue and purple all shot with glittering gold.

The object of her desire lay on his side, one muscled arm outflung as if to wrap someone in against his chest, his hand grasping the pillow. His cheekbone was sharply shadowed, as were his eyes. His mouth was carved as beautifully as a marble statue, his jaw resolute even in sleep.

Jalia's heart was beating in panicked little picket-fence ripples.

Slowly, where she stood, she slipped the thin dressing gown off her shoulders and let it fall to the floor. Underneath she wore the silk pyjamas she had been wearing on their "wedding" night in the valley. In the moonlight the pale jade was the colour of smoke.

Barefoot on the sensuously soft carpet, she crept forward to the edge of the bed. Her shadow came between the moon and his face for only an instant before she dropped to her knees, but as if it had been a touch, he stirred.

"Jalia?" he murmured, in a voice of agonized longing, and her heart kicked so hard the blow would have felled her if she had not already been down.

"Yes," she whispered on a sob. "Yes."

What the devil are you doing here?

She gasped with the shock of the changed tone. Latif sat up, wide awake and furious. The coverlet sliding down his naked chest, he shot one hand out to the lamp on the floor beside the bed.

For a moment they blinked at each other in its glow, his arm still extended to the lamp, frozen in an uncomprehending tableau. Absently she noticed papers and books strewn on the floor beside him, as if he had been working in bed before he slept.

His eyes went from black to green, and anger

blazed from them so hot all the words of argument died on her lips. Jalia shrank from his anger.

"Latif…"

"What the hell do you think you're doing?"

Desperately she sought for courage. "Why shouldn't I be here? I—"

"Get out!"

"It was all right for *you* to make love to me and try and break my resistance!" she pointed out hotly. "You have no right to react like an outraged virgin if I try to do the same!"

He flung the coverlet aside. He was naked, a fact which seemed to make no impression on him, but the golden light and shadow playing with his lean and hungry physique made the breath catch in Jalia's throat.

He grabbed her upper arm in a tight clasp and stood upright, drawing her inexorably with him. "Out!" he said again.

She lifted a hand to drag the heavy fall of hair off her face. "Latif! Can't we—"

Her jade eyes glistened, her full mouth trembled, with passionate tears. "Latif!" she cried. "I miss you so much! Can't you just—"

His hand tightened on her arm as he stooped again, to pick up her robe.

"Can't I what?" he growled savagely. "Forget that you belong to another man? Am I such a fool?"

Her perfume rose from the garment's silken folds, clouding his senses, and he cursed, like a man who does not know he is drunk till he stands up.

"Latif!" she begged again, and watched, her lips

parting, as his flesh responded urgently to the scent and the memory of the pleasure it promised.

"Damn you!" he said and, tossing the robe away, he stepped towards her, drew her against him, wrapped her in a ruthless embrace. His mouth found hers with savage impatience, and then she was falling, dragged down to heaven by his arms.

The hunger in his kiss made her senses swim, and his hands pressed her with the possessive strength that melted her. The heat of his thighs enveloped hers, his body hard and unforgiving as it crushed her.

He lifted his mouth from hers and kissed her neck, her throat, her shoulder, and Jalia moaned with hungry abandon, her fingers twining and luxuriating in the thick curls of his hair as he drew his head up and kissed her mouth again.

With a suddenness that made the breath rasp in her throat, his legs slipped between hers and jerked them wide, his hard body pressing against the million nerve ends that clustered there.

There was a wildness in him, a fury almost, that she had half sensed before, but that he had always kept under tight control; now it was unleashed.

"Love," he murmured, as if the word were torn from his deepest being. "My Beloved."

Her heart soared and sang, and she gave herself up to his fierce embrace with joy like a tidal wave.

He dragged, almost tore off the silk that covered her, till she was naked under his burning gaze. He ran his hand down her body, like a sculptor reminding himself of the lines of a statue he himself has carved, breast, waist, thigh, lost to everything except that she was here, in his bed. Then he drove into her, into that hot home that was his and his alone, over and over, while she moaned and cried out and pushed against him, seeking what he only could give her.

His hands and his body pushed her, pulled her, clasped her, in a ruthless pleasure-seeking that kept her in that intoxicating borderland between pleasure and pain, till she was lost to everything except the world of the senses.

He used all he had learned about her, and with every pleasure-drugged moment he taught her more. She hovered on the edge of blasting sensation for long, agonizing, thrilling seconds, crying and singing with its approach, and at last, with wild determination, he drove her over into ecstasy, and joined her there, so that they clung together as they soared, calling and crying, helplessly giving in to sensation, like two lovers who leap from a cliff.

Drenched with sweat then, he slipped down beside her, and Jalia turned with a grateful sigh to seek his embrace.

He sat up and gazed down at her in silence. She stared at him, seeing nothing but a dark shadow limned against the halo of light that surrounded him. His expression she could not discern.

But his tone of voice said it all.

"This changes nothing, Jalia."

It was like touching cold stone where you had expected living flesh.

"What?" she faltered.

"I play by your rules now. We make love, but it does not touch my heart. If you return to my bed another night, be sure to take no notice of anything I may say in the insanity of pleasure. It is meaningless."

Eighteen

"**O**f course I had no hand in it," Michael said. "Haven't you noticed that the gossip has never been picked up by the *Herald?* Ellin's livid about it."

"Ellin is?" Jalia exclaimed. "She's not the one being made to look a fool!"

"And what about me? Not that it's not totally deserved." Michael tossed down the paper, in which another columnist mauled the tasty story of the Princess's passion. "You're probably going to have to get used to it, Jalia. As I understand it, you should be grateful when what the papers say isn't true. It's when it's true it really bites."

"I suppose so."

Michael looked up, his mouth slowly falling open.

"Ah. My God, how thick I've been! Of course. It is true. That's why you're so bothered."

"No! At least, they're wrong in saying that's why I wanted the engagement. At that time I had no idea how I felt."

He snapped his fingers. "Latif was there at the airport, wasn't he? I should have seen it then, the way he was... But didn't he say he was your bodyguard?"

"You said it. He only agreed."

"Christ! You should have told me, Jalia! Why didn't you just tell me to get on my horse and—"

"Because you had Ellin Black right beside you, Michael."

He closed his eyes and shook his head. "From this moment I renounce champagne. But we've got to find a way out of this. Shall I talk to him? Would it help?"

Jalia shook her head, perilously near tears. "He knows, he just—doesn't care."

"You know, Jalia, now that Noor's home safe, does it really matter so much if Ellin prints some story about a forced marriage? It's what I said before, you know—as long as what they're saying is *not* true, you should be grateful."

"My parents don't deserve the humiliation. Michael. Not while they're still in England, anyway. Imagine what the media attention would be like! I just—I wish there were another way out. For your sake, too."

"Don't worry about me! You know I'm in discussions with the Sultana about old Hafzuddin's collection. If that comes off I'll consider it a fair trade. Anyway, I quite fancy the role of bruised, used, and castaway lover!" he said.

* * *

One of her main concerns now, whether Latif liked it or not, was to find some solution for the various problems facing the women of Sey-Shahin Valley. She had discussed their issues with the Sultan and Sultana, but there was only so far she could go without the Shahin's approval.

"Why are you bothering with this?" Latif said, on a day when she had cornered him in his office in the palace and insisted on talking to him about it. "These women aren't your concern."

"They don't seem to be yours, either, Latif!" she replied smartly. "These women came to me with their—"

"Because they made an assumption that proved wrong," he pointed out coldly. "My wife will be expected to concern herself with these problems. You are not."

"I am not going to be a slave to what is *expected!* Now, I have some practical suggestions and solutions to offer. When are you going to visit the valley again?"

He drew himself up with righteous indignation. "Is one of your suggestions that you should accompany me again?"

"Will you shut up and listen a moment?" She was nearly shouting. Oh, the Ice Maiden had lost her grip, for sure. Sometimes Jalia felt as if she'd spent her life half-asleep, dreaming she was a doe munching in a field, and had awakened to discover herself a tigress gnawing some animal's flesh.

"This could be important to a lot of people and you have no business standing in the way because of personal animosity to me!"

His face hardened, his mouth narrowed, and his eyes glinted with an emotion she could only guess at.

"I have no personal animosity, Princess. Fire away," he said stiffly.

"Thank you. Now, first of all, I've engaged legal advice, both here and in England, to try and sort out that one-sided contract that's tying up the carpet weavers.

"If we're successful, and it's still a big if, the women will need a new agent for their carpets. The Sultana and I have been talking, and we think what's needed—not just in Sey-Shahin, but throughout the country—is a tribal cooperative agent appointed by the palace.

"In other words, one body that will agent for any tribal group that needs representation in markets abroad. I'll be helping Dana set up a team over the next few months. It will take operating expenses only, no commission."

Latif sat watching her, his face a mask.

"We're tentatively calling it the Tribal Arts Co-operative."

"I see."

"With the Sultana publicly involved, it should go over a treat. We think we can produce our own catalogue and organize worldwide distribution. Gazi al Hamzeh will be advising us about publicity on a pro bono basis."

"Gazi al Hamzeh?" he repeated, frowning.

"Don't you know him? He's Prince Karim's Cup Companion, and the hottest press agent going. Dana says he's an absolute wizard at planting information so it gets reported as news, instead of sending out press releases, which get ignored. He organized Ash's press campaign before Ghasib fell.''

"I do know him."

"Dana said you did. We're also thinking about a coffee table book of Marzuqi rugs—we're hoping to get a lot of the world's well-known women who own them to let themselves be photographed with their carpets, and give little interviews."

"And why are you telling me?" He hadn't budged an inch.

"Also a whole series of little cookbooks. If it goes over well, we'd make a complete set, one for each of the tribes. Not just recipes, but pictures of the women planting and picking and cooking, and the tribal area, and the food. Starting with Sey-Shahin Valley."

"Why are you telling me, Jalia?" he said again, with a curious intensity.

"Surely you've noticed you're the Shahin, Latif!"

His eyes burned her. "And what are you, Jalia?"

For a moment her throat caught with hope, but his jaw was clenched and angry.

"At the moment, the Sultana's representative," she said.

"THE PRINCESS I LOVE!"
Forbidden Wedding Will Go Ahead!
The marriage of Cup Companion Sheikh Bari al Khalid and Princess Noor al Jawadi Durrani, which was dramatically halted in Bagestan last month when the bride and groom mysteriously disappeared, is on again, according to sources.

The truth behind the mystery of the wedding couple's flight, only minutes before the cere-

mony was due to begin, has at last come out.
Sources close to the couple have revealed that
the Princess and her fiancé fled because Sheikh
Jabir al Khalid, the groom's grandfather, dramatically withdrew his permission and barred the
union at the eleventh hour. The couple intended
to undertake the ceremony elsewhere. But their
plane was forced down in a storm, and the rest
is history. The couple spent what would have
been their honeymoon on an uninhabited island,
surviving on turtle eggs.

Their disappearance, the search, the dramatic
rescue, and the couple's continuing devotion
have had no influence on the old Sheikh's decision, however.

Bari al Khalid will be forced to sacrifice his
expected inheritance, consisting of vast property
in Bagestan, in order to marry the woman he
loves. The legacy will now probably go to a
cousin.

"My wife and I will build a new legacy together," the handsome Cup Companion has been
quoted as saying. The wedding is expected to
take place next month.

"Isn't it brilliant?" Noor said excitedly. "Bari *said*
Gazi was the man to sort it out. Talk about saving the
brand from the burning!"

It was the best news Jalia had had since the rescue.

"Is it true that Bari won't inherit if he marries you,
or is that—?"

"Not a penny! As if we care!" Noor laughed, and
Jalia smiled. The changes to Noor went very deep. "I

still get the ring, though,'' Noor said, flashing the brilliant diamond, ''because that he inherited from his father. Not that I care, but it is gorgeous, isn't it? It'll be a constant reminder to me of what's not important in life.''

''It is gorgeous,'' Jalia agreed.

''Oh, and did I mention that we love each other after all?''

''Only a few dozen times. Was this story Gazi al Hamzeh's idea? He seems to be an all-around genius.''

''I think he and Bari cooked it up between them,'' Noor said jealously. ''And you're saved, too, I hope you notice! Anything anyone now says about forced marriages is going to look pretty limp, with Bari actually being disinherited—and me so obviously thrilled, of course. Gazi says it's the first time he's ever sorted out two clients' problems with one story.''

''What?''

Noor bit her lip, grinning. ''It was him all along. Apparently, he's been on your case for ages!''

Jalia stared. ''On my case?''

''Don't you get it? Gazi's the one who's been leaking all those stories about you having the hots for Latif!''

Nineteen

The sun was going from the garden, its deep golden light brushing the leaves, glinting from the long rows of arched glass.

It lingered on Latif Abd al Razzaq's black hair, brushing it with glowing fingers as he bent over his desk, working. Jalia thought foolishly, *Even the sun can't bear to leave him.*

She stepped through the open doorway from the courtyard, her bare feet silent on the tiles, and crossed to his desk. His fountain pen scratched across the document as she watched. Then her shadow fell within his line of vision, and he looked up.

They looked at each other for a long still moment; then, as if there had been no pause, Latif carefully lifted his hand and capped the pen. Each movement was precise, as if it were necessary to maintain complete control over every tiniest muscle.

"Was it you?" she asked softly.

With the flick of an eye he dismissed the assistant who entered just then from the corridor. The man moved a fist to his breast, bowed and silently disappeared again.

"Was it?"

"You will have to explain what you mean," Latif said, and Jalia dropped the paper with the latest gossip item about them in front of him. He picked it up and gazed at it.

"Did you enlist Gazi al Hamzeh's media manipulation machine to leak all those stories about me?"

Latif abruptly pushed back his chair and stood, and in spite of herself Jalia stepped back a pace.

"Of course I did." As if he had suddenly tired of the game, he tossed the paper down on his desk and moved to stand in the open doorway.

Outside, beyond the green branches of the trees, a breeze was playing with the fountain. The courtyard was beguiling at this hour, shaded and sweet with the perfume of flowers that did not dare to open in the harsh glare of noon.

It was a moment before the sense of his words sank in, so convinced had she been that he would deny all knowledge.

"You did?"

"The campaign has achieved its goal, hasn't it?"

"What was the goal, apart from humiliating me?"

He glanced at her, then out at the garden again. "Gazi was of the opinion that we had to make a preemptive strike. The story about a forced marriage had to be discredited before it ran. Gazi knows his business."

"And how has it achieved that goal?" she asked.

"Don't you know? Your fiancé and his tame reporter were overheard having a loud argument in the Sultan's Return Hotel this afternoon. She accused him of deliberately misleading her. She has booked a seat to London on the midnight flight."

"It's the first I've heard," she said.

Silence fell. He watched the shadows in the garden, his jaw tight.

At last he turned to face her.

"What do you want out of life, Jalia?"

She blinked and caught her lip between her teeth. A last stray beam of sunshine darted over the roof to catch a spray of water from the fountain and turn it into liquid fire.

Like the beam of hope that suddenly pierced her heart.

"You know what I want. You don't—"

"Tell me again."

"I want the life you offered me before. I want to make my home here, where my people are, where my heart is." She had to press her lips together to stop them trembling. She swallowed.

"I haven't told anyone yet, Latif, but...the Sultana has asked me—she's offered me a position as her Cup Companion. I've thought it over hard, and I'm going to accept it. I think it offers me the best opportunity to make the contribution I want to make.

"So I'll be moving to Bagestan, whether you love me or not. And I guess if you really don't, it'll have to be enough, knowing I'm doing what I can for the people and the country."

She looked up, but still he was silent, watching her with his green falcon's eyes.

"But I want more than that, Latif. I love you. I want you to love me, the way you once did. I want to marry you, and have your children, and give them Bagestan as their home."

A sob caught in her throat. "But you don't want that anymore."

He moved towards her and put his arms around her, and she felt the masculine heat of his hands against her back. Their warmth moved into her blood, her heart, her head, and she lifted her face to smile up at him.

"My Beloved," said Latif, "who has told you such a terrible lie?"

And then she was home, against his heart.

Later, they walked in the garden, where the night flowers tempted the moonlight with their heady perfume. His arm was around her, her head against his shoulder.

"I thought that you did not know your own heart, that you loved me and did not know it. I thought I could teach you the truth of your feelings for me."

She said, "You were right, but it was a long time before I could admit it to myself. Was that why you tricked me into going into the mountains with you? It was a trick, wasn't it? All that talk about Mansour's young son. I finally saw it."

Latif laughed. "There was no hope of teaching you anything if I could not be with you, and you had been very adept at avoiding me before the wedding."

"And my mother knew!" Jalia exclaimed. "She must have been in on it, or she wouldn't—"

"Your parents understood my feelings. When you left the country so suddenly after the Coronation I couldn't hide my reaction from them. They knew what I intended, and what you meant to me."

Jalia shook her head. "That thought only occurred to me way too late. I should have guessed why my mother was so cool about my travelling around with you. 'Tell them he's your husband!'" She mimicked her mother's advice. "I seem to have walked into every trap you set for me."

"Why not?" he said, kissing her softly. "I had already walked into yours."

"And then, just when you thought you had me where you wanted me…"

"Just as I had begun to hope I had succeeded in showing you your heart, Michael was there, claiming you."

The fountain splashed in the darkness and she put out her arm to catch the soft cool drops of water on her skin. Sensation shivered to her scalp, as if at the touch of his fingers.

"When Michael turned up, did you think I'd lied on our…that night when I told you the engagement was invented?"

"On our wedding night," he amended firmly, and wrapped his arm more securely around her. "At first, perhaps. I was so maddened with jealousy I did not know what I believed. But that you had put yourself beyond my reach, stealing from me the chance to show you how strong our love could be, was certain.

And I had to accept that that might be exactly what you intended.''

"But I was appalled when Michael turned up! Didn't you see that?"

"That might have been only your distress at the presence of the journalists. Otherwise, I could see no reason for you not to repudiate the engagement instantly."

A heavy blossom drooped from a branch overhead, offering them its musky perfume as they passed. Its scent mirrored the sweetness she felt in her heart. Jalia smiled and sighed.

"So I decided to play the Western game after all," he continued. "To pretend that I no longer wanted you, in the hopes that it would make you see what you wanted, in order to show you your choices, and make you fear the truth that doors may close when we do not go through them at the right time."

"And all the time you had Gazi on the case."

"I could see no easy way out of that engagement once it was made public," Latif said. "The story of a forced marriage might have dogged us for a very long time, and I thought it would make you and your parents unhappy. Do you blame me for taking steps to protect our future together even when it seemed we might not have one?"

"N-o-o-o. Poor Michael, though. And I look—"

"Michael will be made happy by the Sultan's silver plates. And when we find the Sey-Shahin treasures, I am sure he will be delighted if we ask him to examine them.''

She laughed aloud. "Oh, that'll sort Michael out,

all right. And what about me…was it necessary to make me look such a mad fool?''

He turned to face her. ''Who is not mad, who loves?'' he demanded roughly. ''I am insane for you, Jalia. From the moment I first saw you I have been wandering in the desert like Majnun dreaming of his Layla.''

''But you stopped loving me,'' Jalia murmured. ''When I told you I loved you, you weren't even interested. I was too late. I'd left it too late. All of a sudden, you didn't care anymore.''

She looked up at him, her eyes shadowed with the memory of that dark moment.

''You had learned that you loved me. But you hadn't yet learned that you loved this country. How I wanted to take what you offered, what I had prayed for! But I knew it was a dangerous temptation. What would I do with a wife half-won, only grudgingly mine?'' He spoke as if he were understanding it clearly only as he spoke.

''I saw that if out of love for me you gave in grudgingly to the necessity to live here, we would never be truly happy.

''Life will not always be easy for us, Jalia. There is work ahead. I saw that if you did not come to me from a complete conviction that your home was here in Bagestan, there would be too much room for regret. You had to find your love for the country, too.''

She heaved a deep sigh for the old life—her friends, her students, the university. But she had no doubts anymore. Her life was here, her heart was here, her fate was to be beside Latif all her days.

"So I offered you scope to learn about your heart, and your blood, and your generosity."

"What do you mean?"

"Was it not partly your concern for the women of Sey-Shahin Valley that taught you that your heart was here in Bagestan?"

"Maybe," Jalia began indignantly, "but you can hardly take the credit for that! Offered me scope? If you suggested that I'm marrying you because otherwise the women of your valley won't get a look-in, you'd be closer..." Jalia's voice faded off as the last piece fell into place.

"Oh no! Oh, what an idiot I've been!"

He was laughing and shaking his head. "Did you really imagine, my Beloved, that I could care so little about something so important affecting my people's well-being, simply because it concerned women?"

"You set me up!" she accused. "Right from the start! Right from that day in Sey-Shahin!"

"I only feigned a little indifference in the hopes of engaging your interest on my people's behalf. I hoped that even if you did not love me, Jalia, your love of my people would teach you to love their Shahin."

"Or vice versa," said the Princess, and nestled against his heart.

Epilogue

PRINCESS WINS HER SHEIKH
Princess Jalia al Jawadi Shahbazi, recently appointed Cup Companion to the Sultana of Bagestan, and the Sultan's Cup Companion Latif Abd al Razzaq Shahin are to marry. A palace spokesman said that the possibility of a joint wedding with the Princess's cousin, Noor, and her fiancé, Bari al Khalid, has not been ruled out.

*   *   *   *   *

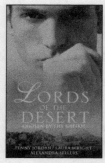 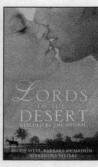 

millsandboon.co.uk Community

Join Us!

The Community is the perfect place to meet and chat to kindred spirits who love books and reading as much as you do, but it's also the place to:

- **Get the inside scoop from authors about their latest books**
- **Learn how to write a romance book with advice from our editors**
- **Help us to continue publishing the best in women's fiction**
- **Share your thoughts on the books we publish**
- **Befriend other users**

Forums: Interact with each other as well as authors, editors and a whole host of other users worldwide.

Blogs: Every registered community member has their own blog to tell the world what they're up to and what's on their mind.

Book Challenge: We're aiming to read 5,000 books and have joined forces with The Reading Agency in our inaugural Book Challenge.

Profile Page: Showcase yourself and keep a record of your recent community activity.

Social Networking: We've added buttons at the end of every post to share via digg, Facebook, Google, Yahoo, Technorati and de.licio.us.

www.millsandboon.co.uk

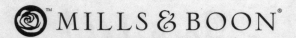